CRYSTAL BALL

LANEY KAY

PART I

CRAZY TOWN...

1

THE MINUTE I PINNED MY HUSBAND'S TESTICLE TO THE garage wall with my car, my day got weird.

I'll give you the details later, but let's make this part short and sweet. Bottom line, after twenty-five years together, my husband fell in love with his twenty-year-old administrative assistant, Barbie, and knocked her up. Yes, Barbie. I know, right?!

Apparently, his next mistake was a big one. He told me about it. I was furious when I realized he'd had unprotected sex with both of us, we were both yelling, I got in my car to leave and then, oops. I thought my car was in reverse, but it wasn't. I hit the gas, the car went forward, he tried to jump out the way, and I accidently pinned one testicle and his leg to the garage with my car. My bad.

When the cops and the ambulance finally got there, he was yelling about me trying to kill him, so the cops arrested me. My best friend, Lola, who is an attorney, was trying to get me out before my dad, the sheriff in this county, came down here and started raising hell. And in the meantime, there I sat. In jail. Being watched over by a big, pissed off woman named Tiffany who looked like she wanted to kick my ass. Or possibly ask me out.

Seriously, how did this happen? How did I go from ordinary wife to criminal in the span of two hours?

You've got to know me to realize how ridiculous this whole scenario is. My name is Daisy Dukes Monroe. I know, I know. My maiden name was Daisy Ellen Dukes, and once daisy dukes shorts became a household term, you can imagine the kind of crap I took as a teenager.

My family never really understood my problem with the name, but irony and sarcasm aren't their strong suits. Don't get me wrong, I love them all to death, but we couldn't be more different. I obviously take after some tiny, smart-ass, great-great-aunt, or second cousin twice removed, because I am nothing like the rest of my family. They're all tall, thin, dark, and serious, and I would be the total opposite of all of those things.

My mom is a Southern housewife, a former debutante and past president of the Junior League, who is always dressed perfectly, and always says and does the right thing— basically the perfect politician's wife. Which works out because my daddy has been the sheriff in Fulton County for about 30 years. He's a huge, quiet, gruff, very nice man. He's always been proud of the fact that I write for the Atlanta paper, but thinks I waste my talent on fluffy topics instead of righting wrongs and fighting corruption. My mom thinks I'm in desperate need of a makeover and should occasionally dress in something other than yoga pants and flip flops. I have two younger identical twin brothers, both of whom live in Roswell, north of Atlanta, and are both dentists. They share an office, and they married twins. They each have two kids, a boy and a girl, and they are very nice, normal people.

I've always been the odd duck in our family. I'm 46 years old, and 4'11" tall, which I prefer to round up to 5'1" because it makes my weight more proportional to my height and doesn't sound so freakishly short. I have curly blonde hair that goes from shoulder to jaw length depending on the humidity, green eyes, huge boobs, and a bubble butt. I have a nice smile. Basically, I'm on the cute side of average looking. Most people just comment on how tiny I am. It's annoying, because I don't really think of myself as small, but let's face it—the reality is that I'm basically a busty, blonde Chihuahua.

I was born and raised in various parts of Atlanta. I grew up a good Southern girl with a bad case of ADHD and I loved the Georgia Bulldogs, softball, sweet tea, and boys, all of which I pursued with equal passion, and not necessarily in that order. By the time I graduated with a degree in journalism from the University of Georgia, Bobby and I had already been married for a year after a quick detour to Gatlinburg on the way back from a football game in Knoxville. My three best friends and roommates, Lola, Mo, and Sara, had been my bridesmaids at a drunken wedding where all of us wore Georgia sweatshirts, Georgia boxer shorts, and flip flops. I thought it was awesome, although my mom was appalled.

My dad was thrilled with not having to pay for a big wedding, so when we graduated, he gave us $10,000 to put down on a house, plus he bought us a washer and dryer. Bobby's folks bought us a big TV so we thought we were living large. We moved our two carloads of possessions into our new home and started our new lives together.

We had a great time in those early years. Bobby is a good old boy, from a good Southern family, so he joined his daddy's insurance business and within a few years was making a very nice living. I got a job working for the Atlanta paper writing a weekly column and occasional articles about Southern culture and traveling in the South. We would travel to out-of-the-way places across the region and the paper picked up our expenses. I always tried to make sure that my schedule coordinated with Georgia football games, so we had a blast the first ten years we were married.

Somewhere along the way, I guess, we settled into a routine. You know how it is when you've been married for a long time--you fall into a rhythm. You get up, you go to work, you go on vacation, you do your usual activities, and the years just pass. I knew that we'd had some down times, but isn't that the way of any long-term relationship? In my eyes, the only way to keep excitement in a relationship long term is to fill it with drama and living that kind of life is my personal idea of hell.

I guess I'm kind of the opposite of a drama queen. I work out of my house writing and I actually like to paint, knit, and play with my dogs. I love to cook, I like to work out, I do yoga, I love SEC football. I've still got the same big circle of friends I've had since I was a kid, my very best friends are all my college roommates, I'm on great terms with my family—really I'm pretty much on good terms with everyone. I'm the type of person who bakes cookies for the policemen and firemen every Christmas. I give money to charities for kids and dogs, I'm nice to old people, and generally, I'm exceptionally cheerful. Of course, now I can add that I also run over people with cars and get arrested by cops. Lawd. My dad will be so proud.

Anyway, so there I sat. In a six by eight foot jail cell. And in case you were wondering, the jail was just as nasty as you'd imagine. The whole place smelled like a combination of various body fluids, BO, and industrial strength Pine

Sol, so I was perched on the edge of the bunk trying to make myself as small as possible, so that I touched as little as possible. My mind was racing as my ADHD kicked in, so I checked my watch, figuring it had to be at least an hour since I got there. Nope. Fifteen minutes. Are you freaking kidding me? I'd been in there 15 minutes? I was in hell.

The rest of my time passed pretty much in the same fashion. Fifteen minutes of intense periods of ADHD-induced stream of consciousness thinking, then a minute of pure panic. I kept wishing they would just come get me, get this done, and let me get the hell out of there.

About three hours later, it hit me that my husband was in the hospital and was undergoing surgery because of me and I was trying not to cry, when suddenly Tiffany was in front of my cell, and she's smiling. More panic. Holy shit, it's like one of those 1970's prison movies. I'm about to become Tiffany's bitch. I could feel my eyes get big and I was trying to decide if I could outrun her, or if she'd leave me alone if I puked on her or wet myself, when she asked, "Hey Martha Stewart, is it true that you found out your husband knocked up his secretary and you splattered his nuts with your car?"

I winced. Well, that really didn't sound so good when you put it that way. I tried to answer, but it came out more like a squeak, so I tried again. Now it was just a big torrent of verbal vomit. "Uh, yeah. I guess that is pretty much what happened. Although, I didn't actually mean to splatter his nuts, and, technically, it was actually only one nut, but yeah, I guess that is pretty much what I did."

A wide grin spread across her face. "You're okay, lady. You look like some little fancy suburban princess, but instead, you are just a tiny little badass. Come with me and we'll get you out of here."

I followed her down the hall. My new BFF Tiffany told me where to stand to get my picture taken and even got me my purse so I could use my brush and some bronzer to make me look presentable. She took the first picture, and then motioned me back when I stepped away. "Get back over there. We're gonna take another picture. You look whipped and I want you to look like a badass so you'll look good on the news."

My heart sank. "What? What do you mean 'on the news'?"

She laughed. "Honey, everyone's talking about it so I'm sure you're gonna be all over the news tonight. I'm going to take a picture that will warn every cheating asshole about what he can expect to have coming if he screws around. Your name will be like Lorena Bobbitt, but instead of cutting it off, you'd just smash it on the wall."

I was appalled. Holy shit. I do not want my name to be synonymous with castration of any sort. What in the hell have I done?

She finished with my picture and did my finger prints. About that time, Lola appeared and told me we could go. I thanked Tiffany for her help and followed Lola toward the door. Before we left, Lola turned around and stopped me from leaving. "Look, there are a lot of news people out there. Do not say anything, just let me do the talking and we're going to get you out of here as soon as possible."

I thought she was kidding. "Lola, you're so full of it. I'm sure there's someone from the paper since I work there, but who else really cares about this stupid little situation?"

And then we walked outside.

It was a zoo. There were flashes and cameras and tons of people surrounding us on all sides, "Ms. Monroe, were you trying to kill him?" "Are you getting a divorce?" "Are you going to hire the same people who represented OJ?"

I couldn't help it, I stopped at that one and turned to Lola. "Isn't that Johnny Cochran, and isn't he dead?"

Lola nodded and put her hand on my back to urge me along, but I couldn't just let that go. I mean, come on, I work for the media and I was embarrassed that one of my colleagues would ask such a dumbass question, so I pointed out, "Uh, no. Johnny Cochran is not only dead, but extremely dead, like since 2005 or so, so no, he won't be representing me."

Lola pushed me along and all the way to her car all I could think about is them matching the bumper impression to the hole in my husband's testicle chanting, "If it doesn't fit you must acquit" and then I realized that there was a good chance I was losing it.

Lola stopped when we got to the front of her car and turned to face the cameras. "Ms. Monroe has no comment at this time, other than to say this was not intentional, it was an unfortunate accident, and no crime has been committed. Mr. Monroe is fine, he's resting comfortably, and we believe that this entire matter will be resolved quickly. Thanks for your time."

Lola pushed me into the passenger seat and fought her way to the driver's door and climbed inside. She looked at me for a minute, trying to gauge if I was really okay. I must have looked all right, because she smiled and put her car in gear. "Where to?"

"I guess we should go to my house so I can grab the dogs."

Lola shook her head. "Not a great idea. There's already reporters there waiting on you. Mo picked up your pups and took them to her house, so why don't you just come home with me?"

That sounded great. I rested my head against the headrest and relaxed for the first time in hours. "How's Bobby? Have you heard anything else?"

"They removed the testicle, but they were able to put in some kind of prosthesis, so he's not going to look like some kind of freaky one-ball wonder. He's got a huge bruise and a hairline fracture on his leg, but he's going to be totally fine. They're keeping him for observation because of the risk of clots, not because there's a problem."

I nodded and thanked her for checking on him for me. She reached over and patted my leg. "Hey, can you tell me what happened?"

I threw up my hands. "Lola, I swear I didn't mean to hit him. Don't get me wrong, I was super-pissed. He'd just told me he'd knocked up some pre-teen slut from work and I just realized that meant that he'd been having unprotected sex with both of us at the same time. He was standing in front of my car and I just wanted to get away from him, so I hit the garage door and threw my car into what I thought was reverse, but apparently wasn't. Next thing I knew, he was pinned between my car and the wall. I called 911, told him to call his skanky whore so she could take care of him at the hospital, and went inside to eat dinner."

She laughed at that mental picture. "So, he's in the garage, rolling around the floor, wailing and grabbing his one intact testicle and you're inside eating takeout?"

That got a reluctant giggle out of me. "I guess so. And you know the rest."

We pulled up in front of her building and she hit the opener and pulled her car into the underground garage and parked. We walked into her private elevator and rode in silence up to her condo and walked in the door.

Lola lives in a reclaimed lace factory between Inman Park and Virginia Highlands that has been converted into loft condos. It is one of those kind of lofts that you see in design magazines, with exposed brick, and exposed air conditioning pipes and free standing walls and reclaimed hardwood floors from a 250-year old Amish barn in Pennsylvania. Lola owns the building, so her loft takes up the entire top floor.

I guess that needs a little explaining. Lola's family is one of the oldest families in Georgia. They were Jewish business owners who came over from Germany in the late 1700s right after Georgia was settled. They moved to Atlanta in the 1800s and were clothing merchants. When the Civil War came, or as my great-aunts called it, "the War of Northern Aggression," they switched over to making uniforms, and after the war was over and a huge portion of Atlanta lay burned and in ruins, they started buying land and putting up buildings to rent. By the turn of the century, their family owned a huge portion of what is now downtown Atlanta, so as Atlanta grew, so did their wealth. Their money had been invested in a ton of already paid-for real estate and they were distributors of illegal alcohol during the 1920s, so unlike many wealthy people in America, when the stock market crashed, they came out just fine.

Anyway, Lola's parents and she and her brother are the only remaining family members, so when they sold most of the family holdings about ten or fifteen years ago, they each ended up with close to a billion dollars, after taxes. Lola promptly bought the old lace factory for next to nothing and had it overhauled. She had our friend Sara, who is a talented designer, design her loft and it is absolutely jaw-dropping. She has a rooftop pool with a terrace patio and an amazing view of the skyline, and built a separate pool and terrace behind the building on the ground floor for her other condo owners. The building was sold out before it was even completely built.

Lola was born Stephanie Markowitz, but hated that name since birth. She staged some sort of hunger strike when she was twelve, refusing to eat until her parents let her change her name. After three weeks, and fifteen pounds that she couldn't afford to lose, they finally gave in and Stephanie Markowitz became Lola Prentiss. Her mother was mortified, stating that the name Lola chose made her sound like some kind of stripper, which made Lola like it even better.

Lola is a lawyer, specializing mostly in criminal law, because she likes being in court and she likes working for herself. She's long and lanky, with blue eyes and olive skin, and is one of those women who always looks pulled together. She drives a red Mercedes convertible and an enormous Ford F-250 Super Duty truck, also red. I don't get the whole truck thing, but she loves it, so that's good enough for me.

We've been best friends since we met at orientation our first day at UGA. She'd deny it, but she's one of the most kind-hearted, generous people you'd ever meet and she's my very best friend on earth. I'm so glad she's on my side.

Other than law, she has a real estate license, she's part-owner of several local businesses, and she also does some real estate investing. She set up a foundation with a chunk of her money that she uses for charitable causes in and around Atlanta. She gives money to various pet rescues, the children's hospital, and to small charities that she thinks actually make a difference. She singlehandedly funds a shelter for women who are trying to turn their lives around and funds medical and dental care for women who have left abusive situations. I can't count how many random people have had their medical bills and tuition paid anonymously by Lola.

She's also been a huge help to all of us, her closest friends. Whenever we need a mortgage, we go to her, she has her lawyer draw up the papers, and we have our money. It's great because we don't have to pay all the bank charges, and it's great for her because we insist on paying one point over standard in interest since there's no hassle and costs, the loan is secured with real estate so her interests are protected, and she's making more interest than she can make in a regular investment nowadays.

I flopped onto my back on one of Lola's huge leather couches. She came in and put a glass of wine on the table. "Sit up, chickie, we need to talk." I sat up, grabbed the glass, settled into the corner, and looked at Lola.

"Here's the deal. You could be in real trouble here. If the TV folks hadn't gotten ahold of this, I'm sure I could have made this go away, but since it's all over the news, and because of who your dad is, the DA has to at least address it. One of my cop buddies just sent me a copy of the initial report, and the investigating officer says it looks like an accident, so if Bobby agrees and doesn't want to press charges, this will disappear on Monday. But if Bobby is pissed and decides to be a dick about it, we may have a problem."

"I'm sure can convince Bobby it was an accident." I chugged the rest of my wine and shrugged. "But, if you want to be real about this, I also thought Bobby would never cheat on me, so what the hell do I know?"

I held out my now empty glass and Lola got up and refilled it. She kissed me on the top of my head and sat back in her seat. "Okay, we all figured you have a lot of stuff to do this week, and you don't need to go to your house until everything dies down, so here's the plan, so far. Mo's keeping your dogs at her house for now. Sara is going to go by your house and pick up the mail, grab some of your clothes, and make sure the house is okay. Mo and I figured that sending Sara was the best idea, because if one of those news people is stupid enough to ask her what she's doing there, the amount of cussing that will ensue will ensure they'll have nothing usable for the news. It'll just be one long bleep."

Lola and I laughed at the thought of what Sara would say to those poor news people and she continued. "Look, Mo told me to tell you she can sneak you into the hospital tomorrow to see Bobby without anyone seeing you." I smiled at that. Mo is a nurse at that hospital, so I have a feeling that my entry will be through the basement and I'm sure that Mo will make sure nobody messes with me.

Mo is a behemoth of a girl who, when we met, was one of the best volleyball players at UGA. The first time I met her, I couldn't get over her size. When she opens her mouth she has the sweetest, softest, most feminine Southern voice you've ever heard. She is married to a man who's even bigger than she is, her husband Harrison, a 6'9" high school football coach and chemistry teacher, whose goal in life is to make sure that his sweet Mo is never upset, uneasy, annoyed, uncomfortable, or even slightly inconvenienced. It's a riot to watch.

It turns out that Mo was always an oddity in her family. She has four sisters, three of them runners up to Miss Georgia. One of them actually was Miss Georgia but lost Miss America to a girl who'd lost most of her tongue in a freak bicycle accident, but still somehow sang like a bird.

And as an aside, what the hell does that mean? How do you lose your tongue in a bike accident? Why did no one else ask this question in the interview portion of the competition?

Anyway, Mo is not a pageant girl. Mo is an athlete. She was recruited by just about every college in the universe for volleyball, but decided to go to UGA and the four of us, me, Lola, Mo and Sara, all met the first week of classes.

Mo was Sara's roommate in the female athletic dorm, which was also the dorm for women in the honors program. Sara is no athlete, unless you consider drinking and cussing to be sports. In fact, Sara is the most uncoordinated human I've ever met. I once saw her fall up the stairs and break her nose. Sober. She was adopted from China as an infant and is even shorter than I am, about 4'9". She has this booming voice with a loud Southern accent and every other word is generally a cuss word. It's always hilarious to see Mo with her big body and her sweet little voice and tiny little Sara with her big booming voice. The first time people see them together it kind of looks like a bad ventriloquist act.

Sara went to school to be an interior designer and got her four year degree at UGA with us. After we graduated she went to Georgia Tech to get a two year master's degree in industrial design. That's where she met her husband Mark, who is now an architect. She does some free-lance design work when she feels like it, but mostly she stays home with her four kids and does the mom thing.

How lucky am I to have all of these women in my corner. They're all wonderful friends. They are sarcastic, they're snarky, they all cuss like sailors, but they are also kind, generous, and loyal, with huge hearts. I can depend on them for anything.

Lola and I sat there in companionable silence with the

lights down looking at the sky line of the city, drinking wine. After a while, Lola turned to me. "You want to talk about the rest of it?"

I felt my throat burn and my eyes started to water. "Nope. Not yet."

Her voice was gentle. "Do you need anything, sweetie?"

I shook my head, fighting back tears. "No. I've got exactly what I need right now. Wine and you."

I saw her smile at me in the dim light. I took a deep breath. "Shit. I'd better call my folks. Last time I checked there were already about ten messages from my dad."

Lola shook her head and got up to grab the phone from the table next to me. "I'll call him. I talked to him for about two seconds while you were being booked, but I didn't have any details then. This way, you won't have to deal with anything tonight, and they won't have to worry about you."

She dialed the number, and obviously my dad answered, because I heard her side of the conversation. "Hello sir, she's fine. Worn out, but fine. No sir. Yes sir. No sir. Aggravated assault. No sir. No sir. I expect to be able to get this dismissed as soon as they talk to Bobby the idiot. No sir. The TV people might have made the connection to you by now, but I made sure the arresting officers and the people at the jail knew before she got there. No sir. No sir. No sir. No, I don't think you need to call anyone over there. They released her on her own recognizance, most likely because of you, and I expect to get this taken care of before she has to make an appearance. Yes sir. No sir. I'll keep you posted. Yes sir, Bobby is a freakin' moron. I'll call you and let you know as soon as I get this taken care of. Take care and I'll be in touch."

As soon as she hung up the phone, I asked, "How are they?"

"Exactly as you'd expect. Your daddy is pissed, and your mom was embarrassed by all the fuss. Both of them were pissed about Bobby."

I nodded. "That sounds about right. So they're fine."

Lola nodded. "Yeah, I think they're fine."

I got up and poured us both a glass of wine. "Thanks for saving me the call. I was afraid my mom would answer."

Lola winced. "So was I, but your dad was easy to deal with, as usual."

At eleven, Lola turned on the TV. "You want to see if you made the evening news?" I didn't really, but I told her to go ahead. She turned on the television and there I was, in all my glory. One story had the title "the Nutcracker", one had pictures of me all over it, at a Georgia game, one from some benefit Lola made us go to last year, my head shot from my newspaper column, and my mug shot.

Lola was impressed. "Holy shit, your booking photo looks amazing. No crazy-eyed, crazy hair, Nick Nolte mug shot for you. That's a great picture."

I looked at it objectively. "Wow. That really is a great picture. You think Tiffany will do my professional picture next time I need one?"

We kept flipping the TV, but holy crap, I was everywhere! Every story seemed to portray me as the poster child for punishing cheating men, and Bobby came out looking like a lying cheating pig, which come to think of it, he pretty much was.

I couldn't believe that I was on every channel. "Oh my Gawd, Lola, how long is this going to go on?"

She shrugged. "Who knows? I mean, it could blow right over or it could linger on depending if the national news picks it up."

My heart sank. "National news?!" I squeaked. "Are you freaking kidding me?"

Lola nodded. "Don't you remember that stupid thing with Lorena Bobbitt? People still know her name. The thing you have to worry about here is that it's like a strike against evil...stupid men that leave their amazing wives for bimbos young enough to be their daughters. It's going to strike a chord among a lot of people."

"Shit. I don't want to be a poster child for anything. I just want to get on with my life. I need to talk to Bobby and figure out what we need to do. Maybe this is just some weird-ass midlife crisis and this whole thing is just a mistake. Maybe she's not really pregnant, maybe it's not his. Who the hell knows what the deal is? All I know is that I really need to talk to him before I do anything stupid."

Lola looked doubtful, but she just nodded her head. "Okay, then. Let's go to bed and we'll figure it all out in the morning."

I guess I did fall asleep because I woke up the next morning to sunlight streaming through huge windows in one of the condos guest rooms. By the time Lola and I got ready and ate breakfast, it was about 9:30. We called Mo, and when we pulled around to the back of the hospital we saw her standing outside by the place they unloaded the ambulances.

She picked me up in a hug that about broke my ribs, and then held me at arms' length so she could see my face. I guess I looked okay, because she hugged me again and then started giving me instructions. "Okay, sweetie, here's what you need to know. I love you and you're going to get through this just fine. Don't worry about your pups. They're having a great time with Harrison and me, so they can stay with us as long as you need. I've put security on the floor where

Bobby is, so you'll be able to get up there without having to deal with any of the news people. And after you see him, if you need me to, I can get assigned to Bobby and I'll be happy to work him over a little myself, so you just let me know."

I knew she would do exactly that. I smiled and hugged her back and Lola and I headed upstairs. When we reached the floor, I told Lola I needed to talk to him by myself, so she nodded and told me she'd be sitting in the lounge by the elevators if I needed her. As I walked toward Bobby's room, my feet were dragging and I felt like my entire life was ending. I got to his room and knocked on the door and heard his voice tell me to come in.

I paused, suddenly thinking, what the hell am I going to do if she's in there? Now I wish Lola was with me. Lola is much scarier than Bobby, especially now that he's laid up with a broken leg and one testicle. Well, one natural testicle.

I pushed the door open and held my breath until I could see it was only Bobby in the room. As I looked at him in the hospital bed, the first feeling I had was worry at how pitiful he looked, and tenderness because I'd loved him since he was a teenager. I waited for the other feelings to surface, but nothing did. I started to feel a little hope. Maybe this whole thing was just a mistake, maybe it was just a bad dream.

As soon as he opened his mouth, that hope went out the window, "Daisy. What, they wouldn't let you up here with a car to finish me off?"

I deliberately shut the door behind me and was a little gratified to see nervousness in his eyes. I took a deep breath and tried to make my voice as neutral as possible. "Hey, Bobby. How you feeling today?"

He looked down and his voice was polite, but he

sounded completely detached. "I'm fine. Thanks for stopping by, but I think you should get going."

I couldn't believe that cold, stranger's voice was coming out of Bobby. My throat started to feel tight and tears filled my eyes. "Bobby, I think we need to talk." When he heard tears in my voice he finally looked at me and softened a little. We looked at each other for a long moment and he sighed and told me to sit down.

I took a deep breath and started toward the bed and sat in the chair by his side.

Despite everything, I really was glad he was okay. I took a deep breath to compose myself, but I was nervous so I started to babble. "Bobby, I'm really sorry for what happened. I swear it was an accident. I didn't mean to hit you. And I especially didn't mean to mutilate your testicle and break your leg. I just wanted to leave, not run you over, but I guess I was just upset and I got confused, and I thought the car was in reverse, but it wasn't, and the next thing you know..." My voice trailed off and I just stared at him with big, teary eyes.

When I was done, he nodded. "I believe you. Once I had time to think about it, I realized that it was an accident. You might be a lot of things, but you're not the type to run people over when you have a problem with them." That made me laugh. "Look, the police are supposed to come by later today to get my statement, and I'll make sure that they know it was an accident so you won't have any problems."

I sniffled and thanked him. "I appreciate that, Bobby. Did you happen to see the news?"

He winced, but then he laughed. "Hey, your mug shot was a great picture."

"Right? Maybe I'll have the jail do my head shots from now on." We both laughed at that.

He sobered and looked at me. "Do you want to talk about all this?"

I didn't, but I nodded that I did. He took a deep breath. "I'm really sorry, Daisy. You always hear people say 'it just happened', but it really did. Another guy in the office and I had to switch administrative assistants and I ended up with Barbie."

I literally had to bite my tongue so I didn't say, "Well of course her name is Barbie. Did her mom tell you that when she brought her over for her first playdate?"

"Anyway," he said. "It happened over a long period of time, and one thing led to another, and, well, now she's pregnant and I love her and I want to marry her."

I just sat there watching the words come out of his mouth, and it still didn't seem real. What I wanted to ask him was, how could he be willing to throw away all those years, all our history, for some little bimbo named Barbie. Seriously?! Barbie?! Didn't he realize what a ridiculous cliché the whole thing was? Didn't he realize how stupid it sounded?

What I actually ended up saying was, "Do you want a divorce?"

"Yes," he said immediately.

I took an involuntary breath. "Bobby, don't you want to try to work on this with me?"

He didn't hesitate. "Not really, Daisy. Don't get me wrong, I love you. I will probably always love you, but it's more like how you love your sister. My relationship with Barbie is true love."

I snorted before I could stop myself. "Bobby, seriously? You're forty-six years old. How can you be in love with some little girl who's less than half your age? What the hell do y'all even have to talk about?"

I was completely serious. How do you fall in love with someone who is just a baby?

At that point, he looked me in the eye, and I swear to God, he said, and I quote, "We're soul-mates and age is just a number." I just stared at him like he was a total idiot, and all I could think is that if he's really that freaking stupid then he totally deserves a skank like her.

But I didn't say that. I'm proud to say I didn't lose it in front of Bobby. I stood up and calmly looked at him. "Well, okay then. I'll call our lawyer to start drawing up some papers and we'll get this done as soon as possible." I stood up, clutching my purse in front of me like a shield. "And thanks for clearing up any confusion with the police and the district attorney." And, with that, I turned and left the room with as much dignity as a woman labeled "the Nutcracker" by the local media, could muster.

Lola didn't say a word when I joined her at the elevator. I made it all the way down the elevator and out to Lola's car before I lost it. Again. I turned to Lola, barely able to get out words through my sobs. "Lola, I don't understand. How in the hell did my life fall apart in one day? Yesterday at this time, it was just a regular day. I was working on my column, I was walking the dogs, I was picking up dinner for my husband, and today, I have an arrest record, and I'm getting a divorce. All in less than eighteen hours. That has to be some kind of record. I don't think I've ever heard of anyone who actually turned her entire life to shit in less than a day. Except for me."

Lola interrupted me to hand me a wad of paper towels she tore off a roll she grabbed from the backseat. "I thought you might need these if I was going to be driving your crying ass around."

I took a handful and laughed one of those stupid little

hiccupping laughs you do when you're trying to stop crying. I wiped my face and blew my nose and took a deep breath. "Okay, that's it. I'm done crying over Bobby Monroe. I'm calling our lawyer and we're going to get this divorce over with as soon as possible."

Lola handed me the roll of paper towels and grabbed my used ones and tossed them in the back seat. "Look, I'm sure there's gonna be a lot more of this before there's less of it. Don't worry about it. You've got your family, you've got a ton of friends, you've got Mo and Sara and the guys, and most importantly, you have me, so you're going to be fine. Did you talk to Bobby about the accident?"

I nodded my head. "Bobby said he was supposed to give a statement to the cops this afternoon and he'll make sure they know it was an accident."

She nodded and muttered, "That's the least that asshole can do." She smiled at me when she realized I'd stopped crying. "As soon as he's done with the cops, I'll go down and get the charges dismissed and that'll be it. Once that's done, the whole thing can blow over and you can get your life back. Or start a newer, better one."

I started to cry again. Lola threw her arm around my neck and kissed me on my cheek. "Come on. Let's go back to my place and we'll call Sara and Mo and make some kickass margaritas and get some enchiladas delivered."

Lola called Sara and Mo from the car, so by the time we got to the house, they were already inside mixing drinks. As soon as they saw me, they both came running over to give me a hug. Mo had brought my three dogs with her, and they were delirious to see me. It was a basic madhouse, which was wonderful and exactly what I needed. Sara had stopped by my house and brought me a bunch of clothes, so I was set for the next few weeks, if necessary.

We ate and drank margaritas, hung out on Lola's patio, and by that evening, I was relaxed and happy. Mo was checking to see if there were any pregame shows for college football the next day. As she flipped through the news channels, there I was. On ABC. On FOX. On NBC. On CBS. I turned to look at them. "Please tell me this is the local news."

They all looked at me, and they all shook their heads wordlessly.

"Shit. Shit. Shit. National news?" I looked at them. They all nodded their heads.

Then Sara started to laugh. Then Lola. Then Mo. Then finally I started to laugh. "Holy shit! I'm on the national news for flattening my husband's testicle with my car." We were laughing so hard we were crying. "Her name is Barbie, she's twenty years old, and I think her mom has to take her and pick her up whenever they want to have sex because she still just has her learner's permit."

By this time we were collapsed on the floor. My dogs were leaping around us trying to lick our faces and we're rolling around laughing like idiots with tears pouring down our faces. It was so ridiculous, it really was hilarious.

Sara sat up and grabbed her margarita. "Hey ladies, check it out. Instead of having a glass jaw, Bobby has a crystal ball—all it took was one shot with Daisy's Volkswagen and he was down for the count, pieces of testicle all over the place."

That made us laugh harder. I grabbed my margarita. "Too bad we couldn't use that crystal ball to see my future, because mine is looking a little uncertain right now."

Sara shook her head. "Once you get past all this shit, your future is going to be awesome." Sara raised her glass. "I'm pretty sure I can't say the same about Bobby. But here's a toast to Bobby and his crystal ball. May the future he deserves be exactly the future he gets." We all laughed and nodded, clinked our glasses and took a huge drink.

I knew it was going to be fine. Eventually. Just fine. Once the rest of this stupid crap died down, we could all get back to our regular lives and I could start getting through and over all this.

2

THE THING WAS, IT DIDN'T GO AWAY. BOBBY AND LOLA talked to the police and everyone agreed it was an accident and the charges against me were officially dropped first thing Monday morning. But, everything else took on a life of its own. Somehow, my stupid accident had become some sort of rallying cry for women who'd been wronged everywhere, and then the other side came out saying that it was some kind of attack on family values, although Sara pointed out it was really more an attack on family jewels, and it just went downhill from there.

Two weeks later, my dogs and I were still camped at Lola's because every time I tried to get near my house I was mobbed by reporters. Now don't get me wrong, there's plenty of room at Lola's but I needed things to get back to some kind of normal so I could start moving on with my life. Bobby had texted me that he got an apartment, and Mo and Sara said the skank was living with him. Apparently, they were bored one night after their respective husbands got home so they made a pitcher of margaritas, paid one of Sara's kids to drive them around, and then followed Bobby home after work. Then, they hung around to see who else showed up. About 10 minutes after Bobby went inside, some young pregnant chick who, they pointed out, looked a lot like I did at that age, pulled into a parking space and went inside.

I felt a little relieved. At first, I had wanted us to get together and talk about it and maybe we could stay together and work things out, but every time I started to call him to discuss it, I just couldn't do it. All I could think about was that he was a liar. Every time he was late or he told me something about where he was and it didn't quite make sense, he was with her and obviously he could look me straight in the face and lie without a bit of problem. I don't see any way to come back after something like that.

And he had unprotected sex with some slut at the same time he was sleeping with me. Every time one of those cheating scandals break, I'm always infuriated on the wife's behalf. Really? These guys have unprotected sex with one skank after another and then they'd have sex with their wives? Endanger your own health if you want, but how can you do that to your wife who did nothing wrong but be loyal to your cheating ass? I'll bet every one of those women did the same thing I did after they found out, which was to run to the doctor and get tested for every skank disease you could get. Every STD I could think of, HIV, HPV, Hepatitis, herpes, syphilis, gonorrhea, crabs, hell everything but Ebola, you name it, I was checked for it.

Loyalty is a huge deal with me, and he proved he can't be trusted, plus I no longer respected him, so the decision was clear. I was done.

So, thanks to my two personal drunken private investigators, I now realize he's also done. Now, I just needed to decide what my personal vision of divorce looks like. And I need to stop crying. The way I have coped with the idea of divorce so far is to cry, then drink and/or eat, then work out, then sleep, watch bad TV, then cry some more. Sometimes I changed the order. My boss at the paper has been very understanding about the whole situation and he's reassigned a couple of stories that have come up. Fortunately, I had about three months' worth of columns already written, so I don't really have to do any work on those for at least another two months, which is a gift. If I had to try to write while this is going on, I'd also have to look for another job.

I made Lola's favorite meal for dinner, baked scallops and shrimp with an heirloom tomato salad and some grilled zucchini, and waited for her to get home. She changed clothes, I served dinner, and we sat down to eat.

Midway through, I put down my water. "Lola, I've got to do something with my life. You know I love living with you, but my pups need a place to run and I've got to get back to a normal life."

Lola nodded. "You're right. It's time. So let's figure this out. First thing, do you want the house?"

I had thought about it and kept going back and forth about it, but I had finally made some decisions in the past couple of days. "I don't think so. We lived in that house together for twenty plus years, and I think it's a better idea for me to start over somewhere else." I looked at Lola. "But I don't know anything about the market right now. Is this a good time to sell? I'm not sure what I should do."

Lola jumped up, excited. "I know exactly what you should do! I have a friend at the courthouse who is desperate to find a place in your school district and your house would be perfect." Lola picked up the phone, called her friend, and set up a time to show her the house the next morning. We polished off dinner and went to bed.

It turned out Lola's friend loved the house. Best of all, she was willing to pay full pop, and had cash up front, so we didn't have to wait for a mortgage approval. Bobby immediately agreed to the deal, so Lola put one of her real estate lawyer friends on it and they had the whole deal wrapped up in a red-hot minute. By the time the house was sold a month later, Bobby and I each cleared about a hundred grand on the deal.

Then, also thanks to Lola, I ended up in the most adorable bungalow in the heart of Virginia Highlands, five minutes from her front door. Lola said that she had just closed on a house that she planned to flip, and it was perfect for me. It turns out that some local contractor had been renovating a bungalow, but he ran out of money and then he pissed off the bank. The bank foreclosed on the loan, and a friend of Lola's from the bank told her about the deal. Lola got it for the remaining amount of the loan, which was fifty thousand dollars, then she paid to have the renovations completed, which cost about ten thousand dollars more, and she let me have it for what she had in it. Sixty thousand dollars.

When I asked her how she managed to find ridiculous deals like that, she said that when you have a bazillion dollars, every banker in town wants to kiss your ass. Good point.

Seriously, though, it was insane. My sixty thousand dollars shouldn't have been able to buy the front door of this house, the most beautiful, cozy little bungalow I'd ever seen. Lola could've made a huge profit if she had sold it on the open market. When I told her that, she looked at me like I was crazy. "Really, Daisy, like I need more money?" She winked. "I'd much rather have you at my beck and call right down the street." She then grabbed my face in both hands and stared into my eyes. "Seriously. I want you to hear me. The first time I saw this house I thought of you, but you didn't need a house then. Now you do. I really want you to have it."

The day after I agreed to buy it, Lola told me to go over and see if I wanted any changes made before the construction guys left. I harnessed the dogs and walked over, went inside and just sat there, soaking it in, loving that this beautiful house would be my new home. That night, I told her that it was perfect, I wouldn't change a thing.

Lola is really more like a fairy godmother sometimes than my best friend. Every time I try to thank her for another wonderful thing she does for me, she just waves me away and says, "Oh please, it's just money." Money to her doesn't really mean anything because she has so much of it, so I'm very careful not to take advantage of our relationship. Most importantly, I do things for her that aren't money related. I bought her a Kindle reader and put her on my Amazon account so every time I see a book I know that she'd like I buy it and we both can read it. She's a great bartender, and she can have food delivered like a champ, but she is a truly crappy cook. Since she doesn't cook and I love it, when I lived with Bobby, I doubled the amount of whatever I cooked and I packed it up in a cooler for her to take home every week. She's completely computer illiterate, so periodically I'll update her computer and scan it for bugs, update her i-Tunes, and load new music into her iphone so she always has the latest workout music. Whenever she needs new equipment like a computer, or a phone, or a tablet, I'll do the research and order it for her and then hook everything up. If we're going somewhere, I research everything and make all the travel arrangements, I order her anything she needs on Amazon, and I periodically help her clean out her closets.

The truth is, more than the money aspect of this new house, I really appreciate the fact that Lola saw it and knew it was for me. If I had built it, I couldn't have made it more suitable for me and what I want in a house. It's cozy, it's colorful, it's full of light, and I love all the little touches like the stained glass around the door and the little doggie footprints in the terracotta kitchen tile. I love everything about it, and the fact that Lola would do what she did to make it happen for me just makes me happy.

That, and the fact there's no big shoes to trip over, and no underwear on the floor. There's no clutter, there's no stacks of paper and newspapers. It's always clean and neat. I just love it. I love the way it looks and feels and smells and the way it feels so comfortable to me. Whatever happens down the road, the one thing I can assure you is that I will not be looking for a man. I might eventually want some kind of friends-with-benefits kind of guy, but I see no reason for him to be living with me.

3

Once I started the process of selling my house and buying another one, I realized I needed to get control of the rest of my life. Monday afternoon, I checked the phone messages from my house. It was still full of messages from a few local magazines, every local TV channel, and holy shit, *People*. Monday night, Jimmy Kimmel actually made a joke about me. Lola was thrilled. She's a huge Kimmel fan and she figures that all she needs is a chance to meet him and he'll come to his senses and realize that she is the woman of his dreams. Well, if he wasn't already happily married with kids.

I turned on the TV the next night and two women had deliberately run their husbands down after finding out they had been unfaithful. One died, and they think one will be paralyzed from the waist down. I was so horrified I immediately turned the channel, just in time to see some late night talk show host say something about that "crazy Southern nutcracker" and that I was an assault against family values. What the hell? How does my husband screwing his assistant and knocking her up make me some kind of assault on family values?

That was it. I went out in the living room where Lola was lying on her sofa in a white silk nightgown, drinking champagne out of a Waterford crystal flute, and eating generic cheese puffs out of a bag. I couldn't help it, I started to laugh.

"Lola, what the hell? You look like some kind of ad for The Ritz-Carlton, or something. Except for the cheese puffs, of course. Beautiful nightgown, delicious champagne, redneck snack. Hilarious."

She laughed. "I love the feel of this nightgown and I love Cheetos. Bite me if you don't like the combo." She tilted the bag up to get the last cheesy crumbs and they rained all over her white nightgown. Unconcerned, Lola brushed off the remnants and smiled at me. "What's up that you're in such a hurry?"

I stared at her. What did I want? Shit. I hate walking into a room and forgetting why I went there in the first place. Oh yeah, the asshole talk show guy. "So, I just saw on TV that two women had killed and maimed their cheating husbands with some sort of vehicle and some jackass TV guy said that somehow I was an assault on family values. I'm tired of being the butt of late night jokes. Somehow this shit is getting twisted around so that now I'm the bad guy? What the hell? I want to set the record straight so everyone will leave me the hell alone."

"So go on TV and tell your story. Once everyone hears your version, maybe this will finally die down." Lola yawned. "Everyone has been given my number as your contact, so my phone's still been ringing off the hook with different folks who want to talk to you about it. The Today

Show, Good Morning America, you name it. Just tell me what you want to do, and we'll set it up."

I was confused. "Why didn't you tell me?"

"I did tell you. About a million times. Every time I said I got another call, you put your fingers in your ears and make that stupid "la-la-la-I-can't-hear-you-la-la-la" noise and told me to tell them to kiss your ass. So I did. I told David Lawson, the host from *The Today Show*, that you said to kiss your ass, I told some chick from *Good Morning America* to kiss your ass, and I even told that annoyingly perky chick on freaking *Great Day Atlanta*, or whatever the hell it's called, to kiss your ass. It's really been exhausting, but a little fun."

I couldn't believe that Lola had told David Lawson I said to kiss his ass. "So I guess I burned all of those bridges, huh?"

She rolled her eyes. "Of course not. Are you kidding, some famous moron and his big ass mouth just said you're a walking attack on family values. They'll want you even more now. You tell me what you want me to do, and I'll take care of it."

I thought about it for a minute. What the hell. "Give me the numbers and I'll give them a call tomorrow. Maybe if I tell my story and people realize it was just some stupid accident, they'll lose interest and they'll leave me the hell alone and even the talk show guys will shut the hell up."

When I got up the next morning, Lola was already gone. She left me a stack of messages on the counter with a note that said she would be in court all day and would see me tonight.

This was it. I was going to make some breakfast, walk the dogs, maybe make a mimosa for breakfast so I can efficiently combine the drinking and the crying all at once, then I'm going to call all these TV folks. I'm going to tell my side of the story.

After breakfast, (just coffee, no mimosas, but no crying either—yay, progress!), and a quick walk, I sat down at Lola's desk and picked up the pile of messages. Where do you even start with something like this? So I grabbed the one from *The Today Show* and dialed. Holy shit, it really was David Lawson's voice on the message. It freaked me out so bad, I hung up and then I was embarrassed because I was so stupid. Before I lost my nerve I called back and left a message, "Hey, David Lawson, Daisy Monroe here. Just returning your call. Sorry about the whole 'kiss my ass' thing, I was having a bad few, okay several, bad days, and you happened to catch me on one. Anyway, I saw some talk show jackass on late night TV and I really would like to tell *him* to kiss my ass, so if you don't mind, could I come on TV and tell you my side of the story? Oh, and it really was an accident, so you might not even think it's that interesting, but if you do, could you call me back? Thanks. Oh yeah, and in case you don't remember calling me, I'm the one who squished her cheating bastard of a husband's testicle and leg with the car. Thanks, and hope to hear from you."

I left my number and hung up and heard a snort of laughter behind me. Sara was leaning in the door frame holding her hand like a phone receiver next to her ear and imitating me in a high, annoying voice. "Okay, so in case you don't remember me, I'm the one who squished her cheating bastard of a husband's testicle...Love you, mean it, bye..." She bent over in the doorway laughing. "That's how you describe yourself now? The one who squished her husband's testicle? So what's on your agenda today, besides harassing David Lawson?"

Before I can say a word, the cell phone rings. There's no name on my caller ID, so I pick it up and say hello and a voice on the other end says it's David Lawson. I just stand there, stunned. Sara mouths, "Who is it?" and I mouth back, "David Lawson" and I'm still standing there.

I can hear him saying hello, hello, Daisy are you there? and finally I have the presence of mind to say something. "Uh, hello, yes this is Daisy."

He was unbelievably nice. I told him I was sorry about the whole kiss my ass thing, and he says he's been told worse than that, and he told me they were still interested in my story, even though it was an accident, and that no, I couldn't actually use the words "kiss my ass" to that annoying talk show host. I said, even if I'm on the section with Hoda and Jenna? He said well, maybe then. We both laughed, and he said a producer would be calling me to set up my appearance. I told him thanks, it was really nice to talk to him, and that I'd see him soon.

When I hung up, Sara and I looked at each other and I squealed. "OH MY God, I'm going to be on *The Today Show*", and we both laughed. Then I said, "Shit! If it's true that the camera adds ten pounds, I'm gonna need me some Spanx, or maybe something stronger like some sort of industrial strength girdle like my grandma used to wear."

Now I'm traumatized. I'm really not very good with clothes because I can't stand anything that's not comfortable. I remember this great quote from Gilda Radner where she said her fashion sense was based on things that don't itch, and I totally get that. As a writer, my work clothes are generally pajama pants, fuzzy chenille socks, and a long-sleeved t-shirt in winter, and a tank, pajama pants and no shoes the rest of the year. I take dressing up as a personal affront, and I haven't worn heels since a friend's wedding in

1995. The few times I do have to dress up, I consider dress clothes to be a cotton dress over leggings with flip flops or flats.

Sara patted me on the shoulder. "Look, make your calls, then we'll go shopping and I promise it won't be horrible."

Whatever. I hate to shop for clothes. Generally, the only way I'll shop is either online, or if I'm drinking, and the problem then is I'll do stupid stuff like buy eight of the same shirt, but in eight different colors and nothing to wear with it. One time I had to buy something for this stupid dinner Bobby and I had to go to, and I went drunk shopping and bought 10 pairs of holiday socks, one edible thong that did nothing but give me a fruit flavored wedgie, and nothing to wear for the dinner. It was completely moronic, but unfortunately, typical. I'm telling you, if it weren't for the Internet, I'd be naked.

Sara was thumbing through my messages and pulled one out and handed it to me. "Here. Call this chick. She's from *Early Morning Atlanta*, and I met her at some function and she was really nice."

I shrugged and grabbed the phone. Why not? Hell, I called David Lawson, why not the local girl done good? While Sara made herself a mimosa, I called and asked for Angie Morgan and she answered her phone, "Angie Morgan."

I was shocked she answered the phone. "Uh, hey Angie. My name is Daisy Monroe, and I'm returning your call."

There was a moment's hesitation and I could tell she was trying to remember who I was, so I gave her a hint. "Um, I'm the one who squished my husband's testicle with the car."

She started laughing. "Now I remember. Sorry for the lapse. So, I wanted to get your side of the story." She dropped her voice and whispered conspiratorily, "Come on, you can tell me. I assume you haven't taken up squishing testicles as a career, or anything..."

That made me laugh. "No, squishing testicles is not my normal job, it's more like a hobby." We both laughed and I told her, "Look, seriously, it was an accident and all the charges were dropped the next day, so it's really not much of a story. I do have a date to talk to David Lawson some-time next week, and I'm hoping once everyone hears that the story is a whole bunch of nothing, this will finally die down."

Angie was sympathetic. "I hope it does, for your sake. Look, our station is an NBC affiliate, so once you talk to David, you can come on with us. Just email me as soon as you know when you're scheduled with David and we'll go from there. "

We exchanged email addresses. "Sounds great. Thanks for your help, Angie."

"No problem, Daisy. I look forward to hearing from you, and I promise I'll do what I can to make this as painless as possible."

Another thing done, and I actually felt much better now that I had talked to Angie. Check. Check. Off the list. Sara asked me what else I had to do and grabbed a pad so she could take notes. I have to meet with Bobby at the lawyer's office to go over what the lawyer has put together for a settlement agreement so I can file. I still have a problem actually saying the word "divorce," so I told Sara to put "saying divorce" on the list so I won't be feel like throwing up every time I hear the word. Apparently, I have to meet with David Lawson and Angie Morgan so people will stop calling me the "nutcracker" and those late-night morons will stop harassing me. And maybe call *People* magazine.

In the meantime, I've got to go buy pants that aren't yoga pants. Maybe a dress. Definitely shoes. I asked Sara if she was ready, and she said sure, so I grabbed my keys, she grabbed a "roadie" by pouring her unfinished mimosa into a water bottle, and we headed out.

PART II

A NEW NORMAL...

4

Mo raised her glass and smiled at all of us at the table. "Here's to Daisy's new house, new marital status, and new job. Congratulations!"

Everyone at the table whooped and hollered and clinked their glasses. "To Daisy!"

I was feeling pretty cheerful, which I think is impressive considering that my divorce was just finalized as of today, exactly eight months and one day after the "vehicular testicular smackdown," as Lola calls it. Honestly, Bobby and I had what is probably the most polite divorce in history. We quietly divided our money and assets, we took our stuff, and we went our separate ways. The only reason it took so long is because we waited for some stock options to vest so we could divide the assets more easily.

In retrospect, maybe the fact that everything was so cordial was a comment on how little emotion was left in the marriage. Sara and I had talked about it late one night, how she said if she found out her husband had knocked up some skank she would have run him over on purpose then backed over him again to make sure he was good and dead, then gone and found that hussy and backed over her, too. I told her that I was furious at first, but then I was just sad. I've come to realize that I was sad that my marriage was over, not so much that Bobby and I were over. I think both of us had gotten to the point that we were more like good friends who shared a nice house and had an occasional booty call. I really liked being married and having a comfortable relationship with someone I had a history with.

On the flip side, that doesn't mean that I don't hope he gets exactly what he deserves for being such a spectacular dumbass.

I've been in my house for several months now, but I still can't believe how painless the whole moving process was, although I have to think that at least some of it was the universe cutting me some slack. Plus, Lola being part owner of the moving company didn't hurt either. Whatever the reason, the whole process was ridiculously easy, starting from the first day I did the house walk through with my dogs.

I didn't see anything else that needed to be done, and they'd already had the final inspection, so as soon as I gave the go ahead to Lola, the construction crew packed up their stuff, took down the permit signs, and moved on. The cleaning crew came the next morning, and by 3 in the afternoon, the house was sparkling clean and ready for me to move in. On Saturday, Lola and I took her pickup truck and moved all of my clothes over to the new house, plus we packed up some breakable things in the kitchen, all my toiletries and personal stuff, photographs, and my wind chimes and yard art and took them over, too. It took a lot of work, but by Saturday night, everything that I had brought over was put away and I was ready for my new furniture to be delivered on Monday. On Sunday morning I spent a few hours at the old house going through my old kitchen cabinets, pulling out all the things that I wanted and leaving the rest in the cabinets for Bobby. That way, everything that needed to be packed was out on the counters and ready for the movers to box it up.

I had asked Harrison and Mark to buy a big TV for the living room, and a couple of nice sized ones for my office and bedroom. They are both great with anything involving technology, and I know nothing about televisions and care even less, so I was thrilled to hand them my credit card and send them on their way. So Sunday afternoon, Harrison, Mo, Mark, and Sara met us at the new house with the TVs in the back of Harrison's truck.

When they piled out of the truck, Mo and Sara saw me and started laughing. Sara rolled her eyes and shrugged. "Just remember, you asked for a big TV."

Oh no. I turned to see Harrison and Mark wrestling a huge, flat box out of the back of the truck. My eyes widened when I saw it. "Holy shit!" The box kept coming. "How big is that thing?"

Harrison laughed and Mark looked at me innocently. "What? You said you wanted a big TV, so we got you the biggest TV that would fit in the space."

That damn thing looked to be the size of a drive-in movie screen. "How big is that?" I shook my head, laughing, because I should have known better than to let them choose the size. You know a man always thinks bigger is better.

Harrison grinned broadly. "It's the perfect size. Seventy inches". He winked at me and said in a low, Barry White voice, "Baby, come on, you know size matters." That made me laugh as he continued. "Seriously, Daisy, we did the math and this size is the perfect size for this space. In other words, this is the biggest TV you get without having to sit outside in the yard to watch it." They carried it past me, laughing as I stood there looking at it with my mouth open.

Mark smiled. "Daisy, I promise you, the first time you watch a Georgia game on this bad boy, you're gonna be loving us and our awesome taste in electronics."

I laughed as they put it down by the bookcases and went out to unload the rest of the truck. They brought in the other TVs, which looked to be much more normal sizes, then they brought in the mounts for all the walls, extra cables, and surge protectors. Three hours later, the TVs were on the walls and the guys had done a great job hiding the wires. By the time they were done, we had ordered Chinese food and ate it on the floor in the living room, laughing and having a great time. When we all left, I told them to plan on coming by Wednesday to check it out, because I'd be completely moved in by Tuesday night.

Monday morning, the cable and phone company people came by to turn on my service and everything worked perfectly. The TVs all worked without any hassle, and I had to admit, I already loved my hugely obnoxious TV. When I turned it on, in that little space, it was like having a jumbotron in my living room. I remember what the guys said about football looking great on a big screen so I found a replay of last year's SEC championship game on the SEC network, and the guys were right. It was fantastic. I couldn't wait for fall. I called both of the guys to thank them again and to tell them how right they were and that I loved, loved, LOVED my new TV. It was actually a little embarrassing how happy it made me.

That afternoon, a team of Lola's delivery guys showed up with my new furniture and my washer and dryer. The new sofa, chair, and the tables fit perfectly in the living room, my kitchen table was beautiful, and my new bedroom furniture was great. I'd gotten a queen sized bed with a tall padded headboard that fit perfectly between the two windows on the bedroom wall. I'd found a beautiful Art Deco dresser that looked great with the bed and fit in the corner by the door and I was planning to put my great aunt's cedar chest across from the foot of the bed. So far, I was thrilled because everything fit like it had been made for my little house.

On Tuesday morning, the movers showed up at my old house promptly at 8 am, ready to go. Here's what I discovered about moving. If you have people pack all of your stuff and then unpack all your stuff and put it away for you, moving is easy. I showed them which furniture pieces were going, so they started with that while I went through my books, stacking the ones I wanted to take on the floor and leaving the rest on the shelves. I shoved the piles on my desk into a tote bag and they packed up everything else. It was kind of magical...like having a team of five really large, sweaty elves. I'm sure it didn't hurt that Lola-the-owner was working right alongside them.

By one o'clock, everything was packed and loaded on the truck and we were heading over to the new house. They placed the furniture where I indicated, put the boxes in the correct rooms, and started unpacking. Lola and I headed to the kitchen and started unpacking that, because I use the kitchen all the time and I'm really picky about everything being in its place. Otherwise, with everything else, so long as it's in the right room, I can figure it out later. Once we finished the kitchen, I went into my office to make sure the furniture was where I wanted it and I hooked up the computer, printer, and scanner, plugged in my phone, and put my piles of research back on my desk. Lola's guys had simply taken out the desk drawers and covered them, not emptied them, so once they put them back in the desk, everything was exactly where it was supposed to be.

Next, Lola and I went out to her truck to get the bags of clean sheets and towels. I'd gone to Costco for new towels and pillows, and ordered all new sheets, blankets, and quilts from Amazon. I'd washed them as they were delivered to Lola's place, so all we had to do was put them on the beds.

By Tuesday at five o'clock, the movers were finished and gone. Books were on the shelves, art was on the walls, the kitchen was completely unpacked and organized, the beds were made, towels were in the bathrooms, everything was done. It honestly looked like I'd lived there for years and it was beautiful. Apparently, all it takes is a team of movers to cater to your every whim, some money, a little work, and a lying, cheating husband to get you the house of your dreams. Who knew?

5

OH, AND I HAVE A NEW JOB, WHICH IS PRETTY hilarious. Yes, I'm still writing my weekly column and occasional feature articles for the paper, but I now have a weekly segment on *Early Morning Atlanta* where I talk to local figures who have done something of interest. Basically, I do fluffy, feel-good pieces. Last month, I did a short test piece on a local lady who saved the park in her neighborhood, and last week, I interviewed a kid who raised $10,000 on the Internet selling virtual lemonade for cancer research. Both segments got great feedback, so my first, full-length story is next week. So far, I'm having a blast.

I know, how ironic is it that the reason I'm doing feel-good pieces is because I ran into my lying, cheating husband with a car? That doesn't really seem right, does it? This does just go to show that life can turn on a dime.

Here's what happened. When I went on *The Today Show*, it ended up that David and I really had a great time together. The interview ended up being really fun, and then I went on the Atlanta morning show, and Angie and I were laughing and kidding around and I had a great time then, too. About a week later, I got a call from the show's producer and they asked me if I would be interested in doing a weekly segment on some local interest stories. I asked her if I had to dress up and she said no, they'd get together and find me something funky to wear that wouldn't annoy me, so I said I'd have to think about it and get back to them.

When I told my friends about it, they were all adamant I should take it. This is a great time to make a change, I should take on a new challenge, blah, blah, blah. I couldn't find a reason not to do it, so I called the producer back and told her I was in, and that was it. Now I write my column and articles for the paper, and I'm also a local TV chick, which is really kind of a hoot.

I keep trying to figure out exactly when it was that our marriage started to go bad. I think it started about five years ago. We both started taking separate trips with our separate friends, then we started doing different things on the weekend. We'd see each other during the week, but it was usually just a combination of eat, hang out a little, go to bed, and go to work, so when we stopped doing things together on the weekend, we started to lose touch.

The thing was, we've always enjoyed each other's company, so it's not like it ever got uncomfortable. When we did go to football games with our friends we'd have a great time. Several times a week, we'd take a walk after dinner and it was always comfortable and fun. We never watched TV together so some nights we'd eat dinner together and then wouldn't see each other again till bedtime. We'd have sex sometimes, nothing exciting, but I always enjoyed it. Again, it was never anything but easy and comfortable.

I'll have to admit, even now, I still don't really see a

problem with that. I've never been a grass is greener girl. My grandmother always used to say that if everyone took all their problems and threw them in a big pile, we'd all take our own back out. No one has a perfect life, everyone has stuff to deal with, and although another person's life might look better to you from the outside, you never really know what's going on behind closed doors.

I totally get that, but I guess some people don't. I guess Bobby doesn't. You always see all those men on daytime talk shows, and when they have affairs they all say the same thing. It's that she "made me feel young," or "made me feel needed," or "made me feel excitement again."

Whatever. Of course you feel that. Because it's new, dumbass. Everything new feels exciting. Everything new is exhilarating. Here's the thing that these guys forget. Once the newness wears off, you're back to the same problem, except now you've traded one set of problems for a new set. I saw a t-shirt online that said, "For every great guy, there's some woman who's tired of his shit." That's so true. No relationship is perfect.

Let's face it, it wasn't just Bobby. I mean, the affair was all Bobby, but what led to it was complacency on both of our parts. I was complacent to the point of not even seeing a problem and he was he was unhappy and wouldn't even put the effort in working with me to make it better.

But, bottom line, I'm not the reason Bobby wasn't happy. Bobby was the reason he wasn't happy, and unless he makes some changes in himself, a couple of years down the road, he's going to have the same thing happen again. But, the difference is that now he'll have a wife young enough to be his daughter and a kid, which he had always said he never wanted because he didn't want to change his lifestyle. And yes, I have to admit I do get quite a bit of pleasure from that.

Does that make me a bad person? Maybe, but mostly I just think that makes me a human. We all want justice, and I think one of the best forms of justice is when the universe gives someone exactly what he deserves.

As I drove around the corner toward my house, I felt the little jump of happiness. My beautiful little home. It's so weird how some things in your life just belong to you from the moment you see them. My little Bug convertible was that way. The first time I saw it, I knew it was mine, and every time I see it, it makes me smile. Each of my dogs is that way. Now, the house is the same way. When I pull in the driveway, I feel peaceful and happy. It's so cute, it's so warm, and it already totally feels like home.

But, as I pulled into my driveway, my peaceful feeling rocketed away. Shit. Why in the hell is Bobby at my house? It actually kind of freaked me out, like I'd somehow conjured him out of thin air. Damn it, my grandmother was right, God don't like ugly. The minute I start to think mean things about Bobby he shows up in my yard.

As I pulled in, Bobby waved uncertainly. Come to think of it, he was probably uncomfortable with him being on foot and me being in the car. The dogs were going crazy trying to get to Bobby since they hadn't seen him in months, which actually made me feel a little bad. Bobby had lived with all of them since they were puppies, and I'm sure they missed him. Of course, they also didn't know that he had left all of us to live with some pre-teen skank, but hey, they are just dogs. I put the car in park, put up the top, and pulled the keys out of the ignition, shaking them in front of Bobby so he'd know he was safe from another incident of unintentional vehicular assault. I grabbed the leashes and we stepped out of the car, just as Bobby rounded the corner of the car and bent down to get his delirious greeting. I pulled the dogs away from him and started towards the front door. "How's the leg? I see you're not limping."

He straightened up. "Yeah, everything healed up fine, no problems."

"Congratulations." I started pulling the dogs up the walk and he followed us to the front door.

When I started to unlock it, he was right behind me. I raised my eyebrows at how close he was and he smiled and backed off a little. "You mind if I come in?"

Actually, I did mind. A lot. One of the things I liked best about the house is that there were no memories of Bobby anywhere in it, which made it much easier in my post-divorce adjustment process. I handed him the leashes and pointed to the gate to the backyard. "No, you take the pups back to the screened porch and I'll meet you there in a minute."

He shrugged and headed to the back. As soon as he rounded the corner, I threw open the door and ran through the house to the back door and opened the door to the porch. He was letting the boys off their leashes to run in the backyard. I told him, "Have a seat, and I'll be right back." I went back inside and grabbed a couple of glasses of tea and came back out on the porch. I handed him a glass and took a seat on the glider across from him.

"What do you want, Bobby?"

He could not have looked more uncomfortable as he avoided my question. "Wow, Daisy. This house is really pretty. Can I get a tour? I'd love to see what you've done with the inside."

By that time, I was getting irritated. "Maybe later. Is there a problem with the divorce or the settlement?"

He shook his head. "No, everything's fine. That was really great that you found a buyer so quickly."

I put down my tea down on the table next to me. "Yeah, well, that was all Lola. I had nothing to do with it. Again, Bobby, what do you want?"

He looked down at his glass and started fiddling with the condensation on the outside. I knew he did that when he was nervous or uncomfortable, so I just waited. Finally, he lifted his head to meet my gaze, took a deep breath, and started to talk. "I just wanted to tell you I was sorry that I hurt you and that, on some level, I'll always love you. I really want us to be friends."

I felt my face get hot and I could tell my blood pressure was shooting up. I clenched my hands together, fighting the urge to punch him in the throat. "Friends? Really Bobby? Yeah, I can't see that happening any time soon, because sneaking around behind my back and lying to my face isn't what friends do."

He hung his head for a moment, then started to reach for my clenched hands before thinking better of it and pulling it back. He met my eyes again. "Look, you're right. What I did was terrible, but I really miss seeing everyone. I know it's way too early right now, but I was thinking that maybe next season we could all join up for a Georgia game. I mean, just because we're done as a couple doesn't mean we can't all still be friends."

I just sat there with my mouth open. Seriously? He thought he and his prepubescent baby mama could join all of us for a game? I really didn't know what to say. How freaking clueless can one stupid man be?

I pasted an insincere smile on my face and leaned forward. "Sure, Bobby, I think that's a great idea. I'll tell you what. You give Lola, Sara and Mo a call and ask them how they'd feel about hanging out with you and Barbie, and if they say yes, we can all hang out together." From the horrified expression on his face, I think the mental picture of what Mo, Lola and Sara would say, and possibly do, to him after a request like that freaked him out. "You'll be lucky to make it out with your remaining testicle intact." I gave a little laugh, leaned back, crossed my arms over my chest and winked at him. "Just let me know when you make that call, because that is a show I would not want to miss."

He sat back and took a long swig of his tea. Monroe had come onto the porch and was sitting by Bobby waiting to be scratched. Bobby absently began scratching above his tail sending Monroe into a happy dance of ecstasy.

I pushed the glider into a slow rock and changed the subject. "The dogs miss you. Any time you want to see them, you're welcome to come take them for a walk. And by 'you', I mean you, not you and little Miss Skanks-a-lot."

He rolled his eyes. "Really? 'Little Miss Skanks-a-Lot'? Nice." Although it did make him smile.

I wasn't ready to make nice. I picked up my glass and drained it, then I stopped the swing as I planted both feet on the floor, narrowed my eyes, and glared at him. "Bobby, here's the way I see it. I'm nowhere near being okay with your girlfriend, so you'd better get used to that. There's not a snowflake's chance in hell that the two of y'all will be going anywhere with all of us. I can't speak for Harrison and Mark, but they're not really thrilled with you at the moment and they sure as hell aren't going to piss off their wives, so you might be out of luck on that front, too."

Bobby slammed his glass on the little side table. "Shit, Daisy, What do you want from me? I told you I'm sorry. I didn't mean for it to happen, it just did."

I was furious. "Oh please, shit like that doesn't just

happen, Bobby. All you had to do was keep it in your pants. What are you saying, you were walking by her desk, for some reason she was totally naked and spread eagled on her desk, you tripped and just fell in? If so, that's a horrible workplace injury and you should talk to your daddy about the agency taking over child support since that's what resulted from your little 'accident.'"

"It wasn't like that."

I felt my blood pressure rising so much I could feel my heartbeat in my ears. Damn it, I would be so pissed if I had a stroke and keeled over dead in front of him, so I took a deep breath and tried to calm down. "Really Bobby? What was it 'like'? You say you've always loved me, you say you've always been my friend, but you were so disrespectful of me and our twenty plus years together that you screwed around behind my back? If you wanted to be with your little trashy girlfriend, you should have had the decency to get a divorce first then do whatever the hell you wanted. I would never have done something like that to you. You don't do that to someone you supposedly care about."

Bobby slumped in his chair. He knew I was right and that there was really nothing left to say. He patted Monroe and stood up to leave. He looked me in the eye. "Daisy, I really am sorry."

I stood up and met his gaze. "I do believe you're sorry, Bobby. But it doesn't really matter because it doesn't change anything. You did a really shitty thing to me and you're going to have to live with the consequences, whatever they may be." He shoved his hands in his pockets and turned to go, but I wasn't quite done. "Oh, and by the way, one of those consequences is that you're no longer welcome to sit in Lola's seats, so you might want to start looking for your own tickets."

He actually staggered back a little. To a good old Southern boy like Bobby, the loss of 50 yard line box seats at the Georgia game is about the worst thing that could happen. He nodded and left.

I leaned back on the glider and started a gentle swing. Monroe and Cletus jumped on the glider with me and pushed their big hound heads onto my lap. I started petting them and scratching under their chins and they immediately fell asleep. Within about a minute, Diego jumped up on the glider, wiggled his way in between the other dogs' heads and went to sleep.

So there I was, in my beautiful little house, with a lap full of dogs on my fabulous glider, and all I felt was sad. I guess that's normal. Lola had commented late one night that losing Bobby is like losing my younger self because he was a part of everything I ever did from the time I was eighteen years old. I miss all of us hanging out together, I miss our get togethers before the game, and I miss our walks after dinner. The truth is, I've started to realize I miss the idea of Bobby more than I miss the actual Bobby, but it's still sad.

I wonder what Bobby's going to do a couple of years from now when he wakes up and realizes what his life has become and what he's lost? The truth is that I'll still have the same friends, we'll all still hang out together and go to games and take weekend trips, and Bobby won't have any of that. Of course, he still has plenty of casual friends he can hang out with, but they're not the same types of friends that he's lost. Interesting. And totally not my problem.

I stopped rocking and told the boys to come inside to get something to eat. They flew off the glider and through the doggie door, I grabbed the empty glasses and followed through the big girl door. I fixed them their dinners and then took the cellphone on the porch to call Lola and tell her about Bobby's visit.

I told her what happened and she was quiet as she thought about what I had told her. "Well, why do you think he actually came over? Was he really just trying to apologize for being such a huge dick?"

Good question. "I do think he feels bad about what happened, but I think his main problem is that he doesn't like that I apparently got all of y'all in the divorce." Lola laughed, and I continued. "Seriously, I think he was seriously bummed when he heard that Mark and Harrison had gone on an all-day golfing extravaganza last weekend and he wasn't included. I think he's gotten a taste of what his life is going to be like, and he doesn't like it, so he'd hoped I'd say we can all be best buds and hang out together."

"He's such a dumbass." I laughed at the disgust in Lola's voice. "As if we'd do anything with him and Baby Skank. I'm pissed that you got to tell him about the tickets. I really wanted to be the one to tell him so that I could see his face."

"I'm really sorry I spoiled your fun, but the timing was perfect. And, Lola, if it makes you feel better, he looked like he'd been shot. It obviously had not occurred to him yet."

"Well, I'm sorry I missed it, for all kinds of reasons, but it is interesting. Maybe reality is starting to bite him on the ass."

"Maybe so. I'm going to tell Harrison and Mark that they didn't have to stop hanging out with Bobby, but please not to do it if I'm around."

Lola snorted. "Yeah, I don't think that'll be an issue. Mark and Harrison are pissed that Bobby would go behind your back like that." She rolled her eyes. "Yeah, basically they think he's an idiot."

I was so lucky to have these people. "That's because he

is an idiot." We both laughed, said goodnight, and I went inside. I was afraid I'd have problems sleeping after my talk with Bobby, but I didn't. I watched some TV and I baked some red velvet cupcakes and cheese straws to take to Lola and the folks at the TV studio, and then I slept like a baby.

6
———

I WOKE UP THE NEXT MORNING TO SUN COMING through my bedroom window. There was a huge patch of sun at the end of my bed and all of the dogs were stacked up in a row in the ray of sunlight. As soon as I lifted my head, little Diego ran up to the top of my bed and tucked under my chin, his hot little tongue trying to lick my nose. I grabbed him and tucked him next to me, rolled him on his back and started scratching his little fat belly which put him in a doggie coma in about 20 seconds. We lay there for a while until my stomach started to grumble. At the sound, Diego's little head popped up and he ran to the bottom of the bed frantically wagging his tail, looking back at me to join him. Cletus and Monroe jumped up and stood with Diego, waiting for me to escort them to the kitchen. I got up and we all walked toward the kitchen to fix our breakfasts.

I filled the boys' bowls, and then went into my office to check my emails and text messages. Apparently, Lola had told Sara and Mo about Bobby's request to hang out with us and his girlfriend, because their return comments were pretty colorful.

By then, the boys were done eating, so I hooked them up so we could walk to the coffee shop and get some breakfast. In the hound dog way, we slowly made our way through the streets of the Highlands sniffing every leaf, patch of grass, and vertical surface, until we reached Java Vino coffee shop. I tied the boys outside and went inside to get a latte. When I came out, a large man in a ballcap and sunglasses was sitting at my table petting my dogs. As I came to the table, he looked up and smiled at me. "Nice dogs."

I smiled back and thanked him and stood there with my coffee in my hand, waiting for him to move. He kept smiling at me, petting the dogs, and obviously didn't get the hint. Finally, I'd had enough. "Pardon me sir, but I'm already sitting here."

He grinned at me. "I assume then these are your dogs, Ma'am?" He stood up and waved his hand toward the empty chair across from him. "Why don't you have a seat and we'll talk?"

I was confused and frustrated. Who in the hell is this guy, and why won't he get out of my seat? Haven't I dealt with enough annoying men in a twenty-four hour period?

I put my drink on the table, looked at him with an insincere smile, and said in a sugary voice, "Sweetie, I'm sorry, but why am I looking to talk to you? I just came here to relax and have some coffee with my pups. No offense, but I'm not really in the mood for company." I stood there with my hands on my hips and waited for him to do the polite thing and leave.

He didn't budge, and as I began to look even more irritated, he started laughing. "Daisy, don't you remember me?"

He pulled off his sunglasses. I looked at him carefully and all of a sudden I saw the face of the boy he'd been when

I knew him in college. I started to laugh. "Lord have mercy, look at you. Luke Mathis."

He stood up laughing and came around the table to hug me. "Yep. Good to see you, Daisy. Sara told me you'd probably be here this morning, so I came by to say hey."

I looked him over and had to admit he'd grown up very nicely. Brown, wavy, hair with a lot of gray on the sides, blue eyes with laugh lines that stood out in his tan face, a big, muscular body with nice shoulders, the kind of lean hard muscles that are made from hard work, not gym muscles, long, strong legs, big hands and feet, and damn how tall was he? 6'3" or 4", at least. Luke is Sara's cousin, something like fourth cousin twice removed, which in the South is just called "cousin." We had all hung out together our first few years at Georgia. He was dating Glenda, who was a pretty girl but kind of mean, and dumb as a bag of hair, and I was dating Bobby, and then he and Glenda moved back to his home state of Louisiana after he graduated early. I hadn't seen him since, but had kept up with him through Sara who said he'd been working in New Orleans, gotten divorced a while back and recently moved to Georgia.

"I hear you got divorced. Sorry."

He smiled at me. "Thanks. I heard the same about you. I hear it even went down the same."

I raised my eyebrows. "Really? So Glenda knocked up her twenty-year-old secretary and then you got in a fight and accidently pinned her to the wall of the garage with your car and it was on the news for weeks and made you the poster child for adulterer castration?"

He dropped into a chair across the table and winced. "Ouch. No, I meant they were both fooling around. Holy shit, seriously?"

"Please. Like I would make that up. Does any part of that like a positive for me?" Luke laughed. "Let's face it, it either makes me sound old, or crazy and pathetic, and I really don't care for any of those things."

He smiled. "I think it makes you sound lucky."

Okay, that's about the sweetest thing I'd ever heard. I found myself staring into his laughing eyes and I mentally shook myself and tried to pay attention. "So what happened with you and Glenda? We're you just as 'lucky,'" I made little quotation marks with my fingers, "...as I was?"

He wrinkled his nose and shrugged. "I think so. She left me for someone else, and I consider that to be extremely lucky." That made me laugh, and he continued. "Basically, she was pretty and I was a teenager with a lot of hormones and not a lot of sense. Once I grew up, I realized that Glenda was a lot of blonde hair, big boobs, and a whole lot of bitch, but not much else, so I buried himself in work and she buried herself in shopping and self-maintenance. After that, we had some issues and she left and I came back here."

"So, does she still live in New Orleans?"

He shrugged. "Who knows? Wherever she is and whatever she's doing, I'm sure it involves lots of parties and having her nails done."

I shuddered. Attending functions and having my nails done is my personal idea of hell. Luke saw my face and laughed. "I can tell you haven't changed much since college, Daisy."

I laughed, too. "Well, I still hate to dress up and I still hang out with the same people and do the same things, except now, I have my own fabulous house and my own car and a job." He grinned at me. "So, why did you come to see me, Luke?"

"Sara told me you were living in the area and I just

wanted to say hey." Diego jumped in his lap and licked his mouth before Luke could react. Sputtering, Luke grabbed his muzzle and kissed him with a loud smack on his mouth, which cracked me up. He smiled at my reaction. "I've spent most of the past twenty plus years running a huge construction business. I was totally fried so I sold it, and I'm looking to do something totally different. Right now, I'm teaching a class on residential construction a couple of times a week at Georgia Tech, which is fun, but for the first time in years I actually have some free time and I want some folks to hang out with."

"Well, you've come to the right place, at the right time. Sara and Mark are cooking out this Saturday and Lola, Mo and Harrison, and I are all going to be there. You know everyone, so you should come."

He looked happy. "I'm in. It'll be great to see everyone again. What time?"

I gave him the details, and we chatted for a few more minutes and I told him I had to go. Tomorrow was my first longer segment on the morning show, and Lola was coming over later to go over a few things and so she could approve my outfit.

He put Diego on the ground and stood up to go. I smiled up at him and he picked up our cups and tossed them in the trash can. "Well, Daisy, it was great to see you, and I look forward to seeing all y'all this weekend." He leaned over and kissed my cheek and then waved as he headed off. I waved bye, gathered up my pups, and then headed home.

The next morning, I stood in the front of the mirror at the station and nervously checked my teeth to make sure I didn't have spinach stuck in them, or more likely Cheetos, since I'd been hanging out with Lola the night before. Teeth fine. Hair not sticking up. Remembered to remove the Kleenex on my neck that kept the makeup off my shirt. Check. Check. Check. I was dressed in black jeans and a light green top the same color as my eyes. I wanted to wear all black because I'd never been a long lanky girl and it was true that the camera does add ten pounds, although if you're short and overly curvy like me, I swear it's more like fifteen. Maybe thirty. My boss told me that all black doesn't make you look thinner on TV, so Lola approved this shirt because it drapes nicely, it's actually stylish, it doesn't wrinkle, and it's a good color for me.

I had found a really interesting woman for my first long segment. Marie White had been a stay at home mom for several years until her husband killed himself. Marie found herself at forty-three with two teenage kids, a mountain of debt and an IRS tax lien on her house and bank accounts. For the next several years she took every job she could find, including a job as a phone sex operator, because she could do that at night from home while her kids were asleep.

Long story short, she eventually bought the phone sex business and franchised it. In fact, if you ever see a sign for Goddess4U, that's Marie's company. Her business is in an office park in Roswell and she has a call center for those who don't want to work out of their home that is beautifully decorated and is ergonomically designed for the operators' comfort with comfortable chairs and neck-saving headsets. She offers medical insurance for all her full time employees, plus a 401K and paid vacation. It's amazing what she's managed to accomplish and she's an incredibly cool chick. I think most of my viewers are going to think she's as awesome as I do, even though my boss wasn't sure about the fact it was a phone sex business. I finally convinced him that most of my followers were women my age who would find this very interesting, and he agreed to let me give it a shot, so long as I focused on the business side and promised there would be no demonstrations or invitations for me to participate. We'll see how it goes.

It turns out the interview was amazing. Marie came across as caring and determined, and I looked like I was having a great time, which I was. My entire life, I've always loved other people's stories, and I'm one of those people that other people will tell everything to, whether we're in a private room or in line at the Walmart. I think I just have one of those faces that makes people want to talk to me, but Lola says it's because I'm friendly to people and there are a lot of people out there who don't have anyone to talk to, at all.

That to me is very sad. I've always had a lot of friends, although Lola, Sara, and Mo are my absolute best friends, so I can't imagine that my only option of someone to talk to is someone in the line at the Walmart. However, it's happened to me enough that I guess Lola is right. There are a lot of people out there without a great support system, so maybe my goofy little interviews will help people realize that there are plenty of other people out there with problems just like theirs.

7

I WAS PRETTY HAPPY ABOUT MY FIRST INTERVIEW, AND was excited to tell everyone about it. When I woke up Saturday morning, it was a gorgeous spring day. The sun was shining, the humidity was low, and it looked like the perfect day for Sara and Mark's cookout. I got up, took a shower, got dressed in an old pair of shorts and my favorite t-shirt that said, "Dogs and Day Drinking," fed the mutts, took them for a quick, well, quick for them, walk, and called Sara to see if I needed to bring anything. She told me to come on over and we'd make a grocery store run and get everything we need. I leashed up the mutts, put down the top, belted them in and headed over to Sara's.

As I came into the backyard and shut the gate behind me, my pups spotted Mark over by the grill and started howling in excitement, so I let them off their leashes. In their experience, Mark is a reliable source of various cooked meats, so they love to hang out with him whenever we get together. I went over and hugged him. "I'm going in to grab some coffee. Want a refill, since it's still a little too early for beer?"

He rolled his eyes and handed me his empty mug. "Yeah, that would be great, but to clarify, it's never too early for beer." I went inside and saw that the pot was almost empty, so I rinsed it out and started a new one. As I waited for the coffee to brew, I looked out at the backyard and marveled again at how beautiful it was.

Sara and Mark's backyard is what happens when you put an architect and a designer together and turn them loose to create whatever they want. It's almost an acre and is a mix of beautiful trees, flowering bushes, and year-round flowers that provide a profusion of colors all over the property. There's a pool that looks like an old swimming hole, with a waterfall. He's always getting leftover rocks and plants after jobs are completed, so there are walkways and patios that meander all over the property. Sara, who is a master gardener, has combined beautiful flower beds along with various vegetables so it's beautiful and functional. Every year I buy her a bunch of flowers and fruits and vegetables to plant, and she supplies me with fresh produce all year. It's fun for her because I try to find unique plants that I know she'll enjoy and I've even gotten her involved with an heirloom seed exchange with a lady I interviewed for the paper last year.

The coffee was done, so I poured us two cups, doctored them, and took Mark's out to him. He was cooking a couple of butts and some ribs on the smoker side, and we were having burgers and dogs on the grill, so he'd set up his area with an umbrella and a book. He'd turned on the outside speakers to classic rock, and had an ottoman to prop his feet on. All three of my dogs were sprawled around Mark's feet, figuring that whenever the meat was coming, they'd be ready. I grabbed a chair and settled across from him so I could share his ottoman.

Mark is one of my favorite people. He's tall with salt and pepper hair, has a runner's build, and is kind of quiet and very laid back, which is a great contrast to his tiny dynamo of a wife. We sat and drank our coffee in comfortable silence. Suddenly I realized it was too quiet. "Hey, where are your kids?"

He laughed. "They all heard about the party and decided to spend the night out so Sara wouldn't be able to rope them into some kind of indentured servitude."

That made me laugh. "Me, too. I saw her out front and hurried past her before she hijacked me and made me clean the fish pond or something."

Mark looked around to make sure Sara wasn't around before he spoke. "Look, if we see her, we need to look extremely busy. She said something last night about wanting to put in a waterfall and I'm not in the mood for that kind of work."

I nodded in agreement. "So who all's coming today?"

He took another sip of coffee. "The usual suspects. Us, Lola, Mo and Harrison, and the kids and their friends will wander in eventually." He got up to check the smoker and satisfied with what he saw, he sat back down. "Oh, and I think Luke is dropping by. He said he saw you out the other day."

I nodded. "Yep. He sounds happy to be back so I'm glad he decided to come".

Mark agreed. "Yeah, me too. He's a great guy and I'm glad he moved back to town."

I was curious about Luke and what happened to him in New Orleans. "He seemed kind of evasive about it when I asked about it last weekend."

Mark winced. "Sorry, Daisy, I think you really need to ask Luke about it. It's a long, bizarre story and I think it really needs to come from him." He scrambled to his feet and made a production of opening the smoker and checking the condition of his wood chips.

I narrowed my eyes and stared at him. "I know why you just did that. And you should know that checking your charcoal won't make me go away, big boy."

He rolled his eyes, very familiar with all of the women in his life and how we worked. "No shit. Nothing makes any of you go away." He poked his pile of chips with long-handled tongs to resettle them, shut the lid, and settled back into his chair. "Seriously, Daisy, it's not a fun story, it was a really bad time for him, and I don't think I should be the one to tell it."

Fair enough. I knew that at some point Luke would tell me what had happened, so I changed the subject to let Mark off the hook.

"Have you seen Bobby?"

Mark shook his head. "No, but he's called me and Harrison every week to see what's going on during the weekend." Mark looked disgusted. "He just doesn't get it. He thinks it's no big deal, that we can just jump back into hanging out like we always did. He actually said that, quote, 'once Daisy calmed down,'" he made little air quotes with his fingers, "'...it shouldn't be a problem if we all hung out together.'"

I felt like my head was going to explode. "Are you freaking kidding me?" I jumped to my feet and threw up my hands. "Like it's my fault? Like I'm having some temper tantrum and am keeping all of y'all from hanging out with him and his baby skank?!"

Mark laughed. "That's pretty much my reaction, too. Last time I talked to him I told him that none of us were interested in hanging out with him and his teenage baby mama, and that he might need to find some new friends to go with his new life."

I was grateful to Mark for his loyalty and felt tears well up in my eyes. I kissed him on the cheek and settled back into my chair. I actually kind of felt bad for Bobby because these guys had been some of his best friends since college and apparently I had gotten all of them in the divorce. He really had no close friends left. "Look, Mark, I love y'all for being so sweet, but I really don't mind if you and Harrison wanted to hang out with Bobby if Sara, Lola, Mo and I aren't around."

He his head. "Yeah, we offered that as an option, but it doesn't look like that will work. Apparently, baby skank doesn't like him going anywhere and doing anything without her, and Harrison and I both made it clear that we were not hanging out with the two of them together."

Okay. I was loving that. She won't let him hang out without her? That's hilarious.

About that time, Sara came into the backyard and Mark and I pretended not to see her and instantly tried to look busy. Mark leaped to his feet and checked the fire and I grabbed our coffee cups and headed toward the house, supposedly to get us a refill. Sara rolled her eyes. "Y'all are so full of shit. I'm not going to make you do anything, so you can relax."

Mark and I froze and looked at each other, unconvinced. She had fooled us before. She sighed and put her hands on her hips. "I just came back here to get Daisy so we can go get groceries. Mark, you need anything?"

We relaxed and Mark dropped back into his chair. "Just some cheap beer. Nothing fancy. Bud Light or Coors Light is good."

I raised Mark's cup to see if he wanted a refill. He shook

his head and smiled and I headed inside. He grabbed Sara's hand and pulled her on his lap, "Other than that, whatever you want is good. Get some hot dogs and buns." He kissed her quickly on the mouth and helped her back up. "And I think we need some buns for the hamburgers and the butts, but we have plenty of burgers."

She smiled and patted his face as she got up and followed me inside.

I went into the kitchen, rinsed out the cups, and put them in the dishwasher. Sara grabbed her purse and keys, and we headed out the door. We decided to take her SUV since my Bug is pretty limited size-wise, and as she pressed the button to unlock the door, I felt my heart rate speed up as I realized she was planning on driving. I casually asked, "Hey, Sara, why don't you let me drive."

She shook her head and started to get into the driver's seat. Now I was feeling a little panicked. "Sara, seriously, please let me drive. I'm begging you..."

She shot me a nasty look. "Just get in, buckle up, and shut the hell up." I rolled my eyes, but I got in, buckled my seat belt, tested it to make sure it was secure, and pushed my seat back as far as it would go so I'd be farther away from the airbag.

The truth is, Sara is a terrible driver and none of us let her drive anywhere if we can help it. One day, when Sara had almost wrecked us trying to avoid a squirrel, Lola told her that as a woman of Asian descent, she should not be such a bad driver because it just perpetuates the stereotype. Sara didn't say a word, just threw up her middle finger, looked in the rear view mirror to stick her tongue out at Lola, and promptly ran into a brick mailbox.

Honest to God, that was about the funniest thing we'd ever seen. She flattened both tires on the passenger side and ripped the bumper off the front corner of the car. Mo took a picture of Sara looking down at the car with the bumper cover in her hand and the most pitiful look on her face you've ever seen. All of us have a framed copy of that picture. Mine's on my desk at home, and it makes me laugh every time I see it.

I think that's what I love the most about these women. They are all so funny and so full of life and just a blast to be with. My mom asked me once if I thought we'd ever grow up, and all I could think of is that if growing up means calming down and not having fun when we're together, then no, we'll never grow up.

It was sunny and warm, so we rolled down the windows, turned up the radio, and headed out. It was going to be a beautiful day. Well, if we made it back in one piece, that is. "Hey, did Mark tell you that Bobby has been calling him every week?"

She snorted. "Yeah, I know it. I told Mark to tell that jackass that he and his skanky whore are never welcome around us, whether you're here or not."

I started to laugh. "Hey Sara, you sure he understood your position on this? I know you're not very confrontational, ha, ha, ha." I had no doubt about her loyalty to me, and I also know if Bobby asked her directly, that would be her actual answer. "Seriously, though, I don't care if the guys want to hang out with him if I'm not around."

Sara shook her head. "They really don't want to. They're as disgusted with Bobby's behavior as we are, and they refuse to have anything to do with the baby skank. Apparently, she won't let him out of her sight, so he can't hang out with anyone unless she's there."

She and I looked at each other and started laughing. She intoned in this deep voice, "Be careful what you wish for, little boy." We yelled at the same time, "Because you just might get it!'"

We got back from our errands to find that Mo and Harrison were in the backyard with Mark. They had all moved onto the screen porch, and Mo was in the hammock and Mark and Harrison were in two rocking chairs with their feet on the coffee table. They all had a beer and were lazily rocking back and forth, chatting about whether we should all take a vacation together this Christmas. I could hear my dogs chasing some varmit in the woods. I indicated that Sara should join them on the porch. "Go sit. I'll unload the car and put everything away."

Instead, Mo got up and followed me and Sara out to the car. It took three trips but we finally got everything inside and started putting it away.

Lola came in just as we finished. As usual, she looked like she had just stepped off the pages of a fashion magazine, even though she was wearing a pair of old denim shorts and a faded UGA t-shirt. I shook my head, marveling about how Lola always managed to look put together, no matter what she was wearing, whereas I was the exact opposite. I could be in a ball gown with professionally done hair and makeup, and within ten minutes, I would look like a hot little mess with some spill on the front of my dress, my hair standing on end and dragging a piece of toilet paper from the bottom of my shoe. Hilarious.

I was just about to tell her how awesome she looked when she casually asked, "Hey, did y'all see Bobby parked out front?"

My jaw dropped. "What do you mean, 'did y'all see Bobby parked out front'"?

Lola shrugged and said she'd seen Bobby in front of the house. "I walked up to the open window, grabbed the front of his t-shirt, and whispered in his ear that he'd better get the hell out of here before I got my car and took out his other testicle. Bobby turned pale and said that he knew we were all together and wanted to talk to all of us. I told him it wasn't a good time and that he wasn't welcome and that if he wanted to talk to us, he could text us and make an appointment."

That was it for me. I saw red. I told all of them to stay there and stalked around to the front of the house and out to the street. Bobby was leaning against a minivan, and I marched up to him, planted my feet, slammed my hands on my hips, and demanded, "Bobby, why are you here?"

Bobby squared his jaw and straightened up, jabbing his finger in my chest. "I want a chance to talk to everyone face to face. You have turned all our friends against me and I'm tired of it." He stepped forward and started crowding me backwards and his voice got louder. "They won't even give me a chance because you told them they couldn't see me."

He grabbed my arms and shook me a little, which infuriated me. "Get your hands off me, Bobby," I hissed. I tried to pull loose, but he was pissed and a lot bigger than me, so I couldn't get away. He wasn't hurting me, but I was getting madder by the minute. "Look you stupid jackass, I never told them they couldn't hang out with you, but get it through your head, they have no desire to hang out with you and your adolescent skank. Do you understand that when you chose to leave me, you chose to leave your old life, too, and that includes your old friends? That's not my problem."

About that time, I felt someone come up behind me and heard a quiet voice above my head. Harrison, all 6'9" of him, was towering over both of us. He tapped Bobby's shoulder, leaned over so they were eye to eye, and quietly said, "Bobby, you need to let her go. Now."

Bobby obviously didn't like what he saw in Harrison's face and immediately let go. I stepped back, rubbing my arms and suddenly Mark was also there and both Mark and Harrison moved slightly in front of me in case Bobby didn't keep his distance. I stood between them, my fists clenched, and narrowed my eyes. "Bobby, it's over. You made a choice and I sure as hell wasn't it, so you have to live with the consequences." I saw movement to my right, looked around Harrison and saw Mo, Sara, and Lola standing off to the side. "But you know what, if you have something to say to all of us, we're all here, so go ahead and say your piece and then you can leave. And I don't want you anywhere near me again."

He stepped back toward the minivan, opened the door, and leaned inside. He motioned for someone and all of a sudden, a small blonde woman who looked to be about seventy-two months pregnant climbed out to stand by him. I couldn't help it. I gasped. Holy shit, I can't believe he brought the baby skank here. Mark and Harrison moved aside as Mo and Sara came up next to me and Lola stepped up behind me and put her hands on my shoulders.

It was just bizarre. The strangest thing was that she looked exactly like me when I was that age, except her face was a little thinner and she was a little taller and her hair was blonder, more of a white blonde like you see on little kids. Which, come to think of it made perfect sense since she looked like she was about fifteen. She had this enormous belly, which she hugged protectively as she stood in front of us staring at a spot on the ground in front of her. Bobby put his arm around her shoulders and casually introduced her as if we'd all run into each other at the mall, or something.

"Everyone, I'd like you to meet Barbie." He then started introducing her to each of us individually, explaining who was with whom and then how we'd known each other since college and had been friends ever since. All of us simply nodded once, too inherently Southern and polite not to acknowledge her, but not wanting to engage her in conversation.

Bobby blathered on, pointing to me and introducing me as "Daisy, you know, my previous wife," and I could feel my friends tense up even more. I patted Lola's hand to keep her quiet and quickly smiled at Mo and Sara to let them know I was okay.

And you know, it was weird, but, I swear I was totally okay. I realized that I really didn't feel anything except relief that the confrontation was actually happening and that I was fine with it. I stepped forward and offered my hand to Barbie, which she took warily. I shook it firmly once and let her go and turned to Bobby, and with a sugary polite voice said, "Well, it has been so incredibly nice to see y'all, thanks so much for stopping by, but we have to get everything ready because we've got some people coming by later. Have a nice day." I then turned away and started walking toward the house.

It turns out that Lola was not so nice. She was furious. Mo later told me that she completely ignored Barbie and walked up to Bobby. She held out her hand and when he automatically took it, she pulled him in close and glared at him with narrowed eyes. "Bobby, I want you to hear what I'm saying. Don't ever try this shit again. Don't ever show up uninvited anywhere near us. You and your skank are not welcome at any function we have, at any of our houses, or at any event we are attending. If you show up, I will have you both arrested for trespassing, I'll get a restraining order, and your baby mama can have your baby in the Fulton County jail." She then stepped back and poked her finger in his chest. "And if you ever do anything to hurt or embarrass Daisy again, I'll take care of the problem myself. Are we clear?" She stood back so she could see his face, which was pale and his eyes were wide. Bobby immediately nodded, because he knew she wasn't kidding. Lola nodded once, and she, Mo and Sara turned and headed back to the house.

Mark told me later that, as soon as we women left, Bobby looked at him and Harrison and quietly asked if that went for them, too. Harrison and Mark apparently told him, in as nice a way as possible, that he was about to have a very different life and that this was probably a good time for all of them to go their separate ways. He would have very little free time and the time he did have would be spent on play dates with other parents and other little kids, so he would meet a totally new group of people he could hang around. After that, Bobby just turned away, silently helped Barbie back into the van, got in the driver's seat and drove away.

By the time the guys rejoined us, Mo and Sara were telling me what happened after I left. "Did you see his face? Damn, Lola, you scared the shit out of him."

Lola laughed. "I just wanted to make sure he understood that it would probably be best if he found other people to hang around with so I politely suggested that."

I snorted and looked at her. "Yeah right. I'm sure that's exactly what you said, so that's why Bobby is probably wetting himself right now."

She shrugged and laughed, and then put her hand on my arm. "I don't care what he thinks. Are you really okay?"

I smiled reassuringly at all of them. "I'm fine. I have to say that seeing her was very weird at first, especially because she looked so much like me at that age," and all of them nodded in agreement. "Can you imagine how awkward it would be running into any of our other friends from college who didn't know what was going on? They would totally assume that she is our pregnant daughter, and Bobby will have to explain that, 'no, this is my current wife, who, by the way, looks exactly like Daisy did in college'. How creepy is that?"

Truthfully, the emotions I was feeling the most were a lot of happiness and relief mixed with maybe just a touch of nastiness. I'm happy because apparently I really have moved on from Bobby. It was kind of freakish seeing the skank, mainly because it was like looking into a very forgiving mirror, but I wasn't upset seeing them together, which I think really does say something about mine and Bobby's relationship.

The guys grabbed some beer from the fridge and headed back out to the grill. Sara started assigning duties to us. Apparently, I was to get started on my "famous baked beans," which, by the way, should be famous, even though they're just doctored Bush's beans. Add some tomato paste, onions, a little dried mustard, brown sugar and molasses, some finely chopped cooked thick bacon and splash in some bourbon. Stick all that in a crock pot and let it cook for a few hours. Try it sometime, it's delicious.

Lola was assigned to be the bartender because she's great with drinks. The only thing you have to worry about with Lola is that her drinks are crippling. Trust me, you can't drive after Lola's been bartending. Or walk, if you're not careful. Fortunately, all of Sara's kids will be here for dinner and three out of the four are old enough to drive, but not old enough to drink, so if things get out of hand we have built in designated drivers, which is great. We call them our KUBERS (Kid Ubers). Even though Sara always tells us not to, we pay the kids for the rides, so they don't mind doing it. It's a great system.

Mo and Sara were washing potatoes for the potato salad and I was putting the last ingredient in the crock pot when the doorbell rang. I said I'd get the door. When I opened it, Luke was standing on the other side with a bottle of bourbon in one hand and a twelve pack of beer in the other.

I'll have to admit, Luke looked great, relaxed, and happy. He was in the typical summer uniform of a middle-aged Southern guy, including cargo shorts, a faded vintage Allman Brothers t-shirt, sunglasses, and flip flops. His hair was a windblown mess and his nose and forehead were a little pink. I saw a bright yellow, jacked-up Jeep with a bikini top and no doors parked at the top of the driveway, which explained the hair and the pink, so I smiled and said, "Nice Jeep."

He smiled back and thanked me. "It was the first thing I bought when I moved back." I stepped back and he came in. He smelled great, like sun, a little sweat, and oddly enough, barbeque. When I mentioned it, he started to laugh. "Yeah, I got stuck at the light by the barbeque restaurant up the street and they had a smoker and a grill going in the parking lot. Apparently, I've picked up the smell."

I leaned in and sniffed him appreciatively. "You smell delicious. Watch my hound dogs, because they're going to think you're a walking buffet."

He laughed and followed me to the back of the house. When we got to the kitchen, Sara had turned up the music and I heard one of her favorite Toby Keith songs blasting from the hidden speakers. She and Mo were singing along while they peeled what looked like a mountain of potatoes, and Lola was hollering that she needed some bourbon to finish off her punch.

Luke smiled and walked over to Lola with the bourbon in hand. "Just ask and you shall receive, Ms.

Lola." She politely thanked him and grabbed the bottle, knowing he looked familiar, but not really sure who he was. Before she could figure it out, Sara squealed and ran over to Luke and jumped into his arms. He managed to catch her as she wrapped her arms around his neck and locked her legs around his waist. "Hot damn, my favorite cousin!" She kissed him on the cheek and hugged him until he begged her to let go before she choked him. She turned him loose and grabbed his hand to drag him over to the middle of us. "Y'all remember my cousin Luke from Georgia?"

Lola smiled at him. "Now I recognize you. Great to see you again, Luke."

Mo laughed at Sara still dancing around him with excitement. "Luke, it is great to see you." Mo handed Sara a potato peeler. "Sara, turn that poor man loose and let him get a beer."

Sara squeezed his hand again, then grabbed the peeler and used it to point to the back yard. "Go take your warm beer outside and put it in the cooler, and you grab yourself a cold one."

He smiled at all of us, and waved the beer in our direction as he headed toward the door. As he passed me, he winked as I opened the door for him, and I winked back. After I shut the door, Lola looked at me speculatively. "Hmmm."

I was confused. "'Hmmm' what?"

Lola squinted her eyes at me. "He winked at you, and you winked back."

"So what? I saw him last week when I was out, and then today. He was just being friendly."

Lola looked at me and slowly smiled. "Hmmm."

I shook my head. "You're such a dork. We're just

friends. Maybe you've forgotten that I'm recently divorced and I'm not even slightly interested in any man."

She didn't look convinced. "Okay. If you say so."

Seriously, I wasn't interested. Not just in Luke, but anyone. Men were not on my list. I turned around to look out the window and saw Luke with a beer in his hand, standing there with Harrison and Mark. My dogs came running over to him, deliriously barking and jumping on him, so he put the beer down so he could pet them all. I smiled as Diego abandoned him to try to get a sip of his beer, knocking it all over in the process. As the beer spilled on the table, chair, and onto the patio, Diego started lapping it up, which I knew was his intention the entire time. I grabbed a roll of paper towels and headed out to clean up the mess with Lola's laughter following me out the door.

As soon as I got outside, I pulled off a bunch of towels and started cleaning up the mess on the table. I wasn't worried about the patio, whatever Diego didn't take care of, we could hose it off later, but I wanted to be able to use the tables without them being all sticky. Luke took the roll from me and tore off a few towels to clean beer off the chair while I cleaned the table. "Sorry," he said. "I wasn't trying to get your pup drunk."

I laughed. "Trust me, it wasn't you. I should've warned you that Diego has a slight problem with alcohol. Every time we all get together, he tries to knock over any unattended drinks so he can have some." I bent over to wipe off the chair leg. "Last time, he had part of five people's beer. By the end of the night, I found his little drunk ass passed out on a pool float with a half-eaten hot dog under his head."

Luke and I were both laughing by that point, and he pointed out that Diego had already managed to lick up all the beer that had spilled onto the flagstone patio. I shook my head. "Here we go again." I bent over to pick up the used paper towels and warned him to watch his beer because Diego was very sneaky and now he knew Luke was an easy target.

I threw the paper towels in the trash and went back into the kitchen. Everyone stopped and looked at me and smiled. I stopped in the doorway. "What?"

Lola smirked. "So y'all seem to be pretty friendly."

I shrugged. "Looks that way. But, hey, you know I'm a friendly girl." I went over to Mo and Sara and grabbed a knife to help with the potatoes. I started peeling, hoping Lola would leave it alone.

As if. "He looks great."

I focused on the potato. "Yeah, I guess he does. You should ask him out."

Lola snorted and took a big swallow from her drink. "He has no interest in me, and you know he's not my type. I want someone who's uncomplicated, young, energetic, and oversexed, but a little dumb. I don't want a talker. I don't need him for conversation. In fact, it might be better if he didn't speak English at all except for a few phrases, like 'Harder'. 'Faster'. 'Wait in the car'."

We all laughed at that, but Sara shook her head. "I'd also add, 'Go get the car' because sometimes it's raining." Lola agreed.

I stopped peeling and pointed the peeler at Lola. "I don't know where you're getting this because Luke has never shown any interest in me before."

Sara disagreed. "Actually, that's not true. When we were in college, he thought you were cute, but you were already with Bobby, then he met Glenda, so it never came up. But when he moved back, you were the first person he asked about."

I was skeptical. "Really?"

She nodded. "Yep. I told him you were divorced and that you liked to hang out at Java Vino on Sunday mornings before eight and that he should go there if he wanted to see you. And apparently, that's exactly what he did because he called me after he saw you and said that you'd invited him to come cook out with us."

"Sara, he just said he wanted to see all of us and hang out because he didn't know anyone else in town. I was just convenient."

Lola shook her head. "Hey dumbass, he thinks you're a cutie. You, not the rest of us." She finished her drink and reached for the pitcher of punch, topping all of us off before she filled her glass. As I started to protest, she held up her hand to interrupt me. "Not that he didn't want to connect with all of us. I'm sure he does want folks to hang out with, so we're a great place to start. But that doesn't change the fact that he'd like to hang out with you the 'hard way,'" she said and made little air quotes with her fingers. She cracked herself up. "Get it? The 'hard' way."

I rolled my eyes. "You're an idiot."

She shrugged and took a swig of punch. "I'm rubber and you're glue..."

At that, I grabbed my drink and went outside to hang with the guys. They were much less annoying.

Mark was sitting back down after checking the meat and Harrison and Luke were lazing in their chairs talking about the Falcons' horrible Super Bowl loss to the Patriots.

I pulled up a chair, put it between Mark and Luke and away from the smoke, and plopped down in it. "Seriously, we're rehashing that awful game again?" I took a sip of my punch.

Harrison raised an eyebrow. "Hey, that's what we're talking about out here. You don't like it, you can go back inside and get to work on those potatoes."

Fine. I made the motion of zipping my lip and focused on my drink. After a few minutes, I felt like someone was staring at me and looked up to see Luke grinning at me. "Are you pouting?" he said.

I really wasn't pouting, but I guess I had gotten remarkably quiet, for me, anyway. I was actually thinking about the confrontation with Bobby and how weird it was that I wasn't more upset. Harrison and Mark were now in deep discussion about whether college players should be paid, and I was completely zoned out, lost in my own thoughts. I must have made a face because Luke quietly asked if I was okay.

I frowned. "I'm fine. I'm just not really in the mood to debate football right now..."

Luke shook his head. "No, the guys told me that Bobby came by with a pregnant lookalike surprise, and I just wanted to make sure you're okay."

I smiled at him and patted his arm. "I'm fine." He looked skeptical and I shrugged. "Seriously, I'm fine. A little weirded out, but pretty good, considering."

He winced. "Yeah, the guys told me she looked just like you did at that age."

"She did. Isn't that just freaky? The chicks all thought everyone would think she was our daughter." I wrinkled my nose and shook my head. "Yuck. That is so freaking creepy." I turned to face him. "What is it with guys our age and twenty-something-year-old girls? I just don't get it!" I pointed to Mark. "He has kids in their late teens. I look at his kids and their friends and think, 'Look how adorable those kids are. You know their mamas just want to eat them up with a spoon, they're so cute!' I can't imagine looking at one of them and thinking, 'Ooh Lawd, he's hot...I'd love to get me a piece of that!'"

Luke started laughing and apparently, I'd gotten a little loud, because Mark and Harrison had stopped talking and were staring at me like I was crazy. Harrison pulled his shades down his nose so I could see his eyes. "I'm sorry, Daisy, what? Which of us do you think is hot and you would 'like a piece of'?" He smiled a cocky smile and winked at me. "I mean, let's face it. It's probably me, and I'm certainly willing to help, but I need to go ask Mo first."

That made me laugh. I leaned forward and grabbed his face in both hands, pulled him down and kissed him a big juicy smack right on his mouth. "Yes, Harrison, you're exactly what I was talking about, so get your ass inside and check with your wife so we can get busy."

He pushed his glasses back up, and, shaking his head, grabbed the tongs from Mark and stood up to check the status of the meat on the grill instead.

I fell back in my chair, laughing, and Harrison shook his tongs at me. "Woman, you leave me alone," he said, laughing. "You are scaring me and making this a hostile eating environment. I'm not some piece of meat."

I stood up next to Harrison and shook my finger in his face, just for comic relief, more than anything. Since I'm 4'11" and he's 6'8", I come up almost to the middle of his stomach, so the idea of me actually scaring him is ridiculous. He could literally stomp me like a grape if he wasn't such a huge, sweet man. "Tease. Don't make me get rough with you, Harrison. I may be the size of a tick next to you, but I'm a scrappy little thing."

He pretended to cower in fear and then said with all seriousness, "Daisy, I've always been terrified of all of you." He tilted his head and pretended to think about it, "Well, honestly, I'm mostly scared of Sara, but you run a close second to the scariest. You little ones are unpredictable."

All of us nodded in agreement of being most afraid of Sara, especially Mark, but I liked the idea that all of those big guys might think I was scary. That's kind of fabulous.

About that time, the door opened and Sara stuck her head out. "How's the meat looking, boys?"

Harrison told her that everything was looking good and would probably be ready in a half hour or so. Sara turned around to tell Lola to grab the pitcher and for Mo to grab the dip and the cheese and crackers and come on out. As always, she climbed onto Mark's lap and got comfortable. "What were y'all all talking about?"

We all looked at each other and laughed. Then, Lola came out with a huge pitcher of her bourbon punch, but this batch looked like pure bourbon to me. She put it on the table and grabbed a chair and put it next to me and dropped into it. Diego suddenly appeared at her feet, and Lola shooed him away. "Daisy, your damn alcoholic dog is making a move on my punch."

He shot her a nasty look over his shoulder and slinked over to me looking pitiful. He whined until I picked him up. "Come here you little drunk." I kissed him on his head and put him in my lap. I felt him move closer to the pitcher, and put him on the other leg so he was farther away. He sighed when he realized he wasn't getting any punch, and curled up and went to sleep.

Mo went up to Harrison and kissed him on the cheek, before sitting in the empty chair next to his. I smiled at both of them, so happy that they had each other. I pointed to

Harrison. "Sorry, Mo, but I unintentionally sexually harassed Harrison, and then I apparently offended him by calling him a tease."

Mo laughed as she patted his leg. "Daisy, don't worry, there's plenty of him to go around." He nodded in agreement. "You know that all you have to do is make him some of your red velvet cupcakes, and he'd be yours forever."

He nodded enthusiastically at the mention of red velvet, and sent a pleading look my way, and I huffed out a breath. "Honey, if that's all it takes, I'll make you a whole cake just for you on your birthday." I shook my finger at him and then winked. "Seriously, you men are so easy."

Everyone looked relaxed and happy. I caught Luke smiling at our verbal play and I smiled back. I knew that he was happy that he still fit in so well with the group, and I was glad that everyone was so comfortable with him.

I felt Lola pinch the side of my leg, and when I turned to her, she winked at me over her drink. I rolled my eyes and tried to ignore her. I know she was commenting on Luke's smile, but I still think she's nuts. We're just friends. Weren't we?

When I looked over at Luke, he instantly looked at me and smiled again. I smiled back and sipped my drink. Holy shit, was Lola right? I'm a good Southern girl who kind of automatically flirts with everyone, but had I been deliberately flirting with him? Had he been flirting with me? Now I wasn't sure. I wasn't interested in a relationship at the moment, so I didn't want to hurt his feelings, especially since he is such a nice guy. Crap. Now, what do I do?

I must have started to look panicked because Lola leaned over and whispered in my ear, "Relax, I'm just giving you shit. He's a great guy, so just have fun and don't worry about anything."

I let out my breath, which I had apparently been holding and looked at her, relieved. She was right. He is just a friend. No big deal. We're not dating, or anything, just hanging out with other friends. I need to relax and not make this a big deal.

Lola winked and leaned forward to grab some cheese. She settled back and took a huge bite and asked, with her mouth full, "So what were y'all talking about?"

The guys and I looked at each other and smiled and I offered, "Football and baby mamas."

Luke said we could let Sara handle Bobby and the skank, but I said it would be like a Texas cage wrestling match. Two would go in and only one would come out, and I assure you, the one would be Sara. Hell, even Harrison wouldn't take on Sara, and he's a full two feet taller and a hundred and fifty pounds heavier than she is.

Harrison swears that his first time meeting Sara was scarier than the first SEC game he played in. He was the starting center for the football team, and at that time weighed about 350 pounds while she weighed maybe 85 pounds. Freshman year, they had a health class together, and the class was discussing self- defense and, purely for entertainment purposes, I'm sure, the professor chose Sara and Harrison to demonstrate self-defense moves. First, he told Harrison to bend over and grab Sara from behind so she couldn't get away. Once Harrison had a good grip, the professor patronizingly asked Sara what she would do to get away. She hesitated, saying that she didn't want to hurt him, and after the entire class stopped laughing, Harrison told her to give it her best shot. Next thing he knew, Sara had grabbed his crotch in a vise-like grip in one hand and a handful of his hair in the other and was showing everyone how she could head butt him backwards in the face while she ripped his testicles off and then snatch him bald-headed if she wanted to. Harrison gently asked her to let go, which she did, and he slowly released her and backed away with both hands raised up by his shoulders and an appalled look on his face.

After class, she apologized if she had embarrassed him and offered to make it up to him by introducing him to her roommate, Mo. I don't know if Harrison had any desire to meet Mo, but he was probably too afraid of Sara to say no, so he agreed to come by the dorm that afternoon before practice. Sara tracked down Mo at volleyball practice and told her that she had found Mo's future husband and for her to come home immediately after practice. She told Mo that not only was he the biggest, sweetest man ever, but he was very cute and she had grabbed a big handful of his crotch and that from the feel of it, he was built right everywhere. That night, Harrison took one look at Mo and it was love at first sight for both of them.

For Sara's birthday two years ago, Harrison bought Sara a documentary DVD about the honey badger. He said that those little 20 pound badgers would eat cobras, kick the shit out of a lion in a fight over food, and basically just do whatever the hell they wanted without any fear for their own safety. You know, just like Sara. Apparently, he thought the honey badger was Sara's spirit animal. Sara didn't find that offensive, at all. In fact, she loved it. Mo's part of the present was a huge t-shirt with a picture she'd drawn of a honey badger getting the crap kicked out of it by Sara, and, that's usually the shirt she wears by the pool.

Tonight she was in a regular tank, and I wanted Luke to see her shirt. "Hey, Sara, where's your honey badger shirt?"

"It's in the dryer. I made sure it was clean because Hannah's friends think it's hilarious." She turned to Mark.

"Did the kids say they'd be here soon when you texted them?"

Mark nodded and told Sara to hop up so he could check the meat, which he pronounced ready to go. We heard a commotion from inside the house and suddenly a hoard of laughing teenagers, including Hannah, came into the backyard, waving hello as they passed us on the way to the pool.

Lola looked at us with big eyes and pointed out how amazing it was that when the food was ready, the kids showed up. "If you cook it, they will come...." Sara laughed and as she went inside to change, she asked Harrison to grab the burgers and hot dogs out of the fridge and throw them on the grill.

Mark took the butt and the ribs out of the smoker and took them inside to pull the pork and chop up the ribs. Harrison came out with the hamburgers and hot dogs and put the meat on the fire, while the rest of us went inside to start bringing the sides and the fixings out to the tables. Within 15 minutes, the kids were wrapped in towels and we were all standing around the table fixing our plates. The kids took their plates to the pool, and we all sat down at the big table on the screened porch. Lola grabbed her punch and everyone else got their drinks, and we all settled in to eat.

I'm not sure how, but I ended up sitting between Luke and Lola again, which Lola acknowledged to me with a knowing smirk. I rolled my eyes and pinched her leg under the table.

Fortunately, the rest of the day was fun and totally uneventful, although Diego did manage to find at least two full, unattended beers, so again, I found him passed out by the pool on a lawn chair at the end of the night. Luke helped me out by carrying him up to my car while I walked my other boys up on their leashes. Diego's a little dog, but when he's wasted, his long little body is dead weight and hard to carry. Luke asked me if I needed to get him into doggie rehab and I laughed, but did tell him that I was concerned enough that I asked my vet about it a few years ago. He said to try to keep him away from alcohol, but the truth is that if we all get together, Diego's gonna get his drink on somehow. It doesn't happen that often, and he seems to be fine once he wakes up, so I've stopped worrying about it. Especially after Lola reminded me that Harrison's college dog ate only pizza, beer, and whatever he could steal off an unattended plate or a grill, and that dog lived to be 18 years old, so I'm sure he'll be fine.

Once I got everyone in and buckled their doggie seat-belts, which attached to their regular harnesses, I hopped into my little car. "Thanks for your help, Luke." I buckled my seatbelt. "When he's passed out, it's hard to handle him with the other two."

He laughed. "No problem." He put his hands on my door and leaned toward me. "Hey, want to meet me for breakfast tomorrow? I was thinking we could meet up at Folk Art and then you could show me your house."

Now that I was a little paranoid about whether he thought I was coming on to him or not, I wasn't sure if that was a good idea, so I hesitated. Of course, he noticed the hesitation. "Look, I had a great time today and I have a few questions about the area. I'm renting an apartment behind a house in the Highlands and my lease is up after the first of the year. I don't know whether I should sign another lease, or start looking to buy something. I figured you've already been through all this and I'd like your opinion on the various options."

He looked so hopeful, I smiled at him and told him I'd

be happy to meet him in the morning. I told him I could be there at 8:30 and we'd leave from there to go to my house. He smiled and turned back down the driveway to Sara's house, waving over his shoulder. I waved back and turned my little car towards home.

8
―――――――

THE NEXT MORNING, I WAS UP AT SIX, AS USUAL. I walked the dogs and then hopped on my bike for some quick exercise. By the time I got back it was seven and it was already hot. The weather folks had said that it was supposed to be ninety-five this afternoon and the humidity was going to be out of control. Great. That meant that by noon, my hair was going to be a curly, sweaty ball of ringlets around my ears. Nice. I decided that after my shower I would just braid it into two stubby little pigtails and call it a day, because they don't make enough product to control my kind of hair with that much humidity.

I ran inside, fed the dogs, took a cool shower, put on my underwear, and stretched out on my bed under the ceiling fan until I finally cooled off, which took forever. At eight-fifteen, I got up, put on some powder and another layer of deodorant, and got dressed in a pair of old shorts and t-shirt, stomped into a pair of flip flops, ran out the door and hopped in my convertible. My plan was to make a grocery run after breakfast and I hate to tote stuff, so I always drive when I run errands. I made it to the restaurant with about five minutes to spare and when I went in, I saw him already seated at a table drinking coffee. His face lit up with a big smile when he saw me, and I was grinning in return. I walked to the booth and slid in the seat across from him.

He put down his coffee and signaled to the waitress to come over to get my drink order. He then smiled at me. "So what have you been up to this morning?"

"You know, the usual. Walking dogs, riding my bike and trying to stop sweating," and he laughed. The waitress came over and I ordered a coffee with a lot of milk and some scrambled eggs with wheat toast.

He smiled at the waitress and ordered the same breakfast. When she left to get our order, he picked up his coffee and grinned as he saluted me with it. "Well, you look like you're doing pretty good after Bobby's little show and tell yesterday."

"Right? Honestly, I didn't even think of that pain in my ass one time until you just mentioned him." I smiled at the waitress and thanked her as she handed me a huge mug of coffee and a carafe of milk. "The only thing I was thinking about this morning was trying to cool off. It's already about a thousand degrees."

"Is that the reason for the cute little pigtails?" He grinned as he reached out and tweaked one. "I had it bad for Ellie May Clampett when I was a kid. Lots of blonde hair and pigtails. That's totally hot."

I laughed. "Whatever blows your skirt up, little boy. This is purely functional, unless you want to see my hair in tiny, sweaty ringlets."

He shrugged and winked. "I like it. Whatever the reason, you look cute." He paused to thank the waitress for a refill.

I was about to make a smart ass comment, then I realized, with only a little panic, he was serious, so I just thanked him and sipped my coffee.

"So, I wanted to get your opinion. Right now I'm renting a little guest house behind a house off of St Charles, and I'm trying to figure out what to do. My lease isn't up for months, not till after the first of the year, but I'm not sure whether I'm going to buy something I can fix up or just renew it and rent for a while. How's the market around here? This still seems to be like the happening part of town."

I nodded in agreement. "It is. The market is still hot and anything that's a decent deal gets snapped up before the average guy would have a chance to get it."

I told him about my ridiculous deal and I could tell he was impressed at the amount she'd paid for the house. "Lola is a great one to talk to because bankers are always calling her about deals before they're actually put on the open market."

He nodded. "I love those kind of deals. I used to know people like that in New Orleans, but I don't really have any of those kind of contacts here."

"That's not true. You have Lola, and that's all you need. Just talk to her and tell you what you want and she'll keep an ear out for you. You want a finished house, or a fixer upper?"

"A fixer upper. Even though I'm not currently in the building business, I love that kind of work, and a project like that would be a lot of fun."

Our breakfasts arrived, and as we buttered, jellied, and hot-sauced our breakfasts, I asked him how he'd originally gotten into the building business.

In between bites, he told me. "My dad and my uncle owned a construction business together, and I worked there from the time I was big enough to hold a hammer. Every summer, every holiday, most days after school, if I wasn't playing baseball or football, I was on a construction site. By the time I was a junior in high school, I'd about decided I wasn't going to college, I was just going to get my contractor's license and start my own business. My mom was furious and, I later found out, she told my dad he'd better make sure I get a degree. My dad convinced me that a business degree would help me deal with banks and handle money, so that's how I ended up at Georgia."

I was curious. "Was it helpful?"

"It was." He nodded. "I think the combination of real world experience and the degree definitely helped me expand more quickly and it gave me credibility with the banks."

"That makes sense." I took a sip of my coffee. "What about your uncle? You never said what he thought about you going to college."

He smiled at the memory. "He told me that I should definitely go because I already knew everything you could learn on a jobsite. I could build things, I could drink, and I could kick the shit out of just about anyone in a fight. Now it was time to learn the business."

I could imagine him as a hell-raising teenager and laughed at the thought. "So you grew the business and now you're here. Why'd you leave? Were you just tired of New Orleans? You needed a change? What?"

He hesitated for a minute, and then he looked at me. "Are you sure you want to hear all this?"

I shrugged and looked at him, confused. "Why wouldn't I?"

He looked down at his plate, forked up another big bite of egg and chewed slowly. Once he swallowed, he looked at me soberly. "Daisy, it's a long, ugly story. I really don't talk about it much."

I snorted. "Really? Is it uglier than your husband knocking up his prepubescent secretary, who looks just like you, by the way, but much younger, you smashing his testicle and leg with your car, being arrested for it, and then being ridiculed for weeks on national TV?" I shook my head. "Please. You're telling me it's worse than that?"

He put down his fork and looked at me with an expressionless face. "Yes. It's actually worse than that."

Holy shit. That must be bad. I finished my eggs and picked up my toast. "Seriously? Worse than that? Worse than being called 'that crazy Southern nutcracker' by every late night asshole on TV?"

He still didn't crack a smile. "A lot worse than that." He forked in another bite of egg and the corner of his mouth tipped up and he amended, "Well, maybe a different worse than that."

I couldn't imagine what could have happened. Mark had said it was a pretty screwy story, but I couldn't imagine what could be worse than my story. I told him to finish his breakfast and we'd go back to my house so he could see it, and then I wanted to hear this story. He looked at me for a minute, I'm sure trying to decide if he wanted to tell me his tale of woe, and then said that sounded like a great idea. We finished our breakfast chatting about nothing of consequence, he paid the check, and then we walked outside. He had walked to the restaurant, so I told him to hop in my car and we'd head to my place so he could check it out. He agreed, so we jumped in the convertible.

I smiled as we pulled into the driveway about a minute later. "Well, here we are."

Luke laughed. "Wow. Good thing we drove or we'd both be exhausted."

"Ha. Ha. I know, I live about 40 feet from the restaurant, but I was going to run some errands right after breakfast, so I drove."

Luke was halfway out of the car, but stopped. "I'm sorry, I didn't mean to screw up your plans. You need to get going?"

I shook my head and pointed up toward the house. "No, it can wait. Now quit being such a wuss, come on in the house, let me show you around, and then you can tell me your horrifyingly-worse-than-mine story."

As we walked through the house, Luke was impressed with the quality of the finish work. "Lola did all this?"

I laughed at the thought of Lola doing any sort of manual labor. "Uh, no. Lola is not a hands on girl, but she is an excellent general contractor." I shook my head at the mental picture of Lola in a toolbelt. "Her skill in life is telling other people what to do, and that really seems to work for her in construction. She's got a good crew now, so it's much easier than it was."

"Was all this trim here, or did she have someone do it? And the bookcases and window seat? Did her carpenter do all that?" He ran his hand over the door trim. "Whoever did all this did a great job."

I told him I wasn't sure what was original and what was added later because Lola had gotten it after someone else had already done a lot of the renovation. "When she got it, all of the kitchen cabinets and appliances were sitting in the kitchen but hadn't been installed, so her guys put in the kitchen and laid my terracotta tile floor with the doggie footprints. I know the bathrooms were already done, the floors were refinished, and only half of the replacement windows had been installed."

He nodded, taking in all of the details. He pointed out that he loved the way the light came through the stained glass sidelights in my front door and made a big fuss over the quality of my built-in window seat. As I watched him go through my house, exclaiming over the same things that I found so appealing, I realized that Lola was right. I like this guy.

His whoop shook me out of my thoughts, which was great because they were starting to freak me out. He was standing in front of my enormous TV with a huge smile on his face. I realized I had no idea what he had said. "I'm sorry, what did you say?"

He pointed to my TV. "I asked how big is this thing?"

I started to laugh. "It's enormous, isn't it? It's seventy inches, courtesy of Mark and Harrison. I asked them to pick me up a flat screen TV, and that's what they brought in here. In this room, it's like I have my own personal Jumbotron." I shrugged. "They told me I'd love it, and they're right. Georgia games on this baby are going to be fantastic."

Typical guy, Luke was thrilled with it. "I can't wait." He finally tore himself away and turned down the hall. "Let's see the rest."

When he saw my bedroom, especially the size of the closet and bathroom, he pointed out that there was no way that was original. "You would never see that kind of space in a house this age. Did they get the space from another bedroom?"

I nodded. "I had actually looked up this plan on the Internet since it was one of the original Sears Craftsman bungalows you could order out of the catalog. It looks like the extra room came out of a large dining room. Most of it was used for my closet and bathroom, but a thin sliver of it is part of the combined living room-eat in area."

His face lit up. "Do you have the plan handy?"

I told him I had printed it off somewhere and we could find it later, after he told me his story. I invited him onto the screen porch and asked him to sit and pet the dogs while I got us something to drink. "Water, or does this story require something stronger?"

Diego hopped up on his lap and the other two stretched out on the floor under the ceiling fan and promptly fell asleep. "I think Diego and I had better just stick to water." I went into the kitchen, poured the water, and added some lemon and mint. I came back out and handed him a glass, and then sat in the glider directly across from him.

"Thanks." He smiled and looked at my backyard, then looked at me. "Daisy, this is an absolutely beautiful home. It's exactly the kind of house I'd picture you living in."

I could feel myself tearing up. "It is, isn't it?" Embarrassed, I brushed the tears from my eyes. "Sorry, I'm such a wimp, but I just love everything about this house. It's been home since the first moment I walked in."

He leaned over and patted my hand. "It looks like you. Warm and comfortable and happy."

What a nice thing to say. I smiled at him and we just rocked in silence for a few minutes. Finally, I looked at him. "Okay, big guy, spill it. I really have to know what could be worse than my stupid story."

He looked incredibly uncomfortable, but he looked me in the eye. "Okay, Daisy, here goes." He leaned back in the rocker and took a drink of water. "The really shitty part happened right after Katrina, but Glenda and I had problems pretty much from the beginning." He settled in and started to talk.

"Deep down, I knew from the beginning that marrying Glenda was a mistake." He start slowly rocking back and forth. "I still remember the first time I saw her, the first day of spring quarter my freshman year. She was asleep by the pool in a tiny pink bikini with her long blond hair pulled up into a ponytail. Even when she was by the pool, I was fascinated that her makeup and nails were perfect, and no matter how she turned, she was carefully posed to make sure that all of her parts were evenly tanned. At that moment I thought that she was the most beautiful, perfect girl I'd ever seen. After a couple of years, I realized that she wasn't the nicest person ever...."

I snorted and immediately felt guilty. "Sorry."

He laughed. "No you're right. I was a typical college boy and I was blinded by a lot of blonde hair, teeth and a perfect appearance. Like I said, I eventually started to realize that she wasn't the nicest person..."

He looked at me and I mimed zipping my lips, which made him laugh. "...in fact, she was selfish and shallow, but I figured she just needed to grow up. By the time we were about to graduate, I figured it was either time to get married or break up, and I definitely made the wrong choice."

"When we graduated, we moved to New Orleans. I started a business as a contractor, and she started her life as a trophy wife. Like most kids, we didn't have a lot of money, but that never stopped Glenda from buying whatever product or jewelry she needed to feel like she was the rich woman she aspired to be. It was ridiculous. Thanks to her spending, we ended up with a mountain of credit card debt and a shitload of resentment. Glenda was pissed that I couldn't take care of her the way she wanted to be taken care of, and I was furious that she kept spending money they we didn't have on what I considered to be stupid crap. Daisy, please explain to me what freaking twenty something needs skin treatments to look younger? How many massages does one woman who doesn't work, really need in a month?"

He sipped his water and took a deep breath to compose himself before he continued. "We went to counseling, which was a waste of even more money, because she refused to see her behavior as a problem. She told me that if I'd just make more money, we wouldn't have these problems. I suggested she get a job, which she found appalling. She said she had never intended to work. Her degree was in interior design so she could help decorators keep her surroundings beautiful, not so she could slave like some...", he made little air quotes with his fingers, "...'common worker bee' every day. Eventually, it got to where we basically co-existed in the same house. We attended fundraisers and other events together, but otherwise we led pretty separate lives."

I was curious. "Why didn't you get a divorce?"

Luke shrugged. "Great question. At first it was because I didn't have enough money to pay her off in a divorce. Then later, it was just easier to keep going like we were going. I know it sounds stupid, but I knew she would have been such a raging bitch about the whole thing that it was easier not to rock the boat." He took a sip of water.

"It also helped that I was always at work building my business. In the late 90's, my best friend from middle school, Nick Watson, had inherited a commercial construction business in New Orleans from his uncle, so we joined up to combine my residential construction and renovation business with Nick's commercial one. We hit the market at just the right time, and in a very short period of time, we had grown those two businesses into one huge company that employed several hundred people and grossed millions every year. Watson and Mathis Construction, Inc., had government contracts, we built subdivisions, we renovated and flipped houses, we built office buildings, and enjoyed a reputation as one of the best builders and renovators in the state. Within a few years, I was able to pay all of my personal debts and Glenda finally had enough money to satisfy her inexhaustible need for shopping and personal maintenance. Most importantly, she left me the hell alone."

He took a deep breath and let it out in a whoosh. "And then Katrina hit."

Luke stopped rocking, leaned forward, holding Diego to make sure he didn't fall, and looked at me with wide eyes. "Daisy, you can't imagine what it was like to see your hometown like that. It was absolute hell, with water everywhere, and snakes and gators and drowned animals and stranded people." He shook his head as if trying to shake the memories loose. "It was absolute devastation."

He sank back in his chair and started rocking again. "As soon as the water went down, we got to work. Money poured in as we were awarded millions of dollars in post-Katrina building funds. We were hired to rebuild levees, we were hired to level neighborhoods full of ruined houses and rebuild them, and we were hired to fix office buildings all over the city."

"At first, our biggest problem was finding enough workers. So many people, including our guys, had left New Orleans after the hurricane that at first, it was difficult to find experienced construction workers. Their homes were destroyed, they were living with family in other states, but once everyone heard that there was tons of work in New Orleans, they all started to come back.

Both the commercial and residential divisions were working like gangbusters. My side of the business got a huge amount of money to tarp roofs until permanent repairs could be done, and I was hiring anyone who could swing a hammer for basic, unskilled work like that. I was trying to oversee everything and ended up running around like a crazy man. We had debris removal teams, tarp guys, home repair guys, we were rebuilding roofs, putting up power poles. We had mold guys. We were working eighteen, twenty hours a day, non-stop for months."

"Nick and I oversaw totally different jobs, so unless it was a really big project, neither of us knew the specifics of the projects the other was working on. We didn't have time to stop and explain, we just kept working. Then I stopped in the office one day to grab some forms for an inspector, and a group of welders that hadn't been paid for the last week were looking for Nick to ask for a paycheck. I called Nick to see what the problem was. When he didn't answer, I took their numbers and told them I would figure out what's going on, and call them later that day.

"Unfortunately, our long-time bookkeeper had been one of those people who had left town immediately after the storm, and as far as we knew, she was still living in Texas with her family. We didn't want to hire a new person because no one had time to train them, so Nick and I had agreed that we would each would pay our own subs and expenses out of our separate business accounts until we could find a new bookkeeper to take over. It wasn't a big deal, because of the way our business was organized. The company already had two separate divisions, commercial and residential. Nick was in charge of the accounts for the commercial division, I was in charge of accounts for the residential division, and we were both signatures on all of the accounts."

"I wanted to make sure we hadn't already prepared checks for these guys, so I went into our bookkeeper's old office, sat down, booted up her computer, and went to see what was going on with the bank accounts."

"I logged into our accounting software, did an automatic update of all of the accounts so all the balances would be current, and then checked my residential account. There was no problem there. All of the money from FEMA and local insurance companies had been credited to the proper accounts and the bank balance was even better than I expected."

"When I opened Nick's accounts, I was confused. I knew that we had been awarded a $13 million contract to replace a levee that had been destroyed by the flood water, and I also knew that the work had not yet started but the materials were supposed to be ordered that week, so most of the money should have been in the general operating account for the commercial side of the business. It wasn't. There was a little more than $2,000, but no other big deposits or withdrawals were showing up."

"Obviously, there was a mistake. I started opening some of Nick's individual commercial accounts to see if the money was there. I saw where the other accounts were set up, I saw where other money had posted and other jobs had been completed, but I couldn't find the $13 million in levee money.

"Now I was confused. I thought that maybe Nick had set up his accounts differently for some reason. Maybe the feds required different accounts for each job over a certain amount to make sure all of the money was accounted for, since federal disaster funds were involved. I backed out of the accounting software and went to the bank's website to see if Nick had set up some different accounts under separate jobs. There were no new accounts that I could see, so at that point, I wasn't really sure what to do."

"I finally said screw this. I picked up the phone and called Nick and it went immediately to voice mail. I then texted him and asked him to call me immediately because something was going on and I needed to talk to him. Nothing."

"Now I started getting worried. I ran outside and jumped in my truck and went out to the commercial building where Nick had been working earlier in the week. Some of his guys were there doing some electrical work, but they said they hadn't seen Nick since the day before. Then I went over to the levee they were supposed to start repairing. There were some markings on the ground indicating where the materials were to be dumped, but nothing else was there, and no sign of Nick.

"Finally, I went to Nick's house and started banging on the door. I was thinking maybe Nick was sick or injured, and that's why no one had seen him at work. No answer. I looked in the sidelights by the front door, but didn't see anyone and I looked in the window in his garage, but Nick's truck was gone."

"I hopped back in my truck and headed back over to the jobsite where Nick had been working. Mike, the foreman, walked over as soon as he saw me, asking if I'd seen Nick because he needed to get his approval for some small changes that needed to be made for an inspection the next morning. I approved the changes and then asked Mike when he'd seen Nick last. He said, 'Sometime yesterday morning. He said he was going to pick up something at your house and that he'd see me later, and I haven't seen him since.'"

"I remember thinking, 'What the hell could he be picking up at my house?' but I tried there next. The night before I'd gotten in super late and hadn't seen Glenda, but, by that point, we hadn't shared a room for more than three years, so that wasn't unusual. She said I snored and disturbed her sleep and I said she was a bitch who drove me crazy, so I had no complaints when she moved into the room down the hall. Well, actually, she had one of my crews combine two bedrooms into one big room with an enormous closet and she had the bathroom redone, so technically, she redecorated and then moved down the hall. I didn't care... the less I saw of her the better. But now I did want to talk to her to ask if she had seen Nick and knew what the hell was going on."

"So I drove up to my house, I pushed the button for the garage door, and the first thing I noticed was that my classic Camaro convertible was missing. I hadn't noticed the night before because I always parked my truck outside. Glenda used the car occasionally, so I figured that maybe she'd taken the car for whatever beauty procedure she was having performed that day, or maybe it was being serviced. I parked my truck and went in to see if I could find her to ask if she'd seen Nick."

"I walked down the hall to her bedroom. The door was locked, so I knocked. No answer. I didn't hear any signs of life, so I took out my pocketknife and popped the lock. I opened the door and walked inside and her room was spotless and perfect, as usual. Then I see a letter on the dresser addressed to me. I picked it up and stared at it, suddenly afraid to open it. Finally, I ripped off the top flap, unfolded the letter, and began to read." He took a sip of his water.

I was enthralled. "So don't keep me hanging. What did it say?"

"I still remember every word." He began to recite it from memory. "Dear Luke, sorry you had to find out this way, but please consider this to be notice that you and I are done. I am tired of your lack of appreciation for all of my hard work to keep myself and our house so beautiful. Nick and I are leaving for a better life together, so I would appreciate if you would do everything to make our divorce and division of assets as easy as possible. You can send my half of everything to my lawyer, who can forward it to me. Sorry it didn't work out, but I need a man who appreciates how special I am. Please get this done as soon as possible. Sincerely, Glenda."

I let out a long, long whistle. "Wow. So what did you do then?"

"I just sat there with the letter in my hand. It made no sense to me. What the hell? She's leaving me to go with Nick? Why would Nick want Glenda?"

"So I got up, shoved the letter in my back pocket, and went over to her closet and yanked it open. There were a few clothes on hangers, but everything else was gone. Obviously, she'd packed her stuff when she and Nick decided to skip town. And put it in my freaking Camaro convertible. Shit. I couldn't believe it. They took my favorite car. Unfortunately, the car was in both of our names or I would've called the cops and reported a theft. I was so pissed."

"I went downstairs and as I ran out of the house toward my truck, I caught a glimpse of blue behind the garage. I hadn't noticed it on the way in, but when I saw it, I realized it was the same color as Nick's truck so I went to check it out. Sure enough, Nick's truck was parked beside one of my work trailers behind the garage. At that point, it was starting to sink in, but I guess I needed more proof. I jumped back in my truck and took off back toward Nick's house. As soon as I got there, I slammed on the brakes, shoved the truck into park, ran up to the front door, and tried to open it. It was locked, so I circled around the house, testing every window until I found a bathroom window that was unlocked. I ripped off the screen, threw up the window and climbed into Nick's house."

"First, I went to his bedroom to see if all of his clothes were there, but they were all gone with just his winter coat left in the closet. Next, I went through the house and noticed that all of his photos were gone, along with several paintings his mom had done. I couldn't believe it. I couldn't believe my best friend and business partner had run off with my wife. Trust me, I wasn't upset about losing Glenda, but I incredibly upset about Nick's betrayal. What did this meant to our business? And most important, where the hell was the levee money?"

"I looked for his laptop, but it was missing too, so I grabbed one of Nick's spare sets of house keys out of the kitchen, locked everything behind me, and headed back to the office. On the way, I called our accountant, Lou Morris, and asked him if he could meet me at the office to take a look at some accounts with me. Even though Lou wasn't our bookkeeper, I figured he'd dealt with our general numbers for so many years that he would have a good idea of how the accounts were set up and what the federal government required its contractors to do. At the very least, maybe he could help me figure out where the levee money was. Lou told me he'd meet me at the office in about thirty minutes, and to put on some coffee."

"We pulled in at the same time. We sat down, and as the computer booted up, I handed him Glenda's letter. I made us some coffee in our office kitchen, and when I came back in, Lou's eyebrows were halfway up his forehead and he kept saying, 'Glenda and Nick? No shit? Glenda and Nick?'"

"Once Lou calmed down, I told him about the welders who hadn't been paid and the money for the levee that wasn't where it should be, and asked him if he could help me figure out what was going on. Lou said he'd be happy to do it and got to work while I wrote checks for the welders out of my operating account so they could get paid. I called the guys to come pick up their checks and then spent a while returning calls and returning some texts and emails."

"After about an hour, Lou came in with a grim look on his face and asked me to come see what he'd found. I followed him back to the computer and pulled up a chair beside him."

"Lou told me I wasn't looking at the correct account initially, and that most of the money for the various FEMA projects was right where it should be. One account had about $2,000 in it, another had a couple of million dollars that Nick hadn't been able to touch because it wouldn't be available for another 5 days, and a few others had $20 thousand here, $30 thousand there."

I was perched on the edge of my seat. "But no $13 million?"

"Nope. Lou showed me where it was deposited in the main account, and where Nick transferred it to the operating account, and then it was transferred somewhere else, but Lou couldn't see where. When I pointed out that $13 million doesn't just disappear, Lou said he was waiting for a call from a contact at the bank, and then we'd know. The guy called back while I was sitting there and told Lou that it had been transferred to a bank in the Cayman Islands and now that account was empty. When I asked him who had an account in the Caymans, he said that apparently it was mine because my name was on it."

I gasped at the idea. "What? What did he mean it was yours?"

"That's what I said. I told him I've never had an account in the Cayman Islands and I had never touched any of this money. Lou said that Nick had apparently set up the account in my name so it looked like I was the one who stole it."

Luke was quiet for a moment and I was sitting there with my mouth open. I finally managed to choke out, "Holy shit, Luke. So, what happened? You've got this huge job you already got money for and that jackass and your bitch wife took everything and set you up to take the fall. What did you do?"

He shook his head at the memory. "It was a nightmare for a long time. The feds came in and told me that they were going to prosecute me for fraud against the government and then they froze our business accounts. I spent the next 5 years digging out from under all of that crap."

I was confused. "How did you manage to dig out from under that with your accounts frozen and having every government agency in New Orleans crawling up your ass?"

He leaned back and Diego growled in his sleep at being disturbed. Luke chuckled and settled him more comfortably in his lap. "Well, I was very lucky that I knew a bunch of the FBI agents in New Orleans, so they were, at least, willing to listen to my side of the story. We had renovated their building a few years back, and several of them later had me build or renovate their personal homes, and I was on good terms with all of them. It was also fortunate that Glenda and Nick weren't exactly master criminals. It didn't take much for them to follow the paper trails and see that I really had nothing to do with it. My lawyer hopped on dealing with the frozen accounts, and we were able to get back up and running within a week."

I was impressed. "A week? That's unbelievable. Usually, working with the federal government takes forever and is a nightmare to deal with."

Luke nodded. "I know. I think someone up there was looking out for us." He looked at me, shaking his head slowly back and forth.

I leaned forward and grabbed his hand, squeezed it and then let go, leaning back in my chair. "It's amazing everything fell into place like it did."

He laughed, and rubbed his hands over his eyes. "Truthfully, a lot of it was just luck, and I never could have done it if it wasn't immediately after Katrina. Everyone was desperate to save whatever they could, people were working around the clock to clear out debris, and we were all trying to get our town back as quickly as possible."

"It turns out that after 9-11, the federal district court in Louisiana had put emergency plans in place and they actually had their shit together, so within a few days after Katrina, they had a bunch of court employees and federal marshals come move their computers and records to Houston, and they were up and running almost immediately."

"Our lawyer filed an order for an emergency hearing in the court, and it turns out that Lou, our accountant..." I nodded. "...His uncle was a district judge in New Orleans. Lou told him the situation and asked him to give us a chance and to hear the motion so we could get back to work. He agreed to the hearing and granted the motion to allow me to keep on doing business, but he did put some restrictions in place. I don't blame them because no one really knew for sure if I was involved, at that point. They put the company in a special receivership situation until everything could be sorted out. The receiver paid all of the bills, oversaw the business, and kept the business going until my name could be cleared."

I put down my glass. "But how could you keep every-thing going since Nick ran off with the $13 million from the levee money? You hadn't bought materials or anything, right?"

Nick shook his head. "No. Before Nick left, we hadn't bought anything for the levee, but fortunately, we had already bought all of the other materials for the other jobs we were awarded. Plus, we had a lot of materials from our warehouse and leftovers from other jobs, so the materials list was nowhere as bad as it could be. Also, because of the way the FEMA folks were awarding contracts, they were paying insane amounts of money if you could just get jobs done in a hurry, which we were great at doing, so my side of the busi-ness had already made a ton of money that was sitting there. And there was still a couple million dollars that hadn't cleared when Nick left. All that gave me enough financial cushion that I was able to complete all of the jobs we had agreed to do."

I was amazed. "Holy shit. You must have been working around the clock."

He laughed at the memory. "All of the time. Day and night. It was insane. It took almost a year before the judge gave me back control over my business accounts, another couple of years before the IRS and the FBI officially cleared me of any wrongdoing and a judge awarded me the entire business, and then another two before all of the jobs were completed, including that levee." He looked traumatized just talking about it. "I actually completed everything on time and on budget, but, honest to God, it just about killed me. All the money that was left went toward finishing these existing projects, so I also had to pick up as much new business as possible so that I could pay myself something and keep my employees' salaries and benefits current. I was running around like a crazy man trying to keep all those balls in the air."

I couldn't believe he'd managed to do all that by himself for so long. He shrugged. "Well, you do what you have to do. Fortunately, we already had great foremen and supervisors, so they supervised the actual work, while I oversaw the different jobs and kept everything moving."

He shook his head slowly. "Looking back, I can't believe we managed to get everything done. The good part was that at the end of that five years, not only was the business still open, but it had actually grown. I worked another couple of years, but I was so fried I needed a break." He laughed, "I told my sister I thought I had post-traumatic stress disorder. Anyway, I had restructured the business after Nick disappeared and so I sold the whole thing for a shit ton of money, put it in the bank, and took six months off to recover. Then, for the next few years, I flipped houses and did some renovation jobs for friends, and finally decided I needed a total change. That's when I came here."

One thought hit me. "Hey wait, so what about Nick and Glenda? Did they get busted?"

He rolled his eyes. "Hell no. I started divorce proceedings immediately, but when I contacted her lawyer to find out where to send the papers, he said he didn't have any contact information and didn't know where she was, so I had to put everything on hold for six months to give her time to respond to the papers I filed. We published a notification, but she never answered. In those cases, Louisiana requires you to select another attorney to represent the spouse's interests in the divorce, which I also had to pay for. When that lawyer asked what I had done to try to find Glenda, I referred her to the FBI agent investigating the case. He told her that Glenda and my business partner had embezzled millions of Katrina funds from our company and then run off together. The FBI knew they crossed the border into Mexico, but then they disappeared, along with my classic Camaro. They theorized that she and Nick were living the high life somewhere like Costa Rica or Belize, but they never had any specific leads.

The attorney turned out to be very reasonable and said that if the FBI said she couldn't be found, that was good enough for her, and she agreed that all assets should go to me since she had illegally taken more than her share when she stole the money from our business. She presented that to the judge, and considering the circumstances, he agreed. So, at the end, I got all of our personal assets, including the full amount for the sale of the business, and I just walked away from New Orleans."

I was outraged that Glenda and Nick weren't in jail. "Didn't they get charged with anything?"

"Oh yeah, they've been charged with all kinds of charges, like false claims against the government; theft of government property; credit card, bank, mail, and wire fraud, but the FBI doesn't have the resources to pursue them. The good news is that they're fugitives, so the statute of limitations for the fraud hasn't run out, plus they've increased the penalties for fraud arising from disaster relief funds, so if they ever turn up, they'll definitely go to prison. The FBI guys I knew worked with the U.S. attorney to make sure that the original levee money was considered to be stolen and I was completely exonerated from any involvement. That case was then closed. Then, FEMA awarded me a separate contract to complete the levee. That way, I could still fulfill my contract, they didn't have to pay someone an additional $13 million, and I was kept clear of the criminal charges. If they ever catch Nick and Glenda, they will be charged with the theft."

I still didn't understand. "So basically, you were awarded a contract for $13 million to build a levee, but you never saw a dime of it?"

He nodded. "Exactly. That original case was closed and the money they stole is considered to still be unrecovered. I was awarded a separate contract to build the levee, I completed the contract, and that way my business and I were completely in the clear. Like I said, it was a nightmare for a few years, but it worked out in the end."

He looked at me and smiled. "So here I am. I sold my house and everything I owned and moved to Atlanta, and now I'm kind of chilling, renting a little furnished apartment, teaching a few classes, hanging out with old friends, and trying to decide what's next. I'm fine money-wise, so I can take my time in deciding what to do."

I smiled back at him. "Sugar, that's a nice place to be in life." I shook my head, amazed by his story. "And, by the way, you totally win. Your story was much worse than mine."

He laughed and rolled his eyes. "Woo hoo, oh yeah, I'm quite a winner."

I laughed and reached over to squeeze his hand. "Luke, that makes you a complete winner. The fact that you went through all that and came out the other side with your sanity and sense of humor intact is an amazing accomplishment."

When I said that, he smiled into my eyes and all of a

sudden I felt a feeling that I hadn't felt in a long time. My heart started beating a little faster, my stomach felt a little nervous, and I stared at him, a little freaked out at the sensation. He stared back, and then his gaze dropped to our linked hands and then to my mouth and his gaze became very focused. He pulled me toward him and started leaning toward me, but just then, Diego yawned and started to stretch in Luke's lap and we both reached for him before he tumbled off onto the floor.

Whatever that weird-ass moment was, Diego broke the spell. I jumped to my feet and excused myself, fumbling through the back door. I ran, panicked, into my bathroom and shut the door and locked it behind me. I stared at myself in the mirror and realized that Luke and I had almost kissed. Holy shit, Lola was right. I was actually interested in him.

I told myself to get a grip. So what if I thought he was a nice guy and kind of adorable? That doesn't mean we're going to start dating. Maybe it was just some weird moment, or maybe I felt sorry for him after his awful story.

I didn't know what to do. I realized my phone was in my pocket so I pulled it out and called Lola. I told her in one long breath what had happened, "...And then we looked at each other and he looked at my mouth and I knew he wanted to kiss me and then Diego almost fell off his lap, so I ran to the bathroom and now I'm calling you."

There was dead silence on the line. I thought I'd lost her. "Lola?"

I heard her take a deep breath. Okay, she was still there. Then I heard her say, "Who is this?"

I thought my head was going to explode. "Ha, ha, hilarious. Lola, be serious. This is not funny."

She sighed. "Fine. So, that's it? So you almost kissed. So, what's the big deal?"

"What's the big deal?" I couldn't believe she didn't get it. This was huge! "I almost kissed Luke, and I'm barely divorced! Oh, and to make it even weirder, I haven't kissed anyone but Bobby since I was eighteen. What if I suck at it?"

I could tell Lola was trying to be patient. "Ooookay. Let's look at this like, I don't know, a normal person, for a minute. Y'all are both single, you've been separated and/or divorced for more than a year, and he's freakin' hot. And I'm pretty sure you don't suck at kissing. Daisy, sorry but I really can't see the problem."

Of course she didn't. Lola doesn't have any issues with men and relationships because she doesn't have relationships with men. She casually dates, and she has lots of sex, but she never becomes involved with anyone, so I could see why she really didn't get what was freaking me out. So, I told her in one long verbal spew. "Lola, you know I don't want a relationship. I like my calm, uncomplicated, man-free life, and Luke is a major complication. He's the kind of guy you end up with, not some casual transition guy, and if I started seeing Luke, it could totally screw up my new life, which I really love. I don't want to mess up a good thing."

Lola laughed. "Hey dumbass, take a deep breath. He almost kissed you, not married you. Don't you think you might be getting a little ahead of yourself?" No matter how much of an idiot I am, Lola still loves me, so she tried to sound a little nicer, knowing that I was really upset. "Look, I know the idea of someone in your life freaks you out, but he's a great guy, so why don't you just roll with it and see what happens? I think you'll have a great time, and maybe you'll finally get a little action." I rolled my eyes at that.

"And you can deal with all this relationship stuff later. Maybe y'all will drive each other crazy and it'll never go anywhere."

I snorted. Whatever. But, I had to admit Lola was right. I was getting way ahead of myself. "Okay, you're right. But Lola, do you realize I've never been on a date as an adult? Bobby and I met at the beginning of freshman year, so I don't even know how to act. And there aren't many things I suck at more than 'roll with it.'"

I heard Lola say under her breath, "That's for damn sure." When I took a breath to finish my tirade, she interrupted. "Look stop making this a bigger deal than this is. Quit being such a damn wimp, and get your ass back out to the porch before he thinks you've fallen and can't get up."

I shook my head, thinking that maybe I should have called Mo or Sara instead of Lola. "Thanks. I'll call you tonight." I hung up, took a deep breath, splashed water on my face and tried to look nonchalant as I walked back to the porch, but I really don't have much of a poker face, so I'm sure I looked more like I was trying not to throw up.

Luke was scratching Diego's ears, and when I came back on the porch he looked at me intently, like he was trying to figure out if I was still freaked out or back to normal. I tried to smile, but I apparently wasn't too convincing, because whatever he saw in my face made him stand up to go. "Well, Daisy, thanks so much for the water. I guess I'd better get going so you can run your errands."

I felt a little bad, but a lot relieved. I stood up, too. "Yeah, I guess I should get going. Thanks for breakfast, but I need to get to the grocery store and then go see my mom, so I guess I'll see you later." I held out my hand for him to shake. Oh, shit, I am such a dork. He smiled and took my hand and started to shake it. "And thanks for telling me your story. It's good to know that I'm not the only one with a bad divorce, although, to be clear, yours is much worse than mine." I was still shaking his hand and he kept looking at me like he was trying to figure me out. I finally snatched my hand back, and I'm sure I still had kind of a sickly, unconvincing smile on my face, so he finally figured it was time to go.

He smiled and turned to leave. "Well, okay. I'll see you later, Daisy." He waved as he walked out the door.

As soon as he left, I collapsed back onto my glider and all three of my boys jumped up with me. I felt kind of guilty because I was rude and didn't even offer him a ride, but hell, he's a big boy and he only lives a few streets over, so I didn't feel that awful. All three pups flipped over so I could rub their bellies, which I did absently as I thought back to that moment when we had almost kissed. I could picture the focused look in his eyes as he leaned toward me and my heart started to beat faster.

Holy shit. I do not need this right now. I need something else to think about. I decided to go see my mother, because I told her I'd stop by, and I know that by the time she starts commenting on my terrible fashion sense and out of control hair, I'll be unable to concentrate on anything remotely sexual. I went inside, made sure the dog door from the porch was opened, grabbed my keys and headed out to buy groceries and see my mom.

I was right. By the time I returned home that afternoon, my mom's visit had done the trick. I was too tired and irritated to think about Luke or anything else. I turned on the ceiling fan in my living room, kicked off my flip flops, and threw myself on my sofa and my dogs all jumped on. We were lying sprawled in a lazy pile when the doorbell rang. I pushed the dogs off and went to open the door.

It was Luke. He looked concerned and asked if he could come in. I was confused. "How'd you know I was home?"

He came inside, and stood in the foyer with his hands on his hips. "You nearly hit me in a cross walk on North Highland a few minutes ago and didn't even slow down. I came to make sure you were okay. Did something happen with your parents?"

I was still confused. "They're fine. I guess I'm just preoccupied. My mom spent her usual time bitching about my lack of ability to dress myself and my ridiculous hair, then once she was done with that, she started in with telling me that I needed to find a man. I told her that I'm not interested in a man, and then I left." I sat back on the sofa, fell back in the cushions and took a breath. "So no, it was a perfectly normal visit."

Luke sat down next to me, looking annoyed. "So, you're not interested in a man?"

I felt my eyes get big and I stared at him. I really didn't want to have this conversation. I swallowed and finally managed to choke out, "Well, I just got divorced."

He looked me in the eye. "Actually, Sara told me you've been divorced more than a year and broken up longer than that."

I started to get irritated. First my mom and now Luke? "That's not that long, buddy, and what's it to you?"

He looked at me and shook his head. "What's it to me? I'll tell you what it is to me...I really like you and we seem to enjoy each other's company, so I thought we could start dating. What's the problem?"

I was speechless for a moment. "Seriously? You never said anything about being interested in me."

He stared at me like I was nuts and raised one eyebrow. "Seriously? You couldn't tell I'd like to spend more time with you?" He looked at me intently. "We almost kissed this afternoon and then you ran away."

I got a little more aggravated. "As far as I'm concerned, I thought we were just friends."

He shrugged. "We are friends, and I like hanging out with you, but Daisy, I also would like to get to know you as more than friends."

I did not want to hear that. I'm sure my eyes were rolling around in my head like a crazy person. I started babbling. "Well, I'm not sure that I ever want to date anyone, and I really like my life the way it is, and I'm not sure I want to change it. I think the whole thing is a bad idea."

I finally had to stop to take a breath and Luke looked at me, as though trying to figure out what was going on in my head and how serious I was about not dating again. He could tell I was panicked, so he took a deep breath and leaned forward. "Look, Daisy, I think you're making this too big a deal." He gently took my hand and stared at me until I looked directly at him. He smiled at me until I finally smiled back at him and started to relax. "I just want us to keep being friends and spend more time together, and we'll just see where it eventually goes." He squeezed my hand, "I don't want to scare you, or pressure you, but we have a great time together and I really enjoy your company. Can't we just hang out and have a good time? I'm still fairly new to the area and I think you're a lot of fun."

I stared at him while my mind raced. We did have a lot of fun, and Lola was right, we're not getting married, we're just hanging out together. It's just like hanging out with Lola or Sara or Mo. Well, except none of them ever wanted to kiss me and they don't scare me to death. But other than that, really, what's the big deal?

He was staring at me intently and I knew he could tell I was considering it. Then, he smiled again and I couldn't help but think how adorable he was when he smiled. I pulled my hand back and looked at him. "Okay. You win. We'll keep hanging out as friends and we'll go slow." I looked at him for confirmation and he nodded. "But I'm not promising anything."

He slapped both hands on his knees and stood up. "Fair enough." He reached down and grabbed my hand to pull me to my feet. I was kind of off balance and tripped against him and landed against his stomach and all I could think was holy shit, I can feel his abs through his shirt. I can't date a guy with abs you can feel through a shirt. Hell, thanks to yoga, mine are strong, but are covered by at least twenty pounds of what I prefer to think of as protective fat. The only way you could feel my abs is to drill your finger into my belly like the Pillsbury dough boy. Why would a guy with a body like that be interested in a little chubby chick like me? He dropped my hand so he could grab my shoulders to keep me from falling, stood me up, and held out his hand to shake. "You've got a deal."

Before I could move, he pulled me closer, pecked a light kiss on my cheek, and let me go. I just stared at him like a total goof. He told me he'd call me in the morning, wished me a good night, and let himself out the front door.

I stood there, trying to take in what had just happened. I took my cell phone out of my back pocket and called Lola as I locked the front door and returned to the sofa.

When I told her what had happened, she was thrilled. "Hallelujah! A man who knows what he wants."

That pissed me off. "Does no one care what I want? Whose side are you on, anyway?"

There was a moment of silence and then Lola sounded

irritated. "Daisy, you know I'm always on your side, and the reason I think this is a great thing is because I think that he is exactly what you want, you're just too chickenshit to admit it."

I felt cornered, mainly because I think Lola was probably right. I did enjoy Luke's company, but I didn't want to rock the boat in my new life. "Lola, I'm not sure I can trust him. Bobby screwed around behind my back after years of being together. How do I know Luke won't do the same thing?"

"You don't," Lola pointed out, "but again, I think you're getting way ahead of yourself. He said he just wants y'all to get to know each other and hang out together. That's not exactly a marriage proposal."

She was right. I thanked her and told her we'd talk in the morning. I called the dogs and turned off the lights. I needed to think about this.

I took the pups outside before we went to bed. I wasn't tired at all, so I put on the Braves game, but I couldn't pay attention. I finally turned it off. I flipped through a magazine, but that wasn't any better. I guess my movements were bugging the dogs, because Cletus scooted his big body alongside me and nuzzled my neck. I know it sounds silly, but he prefers a lot of eye contact and he likes me to talk to him when I pet him, so I turned on my side so we could stare into each other's eyes while I rubbed his neck.

I slowly rubbed his long body as I softly crooned to him in a soothing voice. "Hey sweet boy, I know I can trust you. You'd never screw around behind my back with some skank, would you?" I kissed him on his head and put my nose against his so he looked at me with an adoring, cross-eyed gaze.

"So what do you think, Cletus? You think I'm being a

total wuss? Luke seems like a great guy. Do I need to just chill out and take a walk on the wild side?" His ears perked up at the word "walk", but once he realized that's not what was happening, he gave me a big slurpy lick on my chin and cuddled his face against my neck.

I grabbed his chin in my hand and kissed him between his soulful, hound dog eyes and started murmuring in his huge ear. "What do you think, Cletus? Can I trust him, sweet boy? I trusted the wrong guy last time. You think I should try it again? Give me a sign, boy." He stared at me and his tail thumped once, twice on the bed and then he rolled over with all four legs wide open so I could pet his freckled belly. I laughed as I scratched. "Well, I guess that's a sign. I ask you whether I should consider dating a guy and you flip over and flash me your junk. That's a total guy thing to do." I scratched until Cletus started making tiny little "woof noises" and wriggling his long body in sheer happiness.

Once I scratched him into a doggie coma, I pulled him against by side, kissed his velvety head and reached up to turn out the light. I have to admit, I was feeling better. I just had to keep reminding myself not to freak out and to relax. I'm not looking for a serious relationship. This thing with Luke is just two friends hanging out, maybe eventually doing a little dating. No big deal. I needed to quit looking at this as though going on a date meant I'm going to marry him and then he'd cheat on me. It's not serious, it's just a casual relationship. Easy peasy.

Once I relaxed, I fell asleep pretty quickly. Maybe my subconscious was more at peace with my decision than I was.

9

THE NEXT FEW MONTHS WERE A COMBINATION OF MY usual schedule, writing, working on my TV segments, walking the dogs, working out, with a little, okay a lot, of Luke thrown in to keep it interesting. We walked the dogs together, we went to the gym, we went walking and running, we ate together. One Thursday he wanted to buy a new kayak to take over to the lake at Stone Mountain Park, so we went to REI, and by the end of the day we'd each bought a kayak and he bought a rack for the top of his Jeep. The next day, we took the kayaks to the lake and had a great time, although thanks to me and my usual level of coordination, we both fell off in the middle of the lake while I was trying to avoid a bee. Well, actually, I fell off and then I sort of pulled him off while he was trying to help me back into the boat. I'm sure that, thanks to me, we looked like two of the three Stooges in a kayak, but we had a great time anyway.

I'll have to say, whatever we did, he was a perfect gentleman. When we'd walk, he'd take my hand or put his arm around me and when he'd leave he'd kiss my cheek or sometimes give me a nice quick kiss on the lips, and make another date for some casual activity. He was careful not to crowd me or monopolize my time, and the time we spent together was full of talking and laughing and just getting to know each other.

One evening, we'd just gotten in from a walk and were sitting on the porch drinking some tea I'd infused with pineapple and rosemary and trying some new pastries I'd make that morning. He gave me a quick peck on the lips. "Holy shit, Daisy, these new pastry things are awesome."

I smiled at his enthusiasm. "I'm glad you like them. I made some extra for you to take home."

He hummed as he took another bite. "That sounds great." He swallowed and then stuffed the rest of it in his mouth, chewing and moaning in appreciation. "I think I owe you a dinner for all the times you're always feeding me. That new seafood place up the street finally opened. Want to try it out Saturday night?

At that point, I was finally comfortable with the idea of an actual date. "Sounds great to me. We've been talking about that place."

He grinned at me as he selected another pastry to try. "How about we'll meet at your house and then, depending on the weather, we'll either walk or ride over." He stuffed the mini pastry in his mouth and said, around a mouthful, "Oh my God, this is amazing."

I laughed at his over the top reaction to my cooking. "You're such a goof." I kissed his cheek. "That sounds great."

That gave me a few days to get ready for our date. Mostly, I needed buy something to wear beside yoga pants and my grubby tshirts. And shave my legs. And maybe lose twenty pounds.

By the time Saturday night rolled around, I couldn't believe how nervous I was. I kept reminding myself that it's just Luke, I've known him for a bazillion years, we hang out all the time, it's just dinner, we're buds, it's just like having dinner with any other friend, his cousin is my best friend, blah, blah, blah, but apparently I didn't find myself very convincing. By the time he got to my house, I was a little sweaty, my heart was pounding, and my stomach was queasy. The good news is my new outfit, some super stretchy cropped jeans, a cute, low-cut swingy top with cutouts on the shoulders, and some blinged out flip flops, was just as comfortable as my yoga pants, so at least I had that going for me. I was even wearing some bronzer and mascara, which is almost like makeup, so I was thinking I was looking pretty fancy. I opened the door at his knock, and he was standing there in a pair of nice shorts, a short sleeve blue shirt that made his eyes look amazing and his shoulders about a mile wide, and a pair of casual slide on shoes. I must have still looked a little panicked because he immediately started laughing as he came inside. "Do I make you a little nervous, Miss Daisy?"

I shut the door behind him and I could feel my face turn beet red. I punched him in the arm. "Hey dork, a real gentleman wouldn't mention that. He would tell me some-thing like the nervous sweat on my face makes me glow."

He grinned. "How about, 'Daisy, I've always been a sucker for tiny little sweaty girls'."

I rolled my eyes and tried not to laugh. "Dude, I hate to tell you, but you suck at compliments. That comment is barely above 'you don't sweat much for a fat girl'". He laughed and grabbed my hand, and pulled me in close, which immediately shut me up. He looked down at me, although not as far as usual because my new platform flip flops added at least a couple of inches of height, which brought me up to where I was almost eye level with his nipple. He smiled and kissed me on the lips, not quite a peck, but not a full blown kiss, either. It was really nice and when he straightened up he smiled at me and told me I was still a little sweaty, but I didn't look nauseous any more. I smiled back and told him I felt fine, but I didn't tell him that his sweet little kiss made my lips tingly and my heart pound, because that was ridiculous. I reminded myself that we were just friends on a casual date and told him to just give me a minute to pet the pups and lock up and we could go.

It had finally cooled off some, so we decided to walk to the restaurant. As we turned the corner by my house, he grabbed my hand and put a quick kiss on my knuckles. "You do your usual Saturday morning yoga and breakfast this morning?"

"I did. I even suckered my friend Gina into going shopping with me, which I normally hate, but I figured I could use a new outfit." I stopped and put my arms out to the side and spun around so he could see it. "What do you think?"

He smiled and asked me to turn around again. I laughed and obliged, and when I was done, he grabbed my hand again and we continued walking. "You look great. I know the important question for you is whether it's as comfy as your t-shirts and yoga pants?"

"It is. This may be my new favorite outfit."

Luke gave me a deliberately lecherous look and bobbled his eyebrows up and down. "Mine, too."

I giggled at his silliness. "Okay, you dirty old man. Let's get back to tonight. What have you heard about this restaurant? The only think I've heard is that they make a bourbon punch that comes in an old fashioned punch bowl and is supposed to be amazing."

Luke nodded. "I heard that, too, but I also heard the seafood is great, it has a great bar, and they have a fun outside area."

When we got there, it was already busy, but it did look fun. They said our table wouldn't be ready for about twenty minutes, so we went through the restaurant out to the back patio. Luke got me a Corona Light and got himself a Georgia Brown from Sweetwater and I then proceeded to kick his ass in two straight games of cornhole. I told him not to feel bad about it because it's hard to beat a woman who's spent as much of her life tailgating as I have. By the time I finished my victory dance and Luke bought me what turned out to be a freaking bucket of bourbon punch, our table was ready.

We had a great dinner. I wanted to order the Low country boil, but I hesitated since this was an actual date and that stuff is a total damn mess to eat. Then I thought, oh well, this is the kind of chick I am, so if he's determined that we're going to date, he can take it or leave it, so I ordered it. With extra butter for the crab legs. Luke laughed and ordered the same.

When I looked at him, he was grinning from ear to ear. When I asked him what was so funny, he said, "You are the only woman I've ever met who would order something as messy as a Low country boil on a date."

I crossed my arms across my chest and mock frowned at him. "Oh yeah? Well, you're the only guy that would be rude enough to point that out on a date." That made him laugh. He halfway stood out of his seat to lean across the table to give me a quick kiss, then sat back down. He had dropped his napkin to the side, so when he stood back up and bent over to get it, I couldn't help but notice how nice his shorts looked stretched across his butt. I think he caught me looking, but for once, he didn't call me on it. He just smiled.

I picked up my punch. "Okay, it's been a long time since I've been on a date, so I found an article online that said we should talk about casual subjects so we can get to know each other."

Luke nodded and answered with mock seriousness. "That sounds like an excellent idea, Miss Daisy. So what would you like to discuss?" He took a drink of his punch.

I thought for a moment. "How's your teaching job going?"

He shrugged. "It's fine. It's been a nice break, but I'm about ready to get back doing construction work again." We grinned at each other and started having a normal conversation.

"You mentioned that vaguely a few months ago, but you want to start a new business?"

He nodded. "Yeah, but not a huge business like before. I'd rather do renovation projects for people who really appreciate craftsmenship. I love built in furniture, like book-cases, cabinets, and window seats, so I'd like to design and build those for people. I also like building decks and porches, and I might build an occasional house or put on an addition to a house, but nothing on a large scale."

I was excited for him. "That sounds great, Luke. I know you've already done a few small projects here and there, and you really seem to enjoy it."

"I did. Fortunately, money isn't a concern, so I can really take only the jobs I want. It'll be wonderful not having to deal with a bunch of employees and the headaches that go with managing people. I think this will be great for me."

I agreed. He smiled at me as I took another sip of punch

and asked me if I liked my TV job. I held up my hand and tilted it from side to side. "Eh. Some of it's a blast. I love meeting and talking to people, but I can't see myself doing it full time. Have you ever seen how a short segment is put together?"

He shook his head. "Well, for a tiny little 5 minute story like mine, it takes hours to film, then I edit it, then they edit it, and the process just takes forever. Honestly, I don't like hanging out there for hours, I don't like doing the same shot over and over so they can get it from different angles, and I really hate that I have to wear this makeup that's like spackle so you don't look like Casper the Friendly Ghost on camera." I shuddered. "You know how much I hate makeup, and that crap is so thick you can feel it when you talk. Also, because I'm so short, if we're standing up for any part of the interview I have to stand on a box so that they can get both of us in a single shot. Which would be fine except for my stupid ADHD. I can't tell you how many times I forget I'm standing on a box and have just about busted my ass falling off. It's just a matter of time before I break something I might need. Plus, they make me wear clothes that will 'look good on camera,'" which I did in little air quotes, "which is pretty much impossible for someone like me."

Luke had laughed about me falling off the box, but frowned when I commented that it was impossible for someone like me to look good on camera. Before he could open his mouth to defend me, I explained. "TV cameras are not kind to short chicks with boobs and a butt. I end up looking very short and very round. In fact, after my first segment aired, I asked Sara how she thought I looked on camera and she said she thought I looked good, but I did look rounder than I do in real life, and if she had to choose a phrase to describe me it would be, 'All tits and ass. All the time.'"

Luke was grinning again and I narrowed my eyes at him. "What?!"

He shrugged and started laughing at my expression. "Daisy, trust me, 'All tits and ass. All the time.' doesn't sound like a problem to me, or to any other man."

About that time, our waitress came by and set an enormous platter piled with seafood in front of us. She handed us a basket with claw crackers, hammers, picks for the crab legs and for the blue crabs, and bibs for both of us. I asked her if we really needed the bibs and she nodded so hard her glasses slid down her nose. "Absolutely. We cook this in a butter seafood boil and, trust me, it'll ruin your clothes." Since I'm kind of a hot mess on a good day, and I really liked my new outfit, I quickly tied on the bib.

We dug into the pile of food, and it was delicious. Luke and I were talking and laughing, and I was having such a good time I forgot I was actually on an official date. We were just friends having a great time. When he pounded a crab claw and little crab pieces flew all over his face and hair, I couldn't stop laughing at the look on his face as he picked off what crab bits he could find, so he finally leaned over and kissed me quickly just to shut me up. I waved a crab leg and a claw cracker at him, "Okay, watch and learn, big boy," cracked the claw and somehow managed to sling butter all over my nose and chin. Now he was laughing at me. I tried to wipe off the butter, but I'm sure my face was just a shiny, buttery mess.

I dropped the whole mess on my plate and Luke grinned as I grabbed a handful of paper towels. "Holy crap, look at me." I tried to wipe the butter off my hands and face but I'd managed to get it everywhere.

He shook his head and laughed at my efforts. He waved a huge piece of crab in front of my face, taunting me with his crab-cracking prowess. "Check this out Daisy." I tried to grab it but he was too quick and popped it in his mouth. "Ha, ha. Too slow."

I wrinkled my nose at him. "Showoff. Let me clean this off of me and I'll show you how to pick some crab."

I grabbed a piece of lemon and squeezed it in my hand and grabbed some new paper towels. Luke shook his head doubtfully. "I don't think you have enough lemon and paper towels to complete de-grease yourself."

I agreed and threw down the used towels. "I'm afraid you're right. I think it's going to take some scrubbing with Dawn dishwashing liquid, like they do the ducks in an oil spill to totally unbutter myself." I threw up my hands. "And I think I'm going to need a shower and a big loofah to get me squeaky clean."

At that Luke got quiet. He grabbed a lemon, squirted some on his hands and looked at me intently until he finally said, in a low voice, "A shower, huh? That could definitely be arranged."

We just stared at each other. The tension between us grew and grew and, as much as I thought it would be better for me if I did, I couldn't look away. My brain started racing. Let's face it, Bobby and I had been out of the habit of frequent sex for a while, and we'd been separated and divorced for more than a year, so it had been a while for me. All I could think of is that some friends have sex. Isn't that the whole concept of friends with benefits? I mean, I've never had a friend with benefits, but I'd certainly be willing to think about it. And Luke is a friend. A hot friend, but a friend. Maybe a little recreational sex would be a good idea...

Then I started thinking about the reality of it. All I could think is that I'd have to get naked if I wanted to have sex, and I'm in my mid-forties and I'm a short, chubby chick, and holy shit, how scary is that? Luke is built like some kind of hot jock in a men's fitness magazine, and I'm built like, well, whatever would be the opposite of that, and a middle-aged one at that. I've never been particularly shy or modest, but the whole idea of getting naked with a new man, especially one without a stray ounce of fat or any other physical flaw that I could see, was like a cold bucket of water in the face. And yes, I know that's totally shallow and a stupid thing to worry about, but this whole thing was so new and so weird, I didn't know how to handle it.

I finally looked away from Luke, picked up another napkin and focused intently on wiping off my hands and face. I drained the rest of my punch and poured myself some more and drank some of that, too. It didn't help. I was still freaked. When I finally looked up and met his eyes, I could see he looked concerned. "You all right?"

I smiled unconvincingly. "Oh yeah, I'm just fine." I finally gave up on my hands, scrubbed the napkin between my hands and threw it back on my plate. "I'm just going to run to the rest room and wash my hands and face with some running water. I think I'm finally crabbed out." I jumped to my feet and he stood up to pull back my chair, but I was already on my way. I could feel his stare on my back and I know he was trying to figure out what the hell had just happened.

I washed my hands and face and was relieved to see that there was no butter anywhere else. Shockingly, my hair and outfit seemed to be unscathed. I did touch up my bronzer and debated about calling Lola, but decided I just needed to quit being such a wuss and go back out to Luke. He didn't deserve to have me hiding in the bathroom again. So I took a deep breath and went back out to the table.

He stood up when I approached and once we both sat down, he didn't hesitate. "What the hell was that?"

I looked at him and shrugged. "Luke, I'm sorry. It's not you. This is all really new to me and you know I'm still pretty freaked at the idea of dating anyone." As in, dating-then-getting-buck-naked-with-a-hot-guy freaked out.

He ran a hand through this hair and looked at me, obviously frustrated. "Look, Daisy, I get that the idea of dating anyone freaks you out in general, but we get along great, we're comfortable with each other, and we have a great time together. What is the problem?"

I felt bad, because I know I was acting a little nuts, but I also felt irritated. And still panicked about the whole naked thing. "Look, you've been divorced since 2006, I've been divorced for about a minute. I'm just not in the same place as you. I get that my behavior is frustrating...it's weirding me out, too, but it is what it is." I reached in my purse for my wallet and rifled around for some money. I took out all my cash and threw it in the middle of the table. I told him that should cover at least half and stood up to leave. "I think we should just call this an experiment that didn't work out and I'll see you around."

He was sitting there with his mouth open by the time I was out the door. I turned toward home, trying to get there before I started crying. Within a few seconds, I heard someone run up behind me. Gee, look who it is...Luke. Shocking.

I kept walking, carefully avoiding looking at him, but I was relieved to find that I was feeling less stressed. It figures. Now the stupid bourbon kicks in. "I hope you paid the rest of that bill and didn't stiff that poor little waitress."

He quietly answered me. "I paid the bill while you were in the bathroom because I didn't have a good feeling that you were coming back." He grabbed my hand, pulled me to a stop, put my money in my hand, and closed my fingers over it. "Here's your money back. I asked you out, and I pay."

I knew better than to argue with a good Southern boy over who pays for a date. I shoved the money in my pocket and kept walking, and he silently fell into step beside me. Neither of us said a word until we were back at my house. I dug my keys out of my purse and unlocked the door. I stepped inside and turned to face him with an insincere smile pasted on my face. "Thanks for dinner, Luke. Um, I'll see you around..." My voice trailed off uncomfortably and he just stood there, so I shut the door in his face.

As soon as I did, I took a deep breath and opened it again because it was such a jackass thing to do. He was still standing there with his hands in his pockets and a totally expressionless face.

"I'm sorry." I said.

He nodded silently and stood there looking at me for several seconds. Finally, he said, "You're forgiven. And I'm the one who's sorry. You're right, I forgot that this is all new to you." He sighed. "Can I come in for a little while? I'd like to talk to you."

I stepped aside and motioned him in. "Come on in and I'll make us some iced coffee."

He came inside and followed me to the kitchen. He sat in one of my dining room chairs and watched me as I made our drinks. I glanced at him over my shoulder and asked, "You want some pistachio biscotti? I got it at the farmer's market."

He nodded with a small smile. "Yeah, that would be great since we ran out before dessert."

I grabbed the bag of biscotti, put a few on a plate, and then carried everything to the table. I sat down in the chair across from Luke and we had a few sips in companionable silence. I could feel that the tension had left the room and I felt monstrously relieved.

I figured it was up to me to start the conversation since I'm the one who ruined our dinner. I took a gulp of coffee and smiled at him. "I thought the restaurant was great. The food was fabulous."

He smiled and sipped his drink as I continued. "You've gotta respect any restaurant that serves bourbon in a bucket." He chuckled. "And I love to start off any evening by showing off my mad cornhole skills." I ran out of steam and took a big bite of biscotti.

Luke smiled and winked. "You do have some mad cornhole skills. Let's see how you do with something like bowling or pool, big talker. Something not related to tailgating so I can get my macho bragging rights back."

I laughed at that, and Luke reached over and touched my hand until I looked directly at him. "Hey, we need to talk about this. You want to tell me what suddenly freaked you out at the restaurant? I kidded you about needing a shower and you looked like I punched you."

I didn't want to tell him any of it. There's no way to explain that whole naked thing to a man in a way that doesn't sound crazy, so I told him the partial truth. "You said something about us taking a shower together. My brain starting whirling around and all of a sudden, it just seemed like we were moving way too fast."

He looked at me as though he was trying to figure out if that was really the problem. He nodded at me and said,

"Well you were right in that we are in two totally different places, but I think you're dead wrong about us being a 'failed experiment'." He leaned forward and covered my hand with his. "Let me ask you something, Daisy. Before you got upset, were you having a good time? Because I was having a great time."

I nodded. "Yeah, I was having a great time, too." I smiled at him and I was relaxed enough to tell him more of the truth. "Honestly, Luke, I love when we spend time together because I'm really comfortable with you and we always have fun. We like the same things, you like my dogs, you don't mind that I have no fashion sense and can't stand to dress up, and you pretty much give me as much space as I want, which is a huge deal for me."

What I didn't tell him was that he's not just fun to hang out with. He's hot. And smells delicious. And if I wasn't such a paranoid freak, I would totally love a week-long sex fest with him. Damn it. I took a sip of coffee to distract myself from going down that road right now.

He smiled and turned his hand so that our fingers were laced. "I love spending time with you, too, so let's just keep hanging out. And any time you're not comfortable with me or with something I say or do, just tell me and I'll stop and we'll talk about it. Don't run off and we'll figure it out."

I rolled my eyes. Ugh, how embarrassing. "Wow. That sounds like a blast for you. I can see why you'd think that dating me is a great idea." I could feel my face flush. "How much of a damn wimp am I?"

He laughed. "You're only a wimp because you're just stepping back out into the dating world and it's kind of scary, even if it's with someone you're comfortable with. Let's just take it slow and we'll hang out as much, or as little, as you want." He squeezed my hand. "Look, even though

Glenda and I hadn't really had a relationship for years before she left, it was still weird for me asking someone out and actually dating again, too."

"I appreciate that." I wanted him to understand why this was all so strange to me. "Luke, the worst part of this is that I don't feel like myself. I feel like I've become one of those crazy women that guys always bitch about, and that's not who or what I am. And yes, I'm sure that's what all crazy people say, but the reality is that I'm really not."

That made him laugh. "Daisy, I know you're not one of those crazy women."

"No. Seriously. I'm never moody, I'm not irrational, I'm not overly emotional, and I rarely get mad, but lately I feel like I'm all over the place."

He took his other hand and placed it over both of ours. "Daisy. Seriously. I know that. If it makes you feel better, I think everyone goes through this same process. It's a big deal adjusting to being single and actually dating again after you've been with the same person your entire adult life. The good news is that I'm positive, or at least ninety percent sure, maybe, that you're through the worst of it."

I stuck out my tongue at him. "Ha. Ha. Ninety percent, huh?" He winked at me, squeezed my hand again and then let it go. We drank the rest of our coffee and he ate the rest of the biscotti. Once he was done, he stood up, put both of our plates in the sink, and leaned against the counter. "You feel better?"

"I do." I felt much better and I smiled at him.

He must have liked what he saw because he winked at me and grinned. "So I'll come by tomorrow evening about six so we can walk the mutts?"

I nodded. "Sure. Sounds great." I was so relieved that the tension between us was gone.

I stood up and we walked to the front door then he turned to face me. He looked at me and smiled. "Is it going to freak you out if I kiss you goodnight?" He stuck out his hand. "I'm perfectly fine with one of your hearty hand-shakes, if not."

That made me laugh. "No, I think a kiss would be fine." He carefully put his hands on my waist and pulled me closer and his head lowered to mine.

His lips were soft, but firm, and at first, he just gave me a little peck on the lips. Then, as I relaxed, he moved back in and kissed me a little harder. My hands crept up from my sides to his shoulders and I kind of moaned a little at the way his arms and shoulders felt under my hands. Damn, that man has muscles on his muscles. When my lips parted slightly, I felt his tongue touch mine, first gently and then more strongly as his tongue swept into my mouth.

Lawd have mercy, I've forgotten how hot a kiss can be. Bobby was never much of a kisser and foreplay kind of guy. Don't get me wrong, sex was always fun and I enjoyed it with Bobby, but Luke was a whole different story. I could tell that he was a man who really enjoyed the process.

His hands moved from my waist to my hips as he pulled me closer. My heart was pounding and I could hear his harsh breathing in my ear. I could feel his hard body against the front of my body and I felt like my knees were going to give out. His kisses were overwhelming, and I was just starting to think that maybe sex here against the front door wasn't such a bad idea, when suddenly he pulled back.

We looked at each other, both of us breathless and wide-eyed, and he said, "Holy shit."

We both started laughing and he hugged me tightly. He lowered his head and started kissing my neck, gentle little sucking kisses that just about made me pass out. When my head fell back and I moaned again, he stopped and took a small step back, like he felt like he needed to stop, but I could tell he didn't really want to.

I nodded, mainly because I didn't trust my voice to come out as anything other than a little squeak or a moan, neither of which would be anything but embarrassing. He smiled and kissed me on the forehead, then grabbed my hands from his shoulders and pulled them against his chest. He kissed me one more time, a quick little playful smack on the lips, and then he pulled away. Probably before he changed his mind and started kissing me again. Let face it, both of us knew that if he started again, there was a good chance he wasn't going to be leaving. He opened the door, told me he'd see me tomorrow evening, and left.

I leaned against the door to catch my breath. I haven't felt like that in years. In fact, I can honestly say that I'd forgotten what sweaty, heart pounding, knee-weakening, good, old-fashioned lust feels like. My mouth felt swollen and my heart was still pounding, and I knew if he came back right now, I would probably drag him down onto the nearest horizontal surface. Or vertical.

After a few pleasant moments imagining how great that would be, I shook myself enough to call the dogs to take them outside. I grabbed my phone and called Lola on the way to the backyard.

She didn't even bother to say hello, she just started bitching at me. "For the love of God, why in the hell are you calling me so early?" She barked. "I didn't want to hear from you until tomorrow morning when you called to tell me that you just kicked him out after a big breakfast following a night of drunken, screaming sex."

I rolled my eyes, just as she said, "Don't roll your eyes at me. A girl can dream, can't she?" I laughed and explained to her that he had just left, there had been no drunken, screaming sex, but we had a pretty great time in general, with one small freakout in the middle.

She sounded impatient. "What did you do, you damn chicken? What, did he try to hold your hand and you punched him in the face, what?!"

The mental picture of that made me laugh. "No, there was no punching, and he's been holding my hand, smarty-ass, so that's not an issue." I took a deep breath, because I knew Lola was going to give me hell when I told her my actual issue. "Actually, he made a joke about us both needing a shower after eating Low country boil, and the next thing I know, I'm thinking that, at some point, I'd have to get naked if I wanted to have sex with him, which I do eventually, because, let's face it, he's hot. At that point, my chubby little round self is going to be naked with his big, perfect, beautiful self, and that contrast between us just seems like a terrible idea."

I finally took a breath and waited for Lola to let me have it with a big self-esteem lecture. I was shocked when she actually sounded sympathetic instead. "You know, I bet that is scary. You've only been with two guys in your whole life, and the first was when you were eighteen and then Bobby, and let's face it, everyone looks great at eighteen." She paused, "But Daisy, I gotta tell you, some things never change. The good news is that guys are all simple creatures. They're so excited about having a naked woman in their bed, trust me, all they see is naked. They don't see skinny, they don't see fat, they don't see stretch marks. They see naked boobs, butts, and a hoo-hah, and they are all kinds of thrilled."

I laughed. I know that's true. I've had guy friends all my life, plus, I know when things were good with us, Bobby was just as excited with big boobs at 40 as he was at 20. I could hear Lola smiling through the phone. "Look, if the totally naked thing freaks you out, get you some little short, stretchy, see-through nightie and some candles. Make sure you can pull it down so those huge boobs of yours can pop out over the top, wear a thong that makes that big round butt of yours look fabulous, and he won't even notice you're not naked."

Lola was right, as usual. She knows me well enough to appreciate that I'm a planner by nature, so now that I know how to handle it, if sex ever does come up, I'll be fine. I'll go lingerie shopping, buy some nice candles, and if and when it becomes an issue, I'll be ready. Problem solved. I'm not so good when things come out of left field. Please refer back to the   mutilated-testicle-when-told-about-pregnant-teenage-girlfriend if you want to see some proof of that.

I stayed up and read for a while and was about to turn out the light when the phone rang. I rolled over to look and it was Sara. When I picked up the phone, Mo and Sara were both on the line and they said they'd all been out to dinner together and were back at Sara's house and they wanted to know how the date went. I told them it went fine and that we were going to walk the dogs tomorrow night. And I asked them how many bottles of wine they had shared.

There was a dead silence. "Two, maybe three at the most. Well?" Sara asked impatiently.

I played dumb. "Well, what?"

I could hear both of them whispering and finally, Mo said, "So is he still there?"

I started laughing. "Would I have answered the phone if he was still here? No, he's not still here."

They both sounded disappointed, and I laughed. "Look,

it went great. We had a great dinner, we're getting together tomorrow night..."

I could almost hear Sara's eyes rolling in her head as she interrupted. "So y'all can walk the dogs. Oh yeah, that's totally hot."

I tried to defend myself. "That could be hot. You don't know. Something could happen after we walk the dogs. Or instead of walking the dogs."

I knew they'd never buy that. "Whatever," Sara said dismissively. "I'm sure that'll happen. Did you kiss him, at least?"

I smiled in memory. "Oh yeah. And I have to admit, that was pretty wonderful."

Amazing. That actually shut them up. I heard Mo say, "Hmmm..." at the same time Sara let out a huge "Well, hot damn! Thank you, Jesus! It's like you're finally rejoining the living."

"Look, you dumbasses, y'all act like I've been hibernating like a nun for the past twenty years. It's only been a year or so since 'the vehicular testicular smackdown,' and during that time I've gotten divorced..."

"From a sleazy douchebag who knocked up his skanky 'ho adolescent girlfriend," interrupted Sara.

"Bought a house, moved, started a new job while keeping my old job, and have actually gone on a date." Holy shit, that sounded like a lot when you spelled it out like that. "I think I've done pretty well in about a year."

Mo was supportive, as usual. "That is a lot, when you put it like that."

Sara was not as impressed. "Okay, I guess that is a lot, but damn, now it's time to jump back on the sex horse. Especially when that horse is my fine-looking cousin. We've all seen the way he looks at you and I'm telling you that one tiny yes, and he's all over you."

I asked her to please drop the horse metaphor, because that just sounded nasty, and told them I was hanging up because I was tired. We agreed to meet Wednesday for lunch since Mo had the day off, and Sara said she'd shoot Lola a text to see if she wanted to join us. I wished them good night and hung up, shaking my head and laughing. I whistled for the dogs, they came in, and we all went to bed.

10

————

THE NEXT EVENING LUKE CAME OVER AND WE WALKED
the dogs, and pretty soon, we were walking the dogs every
evening. After several weeks, we had a nice little routine
going. Luke and I would do our own thing during the week-
days, and we would see each other most nights to walk the
dogs. Some nights we'd hang out for a while after we walked
the dogs, some nights he'd go right home. Occasionally, we'd
meet for a meal if we were both free. On the weekends, we'd
hang out with friends, go kayaking or bike riding, and go to
dinner.

We did a lot of kissing and touching and just making out
like teenagers while we were together, but both of us agreed
to take our time before we actually became intimate. I will
say that now, I'm about ready to jump all over him.

It's been wonderful to take the time to really get to
know each other. He's enjoyed getting reacquainted with
our old group, and I know that everyone is happy that we
are seeing each other and getting along so well. He has told
everyone about his issues in New Orleans and about his

plans to start doing construction on a much smaller scale, and Mo has already gotten him a job doing a couple of projects for her sister, Laura. It has been a really a nice, comfortable time.

I went with him to his sister's birthday party and his family was lovely. Luke looked and acted just like his dad, his mom was warm and charming, and his sister still teased him unmercifully. I'd warned him that my family wouldn't be as easy as his, but surprisingly, when he met my folks a couple of times and then my entire family at my dad's birthday party, it was relatively painless. I tried to tell them all we were just friends so my mom wouldn't torment him, but none of them bought it. I could tell my brothers and dad really liked him, although I later told Luke that I was pretty sure that my father would probably run a background check on him. Luke turned a little pasty at that, worried that Dad would freak out about the whole Katrina thing, but I promised him that I would explain it all if Dad asked me about it. Actually, I stopped by my dad's office the day after the party to head off any problems, but I was too late. By the time I got there, he'd already run a check, gotten concerned, and called an FBI buddy in New Orleans who had given him the whole story and assured him that Luke was a great guy. My mom was just thrilled that I was dating a straight man who dressed better than me, as if that was some high bar to surpass, so her goal now was to get me married to him ASAP. Bless her heart, I love her, but that woman drives me crazy.

I like where Luke and I are in our relationship, but I'm not saying it's perfect. He's a great guy, but he's not a wimp and we've had a few incidents where we've butted heads. He can be bossy and overbearing, and I really like to be left alone to do what I want, so when he tries to tell me what to do or we disagree, there can be sparks. The good news is that neither of us holds grudges, so we get past any disagreements pretty quickly.

Our first big blow up was when Luke and I took the pups for a walk and ran into Greg, the guy who owned the landscaping company that took care of my old house. I introduced them, and then Greg turned to me and, in front of Luke, asked if I'd like to grab dinner sometime. Before I could say no, Luke got in his face and told Greg I was with him and for him to butt out. Next thing you know, he and Greg were in some ridiculous pissing contest. I just rolled my eyes and kept walking, ignoring them both.

I had cooled down by the time the pups and I reached my street, but I was still aggravated. I was starting up my front sidewalk when Luke caught up. I kept ignoring him. When I opened the door and started inside, Luke caught my wrist and asked if we could talk. I motioned him inside and then followed him in, stopping to unharness the boys and get them some water. I sat at the table and waved at the chair across from me. "Sit down if you want."

He sat down and it was obvious he was still annoyed. "Daisy, sorry about that."

I raised my eyebrows. "That didn't sound very sincere. What was that all about? You were acting like a total jack-ass. For future reference, I am perfectly capable of turning down a date without your help."

He was looking down, shredding a paper napkin, and muttered. "Yeah, well, I didn't see you turning it down."

"You didn't give me a chance."

He wadded up the paper remnants and sighed as he looked me in the eye. "That's true. Bottom line, Daisy, I didn't like the fact he asked you out right in front of me and you didn't say no."

"I couldn't say yes, no, maybe, or never before you jumped in and started acting like a dick. Look, Luke, we don't have any exclusive arrangement that I'm aware of, so technically, I can go out with whomever I want." I had no desire to date anyone else, but I was mad and wanted to poke him a little.

It worked. I saw his cheeks flush and he narrowed his eyes at me. "That's interesting. I was under the impression that we were dating each other exclusively."

I raised my eyebrows at his comment. "Really? Because I don't remember that conversation. But for the record, as far as I'm concerned, it won't be a problem in the future, because I'm not sure I want to date anyone, especially you." I got up to get myself a drink and didn't offer one to him.

He sat there fuming, drumming his fingers on the table. I poured a glass of tea and sat back down and we stared at each other. Finally, he broke the silence. "Well. For the record, as far as I'm concerned, I don't want to date anyone but you and I don't want you dating anyone but me. So what do you think we should do about that?"

I was fine by that point, but I wasn't ready to cave yet. Any Southern woman can tell you not to give in too quickly during an argument. It sets a bad precedent. I crossed my arms and looked at him. "What do I think we should do? I don't think I should do anything, because that doesn't sound like my problem."

He glared at me and then stood up and headed over to the cabinet. "Mind if I get some tea?"

I shrugged. "Knock yourself out."

He grabbed a glass, got some ice, poured some tea, and returned to his seat. When I still didn't say anything, he took a gulp of tea and then put the glass down. He studied my face, like he was trying to get some idea of what I was thinking. Finally he decided to take another tack. "How about this?" He reached over and cupped my cheek gently. "Daisy, I'm sorry I acted like a jealous jackass. I know you can handle yourself."

I smiled at him. "That was better."

He ran his hands through his hair and then started fiddling with his glass as he chose his words carefully. "I want to discuss something with you. I really enjoy your company, and other than right now, we usually have a great time together. What would you think about us dating each other exclusively?"

I looked at him with big eyes and the most innocent look I could muster. "Really? I pretty much assumed that we were only dating each other, but I guess it's not a bad idea to make it official."

I started laughing at the look on his face. He groaned, stood up, pulled me out of my chair and kissed me. He then turned, grabbed my arms, and swung me up onto his back. I wrapped my arms around his neck and my legs around his waist and I kissed his ear while he galloped me piggy back out to the porch so we could watch the dogs and hang out for a while. That night, he brought me a bag of my favorite coffee and he gave me a foot massage and then he kissed me and we fooled around until I forgot all about being mad. I'm pretty easy that way.

When I told Lola about it, she said that he acted like an ass in that situation because we haven't had sex yet, so he hasn't marked me as his territory. She said I should be happy because that was a better option than him peeing on me, which is how non-humans take care of that problem. Ha! I guess that's true, if those are my only two options.

Our second big fight had to do with work. He had stopped by my house to bring me a biscuit on his way to work and I mentioned that I was recording a segment on this amazing woman named Ms. Edna, an elderly female nurse practitioner who had spent years vaccinating children in India and now ran a health ministry for drug users in north Georgia.

I was excited about finally being able to wear my jeans and a black t-shirt for a story, but all Luke heard was that I was going to the Sandlewood Mobile Home Park in Gainesville and he got upset. Last month, there had been a huge drug bust there, and it turns out that Mexican cartels were funneling methamphetamine into this trailer park for distribution throughout the South by various biker gangs and skinheads. Arrests had been made, but since the bust, there had been multiple shootings in the area and several people had been killed. Luke thought it was, quote, "idiotic to send a tiny little woman traipsing around the worst trailer park in north Georgia with an old woman as your only protection," but I reminded him that I wasn't going by myself. Mandy, my third cousin and producer, would be there and most importantly, so would Billy Ray, my camera guy. Billy Ray is a huge, muscled, ex-professional football player with a shaved head, a bushy, mountain man beard, full sleeves of tattoos on both arms, and piercing blue eyes. He's about the sweetest man ever, but he looks terrifying when he tries. I could tell Luke still wasn't thrilled about the idea, but I reminded him that he had to teach a class and it was too late to cancel, so he couldn't come with me. He grabbed my arms and kissed me, hard, shook his finger in my face and told me to be careful and left, muttering under his breath. I was pretty sure I was glad I couldn't hear what he was saying because I'm thinking it wasn't very complimentary about either my intelligence or my abilities in the art of self-defense.

It wasn't much better when I went to the station. Mandy was out sick with the flu, so Billy Ray had to wire me up, and when he first heard where we were going, he simply refused to take me. Period. He looked me in the eye and told me, "no offense, but I grew up in a place like that and it's a dumbass idea to bring a tiny little unarmed woman into that neighborhood with everything going on," and he wasn't going to be responsible for that.

Mentally, I was thinking, "Lawd, save me from overprotective men," but I looked at him and smiled, touched his arm, and in a sugary voice, said, "Billy Ray, I'm not worried at all. I know you'll protect me." I smiled and stood up, ready to go. "Now come one, we need to get going or we're going to be late."

Billy Ray didn't fall for it. He crossed his arms, perched on the corner of his desk and laid down the law. "Daisy, you can sweet talk me all you want, but there's no way in hell I'm going there, and I'm sure as shit not taking you."

I clenched my fists so I could stop myself from smacking him in frustration. Shit. About that time, I heard a pissed off voice behind me. "If you're insisting on doing this damn thing, let's get going." I spun around and Luke was leaning against the door with his arms crossed, looking unbelievably irritated.

I gritted my teeth. "Seriously? Why in the hell are you here? Don't you have a damn job?"

Billy Ray looked relieved to see Luke. He and Luke had met several times before, and I'm sure he was convinced that Luke would put his foot down and insist that I couldn't go. Ha! As if any of those overgrown buttheads could tell me what I could, and couldn't, do. I imitated his pose, crossing my arms over my chest and glared back at him. "Seriously, why are you here? Why aren't you teaching your class?"

He pushed himself upright and stomped over to me. "When I left your house, I found out that class was already cancelled because of a water main break." He stopped in front of me and leaned so that he was looming over me and we were almost nose to nose. "I knew you'd do this come hell or high water, so I came over to give Billy Ray some backup."

I stared back at him and I could tell it was annoying him that he didn't intimidate me. As if. I knew he'd cut off his own arm before he'd hurt me, so he doesn't scare me one bit. I rolled my eyes dramatically and pretended to misunderstand. "Please. Billy Ray can take care of himself."

Luke looked like steam was going to come out of his ears. He spit out through his clenched teeth, "Of course Billy Ray can take care of himself. But he can't take care of himself and you and Mandy while he's working."

"Mandy's sick and she can't go."

"Whatever. The point is that Billy Ray can't run the camera and look after you, so this way, he can do his job, and I'll look after you both. Problem solved."

I stared at him. He stared at me. Billy Ray looked at both of us, obviously uncomfortable, said he'd meet us at the van, picked up his camera, and pretty much ran out the door. What a wussy. We stood there, neither of us backing down. Finally, I broke eye contact to look at my watch. "Shit. If I don't go now I'm going to be late." I sighed. "Come on then, you can go. But don't think this means that you can tell me what I can and can't do."

He started laughing, saying mockingly, "No shit, Daisy. Let me guess...'You're not the boss of me!'"

I turned and started for the door with him right behind me. "You're not."

He caught my arm and spun me around so I faced him. He grabbed my shoulders and stared unblinkingly in my eyes. "I have no desire to be the boss of you. Daisy, local cops won't go to this trailer park nowadays because it's unsafe, and they're armed and trained for combat. You're not."

I interrupted. "Actually, I'm an excellent shot. I was raised by a cop, after all."

He took a deep breath. "I have no doubt. But you're not armed now, and I'm not letting you waltz into an unsafe situation by yourself just because you're trying to prove a point. If you insist on doing this, I'm going with you to make sure you're safe. Get over it."

I suddenly realized that his attitude was because of fear for my safety, not because he was trying to tell me what I could, or couldn't do. I still thought it was unnecessary, but his heart was in the right place. I grabbed the back of his head and pulled it down and kissed him, and then backed up a step, smiled at him, and patted his cheek. "Awww, you are so sweet."

He stared at me, confused, but looking less irritated. I smiled at him and told him we needed to go. He let go of me and I grabbed his hand and towed him toward the garage. By the time we got to the van, Billy Ray was already loaded up and sitting behind the wheel, so Luke got in the back and I grabbed shotgun next to Billy Ray. As soon as we hit the road, Billy Ray looked at Luke in the rear view mirror. "No luck, huh?"

Luke snorted. "Obviously not. Apparently, in case you didn't know, I'm not the boss of her."

Billy Ray laughed and shook his head, and they kept

talking, both completely ignoring me. "You know, I'm the youngest of four brothers, and all of us played college ball, and two of us went on to play pro ball. In fact, I was the smallest of all of them." My eyes about bugged out of my head when I heard that, because Billy Ray is at least 6'5", and still weighs 260, easy, but I didn't say anything because I wanted to hear this story.

I've known Billy Ray for years because he played high school football with my brothers, but he's one of those people who rarely talks about his early childhood, so I've had to kind of put together his story over the years. I knew that he grew up dirt poor until he was sixteen and his dad inherited a bunch of money and used it to start what eventually became a very successful electrical supply business. I know he played college and pro ball, and I've met his wife, but I never met his parents or the rest of his family.

"My dad was just as big, and my mom is about Daisy's size. Let me tell you what, when we were growing up, all of us, including my dad, always did exactly what she said. Hell, I still do whatever she says. She was never mean, she never yelled, but she ruled that house. Looks to me like you're having the same problem."

Luke laughed and shared a commiserating look with Billy Ray. "Welcome to my world."

What? Why is that a problem? I'm not trying to tell Luke what to do, I'm just saying he can't tell me what to do, either. Then I thought of something and I turned to Billy Ray. "Billy Ray Perkins, you're married and I've met your wife and she's not much bigger than I am. Who rules your house now?"

He snorted. "Who do you think? It sure as hell isn't me. And it's not my two boys. My wife is just like you. I've always told her that she's 5'2", but she plays 6'10", and I'm telling you now, when she says jump, everyone in my house ask, 'How high?!'" As the GPS lady told him to turn right, he steered the van down a narrow gravel road, and checked the doors to make sure we were locked in tight.

Luke hadn't known the details about Billy Ray's football career. "Where'd you play?"

Billy Ray checked the rear view mirror and nervously rechecked the locks. "I played at Florida. Tight end." I made a gagging noise, which made Billy Ray laugh because we discuss our opposing college football allegiances all the time. He ignored me and continued. "I played in the pros for a couple of years. I was drafted by Denver in the second round and played there a couple of years, was traded to Miami, and then blew my knee out in the first game as a Dolphin and had to retire." He shook his head at the memory. "In a few years, I'll probably have to replace it, but it's all good."

I was curious about his brothers. "What are your brothers doing now?"

"My brother was a backup quarterback for seven years and he only played in four games the entire time. When he retired he was much better shape than I was. No blown knees, no bad hits so no worry about future CTE issues. He was careful with his money and is now a high school football coach in Texas, which he loves. My other brothers had gone to work with my dad right out of college, and together they had expanded the business across the entire southeast.

I sarcastically told Billy Ray, "What a shame y'all are such underachievers."

He laughed. "Yeah, well we all knew football wouldn't last forever. Thanks to my dad, I was smart with my money and my wife and I lived like we were still college students the whole time I was in the pros, so we're good. Now, we can do what we want, and I found that I love being a cameraman and photographer." He turned and looked at me. "Well, I love it most of the time."

He and Luke laughed and while he wasn't looking I stuck my tongue out behind his head. When Billy Ray looked at me again, I smiled sweetly at him and patted his arm. "What could possibly go wrong with two such big, handsome men watching over me?"

Luke snorted at my sarcasm, and he and Billy Ray looked at each other, and Billy Ray shook his head. "Famous last words, Daisy." He made another turn and looked at me very seriously. "We're almost there, so promise me we're going to get in and out as soon as we can. You can invite Ms. Edna to the studio to do the actual interview once we get the footage with some of her clients."

I promised him I would do my best. Honestly, we were in a part of Georgia I had never been to, and I couldn't believe how run down everything looked. I'm not the bravest person ever, and I wasn't crazy about filming in an area when Mexican cartels and redneck skinheads were at war, but I think it's important for people to see the reality of the amazing work Ms. Edna does.

When we got there, we could barely see Ms. Edna in the crowd. She was surrounded by people who were waiting in line, some were standing around eating sandwiches and drinking juice, and a few were over to the side getting information about various drug treatment options. When Ms. Edna saw me, she waved me over excitedly, knowing that any publicity helps get donations for her program. I hopped out of the car and hurried over while Luke helped Billy Ray unpack his equipment. Since he'd already wired me up at the station, all he had to do was hook up my microphone, do a quick sound check and we were ready to start recording.

Ms. Edna was incredible. She was even smaller than I am, her head was shaved almost to the skin, she weighed maybe eighty pounds, her skin was a dark caramel brown, and she had beautiful, kind eyes in a face that was almost unlined, despite her being almost ninety years old. She was tiny, but regal, and her voice was booming and very authoritative. Ms. Edna told me where to stand, told Billy Ray to get in close to us so he wouldn't miss anything, told Luke to back up so he wouldn't interfere with the camera, and she started talking. She explained that her ministry provides condoms, Narcan kits to reverse narcotic overdoses, food, and new syringes for IV drug users. For those who were ready to make changes, she helps them get into treatment. She also provides basic medical care for those who have developed infections, HIV, or other physical issues related to their addiction.

After Ms. Edna finished explaining her program and Billy Ray got some great footage of her in action, I started talking to some of the people Ms. Edna was helping. Although they had started to scatter when Billy Ray first took out his camera, Ms. Edna told them to come back and talk to us, so they did. They explained that the gangs pretty much stayed away from wherever Ms. Edna was working, especially in the daytime, like now, but you could still tell everyone was on edge because of the recent shootings. Well, not Ms. Edna, who was cool as a cucumber, but everyone else. Luke stayed behind Billy Ray and kept an eye out, and after about an hour, we thanked Ms. Edna and I told her I would call her to find a time she could come to the studio for an interview. She hugged all of us and told us we'd see her soon.

When we got back into the van, Billy Ray didn't waste any time locking the doors and getting us out of there. Once we were safely on the road, I turned to look at them. "Well? Isn't she an amazing woman?"

They looked at each other and nodded. Luke ruffled my hair and smiled at me in the mirror. "She's impressive and what she's managed to do with so little funding is unbelievable. If you'll give me her information I'd like to make a donation to her foundation, and I'm sure Lola would agree."

Billy Ray nodded. "I'm in."

I smiled to myself. Typical guys. They're all big, bad talkers, but when it comes down to it, they are really just plain overgrown sweethearts. When I told them that, they both looked fairly appalled and started to protest, but I just ignored them. Whatever.

When we got back to the station and started unloading the van, I grabbed both of their hands to stop them for a moment. "Thanks, both of y'all, for coming with me today. I really appreciated that y'all were so concerned with my safety but were willing to come over anyway." Luke stood by as I hugged Billy Ray. "Billy Ray, you and your wife pick a time to come over and we'll have a big steak dinner."

Billy Ray hugged me right off my feet. "You got it, girl." He put me down and picked up some of his equipment to haul inside. "I'll download the footage and send it over to you later today so you can start working on it."

"That would be great." I pulled him down so I could kiss his cheek. "Tell your wife I'll call her later in the week. Thanks again." He waved as he picked up the rest of his equipment and headed inside.

So now it was just us. Luke turned to face me, crossed his arms over his chest, and looked at me with one eyebrow raised. "Well?"

He looked ready for a fight. I guess he thought I was going to bitch at him some more, but I wasn't mad at all. I still thought they were being ridiculous, but having grown up with a cop dad and two older brothers, I knew that big, overprotective men aren't going to change, so I let it go. I smiled at him and said we should go sit somewhere outside and I offered to buy him a burger at Joe's for being such a great bodyguard. Now he looked confused, but he just grabbed my hand, said, "Ookay. Let's go," and we went out to his Jeep. As usual, he had to help me in, because, even with the step bars, it's so jacked up I'd need a running start and a trampoline to get in by myself.

As we drove to the restaurant, I could feel him glancing over at me like he was waiting for me to say something. Every time I'd catch his eye I'd just smile and I finally reached over to grab his hand and just sat back, enjoying the nice weather. When we got to the restaurant, we got a table outside and both of us ordered a loaded burger with fries and a beer. Our server brought our beers and Luke took a big swig and put it on the table and looked at me.

"So?"

I grinned. "So, what?"

He looked at me with narrowed eyes. "So, let's get it over with. I know you weren't too happy with me insisting on coming along with you today, so let me have it."

I shrugged. "No need."

Luke looked at me like I was a bomb about to explode in his face. I finally felt sorry for him and figured I'd explain so he could relax. I reached over and took his hand in mine. "Luke, why did you insist on coming with me today? All kidding aside, we've been hanging out for months and you're not the type of guy who usually gets all Neanderthal about stuff. I've never thought of you as someone who felt like he 'had to be the boss of me'. Was I wrong?"

Luke was taken aback at the idea. "Daisy, trust me, I have no desire to be the boss of you. I love the fact that you're smart, and independent, and a free-thinker. The only reason I insisted on coming with you today is because you were going to a poor, extremely dangerous neighborhood that is having daily shootings because of a drug war. Despite your huge attitude, which I love, by the way, you're physically a tiny little woman who wouldn't be a match for a pissed off, drugged out, man trying to hurt you. I know Billy Ray looks out for you, but the truth is, he can't watch over you and do his job at the same time. I didn't think it was a good situation, so I came to make sure you were safe."

"And that's it? You weren't trying to tell me what to do, or how to do my job, you were just trying to make sure I stayed safe?"

He looked me in the eyes and nodded. "That's it."

I beamed at him. "So I'm good. Thanks for worrying about me. You are about the sweetest thing, ever."

Luke still looked a little confused, but our burgers came out then, and I think he was too hungry to argue any more. He took a huge bite, chewed, swallowed, took a swig of beer and pointed at me with the bottle. "You really are not like most women."

Here we go again. "So you've said. First, when I ordered a messy dinner on our first date, and now. Look, if you're trying to get part of my lunch forget it. I'm eating the entire burger and all of my fries, so trying to shame me into eating like some wimpy, salad-worshiping girl won't work."

He snorted. "Please. I know better than to get between you and your lunch," I lifted my middle finger and smirked at him as I took a huge bite and promptly squirted the entire burger out the end of the bun and all over my plate, with a good bit landing on my chin. He sighed, shook his head, and handed me his napkin. "No, most women would be holding a grudge and making me pay for my transgression for the rest of the day. I'd have to buy jewelry or flowers or something to get out of the doghouse."

I wrinkled my nose in distaste. "Seems to me like your main problem is that you've had bad taste in women." I smiled at the waiter and asked for a few more napkins and a glass of water. "I don't hold a grudge because I don't see the point in it. Once a situation is resolved, why stay pissed?" I shrugged. "And let's face it. I don't like jewelry that much and I'm too easily distracted to remember to stay mad."

The waiter dropped off some more napkins so I started wiping up my mess. Suddenly, I stopped dabbing at my hands. "Oh wait, there is one exception. If all this was so that you can tell me that you just knocked up your teenage girlfriend, we might have a problem." I raised my eyebrows and wagged my finger in his face. "I think you already have an idea how that could turn out."

He laughed as I finished cleaning my face and the table, and my hands, and, damn it, a spot on my pants. Holy crap, that burger made a mess. He smiled at my efforts and handed me another napkin. I dipped it in water and tried rubbing the spot on my pants, but it wasn't going away, so I gave up, wadded up the napkin, threw it at his face and smiled at him as he caught it. "So we're good?"

He drained his beer and smiled back. "We're good." We finished eating, paid the bill, went to his Jeep, and he drove me back to the studio so I could pick up my car. He told me he'd be over tonight to walk the dogs, told me to make sure I put my top up when I got home because the rain was coming in late afternoon, kissed me goodbye, and he drove off.

I stood in my driveway watching him disappear down the road. It turns out that an overly large, grumpy, autocratic man is kind of hot.

By the time Luke got to my house that night, the rain had moved in and it had started to pour. We tried to take the pups for a walk, but my two delicate princesses, Cletus and Diego, refused to go outside because they don't like to get their feet wet. Cletus flopped on his side and refused to move and Diego immediately joined him in his protest. Luke and I gave up and made sure the dog door was open in case they had to go out.

Since the weather was too nasty for a walk, and neither of us had to be anywhere the next morning, Luke and I decided to hang out and stay up late and watch movies on my enormous TV. We settled in with some popcorn and some crispy coconut cookies I had made that afternoon. All the pups came to curl up on the sofa between us, and I felt cozy and comfortable. As usual, Luke was in a t-shirt and a pair of cargo shorts, and as usual, he looked amazing. As usual, I was in shorts and a ratty t-shirt and, as usual, I looked slightly homeless. I kept sneaking glances at him during the movie, and after a while, I gave up and was really just watching him. With my ADHD, I'm not great at watching movies, anyway. When he caught me looking, he frowned. "What?"

I smiled at him and said, "Nothing," although what I was really thinking is that he looks and smells delicious.

He paused the TV and looked at me. "Seriously, what?"

I smiled at him. "Seriously, nothing. I was just thinking that you were looking pretty adorable over there watching that movie."

He grabbed my arm and lifted me up enough to pull me over the dogs and onto his lap. Apparently waking them from a sound sleep annoyed them enough that they all jumped down and collapsed on the rug under the ceiling fan. "Well, you're looking pretty adorable yourself, and you looked lonely over there." He buried his face in my neck and start nibbling where my neck and shoulder meet. "Let's see what I can do to help you feel better."

I smiled as I felt him gently bite me and then he instantly kissed and licked the spot. Let me tell you what, if you ever want to make me instantly hot, do something to my neck. Some women are into nipples. Not me. I'm all neck, all the time. It drives me crazy.

My head fell back, mainly to give him better access, my hands traveled up his arms to his neck and I pulled him closer. I love the way he feels so hard everywhere. You can actually feel each individual muscle flexing with his movements. I felt his hands on my back and they slowly ended up on my hips, then his biceps flexed as he easily lifted me up and turned me so that I straddled his lap.

Now that we were facing each other, he pulled back and smiled into my eyes. "That's better." He ran his hands up my back and into my hair. He smoothed it down and then ran his big hands down my back until they rested on my hips. He pulled me closer and rocked me slowly against him. "Now you don't look lonely at all." He kissed me and tried unsuccessfully to look sincere. "I was really worried about you."

I laughed. "Haha. I'm sure you're worried about me being lonely." And no, I wasn't about to freak out again. I realized a while back that Luke really likes the way I look, which helped me relax about the whole sex thing. Now, I'm actually to the point that I'm thinking that us getting together is a great idea, mainly because he's about to kill me with all this kissing and touching. Over the past few months, we've both lost our shirts and I've lost my pants twice, but he's refused to let me take his shorts off until we actually have sex because he said he's afraid we wouldn't stop and when we finally have sex, he wants it to be my conscious decision and not because we got too carried away. I appreciated his consideration, but the last two times we were fooling around like this, it took me hours to get to sleep because he got me so riled up.

Apparently, tonight was no different. I was so turned on at that point I could barely breathe, but he still just rocked me gently against him and smiled.

We'd already had the birth control conversation, actually over breakfast a week or two ago when we found out one of our 46 year old college friends just found out she was pregnant after she unknowingly jumped her husband while on Ambien. Apparently, she pretty much forgot everything that night, including any sort of birth control, so she was beside herself a few weeks later when a pregnancy test came out positive. Ugh. Anyway, we'd already determined that I'm on the pill for hormone reasons and he'd had a vasectomy years ago while married to Glenda, and both of us had recent blood tests and weren't seeing anyone else so we knew we were both okay.

But that was the last thing on my mind at that moment. Nope, now I had something new to worry about. We were kissing, and I kind of squirmed against him and he wrapped his arms around my hips so tightly that I could feel every inch of him against my stomach. And Lawd have mercy, all of a sudden it hit me...that felt like a lot of inches. Holy crap, how big is that thing? Suddenly, I was more than a little nervous about our size difference. I mean, I'm under five feet tall, and he's way over six foot, so, let's face it, now I'm wondering if us together is physically going to work.

As usual, when my mind goes wandering, I go still, so it didn't take Luke long to realize that I was off on one of my mental tangents. He pulled back and looked in my eyes and asked me if I was all right. I blushed when he asked, because my whole thought process was so embarrassing. I thought about trying to lie to him about what I was thinking, but I'm such a terrible liar I knew that wouldn't work, so I figured I'd just tell him my concerns and we'll see what happens.

I took a deep breath and tried to start. "Well, when we were just kissing, I couldn't help but notice you were excited, I mean...you have an erection."

He nodded. "Okay. Yes I do. Is that a problem?" He stared at me, not really sure where I was going with this. "I mean, you've certainly felt it before and you understand how this whole man/woman thing works, right?"

That made me laugh. "Yes, smartyass, I do know how that works." I looked at him and shook my head and kind of waved vaguely in the area of his crotch. "What I couldn't help thinking was that you, I mean it, seems...um, kind of big." I wrinkled up my nose. "I mean, even though I tell everyone I'm 5'1', I'm actually only 4'11" and I'm kind of short-waisted, and you're 6'4" and all kidding aside, from the feel of things, I'm wondering if we may have run into a compatibility issue."

He tried to look serious, but gave up and started laughing. "I can see your concern. But if it helps, I promise, I'm not too big for you. As a matter of fact, I can assure you, I'll be just right."

I snorted. "Thanks, Goldilocks." I intoned in a high

pitched voice, "And this penis was too small, and this one was too large, but this one was juuuusssst right..."

He lifted an eyebrow and laughed at me. "You want to try it on for size, Goldilocks?" He hugged me close and kissed me a big juicy, smacking kiss on my lips. "I'm willing to sacrifice my body for a scientific experiment if you are."

I looked at him with a mock serious look on my face. "You're such a giver. And so brave." We both laughed, which I love. He's got a great sense of humor, which is almost too much when you consider the fact that he's also smart and gorgeous.

He must have realized that I was feeling better because he went right back to my neck and started kissing it, apparently trying to get me back to the state I was in before. As he kissed me, I pulled back long enough to pull off his shirt and throw it on the floor. I wanted to feel all that muscle and hot skin under my fingers, and Lawd have mercy, I was not disappointed. He had a nicely hairy chest, not too much hair, but enough to go from nipple to nipple and then it narrowed and went down the middle of those abs into his low-slung shorts. Seriously, he looked like something out of a magazine. I felt one hand grab my hips to keep me against him, and the other moved up under my t-shirt to my breast. As soon as he touched it, I felt a groan from deep in his chest. I was startled. "What?"

He lifted his head from my neck and looked at me. His other hand moved up to palm my other breast. "Are you kidding me? I've been wanting to get my hands on these since the first time I saw you at Georgia."

I rolled my eyes, "Oh please...this isn't the first time you've seen them. We've fooled around a lot the past few months."

He smiled. "No, but I never get tired of the view. Daisy,

trust me. There has never been a man alive, including me, that didn't want to see these babies up close and personal."

I laughed and he released me to grab the bottom of my shirt. "You mind if we lose this?"

When I said sure, why not, he whipped the shirt over my head so that it was just me in my bra and cut off shorts straddling his lap. He cuddled my breasts with both hands, staring at them with an intent look on his face. I reached behind me, opened the clasp, slid the straps down my arms and pulled the bra off and threw it on the floor, telling him that now he could look all he wanted without any distractions. He absently thanked me without looking up and gently squeezed them together and took one of my nipples in his mouth.

Normally, like a lot of large-breasted women, and unlike my neck, my nipples aren't very sensitive. But watching him lick and kiss and suck them in turn, enjoying every minute, was incredibly hot. I could feel myself getting hotter and wetter, until finally I felt like I was going to explode.

I grabbed his shoulders and pulled him closer. He groaned and continued licking and sucking and squeezing my breasts while still moving rhythmically against me. I wrapped my arms around his head to hug him and whispered in his ear if he would like to go to the bedroom.

He pulled his mouth off my breasts and drew back, breathing hard. He searched my face. "Daisy are you sure?"

I nodded. "Luke, I'm absolutely sure. If we don't do something about this tonight, I will never get a lick of sleep. We've been dating for months, and it's time."

He was not arguing with that. He stood up easily with me still straddling his lap, so I grabbed his shoulders and locked my legs around his waist to make sure he didn't drop me. He walked us back to the bedroom, stopping occasionally to pin me against the wall and kiss me until I couldn't breathe. I'm small, but I'm not a lightweight, and I can honestly say that, for whatever reason, it turns out I really like a guy who can toss me around and put me exactly where he wants. Hey, don't be all judge-y. I take my thrills where I can get them.

It's also pretty handy when you have a height difference like we do. When you're 4'11", sex can be a challenge. In my extensive experience, well, okay, mostly Bobby, for a lot of positions to work, the guy either has to bend down, lift me up, or put me on some kind of ladder or stepstool or something, so everything lines up right. Fortunately, Luke and I are problem solvers and I have no doubt he'll rise to the challenge.

When we got to my room, he kicked the door shut behind him to keep out the dogs, then he put one knee on the end of the bed and lowered me down to the covers. He stood over me looking down with a very focused look on his face. I asked him to turn on the ceiling fan, and as he walked over to the wall switch, I lit a couple of candles on my bedside table. Now, we had a soft glow that was light enough so we could see each other, but it wasn't obnoxious like an overhead light.

For a moment, he just stood there at the end of the bed staring in my eyes. When I smiled at the intensity on his face, he smiled gently back at me and stepped closer. He climbed on the bed and knee walked over until he straddled my thighs. He put both hands on either side of my shoulders and lowered down so he could kiss me. He kissed me gently at first, one quick kiss on the forehead, one on the nose, one longer one on my lips. He then lowered himself until he could prop himself on his elbows and smiled into my eyes. He started kissing my neck, which took about two seconds to get me back to the level of excitement I'd felt while we were on the couch. I grabbed his ribs with both hands and squeezed as I moaned in his ear. When he realized how excited I was, he moved up and his mouth slammed down on mine, tongues wildly tangling, and both of us straining against each other. My hands were all over his back, and even as crazy aroused as I was, I still marveled at the muscles on his back and shoulders, and honest to God, his butt was ridiculous. High, tight, and rounded with muscle.

I tried to unbutton his shorts, but he was pressed so tightly against me that I couldn't get my hands between us. Finally, I jerked my mouth free and told him he needed to lose the pants, now. He reared back and stood at the end of the bed. He leaned forward, unbuttoned my shorts, and yanked them and my panties off in one motion. Okay, I actually meant his pants, but, whatever, this was a good start. I could hear his harsh breathing as his eyes moved over every inch of me. Suddenly, I felt very exposed, and I raised up on my elbows, bent my knees, and pulled my legs together as I stared up at him.

He smiled and said, "Nope," and joined me on the bed. He kneeled by my feet, grabbed a knee in each hand and slowly pulled them apart so he could see all of me. I collapsed back on the bed so I could see his face as he stared between my legs with a serious, absorbed look.

He then raised his eyes to mine, his eyes hot and greedy, "Baby, I can see how wet you are already," and I felt both of his thumbs there, spreading me apart. The next thing I know, he was kneeling on the floor. He grabbed my hips in both hands to raise me up and he pressed his mouth against me.

Holy. Shit. I felt my eyes roll back in my head as he got

down to business. Long licks up both sides. A gentle nibble here and there. He pushed his big finger inside me and moved it in time with long laps of his talented tongue. As he added another finger, I could feel myself getting closer and closer to the edge, but he refused to let me finish. I grabbed his hair and pushed him down harder, but he slowed down. Finally, I was just about whimpering, please, please, please and suddenly, he sucked hard on just the right spot and, at the same time, he pressed hard inside me with both fingers.

That was it for me. I was hollering and moaning, and still he wouldn't let up. Finally, I went limp. My legs just flopped to the bed and my hands rested on his head. He pulled out his fingers and gave me a couple of gentle laps with his tongue and raised his head to smile at me, "You okay, baby?"

I could barely lift my head to see his eyes. When I saw him smiling at me, I smiled back and my head dropped back on the bed. "Okay? Yeah, you could say that." I ran my hand through his hair and let it drop back on the bed. "Except you just about killed me. I'm sorry, but I'm just too tired. I think I'm done for the night."

I heard him chuckle and he looked very satisfied with himself. "Want to bet I can change your mind?"

I closed my eyes and gave a huge yawn and pretended to snore. He scooted up between my legs and propped his head on my stomach, laughing at my antics. When I continued my fake snores, he turned his head and bit my stomach and my eyes flew open. He laughed, kissed me where he'd bitten me, then pushed himself off me and stood up next to the bed. I smiled at him, curious about his next move. He waited until he had my full attention and then he slowly unbuttoned and unzipped his shorts and I sucked my breath in when I could see he wasn't wearing underwear. Nice.

Finally, he let them drop to the ground. Lawd. Have. Mercy. I propped myself up on my elbows to get a better look. Then I took a deep breath and sat up, because I wanted my hands on him. "Why don't you come over here so I can take a closer look."

He moved closer and he reached for my breasts with both hands and started squeezing and massaging them. I sucked in a breath and let him play while I reached out and wrapped my hand around him. He was every bit as big as I thought, but at that point, I didn't really care. I mean, it wasn't mutant big, it was manageable, and I figured we'd make it fit somehow.

Now, in general, I think most women agree that a limp dick isn't that exciting, and, let's just say it, testicles in and of themselves aren't much to look at. That being said, get the right man and the right circumstances, and I think a full blown erection can be a thing of beauty, and Luke's was definitely that. Huge, smooth, and thick. So hard it was actually pointing upward, and it bobbed in time with his harsh breaths.

Anyway, when I squeezed him tighter and started to stroke him slowly from the base to the head, he pulled my hand away. When I complained, he kissed me. "Baby girl, you can do whatever you want to me later, but right now, this is my show." He grabbed my ankle to pull me flat on my back and dragged me farther down the bed. He lowered himself against me, propped himself onto one elbow and grabbed himself with the other hand. He rubbed himself against me, up and down, and he pushed himself in, just barely, and grinned at me confidently, "So what were you saying? Do you think you're awake enough now to go another round, or are you just too tired?"

I pretended to think about it for a second and he started to draw back. I grabbed him to keep him from pulling back and said magnanimously, "Well, since you're already here, you might as well go ahead and come on in." He grinned at that as I pulled him closer. "Come on. I don't want you to think I was being inhospitable."

He laughed and slowly started to push his way inside. Even as wet as I was, and as soft and relaxed as I felt inside, it had still been a long time for me and it wasn't an easy fit. I protested. "Damn, Luke, you've gotta go slower. That thing's as big around as a damn Coke can and I'm just not sure this is going to work."

He laughed and shook his head as he kissed me gently. "Baby, it's fine. Just relax and I'll go slow, and I promise it'll fit just fine."

Well, shit. I tried to relax, but it wasn't easy. I took a few deep breaths to try to get my muscles to loosen, but it didn't seem to help. He pushed in a little, then pulled back, then pushed in a little more, and then he started kissing my neck while rocking gently inside me, a little farther each time, murmuring how good I felt and how much he wanted me. At first, it still wasn't all that comfortable, but as he worked his way in, it started to feel better and finally, when he was all the way inside me, I held him close and asked him just to stay like that for a few to give me a little time to adjust before he started moving. After a few moments, I still felt stretched to the limits, but it wasn't really uncomfortable any more. He lifted his head and smiled at me. "How you feeling?"

I smiled up at him and ran my hands down his muscular back. "I feel better. Very full but it feels good." And it did. I could feel every thick inch of him inside me, and the way he filled me up was like nothing I'd ever felt before.

He raised an eyebrow. "You think you could take a little movement?" He slowly pulled back very slightly and then slowly pushed back in.

I pretended to be upset and huffed, "Well, not if that's the best you can do." He growled as I laughed, slid one arm under me to raise my hips higher and pulled out about half way and thrust in a little harder, watching my face to make sure he didn't hurt me.

There was still a little discomfort, but it was far outweighed by pleasure, and he saw it, because that's when his control left him. He started with a slow, steady rhythm, but within minutes he began moving harder and faster. In. Out. In. Out. Then he added a little grinding twist at the end of each stroke that made my eyes roll back in my head. At first, I was just hanging on for the ride, adjusting to his size, his movements, but after a few minutes, I was grinding against him as he pounded into me. I heard myself whimpering and moaning, until finally I was moaning his name as he cursed and groaned as he thrust inside one last time. After a few moments, he hugged me to him and rolled us onto our sides so he didn't squash me into the mattress.

We lay there, breathing hard, sweaty, and very relaxed. He was still inside me, not as big as before, but I could still feel him. Neither one of us said anything, we just held and cuddled against each other, occasionally kissing or giving an absent pat or rub to whatever part we could reach. After a few minutes, I raised my head to look up at Luke. "You awake?"

He opened one eye and closed it as he yawned. "Kind of. You cold? Want to get under the covers?" He snuggled closer.

I wrinkled my nose. "I don't think so. I don't know about you, but I'm not so much cold as kind of goopy and sticky. I think I need a shower before we end up being permanently stuck together."

His eyes popped open and he looked at me, suddenly wide awake. "That's a great idea. I think we both need a shower."

I started laughing and punched him on the shoulder. "You're such a guy. You know, sometimes, a shower is just a shower."

He sat up and looked at me, raising an eyebrow. "Really? Just out of curiosity, is this one of those times?"

Hey got me there. "Okay, probably not. In fact, if you think you have the energy, I could probably use a little help getting cleaned up." I then winked at him. "But only if you're interested, of course."

He didn't bother answering. He just jackknifed up, stood up next to the bed, reached over and picked me up and carried me in the bathroom before I had time to protest that I could walk.

He lowered me to my feet on the bathmat and grabbed a towel to wrap around me while the water heated. My legs were still kind of iffy, so I sat on the toilet while he turned and adjusted the shower, enjoying the novelty of having a large, naked man in my bathroom. Once the water was hot, he turned and extended his hand with a warm, inviting smile and a formal bow. "May I have the pleasure of your company in the shower, madam?"

I giggled at his silliness, batted my eyes, thanked him, took his hand, stood up, and stepped into the shower with him. As soon as the door shut behind us, he pulled me up against him, grabbed my bottom with both hands and lifted me up so he could kiss me easily. I threw my arms around his neck and kissed him back, enjoying the feel of the hot water as I rubbed our chests together. Finally, he lowered me to my feet.

He grabbed the bar of soap, lathered up his hands and turned so that he was between me and the water. "Let's get you cleaned up, missy." He placed his soapy hands on my neck and then began a very thorough job of sudsing me up, the whole time kissing me intensely. He wrapped his arms around me so he could wash my back first, and then spent a ridiculous amount of time on my butt and between my legs.

I gave him a stern look. "Um, excuse me, Mr. Mathis, but that feels a lot more like fondling than washing."

He ignored me and continued soaping me up. "Hey, when it's your turn, you can do it however you want. This is my turn, and you just need to let me do my thing. This is a highly efficient showering system and you need to trust me as to how well this is going to work."

Once he was done with my back, he turned me around, then told me to lean back against him so he could do my front. I leaned back and felt that he already had another erection. I pressed against it and wiggled so I could feel it slide against me, hard and hot. He held me still. "Don't go starting anything. It's still my turn."

I grumbled. "You need to get busy, mister. This doesn't seem very efficient to me."

He ignored my comments and rinsed my back before he grabbed the soap again. Once he had a huge amount of foamy lather, he started below my neck and slowly worked his way down to my breasts. As he rubbed them together and squeezed them with his soapy hands, fingering my nipples and pinching them lightly, he also began kissing my neck. One hand wandered down my stomach till he reached between my legs, and the other continued to squeeze and fondle my breasts. By this time, my legs felt like jelly and I could hardly stand up. I reached back and grabbed Luke's hips and ground against him and begged him to get inside me right now.

I have a built in seat in my shower, and a long, narrow, teak bench that puts me high enough so I can reach the shower head, so Luke moved the bench so it butted up to the seat. He moved me forward so I stepped up onto the bench, and then he pushed me forward so that I was bent over leaning on my hands. My arms also felt like noodles, so I lowered myself to my elbows, which raised my hips even higher. Fortunately, I'm pretty bendy, so the position was comfortable. He used the handheld shower to rinse off my butt and backside, then turned up the pressure and used it between my legs until I thought I was going to collapse.

Finally, I felt Luke move in behind me and he rubbed his hands all over my bottom then squeezed it, hard, and rubbed his fingers between my legs to test if I was ready for him. I was still kind of swaying from my run-in with the showerhead, so he grabbed my hip with one hand to steady me, took himself in the other, lined himself up, and started to push inside me. It was much easier this time and he seated himself to the hilt in one slow thrust. He then grabbed my hips with both hands and started moving.

Wow. That position was amazing. Not only was it incredibly deep, but the angle, especially with me on my forearms, made it so he hit me right on that hotly debated g-spot area every time he thrust into me. And by the way, as far as I'm concerned, the debate is over. That spot is awesome. Within a couple of minutes, I just about passed out, it was so intense. It was insane. His hands clenched on my hips as he drove into me and when he pounded into me one last time, I heard him groan like it was being ripped out of his chest. He collapsed against my back, probably trying to stay on his feet, then straightened up, pulling me with him, and he pivoted back on the bench with me on his lap and him still inside me. We sat like that, both trying to catch our breath. He wrapped both arms around me and buried his face in my hair, which was still pretty much dry, oddly enough. I rubbed his forearms where they crossed my belly and leaned my head back against his. "You okay?"

I could feel him shake his head. "I'm not really sure."

I felt the same way. I turned my head and kissed him on the cheek. He smiled and I squeezed his arms until he opened his eyes. "Hey. I just want you to know, I never remembered sex being like that."

He smiled and squeezed me back. "I agree."

"Also, I'd like to lodge a complaint." When I turned my head so I could see him, he looked at me with one raised eyebrow and I waved my hand to point out the soap that still covered the front of my body. "I'm all covered in soap, plus now you've got me all messy again. Since I'm not any cleaner than when I originally got in the shower, I think this means that your 'highly efficient showering system' has a serious flaw somewhere."

He laughed and kissed my temple. "Maybe so. We'll try it again later and see if I can make some modifications to make it more efficient." He patted me on my hip. "Think you can stand up?"

I shook my head, no. "No way. Not without help." So he grabbed my waist and lifted me off of him and stood me on my feet. We were both a soapy, sticky mess, and as he unsteadily started to stand up, I held up my hand in warning. "Stop right there. You sit back down and don't you touch me, Luke Mathis. This time I actually want a shower and I can't trust you to keep your hands to yourself."

We both laughed and he dropped back on the seat and promised he'd be good. We took turns under the water, which was still hot thanks to my fabulous tankless water heater, and started to rinse off soap and, well, everything else. We quickly cleaned up, dried off, and went back to the bedroom, where I opened the door to let the dogs in before we pulled back the covers and both fell into the bed. We curled up together, then the dogs hopped on the bed, still a little miffed at being locked out of the bedroom, and all of us went to sleep.

The next morning, I was awakened by a cold, wet dog nose in my face, and a large, aroused man against my back. He, (the man, not the dog), mumbled good morning as his hands automatically went to my breasts and his erection rubbed against my backside. He mumbled, "Nice," lifted my leg onto his hip so he could easily touch me between my legs and started gently stroking me. I was still only half awake as he tested me with one big finger to make sure I was ready, and slowly pushed himself inside me. He thrust slowly all the way in and pulled almost all the way out over and over, the whole time lazily fondling me and kissing my neck. I grabbed his hip behind me to pull him closer as I slowly writhed against him, both of us still half asleep, neither of us in a hurry, and neither of us wanting to finish too quickly. It was a slow buildup and a nice, calm, but oddly intense experience for both of us. I must have dozed off again afterwards because when I woke up again I was alone in the bed.

I could hear Luke talking to the dogs in the kitchen so I jumped up and went into the bathroom. I brushed my teeth and took the world's fastest shower, dried off, braided my wet hair into two stubby pigtails, and got dressed.

By the time I got to the kitchen, the dogs were already

eating and Luke was standing by the stove wearing nothing but his shorts.

What a nice way to wake up. The smell of bacon and coffee and the visual treat of a half-naked Luke. Yummy. I came up behind him and grabbed him around the waist and hugged him. He smiled at me over his shoulder as I let him go and snagged a piece of bacon as I went to sit in my small dining area. I do love to watch a man doing anything domestic, especially a macho guy like Luke. There's something about the contrast of a big muscled body making an omelet or, ooh better yet, doing dishes. That is just sexy.

He looked over at me and grinned. He grabbed two plates, cut the omelet in half and put a piece on each plate, along with a couple pieces of bacon and walked them over to where I sat. He put one plate in front of me and sat down with the other. He'd already poured coffee and fixed mine perfectly, lots of milk and a couple of Splendas. I took a sip and smiled at him over the top of my mug.

He looked at me expectantly. "Okay, let's have it. Was that the best sex you've ever had, or what?"

I started to laugh. He shoveled a huge bite of omelet in his mouth and crossed his arms over his chest as he chewed. He looked very large and very proud of himself, so I decided to mess with him a little. I looked at him with a mock serious look on my face and took one hand and rocked it from side to side. "Eh, it was okay. I mean, it wasn't bad, but I'm sure we could do better with a little practice." I pursed my lips and airily waved in the direction of his lap. "I mean, you know what they say about size not mattering..."

He raised one eyebrow and looked at me. "Really? You want to go there? Why don't you come over here and say that to my face?" He reached over and grabbed my wrist and started to pull me toward him but I shrieked with laughter and held onto the table yelling that I wanted to eat my omelet. He laughed and called me a chicken, but let me go.

I took another couple of bites and then put my fork down. I reached out and squeezed his hand and waited until he looked directly at me. "Last night was amazing, and honest to God, Luke, that was the best sex I ever had."

He grinned and leaned over to give me a quick kiss. "I agree. I'm really glad you decided to give us a chance, Daisy."

We smiled at each other and finished our breakfast. I cleared the table and he started loading the dishwasher. I was right, he was even hotter doing the dishes. When we finished in the kitchen, we took the dogs for a quick walk and then we poured some ice coffee and went to sit on my screen porch. I needed to do some grocery shopping and cooking, but neither of us was ready for the morning to end. We sat next to each other on the glider, chatting and sharing an occasional kiss.

Finally, I looked at the clock and groaned. "Damn it. I have to get going if I want to have enough time to get everything done."

Luke looked up from the magazine he was flipping through. "We still cooking out with everyone at Sara and Mark's house?"

"Yes, and I wanted to get there early enough to help Sara get the food together." I grabbed our empty cups and started into the kitchen.

Luke and the dogs followed me inside. I put the cups in the sink, opened the dishwasher, and loaded the cups inside. "So what are you doing while I go to the grocery store and get the food together?"

He leaned against the counter next to the sink. "I'm going to run by Mo's sister's house and finish installing that window seat. All I've got left to do is a little trim and touch up paint, but she's having some meeting at her house on Wednesday so I told her I'd have most of it done this weekend and I'll finish up on Monday." He smiled at her. "I'll be back by three so we can get to Sara's and get started on dinner."

I smiled at him and he grabbed my hand as we both started walking toward the front door. When we got there, he pulled me against him, intending to give me a quick kiss goodbye. Instead, I found myself pressed between him and the door, both his hands on my butt, and his tongue in my mouth. I kissed him back for a few seconds and then, coming to my senses, I pulled my head back and covered his mouth with my hand. "Stop!" His tongue came out and poked suggestively between my fingers. I snatched my hand back as he laughed at me. "If you don't stop, we're never going to get anything done today!"

I felt one of his hands start to trace down my butt and between my legs and he looked at me innocently. "Would that be such a bad thing?"

I felt myself wavering, because no, I think it would a great thing, but I pushed against his shoulders and he let me drop to my feet. I was already missing the feeling of him plastered up against me, but we really did need to get going. "How about this? I'll make you a deal. If you let me go now so I can go to the grocery store and get the food taken care of, we'll come back here after dinner and I'm yours till Monday. After all, I still haven't had my turn to play with you, and I promise that I'll make it worth your while."

He pretended to think about it for a second. "Hmmm. I think I like the sound of that. Okay, it's a deal." He kissed me quickly and let me go. "I'll stop and grab some beer and wine for tonight and I'll come pick you up later this afternoon." He gave me another quick peck and left. I grabbed my purse and headed out the door.

I was home from the store in about an hour and I spent the rest of the afternoon baking some muffins for the weekend, and some dishes and treats for that night, including a batch of red velvet cupcakes for Harrison. I made an Asian noodle salad with peanut sauce, a pasta salad, and strawberry shortcake with a real shortcake and homemade whipped cream for dessert. I changed into a bathing suit with a tank top and a pair of shorts, pulled on a cowboy hat, and had just finished packing all the food into a big cooler when the doorbell rang. I ran and opened the door to let Luke in, who looked amazing as usual in a long, baggy bathing suit and a ragged t-shirt with the arms ripped off. I stared at his arms, thinking it was ridiculous what that man could do to a shirt, and then shook myself out of my reverie and went back to finish getting everything together. He followed me into the kitchen as I finished cleaning the sink and then absently palmed my butt as I bent over to stack my coolers. I couldn't help but smile. I straightened up and turned to face him. "You are just a mess. Why don't you use those hands to grab these coolers instead of my ass and go put them in your Jeep?"

He sighed as if very put upon, grabbed my butt with both hands to pull me against him and gave me a kiss that just about made my eyes cross. He looked very satisfied with my reaction and let me go, smiling when I swayed on my feet. "Fine. I'll put this in the car, but I'm telling you right now, you're mine tonight, and you're not putting on a stitch of clothes or leaving this house until Monday morning, so you'd better take it easy today and maybe do some carb loading or something so you'll have enough energy to keep up."

He grabbed the coolers and headed out to the car. I stepped in front of him and reached under the cooler to rub him through his shorts. "Oh, I'll be ready." I gently squeezed and fondled him and rubbed my breasts against his side. "Feels like you will be too."

He started to sweat. "Damn it, Daisy, you'd better stop that right now, or we're not going anywhere."

I laughed, gave him one last squeeze and backed away from him with my hands in the air.

He was gritting his teeth as he spun around and went out to the Jeep, muttering under his breath something about me being a tease and about payback, and how I wasn't going to think it was so funny when I couldn't walk at work on Monday. I was laughing as I called the mutts and got them harnessed and ready to go. Luke came back inside, grabbed their leashes in one hand, my hand in the other, and we left.

When we got to Sara's, we put the pups in the backyard then we went inside to unpack the salads and the shortcake. We went out to the pool to say hey to Mark and Sara and to put the beer and wine in the cooler. Sara was in the pool asleep on a float in a bathing suit and her honey badger shirt and Mark was asleep in a chair with a book on his stomach and a beer on the ground next to him. Before I could grab him, Diego came out of nowhere, knocked over the beer and had downed most of it by the time I could wrestle him away. Luke was laughing and shaking his head as I struggled to pick up Diego and manage the other two. "Here we go again."

He grabbed Diego from me and ruffled his fur, laughing as he asked, "Why don't we just get him a bowl and his own beer and maybe he'd leave everyone else's alone?"

I shook my head. "Lola tried that, but he emptied his bowl and then he still went after everyone else's. I've about decided that he was some frat boy in a former life and his goal is to drink until passes out." Luke laughed, but for a while I had been really worried about him. "When I first noticed the whole drinking problem, I was scared about him being drunk around the pool, but watch him. He swims like a fish and is constantly in and out of the pool, so I stopped worrying about it." As if to prove my words, as soon as Luke put him down, he jumped into the pool, swam out to Sara and climbed on the float with her, waking her up with a cold nose in her neck.

She grabbed him and planted a big kiss on his head and petted him as she looked around for us. "Hey y'all! Hey Daisy, your damn dog already has beer breath. How long y'all been here?"

We both laughed. "Long enough for Diego to start his day drinking, so about a minute."

Mark stood up, yawned, waved to both of us, and popped me on the butt as he passed me to go inside. I smacked him back. "Hey, sorry for Diego drinking your beer."

He shook his head. "Wouldn't be the first time, and there's plenty more. Y'all grab whatever you want."

He continued inside and I grabbed a towel and sat down on the end of the closest lounge chair and Luke swung his leg over so he straddled the chair and sat behind me. He pulled me back against his chest and Sara immediately sat up, almost knocking Diego in the water, and looked back and forth between us. I shrugged, trying to look casual. "What?"

She jumped into the water and towed the float with Diego on it until she was right in front of us. She stared at

Luke and then stared at me, and I could feel my face turn red. "What is your problem?"

She grinned and screamed. "Yee haw! Y'all finally had sex!" She put her hands on the side and levered herself out of the pool and threw herself on both of us, hugging us and laughing. I pushed her away as she grabbed my neck and kissed my cheek and then she let me go and climbed on Luke's lap, smothering his face with loud kisses. We were both protesting, and laughingly trying to push her off of us, but she completely ignored us. Mark came out to see what the ruckus was all about and Sara screamed to him that we'd finally gotten horizontal, and it was about damn time, and how she knew we would be good together and he just smiled, congratulated us, grabbed a fresh beer and jumped into the pool.

Right about then, Lola, Harrison, and Mo came out of the house. We were still trying to get Sara off of us, but she was still carrying on. "...It's about damn time. I was worried poor Daisy was gonna end up some kind of born again virgin, but it looks like we don't have to worry about that anymore." They all stopped dead in their tracks and looked at us. Luke and I looked helplessly at each other over Sara's head and shrugged as we started laughing. Oh well, it didn't take long for that cat to get out of the bag.

Mo screamed and Lola yelled holy shit and they both dropped what they were carrying and ran over to us and piled on. At that point, I couldn't stop laughing and Luke just shook his head and tried to keep all of us from falling off the chair. Finally, I pulled myself out of the pile and stood up next to the chair, still laughing at their reaction. "Y'all get off Luke and let the poor man breathe." Harrison bumped me with his hip and smiled and winked as he went by carrying all the towels and stuff that Mo and Lola had dropped when they jumped on us. Luke grabbed Sara and lifted her off of him and managed to stand up without the other women knocking him over. He made a hasty retreat, muttering that he needed a drink and got the hell out of there. He got a beer and jumped in the pool with the other guys, probably to put as much distance between us and him as possible.

As soon as he left, Sara, Lola, and Mo grabbed me and pulled me back on the chair with them and stared at me. I'm never that comfortable being the center of attention, and I could feel my ears get hot and my face turn red. Finally, I couldn't take the pressure. "What? What do you want from me?"

They all looked at me like I was crazy and Lola said, "Duh, details?"

I dropped my head and sighed and asked them what they wanted to know, and Lola looked at me like I was an idiot and started counting them off on her fingers. "The basics. How was it, was he as good as you'd hoped..." She looked at Luke with a speculative look as he climbed out of the pool, his shorts clinging as he walked back to the cooler to grab another beer after Diego had tipped his over on the side of the pool. "Damn...bonus question, is that dick as big as it looks?" I smacked her as Mo and Sara burst out laughing and I saw Luke freeze as he overheard her question and then he just sighed and kept walking, shaking his head. Lola continued. "Are you finally going to admit y'all are officially a couple now, and when are you going to do it again?"

I knew they'd never leave me alone until I filled them in. I was just thankful Luke had managed to get out of their clutches, because I know they would've asked those exact same questions if he was still sitting there, poor thing. I took a deep breath and answered, also ticking off my answers on my fingers. "It was amazing, and he was even better than I could've imagined." I saw Luke jump back in the pool and soon the guys were all laughing and slapping Luke on the back. I don't know if they were congratulating him on us being together or commiserating about their women having no filter and talking about personal things like dick size. "It's actually bigger than it looks, yes, we're officially a couple, and tonight when we leave here, he's apparently locking us in the house until Monday morning."

All of them turned to look at Luke with big grins on their faces, and when he realized he was the center of their attention, he just swigged his beer and turned his back to us. I know he had an idea of what we were talking about because later, when he got out of the pool, before he sat down, he pulled a beach towel around him and tucked it securely around his waist. We all burst out laughing and he yelled "Perverts" and flipped us off, which made us all laugh harder.

We had a great day hanging out at the pool, talking and enjoying each other's company. We ate kind of a late lunch/early dinner, and Harrison was ecstatic that I had made red velvet cupcakes, even though it wasn't his birthday. I think he and Luke and Lola ate most of them. Afterwards, we threw out all the paper goods, put away the leftovers, minus some hot dogs and pimento cheese that my dogs knocked onto the ground and scarfed down, and went on the screen porch to avoid the bugs.

I was thrilled that everyone was getting along so well and that everyone was so happy for us. It was still hard to believe how much everything has changed in the past year. Speaking of which, I told everyone that my mother told me that she'd run into Bobby's mother at some benefit and it turns out Bobby and the skank had a baby girl. I told my mother good for them, and that was it.

Lola was curious. "Does Bobby's mom like the skank?"

I told her that his parents were still fairly appalled at the entire situation and that when I had run into them a couple of times, they were lovely and very apologetic to me. Apparently, according to my mom, they weren't too crazy about the skank, but they were thrilled about a grandchild, so I guess it worked out okay for them.

When Lola and I went inside to get more vegetables and dip and some cheese straws I'd pulled out of my freezer, I remembered to ask Lola about the story I was doing that week. I had met a local woman, Bella Varnedoe, who was trying to raise funds to rebuild water treatment facilities and an orphanage in Belize that had been decimated by a recent hurricane. She's apparently some wealthy widow who does all kinds of charity work around town. "Lola, you know her?"

Lola nodded. "Yep. Cool chick. Bella's maybe a little older than us, maybe early 50s, and she's like me...you know, a trust fund baby who tries to use her money for good instead of evil." I laughed at that, and Lola continued. "Seriously, I like her a lot. She's funny, warm, personable, and a fundraising machine. And I'll bet she'll be great on camera."

As we walked back outside to put the food on the coffee table on the porch, Sara overhead the last part of the conversation and asked who we were talking about. "Bella Varnedoe. I'm interviewing her for my story this week."

"Oh, I've met her several times. Nice lady." Sara grabbed a piece of carrot and popped it in her mouth. "What are you wearing for the interview?"

Oh no. Here we go again. Lola and Sara ask me every week what I'm wearing, because they know that, if left to my own devices, I would wear a black t-shirt and a black pair of jeans and call it a day. They consider it their purpose in life to keep me from looking like a walking "fashion don't." I actually appreciate their advice, even though they can be pretty rough. Mo is very sweet, so I can't trust her to tell me when I've made a bad choice. She'd never look me in the eye like Lola and Sara do, and say things like, "Ohmy-GAWD, take that off right now, that skirt makes your ass look huge" or, my personal favorite from Sara, "Girl, if you're looking for an outfit that makes you look like an ad for 'Extreme Tits and Ass Magazine', you found it. Take that shit off." Brutal, right?! But always honest, always hilarious, and considering my lack of ability to dress myself, I really do need all the help I can get.

As the afternoon waned, I could tell Luke was getting antsy. He constantly touched me, a pat here, a rub there, a subtle hand on my butt when no one could see. By the time 6:30 rolled around, he was obviously past ready to leave, and I'll have to admit, I was ready to go, too. We both stood up at the same time. "Hey guys, we're out of here. We've got some stuff to do..."

"Like each other." Sara interjected, and everyone laughed.

I ignored her. "...So we'll see you later." I started picking up my purse and towels, and Luke grabbed the cooler. We grabbed the dogs, (for once Diego was only tipsy and was still upright), and headed home.

I tried to make small talk with Luke but he wasn't interested. I could see his jaws were clenched and his entire body looked tense. I put my hand on his leg, hoping to make him feel more relaxed, and he just looked at my hand and then looked at me with a very single-minded, intense gaze. I moved my hand up his leg, under the edge of his shorts, and he grabbed it so it couldn't go any higher. "Daisy, we're almost home and I'm about to lose it here, so hang on a few minutes more."

Wow. I didn't realize he was quite that close to the edge. This was fun. I smiled at him. "So what do you want to do first when we get home?"

He shot me a don't-screw-with-me look, and I smiled at him innocently. "How about this? Since you don't really seem like you want to talk about it, I'll tell you what I'd like to do to you." I leaned over so that my breasts were pressed against his arm and I put my lips next to his ear and softly bit his earlobe. Goosebumps broke out on his arms and I could see that his bathing suit was starting to tent in the front. I pulled my hand out of his grip and started rubbing his leg, slowly, teasingly sliding my hand slightly higher, under his shorts. "As soon as we get in the door, I want us both to get out of these clothes as quickly as possible. Tonight, it's my turn to play with you, so I just want you to relax and then I'm going to kiss you all over." He made an involuntary groan in the back of his throat and I moved my hand higher as I kissed his neck.

He was so distracted he almost drove past my street. He yanked the Jeep into the turn, screeched into my driveway, and jerked it in park. He hopped out and reached in the back and unbuckled the dogs while I came around from the other side. He grabbed my hand and we literally ran up the driveway, the dogs jumping and barking madly. I shoved the key in the door and threw it open, immediately dropping to the floor to get the dogs out of their harnesses. Luke slammed the door behind us and locked it, and as soon as the dogs were free and the dog door was open, he picked me up, threw me over his shoulder, and started toward the bedroom. I was laughing so hard I could barely breathe. He kicked the door shut, threw me on the bed, and told me to take my clothes off now or he was going to rip them off me.

I tore off my clothes and my bathing suit while he did the same. In about two seconds we were facing each other naked on either side of my bed. He put a knee on the bed and started coming toward me, but I held up a hand to stop him. "Wait! It's my turn first."

He stared at me as if debating what he wanted to do, then he flopped on his back in the middle of the bed. "Fine, but you'd better get over here right now and get busy or I'm taking over."

I jumped on the bed and looked at him lying there. Seriously, I think he's the sexiest man I've ever seen. I put my leg over him and straddled his waist so I could reach his mouth. As usual, he grabbed my backside and started squeezing and fondling it. As soon as our lips touched, the kiss went out of control and I finally pulled back before I got too distracted. I licked his ear and bit his earlobe and I felt him shiver. I started kissing my way down his neck and he started moving his hands from my bottom down between my legs, but I quickly slid down so he couldn't reach me. I licked my way down his chest, kissing and sucking his nipples, rubbing my breasts against his chest, running my tongue down the middle of those crazy hard abs. I could feel him hard against my chest, as he grabbed an extra pillow to prop up his head so he could watch what I was doing. I smiled at him and grabbed my breasts and surrounded his erection. I rubbed myself up and down, massaging him with my breasts while he watched intently, clenching his hands on the pillow behind his head. The next time his penis emerged, I squeezed harder, lowered my head and gently licked the tip. His entire body froze and then he deliberately relaxed as he watched me.

I smiled and scooted down a little farther, grabbing his erection with both hands. I have to admit, I was a little unsure of how much of that I could actually get in my mouth, because he somehow seemed even bigger than last time, so I licked around the top and sucked the head in, squeezing him around the base with both of my hands. I moved down as far as I could, using my tongue as much as possible and sucked hard as I pulled back. Suddenly, I felt his hands in my hair guiding my movements, but being careful not to push me down too far. I slowly went up and down, taking a little more of him each time, licking around the head and the sensitive underside as I went down, and then applied a lot of suction as I pulled back. I took one hand and gently massaged his balls as the other hand squeezed him and stroked up and down. After a few minutes, he grabbed my head and tried to pull me back. "Baby, that's enough. I can't last much longer."

I shook my head and kissed the tip of him, told him I wanted him to finish this way, and then went back to it. A few more strokes and he was wild. I could feel his whole body clench and he finally let go with a loud groan. I stayed with him, moving more slowly and gently as he gradually relaxed. One more light lick and a kiss, and I moved up his body and then laid down next to him. His breathing was still loud and harsh and his body lay limp against the bed. I watched him as he recovered, his breathing slowing. Finally his eyes opened and he looked at me and smiled.

I smiled back. "So how was that?"

He raised one hand and rocked it side to side and said, "Eh."

We both laughed and he rolled to his side and hugged me to him. He smiled into my eyes as he ran his hand through my hair. "Baby girl, that was amazing and you were right, it'll be much better now that we took the edge off."

We started kissing and fondling and, within a few minutes, I could feel him getting hard again against my stomach. I smiled and rubbed myself against him as we kissed, and he moved one hand down to see how ready I was. He smiled when he realized I was already wet. "You liked doing that, baby?"

I nodded and gently bit his earlobe then kissed down his neck. "Absolutely. Getting you off is just as exciting for me." We played around a little more and it got out of hand quickly. He rolled me on my back, got on his knees, pulled my feet up to his shoulders and started to push himself inside me, which fortunately, was getting easier each time. Once he was fully seated inside me, he started moving hard and fast. I writhed against him, but eventually I wanted him deeper, so he dropped my legs down, he draped my knees over his elbows as he put his hands on the bed on either side of my shoulder, and shoved in me as deep as he could go. Wow. He gave me a second to adjust, and then he was pounding in as hard as possible. I could hear myself moaning, and finally I was begging him, and finally I was screaming his name like a crazy woman. Note to self, this is why I don't live in a condo. I heard him groan this low growl, he dropped my legs, and then finally we were both still, with him on top of me and still inside of me, and me squashed under his weight. We kind of half way dozed under the ceiling fan, both of us too exhausted to move.

He stirred after a few minutes and started to lift himself off me. "You okay? I know I'm heavy, you need me to get off you so you can breathe?"

I pulled him back down and kissed the hollow of his neck. "Nope, I'm just fine. I want you to stay just like this."

He rolled partially up onto one elbow to take a little weight off and cupped my cheek in the other hand as he gave me a gentle kiss. We smiled at each other and stayed that way for a while, just talking and idly touching. I looked at the clock and saw it was eight o'clock.

I groaned. "Damn it. I forgot to feed the dogs when we came in."

He looked at the clock. "Oops." When I patted him on the butt to tell him to let me up, he didn't move. "Wait. I wouldn't give them anything else. The three of them ate all of those leftover hot dogs and pimento cheese they knocked on the ground. I don't think they need extra food."

"I forgot about that. Good point. I just wanted to make sure Diego wasn't drinking on an empty stomach."

A few minutes later, we got up to take a shower, which turned into another not-very-useful-but-very-fun shower that required a no contact shower afterward. I pulled on a big t-shirt and he pulled on his shorts, no underwear, as usual, and we went into the kitchen to grab a snack. Apparently, I'd forgotten how an overabundance of sex can work up an appetite.

We decided we weren't sleepy, so we found "Ferris Bueller's Day Off" on one of the cable channels and settled in with the dogs to watch it in bed. Of course he pulled off my clothes as soon as we got the in the bed, insisting that he'd keep me warm. We both fell asleep right in the middle of Ferris' big day, and slept for a few hours, until Luke woke me up kissing my neck with his hands busy between my legs. I returned the favor around dawn, and then we both slept until nine, which I honestly don't think I've done since I was six.

True to his word, that was pretty much the whole weekend. He was also right that I could barely walk by Monday.

My legs felt rubbery, I had a huge hickey below my collarbone, whisker burn pretty much everywhere, and I felt like I'd been rubbed raw between my legs, but to be fair, I don't think he was doing any better. I wasn't complaining. This had been one of the best weekends I'd ever had and every sore spot was totally worth it.

11

We both had to work on Monday morning, so we woke up early, fooled around again, "one more for the road", as Luke put it, took quick, separate showers, and went into my room to get dressed. I tried on a couple of the outfits the stylist had sent over and let Luke help me pick one out, making sure it covered my hickey, then I put on my usual shorts and tank top, because I didn't want to screw up my outfit before I got there. Luke and I made breakfast and fed the dogs. I made two to-go cups of iced coffee, packed some stuff in a cooler for my parents, and we were ready to go by 8:30. I told him I was going grocery shopping after my interview and needed to drop off some stuff for my folks, and I'd be home early afternoon. He said he was teaching this morning and then he was going to finish up Laura's window seat and then he would be back this evening before dinner. We kissed, being careful not to let it get out of hand, and headed out the door.

Atlanta is known for its terrible traffic, and because of it, I didn't get to Ms. Varnedoe's house until almost nine, despite the fact that it was only about three or four miles from my house. She has one of those beautiful, restored Victorians that is regularly featured in the annual spring festival and tour of homes. I parked in front and ran up the front steps with my big tote bag over my shoulder, my iced coffee in one hand, and my outfit in the other. I knocked on the door and Ms. Varnedoe opened the door and greeted me with a warm smile as she waved me in. "Hey I'm Bella, so nice to meet you."

I saw that my coworkers were already inside, and I waved. "Bella, do you have any preference as to where we do the interview?"

She thought about it for a second and then beckoned us to follow her down the hall. "See if y'all think this room would work." We walked into a huge hexagon-shaped room with windows all the way around and a beautiful view of her manicured rose garden. There was tons of natural light, it was beautifully decorated, and there was plenty of room for the two of us, plus Billy Ray, and Mandy.

Billy Ray looked around. "The room is beautiful and the light should be perfect, Ms. Bella."

He started setting up his camera and I held up my clothes. "Bella, I'm sorry to impose, but do you have a place I could change." I pointed down to my shorts and tank. "I can't be trusted not to spill something on myself before the interview starts." I heard Mandy try to muffle a snort of laughter, but I ignored her.

Bella grinned at me and pointed down the hall. "Third door on the left."

As soon as I shut the door, I snatched off my shorts and tank and stuffed them in my tote bag, pulled on my clothes, and then realized I'd forgotten any shoes except for the flip flops I was wearing. Oh well, I guess they'd just have to keep my feet out of the shot.

I rejoined the group, put my tote bag out of the way, and sat down in a folding chair so Mandy could do my makeup. She immediately came over and put a bib over my shirt, but stopped when she saw my feet. I shrugged. "I forgot my shoes, so I'll just wear my flip flops, no biggie."

Mandy didn't say a word. She just sighed, went to her duffle bag and handed me a pair of cute platform sandals in my size that looked great with my outfit. When she bent over to drop them by my feet I kissed her on the cheek and winked at her. "Thanks, Mandy. I guess I'm walking proof that it does take a village." She rolled her eyes, put on my makeup, Billy Ray wired me up, and Bella and I started talking while Billy Ray did last minute adjustments to his equipment.

"Bella, before we start, is there anything in particular you want to talk about, or don't want to talk about?"

Bella wrinkled her nose. "I'd really prefer we not discuss the fact that I have family money or my own charitable giving because I don't want the focus to be on me. I'm hoping the story would bring some attention to some of the great charitable work that's going on in Atlanta, and I also want people to get involved with my current project involving hurricane relief."

"Not a problem. Unless you bring it up, we won't talk about any of that stuff."

It was a great interview. Bella was charming and funny, we got along really well, and her story was very interesting. She said she had gotten a degree in advertising and public relations and had worked in that field for several years while her husband, Max, got his construction business off the ground. Over the years, she turned to fundraising for various charities and her husband built some of the tallest buildings in Atlanta. He had just finished the renovations on this house when he died of a heart attack right before they were about to move in about five years ago.

Bella had focused on decorating the house to keep herself busy after his death, and once it was done, she threw herself into her charity fundraising even more ferociously than before. I asked her about her success as a fundraiser, and commented on the fact that she was known in charitable circles as "The Socialite Whisperer."

She laughed. "Yeah, I've heard that. The truth is, I was born in a family with money, so I grew up in this environment so these are my people, and I'm comfortable with these kinds of events. We're lucky in Atlanta that most of the people who give money to various projects are good, kind people who like to contribute to projects that make a difference, that make the world a better place. I just know how to set up fundraisers so they're both fun and get the job done."

"So what are you involved with now?"

"Now, I'm helping to raise money for hurricane relief in Belize."

"Why Belize?"

"My sister lives in Belize in the winter and she talked me into buying a small condo on the beach in the same complex. After the hurricane, we went down to check out our places, which were pretty much fine, but other parts of the country were devastated. Once we found out that an entire orphanage full of kids had lost their home and school and that there was little clean water for the poor people in the area we live in, I knew we had to do something."

We were done in a couple of hours and Mandy and Billy Ray left to cover a story about a fire on the south side of town. I had scrubbed my face and changed back into my shorts and tank and went to find Bella to thank her again before I left.

"Daisy, I'm about to make some tea. Do you have some time to hang around for a while?"

"I'd love to. I still have a few questions, anyway." I followed her into her kitchen as she filled a beautiful, magnolia-shaped teapot with hot water. I grabbed a pad of paper from my tote so I could write notes, and sat down at her kitchen table as she bustled around. She placed loose tea leaves in an infuser and dropped it in the pot, grabbed a couple of matching cups and some lemon, honey, milk, and sweetener, put it all on a matching tray, and set it in the middle of the table to steep.

As we waited, she handed me a flash drive. "This is documentation for your story that I thought you'd find useful. It's photos and a video of the devastation, plans for the buildings, photos from all of the Belize fundraisers, a tally of how much we've collected from each event, and how the money is being used." The timer dinged, she removed the infuser, put it in the sink, and poured us each a cup of tea. She handed me one as she sat back down across from me and added sugar and milk to her tea. "I always want people to be confident that the proceeds from fundraisers are being used correctly."

I grabbed my laptop and plugged in the flash drive. When the pictures came up, we started to go through them.

The first few pictures showed a large building that was an almost competed shell. "That's the orphanage."

"That's amazing." I flipped through a series of several pictures. "You're almost completely done on the outside."

She nodded. "We've been super lucky with weather since the hurricane, so we've been able to get a lot done in a short period of time." She scooted closer. "May I scroll through and show you some things?" I nodded and she flipped to a view of the back of the building. "See this wing? The local schoolhouse was also destroyed, so we added a wing with school rooms that will service both the orphanage and the surrounding neighborhoods."

"That's a great idea. I take it that saved on construction costs?"

"Yep." She flipped to the next series of pictures. "Check this out." She showed me a beautiful beach with a huge open lot that backed up to the jungle. "Guess what this is going to be?"

From the looks of the location, I guessed it would be something fancy. "You're rebuilding a resort?"

She laughed. "Nope. Believe it or not, this is one of the sites for the water treatment plant. It's actually a desalination plant that can treat seawater to be used for drinking water. This location is perfect because the water can be collected right here. No transport costs." She then showed me plans for another plant that converted groundwater and rainwater into drinking water and would be located inland.

"Bella, this is amazing. I can't believe how much y'all have already done."

She nodded. "We've been lucky. We've been able to do a lot of this using private funds, so we haven't had to deal with the local government for anything other than permits, and luckily, those people haven't given us any problems." She amended. "Well, just the usual bribes you deal with as a cost of doing business in that area, but at least they gave us the permits."

"Where did the private money come from?"

"Well, we've already had a couple of functions here in Atlanta that raised a good chunk of money, plus we've had a couple of functions locally that also did well."

"I thought Belize was a super poor country. Is it hard to raise money there?" I sipped the tea. It tasted like an Earl Gray, but with something else. Lavender, maybe? Delicious.

"It's like a lot of Caribbean and South American countries. You have rich folks and poor folks and not too much in the middle. In Belize, about forty percent of the country is very poor, but there's also a bunch of rich people who live there because the cost of living is low and they can get beachfront property with amazing houses for only a percentage of what they'd pay here."

Bella clicked through several pictures until she got to pictures of an event where people were very tan and dressed in what looked like expensive resort wear. "Here are the pictures of some local events." There were pictures of a dance at what looked at a country club on the beach. "You can tell it's not from here because you know no rich woman in Atlanta would be caught dead in front of a camera with flat hair and no Spanx."

We both laughed. The next set of pictures were of a group of well-dressed people wearing hard hats and sunglasses and holding ceremonial shovels in front of a large open field. "That's the ground breaking ceremony for one of the water treatment plants, which was followed that night by a casino night fundraiser." She identified some of the smiling faces, pointing at each in turn as I recorded the information in my notebook. "That's Jose Moya, the mayor of Belize City, that guy is the president of one of the local banks, I can't remember his name, I don't know who that guy is, that guy is Nicholai Wilson, Watkins, something like that, anyway, he's in charge of something with the construction, the blonde next to him is his wife, Glynn, not my favorite, and the guy on the right is Darrell Lugo, and he's the previous plant manager." She sat back. "It's important to get these people involved because there are so few resources and there's a ton of corruption, so if you don't know the local power people in charge, you can't get anything done."

I'm not surprised. We have the same kinds of corruption problems here in Atlanta, but probably on a much lesser scale. I clicked through the rest of the pictures, all of them from the casino night party, and I stopped on one. "This is that Glynn chick and her husband?"

Bella looked at the screen and wrinkled her nose in distaste. "Yeah, that's them. I've had a couple of meetings where I had to deal with her. She's one of those rich chicks who's only involved so she gets her picture in the paper, and she's kind of fake and really bitchy." She shook her head. "I hate having to deal with people like that, but unfortunately, that's part of any fundraising." She sipped her tea, leaned forward, and pointed to the husband. "And I don't know anything about him."

I'd never seen him before, but the woman definitely looked familiar. Probably because she looked a lot like Gwyneth Paltrow. Well if Gwyneth Paltrow was overly tan, had big fake boobs and lips, and a whole lot of Botox and fillers, that is. I mentally shrugged and put it out of my head as we went through the last of the pictures.

We finished our tea and I packed up my laptop and notebook. "Bella, thanks so much for your time and your hospitality. I really enjoyed today. The segment will be on the end of next week, and I'll send over a copy before it airs to make sure you're good with everything. "

I held out my hand and Bella shook it firmly. "I really enjoyed today, too. Please tell Lola and Sara I said hello, and maybe all of us could get together for coffee."

"I would love that." I was serious. Bella was a lovely woman and I'd really enjoyed talking with her. I really liked the fact that she looked like a generic, fancy, Buckhead matron, but was actually very funny and down to earth. She'd be fun to hang out with outside of work.

After I left, I headed over to my parents' house. My mom had asked me to make her some snacks for her book club, so I dropped off some of my bread and butter pickles and cheese straws. Fortunately, she wasn't home so I didn't have to hear about how inappropriately I was dressed and how a little lipstick wouldn't kill me.

I also saw a note for me thanking me for the food and telling me that she and dad expected to see Luke and me again sometime soon. Crap. My mom's goal in life has been to harass me until I finally give up and become some well-dressed, proper socialite type, but so far I've been a constant disappointment. And it's much worse now that I'm divorced. Before, I was a disappointment, but at least I had a husband, so I know she's not going to rest until she's gotten me married off again.

I dropped off some leftover blueberry muffins at my dad's office so he could enjoy them without my mother yelling at him about his cholesterol. Then I went to the grocery store and picked up food for the week and some steaks and big baking potatoes for tonight.

Finally, I made it home, let the dogs out, and put all of the groceries away. It was only about two o'clock, so I had plenty of time to cook. I made a huge pot of jambalaya, Lola's favorite chicken enchiladas, and some vegetable soup and cornbread. I made a batch of blueberry scones, biscuits, and a couple dozen red velvet cupcakes, since Luke had requested them and I know Lola loves them almost as much as Harrison. While everything was cooling, I texted Lola to tell her to stop by to pick up her dinners for the week because I'd been running around all day and didn't feel like going back out.

She texted back that she was almost done in court and would be by as soon as she was done. I was actually dozing on the sofa when Lola came by about a half hour later. She let herself in, moved Monroe over, kicked off her shoes, and collapsed on the sofa with a sigh of relief. "Damn, I'm glad today's over. My entire day was one shitstorm after another."

I sat up and patted her leg. "Unusual shitstorms, or the usual shitstorms?"

"The usual. Nothing interesting." She put her feet on the coffee table and I asked her if she'd like a drink.

"Please."

"You want some tea?"

"Not unless it's a Long Island Iced one."

I laughed. As I got up, I playfully tugged her hair. "How about some bourbon? I could make you a Kentucky Mule." She nodded enthusiastically, and I headed into the kitchen.

I made the drink with some ginger beer, fresh squeezed lime juice, and bourbon, put it over ice, and brought it out to her. She smiled in appreciation as I bent over to hand it to her.

As I went to straighten back up, she shot up and grabbed the top of my tank and pulled it down. "Nice hickey, Daisy," she smirked.

I rolled my eyes and sat down. "Ha, ha, thanks." I pulled my shirt a little higher and tried to ignore her. Of course she wouldn't leave me alone.

She reached over and pulled up the leg of my shorts, "Hmm, and your inner thighs look a little chapped." I smacked her hand away. "What happened there? I'm guessing a friction burn of some sort? Beard burn, maybe? Nice." She bobbled her eyebrows at me and winked.

I crossed my arms and stared at her and asked her if she was done. She shook her head and grinned at me. "Nope. I'll bet you have some nice fingerprint bruises in a few places, too. Let me guess, hips, tits, and butt maybe? Let me see."

I had to laugh. She is so ridiculous. "Okay, hands off, Buttercup. Yes, I'm a little 'banged up,' haha, but we had a great weekend and if it makes you feel any better, I don't think Luke is in any better shape than I am." She smiled and looked at me and grabbed my hand and squeezed it. I squeezed back, and we smiled at each other.

"You know how happy I am that you're doing so well. And we all love Luke and the fact that he's so obviously crazy about you."

I nodded. "I know. He's a great guy. I'm really lucky. And you know I always love you, crazy girl."

She snorted. "Obviously. I mean, come on, what's not to love? I'm damned delightful."

"You are."

We both laughed and we sat there for a few minutes, petting the dogs, and chatting about nothing important.

After a while, I got up to frost the now cooled cupcakes and light the grill and Lola went to her car to get the cooler and clean covered dishes from last week's meals. I asked her if she'd like to stay and eat steaks tonight with us, and she said she'd love to. We put her food for the week in those containers and stuck them all on the bottom shelf in my fridge so she could grab them when she left. I took out the steaks and cut my ribeye in half to share with her. I put some seasoning on the meat, rubbed the potatoes in olive oil and salt and wrapped them in tinfoil, and went outside to put them on the grill. She changed into a pair of shorts and a t-shirt she keeps in my guest room and sat down at my little dining table with her feet in the opposite chair to keep me company while I made a salad.

There was a knock at the front door. Lola stood up and padded to the door to open it for Luke. She went to hug him, but he was covered in paint and sawdust, so she settled for quick whack on his hip as he came through the door. He had a duffle in his hand and came over to give me a quick peck on the forehead. "Mind if I take a quick shower and then I'll come help with dinner?"

I smiled up at him. "Of course." He ruffled my hair and headed down the hall.

As he disappeared toward my room, Lola winked at me. "Watch this." She called down the hall. "Hey Luke, you need any help with that shower since Daisy is busy with dinner?"

He pretended like he didn't hear her, but I did hear the lock on my door click as he closed it. We both started laughing. "I guess he still hasn't completely recovered from your question at the pool. He's probably afraid he'll be taking his shower, minding his own business, and you'll pop into the bathroom with a tape measure."

She bobbled her eyebrows and laughed at the thought. "That's right, Luke. Be afraid. Be very afraid."

He was back in about ten minutes, all squeaky clean with damp hair. "What can I do?"

I pointed to the fridge. "Go grab a beer and sit and relax with us until the steaks need to go on." He got his drink, sat in the chair at the end of the table, put his feet up next to Lola's, and took out his phone to show us a picture of Laura's new window seat, which was beautiful.

I finished the salad and asked Luke to go check the grill

to see how the potatoes were doing and to see if it was time to put on the steaks. As he disappeared onto the back deck, Lola turned to me. "So how was the interview with Bella?"

"You were right. She was absolutely delightful and I was really impressed by the work she does. You might want to take a look to see if you're interested in donating." Lola took down a couple of glasses and grabbed a bottle of wine to open. I went to my office to get my laptop so I could show her some of the video we'd shot today, plus the pictures and videos Bella had given me of what they were doing in Belize. I called over my shoulder. "She said the three of us should get together for coffee and I said we'd love to."

As I came back into the kitchen, Lola put two glasses of wine on the table. "Sounds great to me. She's a lot of fun and I'd like to get to know her better."

I had just sat down at the table and Lola and I had started scrolling through the photos when Luke came back in the kitchen to tell us the potatoes were looking good and that he'd put the steaks on in a few minutes. He washed his hands as he curiously looked over at us. "What are y'all looking at?"

"It's pictures from my story today." I looked over at him. "Remember, it's that lady who's rebuilding an orphanage and two water treatment plants in Belize?" He came to look over my shoulder as I clicked rapidly through the pictures. "Hey Luke, I know you've built stuff like water treatment plants in your previous life. Check out this location." I laughed as I showed him the lot located right by the beach. "A beachfront water treatment plant. That tells you how cheap you can get land there."

He laughed and agreed that no one could afford that in the States. I flipped through the pictures of the fundraising event at the beach. Lola commented on one bathing suit that she said she'd seen in *Vogue* and said it cost over a thousand dollars, which completely freaked me out. We came to the ground breaking ceremony picture. "These are the local muckety-mucks, you know, the town mayor, the bank president, some local fancy people, blah, blah, blah..." I started to click to the next picture, but Luke suddenly grabbed my arm. "Stop. Who did you say these people are?"

He leaned over my shoulder so he was closer to the screen but he still had ahold of my arm. In fact, he was squeezing me so tightly that it hurt, so I put my hand on his so he'd stop. He immediately let go, but I looked at his face and he looked pale and his jaw was clenched as he stared at the screen. I started to worry something was very wrong. "Luke, are you okay?"

He ignored my question and pointed at the screen. "Can you blow this up?"

I shrugged. "Sure." I zoomed in on the picture so that you could see the people's faces. The hardhats and sunglasses made it hard to make out details. Luke looked like he was about to fall over and Lola and I exchanged a look. I stood up, pushed him down in my seat, and went to get him a glass of water. "Luke are you okay? Do you need a doctor or something?"

He ignored me, grabbed the mouse himself, and stared at the picture. "Are there any more pictures of these people?"

I was confused and worried. What the hell was going on? "Uh, yeah. Keep clicking and you'll see them at a charity event." When he reached the one of the bitchy woman and her husband, Luke stopped scrolling and immediately enlarged the picture. He leaned forward and whistled long and low. "Son of a bitch. I can't believe it."

Lola and I looked at each other. She shrugged at me,

and I pointed to the picture. "I thought she looked familiar, but I finally realized it's because she looks like a trashy, overly tan, overly botoxed and filled, Gwyneth Paltrow."

He leaned back in his seat, staring at the picture. "She does look like a totally overdone version of Gwyneth Paltrow, but that's not why she looks familiar." He started smiling, then grinning, and then laughing. He stood up and grabbed me and pulled me up against him and kissed me and then whirled me around the kitchen, then grabbed Lola, too, and started hugging us both off our feet. By this time, we were all laughing, but we were very confused, and finally Lola asked him what the hell was going on.

He turned back toward the computer. "Daisy, do you remember who Bella said these people are?"

I shrugged. "I'm not sure about the last name, but Bella said they were some fancy couple named Glynn and Nicko-lai, and she said that Glynn was bitchy and only in it for the publicity and she didn't know the husband, but he was doing something with the construction projects."

Luke snorted. "Yeah, that sounds about right." He pointed to the people in turn. "Try Glenda Mathis and Nick Watson. My ex-wife, my ex-business partner, and current fugitives from the US government." He nodded with a self-satisfied look on his face and grabbed me and kissed me again, hard. "She looks familiar because you knew her in college. Daisy, you actually found those assholes."

Lola and I stood there with our mouths open and stared at the pictures. Now that he said it, even though I hadn't seen her in years, I could totally recognize Glenda, even though Lola didn't. Neither Lola nor I had ever seen Nick, so Luke went on the FBI's website and pulled up their pictures so we could confirm that it was actually them. It was. I couldn't believe it. "Have y'all ever had any leads on their whereabouts before?"

He scratched his chin as he thought. "Right after it happened, the money trail disappeared after the money went from the Cayman Islands and then to Brazil or Argentina, I can't remember exactly where, and they knew they'd crossed the border into Mexico. That was really it. There had been rumors over the years that they had been seen in Costa Rico or Belize, but nothing was ever confirmed."

He threw up his arms and let out a whoop. "We've confirmed it now. Hot damn! Now that we know where they are, maybe we can make their lives as fun as they made mine for all those years."

We all sat back down and watched as Luke flipped through the rest of the pictures, but there were no more pictures of Glenda and Nick. Lola sat there quietly, lost in thought. Finally, she looked over at us. "Okay, here's the little bit I know about extradition. The good news is that I'm 99.9% sure that we have extradition agreements with Belize and I'm pretty sure I remember seeing a few cases where the Belize folks sent some rich American assholes back to the States so they could go to prison. However, I do see some potential problems in this case. First, since the hurricane, I'll bet everything is such a mess that it will be super difficult to get anything done, especially because extradition is a bureaucratic, paperwork-intensive nightmare on a good day. Also, if these are prominent people in the country, the local police and courts may be happy to take a little money to tip them off. They might just end up getting 'lost' or 'escaping' while in custody or while being transported." She rolled her eyes. "Then they'll just disappear again." She looked at both of us. "We've got to figure out a way that they won't see us coming and they can't bribe their way out of trouble."

Luke nodded as he considered what she said. "You're right. I've got the number of the FBI agent I dealt with in New Orleans and I'll ask him what he thinks about all this." Lola and I agreed that was a great idea. "Email me those pictures and I'll send them over to Agent Prince as soon as I talk to him."

He grabbed his phone from his back pocket, flipped through his contacts, and dialed Agent Steve Prince. Agent Prince apparently wasn't answering, because Luke left him a message. "Hey Agent Prince, Luke Mathis here. Thought you might want to know that I just ran across Glenda and Nick in Belize, and I wondered what we should do about it." He left his callback number, sent the pictures to Prince's email, hung up, winked at both of us, and went to grab his beer and then he took the steaks out of the fridge.

He was grinning from ear to ear as he took the steaks to the patio. My three dogs followed him, also very happy, mostly about the thought of steak. Okay, Diego was happy about steak and beer, but bottom line, everyone was happy.

Lola and I looked at each other, amazed at what had just happened. "Holy shit." Lola took a big swig of wine. "I can't believe he actually found them."

I got up to grab the bottle of wine and brought it back over to the table. I topped us both off and sat down. "Do you think they'll be able to get them back to the States?"

Lola shrugged. "I really don't know. I know some of these cases have dragged on for years, and I know that sometimes the outcome wasn't in favor of our government." She wrinkled her nose. "I'd hate for Luke to go through all that and then they just get away with it."

I agreed. "No shit. Letting them get away would be

worse than never finding them, at all." We looked outside to see Luke talking animatedly on the phone with someone. As we watched, he hung up the phone and came inside.

He kissed me on top of the head and threw himself in the chair next to me. "I called Lou, our old accountant, to tell him what's going on." he took a sip of his beer and smiled. "He was hollering like a crazy man, he was so excited, and told me to keep him posted about what we decided to do."

"I can't imagine how you must feel, realizing that you finally know where they are." I bumped his shoulder with mine and smiled at him.

"It doesn't feel real. This has been going on for years, and I can't believe that I finally have a chance to give those jackasses the justice they deserve." He shook his head. "It's been a long time coming."

Lola and I exchanged a worried look, and Lola leaned forward to get Luke's attention. "Luke, let me know as soon as you hear from your FBI buddy. I have a couple of friends in the State Department and Daisy's dad knows people all over the world in various law enforcement agencies, so we can figure something out."

Luke smiled at Lola appreciatively. "Look Lola, I know that there are a lot of potential problems here, and I'm not naïve that this may not work out." He grabbed my hand, flashed me a quick grin and raised my hand to kiss my knuckles. "I just want to see what our options are, and if there's any way to make Glenda's and Nick's lives a little less pleasant in the long run, it's all good to me." I smiled back at him and squeezed his hand in return. He grabbed his beer and went back outside to tend the steaks, and Lola and I started setting the table.

We had a wonderful dinner and took the dogs to walk

afterwards, talking about everything except the situation with Glenda and Nick. We agreed that we'd worry about it after Luke had talked to his FBI buddy and we had an idea of what we were looking at. When we got back, Lola grabbed her food for the week, hugged us both, and went home.

As soon as she left, I convinced Luke to take a bath with me so he could relax. I filled my tub with lavender bubbles, lit a bunch of candles, got us each a red velvet cupcake, and put it on a tray on the shelf next to the tub. I brushed my teeth, undressed, got in the tub, and called Luke to come on in.

When he came in, it took him a minute for his eyes to adjust, but once he did, I saw him smile and he pulled his shirt off and came over to the side of the tub. I smiled up at him and told him that the water was nice and he should join me. We were smiling at each other, and he stood up, unbuttoned his shorts, and they dropped to the floor. He kicked them out of the way, and I could see he was already getting excited and I could feel my heartbeat speed up. He climbed into the tub and sat down facing me with my legs draped over his. "This feels really nice, Daisy."

Uh, yeah. I smiled at him and handed him a cupcake, telling him I was saving mine for later. He settled back against the side of the tub and took a huge bite, making ridiculous groaning noises and saying how good it was. I was laughing and rolled my eyes. "Mathis, nothing tastes that good."

He immediately snapped to attention. "Oh really?" He took a big swipe of frosting on his finger and wiped it across my lips. Before I could get a taste of it, he held the rest of the cupcake up with the other hand so it wouldn't get wet and pulled me forward so I was straddling his lap. He kissed me, nibbling and licking the frosting off my lips, and then finally thrusting his tongue inside my mouth. Wow. I guess he really did like the frosting. When I pulled back and started giggling at how silly he was, he got another fingerful of frosting and smeared it across my chest and put a blob of it on each nipple.

I shook my finger at him. "Now look what you did." I tried to look serious, and he tried to look sorry, but neither of us was very convincing.

"So sorry. But I don't want to waste any of this amazing cupcake, so let me take care of that for you." He bent his head and took my nipple in his mouth and licked and sucked it until the frosting was gone, then he slowly moved across my chest to the other side. It took him a while, but he did a great job of removing every bit of frosting. When he finally got down to his last bite of cupcake, he offered it to me. I swallowed the bite of cake and then grabbed his hand and licked and sucked every bit of icing suggestively off his finger, until both of us were breathing hard and staring at each other.

Luke kissed me until I was about to collapse, and then he lifted me off his lap and turned me around, pulling me so that I was actually lying with my back to his chest. I picked up a washcloth from the side of the tub, along with some body wash, and Luke held out his hands for me to give them to him. He soaped up the washcloth and lazily started running it across my chest and down my body while he kissed my neck.

Next thing you know, water was all over the bathroom floor, my cupcake was an inedible, soggy mess, and once again, I needed a real shower after our bath was done. Eventually, we got out of the tub, took a quick shower and I laughed as we stepped out and both grabbed a towel. "My water bill is going to be insane this month."

He looked at me with a raised eyebrow. "Are you complaining?"

I pretended to think about it, and finally let out a heavy sigh and admitted. "I guess not. I suppose the amazing sex is probably worth the extra water."

Once we were dried off, he threw me over his shoulder, went into the bedroom, and tossed me in the middle of the bed. "'Probably worth the extra money', huh?" He leaned over with his hands on each side of my hips, trapping me under him on the bed. "Girl, I'm going to make you eat those words."

I looked at him primly and told him that it wouldn't be easy to eat anything since my mouth was about to be full, if he would like to join me. He laughed and we spent the next few hours enjoying each other.

He fell asleep first. He was spooned around my back with his arm anchoring me to the bed and his hand between my breasts. As we lay cuddled together, all of a sudden, it hit me like a ton of bricks. I was head over heels in love with this man. It had happened so gradually over the past few months that it kind of snuck up on me, but there was no question. I was in love with Luke Mathis.

Was I freaked out? Was I worried? I thought about it and then I realized that I totally fine. I just felt warm, happy, and content. Thanks to us taking so much time getting to know each other, I knew he was a good, kind man that I could trust completely, and bonus points, he was hilarious and incredibly hot, too. If this was how karma works, and Luke and my new life are payback for all the crap I had to go through, I was incredibly grateful.

That night, I fell asleep with a smile on my face.

12

A FEW DAYS LATER, I HAD TO GO TO THE TV STUDIO TO do some final editing on Bella's story, and Luke was going to the next door neighbor's house to do some measurements for the screen porch she wanted him to build. He also planned to speak to the head of the department at Tech and tell them that he was done with teaching after this year so he could start working full time on his construction business before next summer.

We went to the kitchen to grab some coffee to go, and as we fixed them, I reached into a drawer and got an extra key and held it out casually, like giving him a key was no big deal. "Here. Why don't you take this in case you get back before I do?" I hoped he didn't notice my hand was actually shaking a little and my voice kind of caught.

He looked at the key and then looked at me like he wasn't sure if I meant it. "Are you sure, Daisy?" He reached out and took the key and put it in his palm and looked at it and then smiled at me. "You don't mind me having this?"

I busied myself pouring coffee into the UGA Yeti cup

that Mo had bought me for my birthday last year. "It's just an extra key. Lola, Sara, and Mo all have one, and since you're over here all the time and you live around the corner, I thought it would be a good idea if you had one, too." I looked up to see him with a satisfied smile on his face as he placed the key on his key ring. "No biggie." I put the top on my Yeti, reached up to give him a quick peck on the cheek. "Call me if you hear from your FBI buddy." I petted the dogs and headed out.

The weather was beautiful, warm, and sunny, but with no humidity for a change, so as I got in the car, I put the top down and headed for the studio. By the time I got there, Mandy had already done most of the editing of the interview itself, and I brought her the flash drive so we could use some of the photos and hurricane footage in the segment. I had already saved the flashdrive to my laptop and emailed the Belize pictures to Luke, but I wanted to use the studio's high definition printer to print some photos of Glenda and Nick. I put those in my bag and then we spent the next few hours editing the story, which came out really fun. I sent it to Bella for her final approval before the story aired later in the week.

When I got home, I changed into my usual work clothes of yoga pants and a t-shirt, made myself some lunch, and worked on my column for a few hours. I always try to stay way ahead so I'm never in a time crunch, and so if something happens like, oh I don't know, I try to castrate someone with a VW, I always have at least three months of columns ready to roll. Right now, I have almost four months' worth done, so I'm good to go.

When I was finished, I checked my phone and my email. I sent my boss my columns for this week and next week, and took care of some administrative stuff, which I hate. I was sitting there debating whether I should do some bookkeeping, which I also hate, when my dogs ran to the front door, barking like morons, so I figured Luke had gotten home. I heard the door open. "Luke? I'm back here."

He came in, looking tired and irritated and threw himself in my big overstuffed chair across from my desk, while the dogs jumped all around him. Uh oh. "Did you finally hear from Agent Prince?"

He nodded. "Yeah. I just hung up with him. He apologized for not getting back sooner, but he's not sure what we can do about this." He closed his eyes and rubbed them. "Prince was very happy to know where they were, and he loves the idea of throwing their asses in jail, but he doesn't see any way to do it right now."

I was pissed. "So you did their job, you found them, and the damn FBI can't be bothered to do the freaking paperwork to get them back here?"

He shook his head and frowned as he raked both of his hands through his hair. "It was exactly what Lola said. It's a paperwork nightmare down there on a good day, and after a hurricane destroyed courthouses and everything else, there's just no way to get something like that done anytime soon."

I couldn't believe someone could steal $13 million from the U.S. government and no one thought that was worth pursuing. "So there's nothing we can do?"

"Not any time soon." He closed his eyes and dropped his head against the back of the chair. "He also said that Lola was right and that if we made a move, that there's a good chance the local authorities will tip them off and they could disappear before we could make anything happen. And that leaves us right back where we started."

I came around my desk and climbed on his lap to hug

him. He put his arms around me, squeezing tight, and buried his face in my hair. "This is so damn frustrating, Daisy. It sucks that we know where they are but can't do a thing about it."

I pulled back and kissed him on his nose and brushed his hair back. "Let's go take the dogs to walk. It's beautiful out, and I think you could use a little fresh air. Then, I'll make you a drink and we'll sit on the porch. Maybe we can figure out a way around all this."

We took the dogs to walk and then came back to the house. I made a pitcher of bourbon punch and added some mint. It grows along my neighbor's fence, but it stuck through my side of the fence so I figured that part of the mint was mine. Luke was already on the glider, out on the porch, surrounded by dogs. I poked Cletus so he'd move over, sat down, and handed Luke his drink. "You okay?"

He shrugged. "Yeah, I'm fine."

Obviously, he wasn't fine, so I figured I'd change the subject. "Hey, so how'd it go today over at Tech? Can you finish after this semester or do you have to wait till the end of the school year?"

He took a sip of his drink. "It actually went great. It turns out they're going to reorganize the department anyway, and they gave me the choice. I told him I'd like to leave at the end of the semester and the department head said that was fine and that I was always welcome if I wanted to come back."

I bumped my shoulder against his. "That sounds great."

He grinned. "Yeah, it is. I want to get going with my new business after the first of the year, and now I won't have to wait."

"Did you finish getting the measurements on the porch next door?"

He nodded. "Yep. I'm going to dig up some of my old forms tonight and reconfigure them for my new business."

"What kind of forms?"

"Cost projections, estimates, completion checklists, punch lists, stuff like that." He took a drink. "Is this green stuff mint?" I nodded. "It's really good." He continued. "I can use the old originals and make them work for smaller projects like what I'm doing now. That way, I don't have to start over with the forms."

That made sense, no reason to reinvent the wheel. "You did a lot of residential renovation before, didn't you?"

"Oh yeah. We did everything from small renovations to building subdivisions, so I can do anything I want."

"But you don't want a big company with a bunch of employees again, do you?"

He shook his head. "Oh hell, no. I don't want to do huge projects. My goal is to hire a couple of talented carpenters I can depend on, and then I'm using subs for everything else. My goal is to only do projects that interest me. And I want to work with people I like."

"So your goal is fun work only, no assholes allowed?"

He took another sip of his punch and started slowly rocking us. "Exactly. How was your day? Anything exciting?"

I snorted and shook my head. "Not unless you think reading syndication agreements is exciting, which I don't." He agreed that didn't sound fun at all.

"I'm done drinking. You want some tea?" When he nodded yes, I moved Cletus and Diego off my lap and stood up and grabbed both of our glasses. When I came back out he was almost asleep and covered in dogs who were all on their backs, paws in the air, while Luke lazily scratched them.

As soon as he heard me come back on the porch, he half smiled at me, and asked me if I wanted to go inside and lie down for a while. I looked at him with my eyes narrowed, trying to decide whether he meant he wanted to take a nap, or "take a nap," as Sara would say with air quotes and a nasty wink. Before I could answer I heard a knock. The dogs flew off the porch and I heard Lola's voice. "Hey, where y'all at? Are you decent?"

Lola's head popped into view around the corner. She looked disappointed. "Awww, y'all are decent. That is just a shame."

I laughed at her goofiness. I told her to grab some tea, or there was some punch in the fridge and some mint on the counter, so get whatever she preferred. She disappeared down the hall, hollering over her shoulder, "Hey, I might have some interesting news. Save my place."

When she came back, she had changed into her shorts and t-shirt from my guest room. She held a glass of tea with a sprig of mint and dropped into a wicker rocker with a sigh of relief. "Shit, I had a long day."

She looked at Luke. "Did you hear from your FBI buddy?"

Luke nodded. "Yep. And it was exactly like you said it would be. No one can touch them any time soon because of the hurricane flattening the courthouse and if we went ahead and filed the paperwork, odds are they'd be warned and would disappear." He shook his head. "It pretty much sucks."

Lola nodded. "I totally agree, but I did hear something kind of interesting today. Daisy, I ran into your dad at the courthouse, and I knew he'd dealt with extradition with some pedophile that he was trying to get back here from Mexico a couple of years back. I told him what was going on with Luke and he gave me an idea. He said that when they were looking at the options to get that, quote 'baby-raping asshole' back here, one of his captains suggested that they should take up a collection to get enough money to hire a professional kidnapper. Your dad laughed it off, but he said if he could have found a way to kidnap him back to U.S. soil without breaking a million different laws, he'd have done it in a heartbeat."

Oh shit. Lola was pissed, and I know from experience that nothing good comes from that. I hope that didn't mean she wanted to have them kidnapped, but I wasn't really sure, and she certainly had enough money to make it happen. Luke apparently had the same concern. "Uh, Lola, I appreciate the thought, but I'm thinking that kidnapping them is not the way to go."

She laughed and rolled her eyes. "No, you jackasses, I'm not saying kidnap them. I'm saying we need to get them back on U.S. soil. Voluntarily."

Luke shook his head. "They've been out of the country for years. I can't imagine they'd come back here willingly."

Lola smiled at him. "But what if they didn't know they were in the States?"

We both looked at her blankly. "What?"

She smiled at us. "Okay. Hear me out. While I was trapped like a rat in court today, I kind of came up with an idea. It's not ready yet, but I think we can make it work if we can figure out some of the details." She took a big gulp of her tea and put it down on the side table. "Okay, y'all follow me here."

Lola leaned forward and began to outline her plan. "First, let me recap to make sure I'm not missing anything. They committed fraud on the U.S. government to the tune of about $13 million. They left the country and ended up in Belize. Prince can arrest them if they're on American soil but that's not as easy as it sounds. Belize has an extradition treaty with the U.S., but there have been many cases that show that Belize is kind of an asshole about sending people back on a good day, and now they've been nailed by a hurricane, they have no federal courthouse, no infrastructure, and the people we're dealing with have a lot of money to bribe officials with, so getting them back through normal channels probably isn't going to work."

We were nodding as she spoke, agreeing with everything she said. She continued. "If they return to American soil, they can be arrested and because they've already proven they are a flight risk, they'll probably stay in custody until they can be tried. "

We were still nodding, but I still saw the same roadblock. "But how, without kidnapping them, are we going to get them back on American soil?" Then I thought about who I was talking to and covered all my bases. "And Lola, I mean without us, or anyone related to us, dealing with us, hired by us, peripherally involved with us, or anyone who ever met us, kidnapping them and returning them back to American soil."

Lola tried to look hurt. She put her hand on her chest and looked at me with big eyes. "What...Me? As if I would be involved with something illegal like that!"

I snorted. "You would do whatever you thought was necessary to take care of an injustice, and you wouldn't think twice. And this is one hell of an injustice."

She smiled. "You're right. But I don't think we have to kidnap anyone." She looked at Luke. "Luke would you say that Glenda and Nick are smart?"

Luke snorted. "Well, apparently they are smarter than I

am. I mean, I had no idea of what they were doing right under my nose."

She patted his knee comfortingly. "You just assumed that everyone is honorable like you. What I mean is, are they generally smart people?"

Luke thought about it for a minute. "Glenda was extremely manipulative, and she was very good at getting men to do what she wanted, but no, she's not generally smart. Nick is great with construction, but I don't think he's particularly smart, either. Neither of them are book-smart at all, and I know for a fact that Glenda never read anything more complicated than *People* magazine."

Lola looked satisfied. "Okay, this might work. Daisy, didn't you say that Bella said that Glenda is only into charitable events if she gets something out of it? She likes the personal recognition?"

I nodded, and Lola continued. "So here's what I'm thinking. What if there was a banquet or an awards ceremony dedicated to recognizing individuals who perform extraordinary charitable acts? And Glenda was one of the people recognized? And the ceremony was held on U.S. soil?"

Luke looked skeptical. "You think she'd come back to the States to receive an award? Agent Prince said they were monitoring events like her parents' fiftieth anniversary party, and as far as they know, they've never set foot back in the States."

Lola smiled. "But we wouldn't have it in the States. We'd have it in the Caribbean, specifically Puerto Rico. Do you think they'd come to a Caribbean country? Lots of people don't realize that Puerto Rico is a U.S. territory and is legally American soil, even though it's not a state."

By the time she finished explaining, Luke was grinning

from ear to ear. "Holy shit, Lola, that might actually work." He sat forward. "She's vain enough to want to get the award, and I would bet that she doesn't realize that going to Puerto Rico is legally the same as coming home. Even if she does, I don't think she'd feel like it was risky, as opposed to coming to the U.S. mainland."

I was getting excited. "Lola, we need to get Bella involved. If she's the one who brought it up to Glenda, she wouldn't think a thing anything about it. Bella has already been dealing with her for months with these fundraisers, plus Bella and her sister both have places there and run in the same social circles. She'd have no reason to think it's not completely legit."

Lola nodded enthusiastically. "We can do it as a combination of awards banquet and fundraiser for Belize. I'll be happy to put up the seed money for the fundraising and we'll actually give it to Bella for her foundation."

Luke shook his head. "That's a great idea, and I appreciate the thought, but Lola, you don't need to front the money. This isn't your fight. I'll cover the costs for the benefit itself, and then I'll put up an chunk of change so Bella will be able to show how much has already been pledged from her 'benefactors.'"

Lola waved away his protest. "Luke, I'd already told Bella I'd make a big donation before this situation ever came up. Anyway, it'll be better if both of us donate, because the two of us can put together a hell of a pot of money. Someone like Glenda would love to be the one to get the credit for such a huge fundraising effort."

I agreed. "Luke, she's right. The bigger the pot, the better. Just make sure your names aren't mentioned as donors, or it'll tip her off."

We all were turning the idea over in our heads, trying to

find any potential problems. Luke asked about Bella. "Do you think we can trust her not to tell Glenda and Nick what's going on?"

Lola and I looked at each other and we both shrugged. Lola wrinkled up her nose and looked directly at Luke. "Luke, I'll be honest, I really don't know her all that well on a personal level, but I've known her casually for years and my gut says she's good people. I've never heard anything but positive things about her from everyone, and, personally, I like her a lot. Plus, I really like the fact that she doesn't need money so she's less likely to be open to a bribe."

Luke looked at me. I shrugged and then nodded. "I agree with Lola. I really don't know her at all, but what I know I really like. She described Glenda as cold and fake and said that she didn't like dealing with her, and that seems to confirm everything you've ever said about her." I shrugged again. "I couldn't say it with a hundred percent certainty, but my gut also says we can trust her."

Lola looked Luke in the eye. "Here's our worst case scenario. Whether we somehow blow it, or Bella rats us out, or Glenda won't leave Belize, the bottom line is that no matter what happens, we wouldn't be any worse off than we are right now. They'd still be free and we'd still be pissed. I think we should go for it because we have nothing to lose."

Luke nodded. "I agree. Bottom line, we either do this ourselves, or it can't be done. Not any time soon, at least." He grabbed my hand and squeezed it as we all smiled at each other. "So what's next? We talk to Bella?"

"Yep." Lola nodded and took out her phone. "Let me see when we can all get together. I'll text Bella and tell her I'm with you and we have a project we think she'll be interested in and see what day is good for her." She tapped in a message and sent it off. About a minute later a message dinged in. Lola read it and laughed. "She's available tonight and is apparently extremely bored. Y'all up for it?"

Luke and I looked at each other with raised eyebrows. We both shrugged and looked at Lola. "Good for you?" When she nodded, we agreed. "Tell her to come over and I'll make something." Lola texted an answer and said, "I sent your address. She'll be here in a few."

I took a frozen pan of chicken enchiladas out of the freezer and put it in the microwave to thaw and put the oven on preheat. I threw together a salad and Luke and Lola set the table. She put rest of the bourbon punch in this ridiculously ornate punchbowl I'd inherited from my great aunt, which I love, and put the rest of the red velvet cupcakes and some little pastries on a little cake stand I'd found at a shop in Charleston. Yeah, okay, I know, when it comes to fashion, I'm a total trainwreck, but when it comes to food I really am freaking Martha Stewart.

Bella was there within thirty minutes, and I made the introductions. We ate dinner while everyone got to know each other, and by the end of the meal, I could tell that Luke and Lola were comfortable with including Bella in our plans.

When we were done, we all took our drinks back out to the living room and took a seat. Bella looked at us expectantly. "So what's this project y'all think I'll be interested in?"

We all looked at each other and Luke leaned forward. "Bella, would you mind if I asked you a few questions about your projects in Belize?"

She looked confused, but she shook her head. "No, I don't mind. I'll be happy to tell you whatever you want to know." He reached into my bag and took out a folder and showed her the pictures she had taken of Glenda and Nick. "You know these people?"

Bella looked at the picture. "Yes. That's Glynn and Nicholai Wilkins, or Watkins, Walker, something with a "W" but I can't remember the last name. They're both some big deals in Belize."

Luke looked at her closely. "What do you know about them?"

Bella shrugged and looked at him, obviously not understanding what he was asking. "Nothing really. Like I told Daisy, she's been helping over there with fundraising and he has something to do with all the new construction." She looked confused. "I don't know the husband at all, but I've been in several meetings with her." She hesitated, not wanting to say anything negative about her in case Luke knew her personally. She looked at me, and I nodded and told her to go ahead tell him anything she knew about her, including her personal impressions.

She wrinkled her nose, obviously not too fond of Glynn. "She's not the nicest person I've ever dealt with. She's one of those people who's very impressed with her status in the community and I'm pretty sure that if she wasn't getting public recognition for her actions, she wouldn't be doing it." She took a deep breath and looked directly at Luke. "Look, I'm sorry if she's a friend of yours, but she's really kind of a bitch. I always dread working with women like her because she's the type who makes my job much more difficult and a hell of a lot less fun."

She looked around at all of us. "What's this about? Is there some kind of problem?"

Lola and I looked at Luke and nodded our heads at him to continue. He looked at Bella. "We don't think this Glynn and Nicholai are who they say they are." He then launched into a short version of the whole story, and when he finished, he said, "So Glynn and Nicholai are actually Glenda Mathis and Nick Watson, my ex-wife and ex-business partner, and they are wanted by the U.S. government for stealing $13 million in Katrina funds." He opened the folder to show her pictures of them he had pulled off the FBI website so she could confirm their identities.

At that, he leaned back in his seat. Bella was sitting there with a stunned look on her face, looking back and forth between the pictures. Finally, she looked up at us and said simply, "Holy shit."

We all laughed and told her that was all of our reactions, too. She slowly shook her head. "You never think you're going to be the one who sees someone who's wanted by the cops. This is so weird." She looked at Luke and snorted. "One thing for sure, you've certainly gotten better taste in women since then." He nodded in agreement and Lola and I laughed. "What can I do to help?"

Lola took over. "Here's the problem. We now know where they are, and Belize has an extradition treaty with the U.S., but as you know better than anyone, there's no way to proceed right now. There's no courthouse, there's no place we could even physically file extradition papers. On a good day, it's a totally painful, bureaucratic process that takes forever, but after the hurricane, there's no actual way to do it."

Bella looked incensed. "Seriously? So you know exactly where these assholes are, but you can't have them arrested and make them stand trial?"

We all laughed, and I said, "Yeah. We can't believe it either."

Lola leaned forward. "Bella, we're also worried that the local authorities would tip them off, probably in exchange for a bribe, so they could disappear before they could be apprehended. What are your thoughts on that?"

Bella nodded emphatically. "Unfortunately, I totally agree. Tons of the local governments in Belize are corrupt, but it's much worse now that everyone is in such dire straits. I'm afraid that it's pretty likely they'd be tipped off." She looked at us with a serious look on her face. "So, what do we have to do to get them arrested?"

Lola told her about her idea about getting them onto American soil. "Do you think that she'd leave Belize to go to Puerto Rico to receive an award and to host the benefit? Luke and I will front the money for the cost of the event and to start the pot for donations, and we'll donate the money to your fund after this is all over."

Bella was quiet, tapping her lip with her index finger as she thought. Finally, she nodded. "I think we can make this work. You know, this hurricane first hit Puerto Rico and the Virgin Islands, then it meandered around the Caribbean for a while gaining strength, and then it headed straight for Belize. I had already mentioned to the Belize organizers that some of the fundraising organizers in Puerto Rico and St. Croix had contacted me about combining some of our events, so maybe we can work with that."

She thought about it for several moments, then she sat straight up with an excited look on her face. "I've got it. I'm supposed to go back to Belize in about three weeks to meet with a bunch of folks there to decide how to allocate the money we've already raised and to organize the next fundraiser. There's a lady there who has put together a weekly newsletter for all the people involved with fundraising so we can all stay in touch. I'll get her to put an item in the newsletter next week that says that we're going to do a huge benefit with the people in St. Croix and Puerto

Rico, and we'll divide the proceeds between the three areas." She was getting more animated. "I know the St. Croix and Puerto Rico people will be all over it, and since I've already talked to the Belize people about this being an option, it won't be anything new. Trust me, I'll make sure everyone knows it'll be the event of the season. By the time I get to Belize, everyone there will have been talking about it for a couple of weeks and will be dying to be involved. There's no way an attention whore like Glynn," She looked at Luke apologetically. "Sorry, Glenda."

He shook his head and grinned at her. "No, she's Glynn as far as you know, so you're fine."

She smiled and continued. "...So there's no way an attention whore like Glynn will be able to turn down an invitation to be one of the hosts of a function like that."

We were all sitting there quietly, trying to figure out if we'd overlooked anything, but none of us could come up with a problem. Lola turned to Luke. "If we get them to Puerto Rico, will your FBI guy arrest them?"

Luke shrugged. "I'll confirm it, but he said if they were on American soil he would arrest them, so I don't see why not."

I snorted and rolled my eyes. "Please. If he can't get off his lazy ass to make the world's easiest arrest, he doesn't deserve it. Look, worst case scenario, we'll go talk to my dad. He was actually deputized by the FBI for some drug task force thing he was working on several years ago, so I know it's possible, but I don't know the details." I laughed. "One way or another I'm sure he can get something done. Did y'all know the current U.S. Attorney General was his college roommate? Trust me on this, all it'll take is a phone call and I'm sure we can get some kind of help if we need it."

Luke grabbed the back of my neck and dragged me forward for a quick kiss. "Nothing quite as hot as a powerful woman."

I batted my eyes at him, fanned myself with my hand, and told him with a syrupy accent, "Who, little ol' me?" I patted his leg. "Hate to break it to you, sweet thing, but my dad is the powerful one. You owe him that kiss, not me. I was just sharing a little information."

Luke smiled. "Look, I like your dad just fine, but I think he and I are going to keep things on a platonic level."

Lola grinned and shook her head. "Hopefully, it won't come down to you having to make out with Daisy's dad. There's no way Agent Prince won't want to take care of this himself. His problem was the extradition issue, but we're delivering them directly to his hot little hands and all it'll cost him is some travel funds. I'm sure he wouldn't want to miss this."

The rest of the evening was very relaxed. Lola, Bella, and I made plans to go to lunch the following week and I told Bella we'd let her know the next time our entire group was getting together so she could meet everyone. Around ten, Bella stretched and yawned. "I've got to get going. I've got to get up early tomorrow so we can start the process of getting your exes exactly what they deserve."

Everyone stood up and started moving toward the door. Luke leaned forward and kissed Bella on the cheek. "I'll call Agent Prince in the morning."

Bella smiled. "As soon as I hear from y'all, I'll call the people in St. Croix and Puerto Rico to get the ball rolling." She picked up her huge bag and slung it on her shoulder as Luke opened the door for her. "Thanks for the great dinner and the most interesting evening I've had in a long time."

She waved and left, with Luke following her to walk her

to her car. When he came back in we had refilled our drinks and we all settled onto the couch with Luke and Lola on the ends, me in the middle, and Lola with her legs propped over mine. Luke drained his glass of punch, then grabbed Lola's ankle and shook it gently till she looked at him. "Lola, I want to thank you for your willingness to dive into a pretty screwed-up situation. I really appreciate you and all your help."

Lola has never been comfortable with compliments. She rolled her eyes. "Oh please. This is a chance to screw over that skank Glenda for what I consider to be the ultimate sin...taking advantage of people after a disaster. There is a special place in hell for people like her, and if I can make her life a more shitty place to be, I don't think it can get better than that."

At that, she pulled her ankle loose, uncurled her long legs off the sofa cushion and stood up. She looked at me and winked, and then looked at Luke and said, "Plus, you're in love with my best friend in the world, and I'd do anything for her, so now I'll do anything for you, too."

He didn't even flinch, but I was sitting there with big eyes and my mouth hanging open. This is not the way I wanted this subject to come up. I was thinking over a nice dinner this weekend, or maybe after having him for dinner. I hadn't decided yet.

Luke nodded and stood up in front of Lola, grabbed both her hands, and looked her in the eyes. "That's true. So thanks for being such a good friend to both of us." He pulled her in and hugged her tight. They broke apart, she kissed him on the cheek, bent over and kissed me on the top of my head and headed to the door, tossing a "good night" and a wave over her shoulder. Luke grabbed her stuff from the kitchen and followed her outside to make sure she got to her car okay. I just sat there. I was sure Luke loved me too, but this all was so matter of fact that it was kind of anticlimactic. Yeah, of course y'all are in love, whatever. Gotta go, see you later...

The door opened and Luke came back in, shut the door, and came to sit beside me. He smiled and looked at me, worried that I might be freaking out, and relieved to see I wasn't. "You okay?"

I smiled back at him. "Fine as frog's hair, big boy." I scooted over closer to him and he pulled me onto his lap so that I straddled him. I cupped his face in both hands and kissed him gently on the lips, then pulled back to look into his eyes. "So you love me, huh?"

He looked at me, unsmiling. "Yes I do." He hugged me tightly and then pulled back so he could see my face. "What about you?"

I felt so happy and so free I answered with a smile and with no hesitation. "I love you too." He started to smile as I continued. "I never wanted to have a relationship again after what happened with Bobby, but I didn't figure on you." I unbuttoned his shirt and pulled it wide open when I reached the bottom, all the while kissing his neck with nibbles and little sucking kisses. I pulled back and shrugged. "Honestly, I finally figured out I had been in love with you for a while before I really realized it. You were always so patient, you were kind, you didn't crowd me, and you didn't push before I was ready. We got to know each other and hung out as friends for months and I just enjoyed your company. It really hit me the other night, and all I could think is how lucky we are to have found each other."

He laughed and kissed me until I felt like I was melting into the couch. He finally broke it off and leaned back against the couch with his hands clasped behind his head and a huge grin on his face. "This has been a hell of a day. You finally told me you love me and there's a good chance that Glenda and Nick are going to prison. I can't think of anything that could make this day any better."

I smiled at him with a pitying look on my face. "Really? You can't think of one thing that could make this day any better?" I looked up at the ceiling and pretended to think and tapped my finger on my pursed lips. "Hmmm. Not one, single thing? Bless your heart, let me help you out." I grabbed his head with both hands and we kissed until both of us were out of breath and our hearts were pounding. I sat up, pulled my t-shirt and stretchy bra over my head and threw them over my shoulder.

He smiled as I slid off his lap, rubbing myself against his bare chest on the way down to the floor in front of him. I grabbed his knees and pulled so he'd scoot down lower on the sofa so I could reach the button on his shorts. Once I got him unbuttoned and unzipped, I peeked inside his opened shorts, grabbed him with one hand to give him a quick squeeze and stroke and, with the other hand, shook my finger in his face. "Shame on you, Luke Mathis. Not a lick of underwear, as usual. You're such a bad boy." I asked him to lift up and I pulled his shorts off and threw them behind me.

He shrugged, unrepentant. "Well, Miss Daisy, if you have a problem with that, what are you going to do about it?"

So I grabbed him with both hands, gave him a long lick, a quick nibble, and showed him until he just about collapsed.

Then he returned the favor. By the time we were done, we were both happy, sweaty, smiling, and we were both ready to head for bed. We staggered down the hall together, brushed our teeth, and went to the bedroom. I reached for my nightshirt, but he pulled it out of my hands and tossed it back in my closet, telling me he'd keep me warm. He cuddled me close and turned off the light. But this time, before we fell asleep, he mumbled, "Good night. Love you." And I mumbled back, "Love you, too," and we were both asleep immediately.

13

THE NEXT MORNING, AS SOON AS WE GOT UP, I TEXTED Mo and Sara and Lola, and asked them if we could all get together for dinner that night because we had some news about Luke's Katrina situation. They all texted back and said dinner sounded great, they'd see us around six and we could talk then.

Luke made us breakfast and told me he was going to spend the day getting his forms in order and finishing the proposal for my neighbor's screen porch. I was doing the final video editing on Bella's interview, so I told Luke I was going to work on the porch and he was welcome to join me there with his laptop or he could use my desk, if he needed it.

It ended up we both took our iced coffees outside to work on the porch. The dogs stretched out on the floor, under the fan, as usual, and Luke and I worked in companionable silence for most of the day. He got up once to print a proposal and take it next door for my neighbor to look at, but other than that we just worked together. I put the finishing touches on Bella's story, and when I was done a little after five, I showed it to Luke, who told me it was a great segment and that Bella and I both looked fantastic. I sent it off to my boss at the station and went inside to get started with dinner.

Luke joined me a few minutes later and we finished making dinner. We cleaned up and I had just popped a chicken caprese casserole in the oven when I heard a loud knock as the door opened. Lola hollered that she hoped we were decent. We looked at each other and laughed as she came into the kitchen with Harrison and Mo right behind her. We all hugged as Mark and Sara knocked on the door and came in waving a bottle of wine. I waved them into the living room. "Y'all go sit. The casserole will take about forty-five minutes and we have time to get y'all up to speed before dinner is ready."

Harrison opened the wine as Sara brought glasses from the kitchen and we all sat down in my living room. Mark took the chair and Sara climbed on his lap, Harrison pulled up a kitchen chair next to Mo on the end of the sofa, and Luke and I took the other end, with Lola in the middle. We all got a glass and sipped, but Sara couldn't take the suspense. "Okay, so what's going on? Is there a problem again with the Katrina money?" Sara's brows drew together and she started to look angry. "I hate the damn government! Are they messing with you, cuz, because we'll get you a great lawyer and..."

Lola leaned forward and patted Sara's knee. "Hold on honey badger, it's good news."

Sara looked at Luke for confirmation and he nodded, so she leaned back against Mark and relaxed. "Okay, y'all go on and finish your story. Sorry I interrupted."

Luke smiled. "Thanks, cuz. It's good to know you have my back." He patted my leg and relaxed back into the sofa.

He told them how he'd accidently spotted Glenda and Nick in my story about Bella's fundraising, Lola's idea about how to catch them, and what Bella was going to do for us. By the time he was finished, everyone was just silently staring at him.

Sara was the first to break the silence. "Holy shit. I can't believe you actually found that skank and your dick of an ex-partner."

Mo and Harrison asked if we were planning on going to the fundraiser, and Lola said that she and Luke and I were definitely going, but we'd all have to stay hidden until after the arrest so we didn't tip off Glenda and Nick. Sara looked at Luke with a belligerent look on her face. "Well, if y'all are going, we're going."

Mo took a big swig of wine and echoed Sara. "Well, if y'all are going, we're going."

Harrison nodded in agreement, winked at me, and added, "Y'all can probably use a little backup, so just let us know the date."

Sara looked at me and smiled an overly sweet little smile and clapped her hands in glee. "And Daisy, you know the best part? This is so lucky! We all get to go shopping for something to wear."

My heart sank and I guess I looked traumatized, because everyone started laughing. Luke put his arm around my shoulder and squeezed, and I rolled my eyes. "Fine. Hey, if it takes me shopping for an outfit and wearing it to a fundraiser so that Glenda and Nick go to jail, I'll take one for the team."

Amid comments of, "Awww, you're so brave," and "Look, she's willing to do whatever it takes, even shopping, to put away criminals," I flipped them off as I went into the kitchen to check on my casserole. Ha. Ha. Ha. They're all so damn funny.

Luke followed me in and hugged me from behind as I shut the oven door and set the timer for another ten minutes. He buried his face against my neck and gave me a quick smooch. "I appreciate you being willing to go shopping. I think you're very brave because I know how much you hate it."

I laughed and hugged his arms across my belly then pouted. "I know you do. You're my only real friend here. The rest of those buttheads don't understand real sacrifice." I turned and put my arms around his neck and pulled him down for a quick kiss that, as usual, started to get out of control.

We both realized it and pulled away just as Lola came in to grab a new bottle of wine out of the fridge. "For God's sake, don't make me turn the hose on y'all." She tried unsuccessfully to open the bottle, so she wordlessly handed it to Luke who yanked out the cork with one easy pull. She turned to leave, batting her eyes and saying, "My hero," as she left the room.

Luke let me go and laughed, shaking his head. "Good God, all y'all women are crazy as shithouse rats."

I shrugged agreeably. "Yep, pretty much. I know." What else was there to say? Yeah, they're crazy, but they're my crazies, and, after all these years, I know they don't make friends any better than these people. They're nuts, they're nosy, they can be unbelievably intrusive, but whatever comes up, they're all in and I love them.

At dinner we discussed our plan. They were all interested in meeting Bella, and I told them that if Glenda took the bait we'd all get together to finalize details. Either way, I promised to keep them posted. We all said good night and everyone went home. Well, except Luke.

As soon as the door shut behind them, Luke pinned me up against it and started kissing my neck. "Alone at last."

I started giggling, but the giggles quickly turned into a moan. Lawd, what that man can do to a neck was insane. I felt my knees get weak and he pushed harder against me to keep me upright, until I managed to croak out, "Luke, let's move this down the hall. I'm about to fall over."

He let my feet drop to the floor and then scooped me up and ran us down the hall. We were both laughing like crazy, and he dumped me face down on the bed and fell on top of me. He pulled my hair to one side and started kissing my neck again as he reached under me to undo my shorts. He managed to unbutton them and then he stood up at the end of the bed, dropped his shorts, pulled my shorts and panties down in one quick movement, and pulled my legs apart and knelt in between them. I looked over my shoulder and saw he was staring intently at me. "Can't decide where to start?"

He laughed but never took his eyes off me. "It's like you're a Thanksgiving buffet and I can't decide what I want to eat first."

That tickled me. I tried to roll over, but he put a hand on my lower back to hold me in place. "Nope. I want you just like this." I could feel him bend over me and he took a quick bite on my bottom and then licked over the spot. He took both hands and started to massage my lower back and slowly moved down toward my thighs and down between my legs. He slid his arm under my stomach and pulled me up onto my hands and knees, placing a thick pillow under my knees. I felt him touch me lightly with one finger, just barely rubbing over me until I opened my legs further to give him better access. He teased me with it, just barely putting the rough tip of it inside me, then withdrawing and moving it slowly up and down. He was driving me nuts. I glared at him over my shoulder. "Stop being such a tease, Mathis. You know payback is hell." He didn't say a word, he just winked and smiled and kept doing it.

Fine. You want to play that way? I tried to reach back and grab him, but he pulled my hands above my head and pinned them to the bed with one big hand, then went back to slowly fondling me with the other hand. Finally, he pushed one big finger all the way inside me to see if I was ready for him, and he must have figured I was, because he let my hands go, lined himself up, and pushed himself in to the hilt in one long thrust.

I realized I had been holding my breath. He stood up on his knees and grabbed my hips with both hands, and started moving slowly, pulling almost all the way out and then back in just as slowly. He started rotating his hips against me at the end of each long stroke, and after a few minutes of that, I was going crazy. "Harder," I begged and, finally, he started pounding into me, and after about a minute of that, I was a goner, but he kept going. I felt like a noodle and my arms gave out, but he just kept going. Faster. Harder. Finally, he grabbed my hips so hard I knew I'd have bruises, but trust me, at that point, I didn't care. He slammed into me and I could feel him get even bigger and harder inside me as he finally let go, which pushed me over the edge again, as well. We both collapsed on the bed, totally wrung out and I wasn't sure, but I may have become slightly, hopefully temporarily, blind.

After a few minutes of lying there trying to catch our breath, Luke rolled off me and onto his side and pulled me close to him. He says he's always afraid he's going to squish me like a bug, so he's always a little afraid to lie there with all his weight on me, but I like it. Finally, he rolled onto his back and groaned like an old man. "Girl, you're trying to kill me." He sat up and slapped me on the butt. "Wait here and I'll be right back."

I'm not sure I could've moved if I wanted to, so I didn't argue. I heard him go into the bathroom, heard the sink running, and soon he was back. I was relaxing with my eyes closed, and he rolled me onto my back and spread my legs, and I started to protest until I felt the wet, warm cloth. It felt wonderful. I opened my eyes and smiled at him as he carefully and gently started to clean me up. "Just relax and let me take care of this, baby. Trust me, you'll sleep better if you're not a sticky mess."

When he was done, he went to the bathroom door and tossed the washcloth in the sink and then opened the bedroom door so the dogs could come in. I managed to rouse myself enough to pull back the covers and we got in bed. He pulled me up against him with one arm under my head and the other hand idly fondling me, just rubbing slowly, up and down, a breast here, over my butt, my stomach, my hip, my thigh. I felt him kiss the back of my neck, we both mumbled a quick good night, and fell asleep almost immediately.

We got up the next morning at about six, as usual. We took a quick walk and a shower, then Luke had to teach his class. He also had a couple of meetings with some local subcontractors whose work he wanted to see, so he would be busy most of the day. I needed to figure out the subject for my next segment and I had a great idea for a new column, so I was going to work on that all day. We kissed goodbye and went our separate ways, each telling the other to call if either of us heard from Bella.

Luke called after his class ended at noon. "Hey baby girl."

"Hey, hot stuff. You got some good news for me?"

He chuckled. "Yep. Bella called the folks in Puerto Rico and St. Croix and they're all over the idea of combining their resources for some kind of award ceremony and benefit. Then Bella called the lady in Belize in charge of the newsletter and told her about the idea and she said it was a great idea and that the information would go out in the next newsletter."

I whistled long and low. "Lawd, that chick don't play. You can tell this isn't Bella's first rodeo."

"No shit. She already wrote a press release announcing that Puerto Rico, St. Croix, and Belize were combining resources to put together a great fundraiser and that everyone could submit ideas for the next three weeks and they'd vote on the best ones and finalize details when she got down to Belize next. When I asked her what our timetable looked like, she'd said that there's a sense of urgency because everyone needs help immediately, so the timetable would be much faster than usual, hopefully a month, no more than two, after their next meeting.

"Seriously?" I couldn't believe they could get it done that fast. "So about two to three months from now, at the most?"

"Yep. Bella said everyone is so desperate for work that the hotels and caterers will work on whatever timetable we want."

"That's amazing. Did she say that the event is also to recognize those individuals who've been helpful with the fundraising?"

"Yes. So any attendees who are all about the recognition will love to be involved."

"So an attention whore Like Glenda will be all over it?"

"Exactly." He sounded very satisfied but a little dazed

that everything was happening so fast. "You know, Daisy, I really think this crazy idea might work."

I was sure it would work, especially with Bella on our side. "I told her to just let me know when she needed the money and I'd send it over immediately. She said that sounded great and she'd be in touch."

I couldn't believe Bella had managed to do all this today. "So that's it? We'll have all the specifics after the meeting in three weeks when she meets with everyone and until then we just hang tight?"

"That's what it sounds like. Once they decide exactly when and where and who's in charge of what, we'll have a good idea of what we need to do next."

We both sat silently on the line, thinking. My only concern was whether or not Glenda's need for attention outweighed her sense of caution. "So the big question is whether Glenda takes the bait?"

I could hear the anticipation in his voice. "Bella is pretty confident that Glenda will be all over it once she hears the details. She says she deals with women like her all the time and knows exactly what buttons to push to get her to do what she wants."

I laughed. "Hell, I believe it! When I did my segment, everyone I talked to said they call her the 'socialite whisperer' for a reason. The more difficult they are, the better Bella is at handling them."

Luke snorted. "Better her than me. See you in a few hours, baby girl."

We hung up and the rest of the day was a typical day for me. I walked the dogs, worked, went to my yoga class, had lunch with a friend, and called Lola to tell her what Luke had found out from Bella. As soon as we'd hung up, the phone rang again and I snatched it up.

"Hola, Lola, what'd you forget to tell me?"

My mom's calm voice answered. "It's your mother, darlin' and I was calling because I haven't seen you in weeks and I wanted to see if you and Luke would like to meet your dad and me for supper."

Crap. Busted. But I knew my mom wouldn't let me off the hook. She probably wanted to make sure I hadn't run Luke off yet. "Sure mom. Let me check with Luke to make sure he doesn't have other plans and I'll call right back."

I hung up and called Luke. "Sorry big guy, but my mom is guilt tripping me because I've managed to avoid her for almost three weeks so now she wants us to meet them for dinner. Would you mind?"

He was his usual agreeable self, so I called my mom back. "Hey Mom, that would be great. When and where?"

She named a restaurant near my house and I said we'd meet them there at 6:30. Since we'd be tied up for dinner, I took the dogs for another quick walk and was home right before Luke walked in at 5:00.

I made us both a glass of tea and we went to sit on the porch and hang out for a little while before we had to leave for dinner. Luke put on a pair of old jeans and a buttoned-down shirt the same color as his eyes, so he looked amazing. I grabbed an embroidered pair of jeans and a cute, green, swingy cotton sweater that my mom would find only mildly objectionable and we headed out to Luke's Jeep. He boosted me into the seat, as usual, and we were off. The entire way, I tried to remind him about what a pain my mother could be, but he wasn't worried about any of it. I, on the other hand, was a hot, babbling mess. "...And you know she's gonna ask you when we're getting married and if we do get married what am I going to wear, and why can't you get me to dress like a lady instead of some 'homeless ragamuffin...'" I made little air quotes and was about to go off again when Luke grabbed my hand and squeezed it to distract me from my tirade.

"Hey, what the hell is a ragamuffin, anyway?"

I shook my head and threw up my hands. "Shit if I know. But whatever they are, they apparently spend most of their time trying to kill their mothers with their inattention to fashion."

When we got to the restaurant, Mom and Dad were already seated on the patio with an assortment of tapas and drinks. As we walked up to the table, I hugged Mom while Dad stood up to shake Luke's hand and then he hugged me and Luke leaned over to kiss my mom on the cheek. We sat down and Luke ordered a carafe of white sangria for me and a beer for him.

I saw Mom focus on Luke like a laser beam. Uh-oh. Here we go. I grabbed Luke's leg under the table in warning, but he just patted my hand reassuringly. She smiled sweetly at him and off she went. What are your plans for the future, are you planning on staying in Atlanta, are you going to buy a house, oh, and when are you getting married?

I choked on my sangria. Luke helpfully pounded on my back until I could catch my breath, and then handed me some water. I could almost breathe again and was about to let my mom have it, when Luke patted my leg under the table, winked at me, and answered my mom with a charming smile. "Well, Carol Ann, I do know I'm staying in Atlanta, but with everything else we haven't really gotten that far. Once we make some sort of decision, I'm sure you'll be the first to know."

She leaned back in her chair and looked at him shrewdly. "So it's just a matter of time, is what you're saying? You do realize you've been dating for several months now and it's time to get your ducks in a row." She rolled her eyes and pointed her head in my direction. "I assume Daisy is the holdup?"

I was about to beg my mother to please shut up when my dad leaned over and put his arm around her shoulders and gave her a warning squeeze. "Now, Carol Ann, that's enough. They're grown and they seem to be doing just fine without your help. I'm sure if something momentous happens they'll let us know." He looked across at me and I mouthed a silent "thank you." He winked at me and then focused on Luke. "I am interested in your new business, son. I'd like to add a big screened porch on the back of the house attached to an outdoor kitchen if that's something you can do."

"Clayton, I'll be happy to come take a look, but I can't get to it till after the first of the year."

He smiled at Luke. "No rush."

Mom turned her attention to me, and as soon as I felt her focus point my way, I started to get tense. Luke moved his hand under the back of my shirt, rubbing my lower back comfortingly until I relaxed. When I flashed him a grateful smile, he winked at me, just as my mom started her interrogation. "So, I saw your story on Bella last week and I thought you did a nice job."

I was confused. "I didn't know you knew Bella, Mom."

She nodded and sipped her drink. "I've worked with Bella several times to raise money for various children's charities and she also helped your dad apply for multiple federal grants for new tactical gear." My dad nodded as she continued. "We both think she's wonderful at what she does and is a genuinely nice person." My mom reached for a piece of bread. "Now she just needs to put herself back out there and start dating again."

I stuffed a big bite of calamari in my mouth and avoided the topic on Bella's behalf.

The rest of the dinner was relatively uneventful. Mom only commented on my hair twice, my outfit once, the fact that I wasn't getting any younger three or four times, and she somehow managed to work in over a cheese plate that it wasn't too late for me to get a breast reduction, so all in all, I considered the evening to be a total success.

By the time we left, I was tired, and slightly aggravated, from fending off my mom's usual snarky comments but it had been great to see my dad. When we got in the Jeep, I noticed that Luke looked irritated, too, which made me feel gratified. "Ha, ha, look, my mom even managed to piss you off. What was it? The marriage comments?" I nodded knowingly. "Sorry, just ignore it. I know she's pretty annoying about that. She thinks every woman needs a husband to take care of her. Last time she said it, I reminded her that Lacey Peterson had a husband, and look how well that turned out, and she didn't find that amusing at all."

He ignored my comments. "You've been thinking about a breast reduction?"

I started laughing. "Out of all that, that's what bugged you?" He's such a guy. Holy crap, whatever you do, don't mess with his toys. "No, I don't want a breast reduction. She wants me to dress better and thinks clothes would fit me better if I got a reduction, so she's always suggesting it. I tell her you don't have to worry about how your clothes fit if you only wear t-shirts and yoga pants, which just irritates the shit out of her."

He still looked annoyed. "So you're not really considering it?"

I shook my head, still amused. "Not really. I'd thought about it over the years because big boobs are a pain, but I don't have any physical problems, like headaches or back pain, so I really don't see the need for surgery."

He still looked irritated, but seemed more relaxed. I was curious, though. "What if I was having problems?"

He glanced at me as if surprised because the answer was so obvious. "Well, then you'd need to have surgery. I just didn't want you doing something just to satisfy your mother."

I snorted. "Please. There's nothing I can do to satisfy that woman, so I gave up on that a long time ago." I was surprised at how casual he was about the topic. "So you wouldn't care if I got a reduction?"

He rolled his eyes. "For completely selfish reasons I don't want you to, but if you were having health problems, I'd miss them, but I'd get over it." He reached over and took my hand. "I love you, not your tits." When I raised my eyebrows and gave him a get-real look, he amended. "Okay, I do love them, but I love the whole you, more."

I laughed and squeezed his hand. "That was completely lame, but I know what you mean, and I appreciate the thought."

Luke started the Jeep and drove toward my house. I looked over at him and he looked the same as usual, calm and unworried—okay and also extremely hot—but I know that he was stressed out about this whole situation with Bella. I reached over and grabbed his hand. "You okay with having to wait on Puerto Rico? I know you're not the sit back and let someone else handle it kind of guy."

He smiled and shrugged and lifted my knuckles to his mouth for a quick kiss. "Nothing else we can do. I figure we'll know in a few weeks whether it's a go, and until then, we'll just keep doing our thing."

I knew he was right, but I hated the fact that there was

nothing for us to do. I squeezed his hand until he looked at me and then I bobbled my eyebrows and shot a finger gun at him. In the cheesiest voice I could manage, I said, "Heeeyyy big guy, if you're in the mood for something you can control, you know I'll try just about anything once, and maybe more than once if you're lucky. Especially if it involves you completely naked." I winked. "That's the one time you're welcome to be the boss of me."

That made him laugh and he looked much more relaxed. "Despite the fact that I now feel like I've been propositioned by the world's sleaziest used car salesman, oddly enough, that sounds like an excellent plan. Let's get home and see how much you really like to be bossed around."

I threw both my hands in the air and yelled "Woo Hoo!" and Luke laughed as he turned onto my street. In a couple of minutes we were home, and then I proved to him that there are times that him being the boss of me was great for both of us.

14

<hr>

DESPITE OUR CONCERNS, THE NEXT FEW WEEKS FLEW by. I was way ahead on my columns, my latest article had gotten great feedback, and I had enough ideas for my TV gig for the rest of the year, so I was coasting through the fall. Luke, on the other hand, was freakishly busy. Because he was getting his business ready to start after the first of January, he had to get a business license, tax ID numbers, worker's comp coverage, liability insurance, pass a test for his Georgia contractor's license, get his corporation set up and registered, and get established with a bank. On top of that, he already had a waiting list of people who wanted work done, so he when he wasn't at school or at City Hall, he was putting together proposals for potential clients. Whenever I had time, I was helping him fill out paperwork and put together packets for the insurance companies and banks.

One night, Luke and I were hanging out after dinner doing some paperwork and we heard a knock on the door. We looked at each other, and he asked, "Were you expecting someone?"

I shook my head and Luke got up to answer the door. It was Bella. He stood back and motioned her in. "Hey Bella. Come on in."

She was grinning and danced into the house, punching both hands in the air and humming the theme from *Rocky*. "Hey. Sorry I didn't call first, but I have something to tell you." She could hardly contain herself. "Guess who I just got off the phone with?"

Luke and I looked at each other and he started laughing. "From your reaction, I assume you finally heard from Glenda?"

"Hell, yeah, I just heard from Glenda. Guess which two assholes are the new co-chairs for our fundraiser?" She didn't wait for our answer. "That's right, Glynn and Nicholai."

I jumped up to hug her and we hopped around yelling while Luke watched us and laughed. "Okay, Bella, tell us the details. How did you hook her?"

"Not just her, them. It was a carefully planned, diabolical plot that freakin' worked! Right after the news release, I had one of the local event planners call her and a couple of other people. She told Glenda—wait, Glynn, so I don't get mixed up--Glynn that she was one of the three people we were considering to be hosts of the gala, but we really weren't sure who we were going to pick, so someone would be in touch later. It turns out that as soon as Glynn got that call, she started campaigning with all of the local planners to try to get selected as host for the event. I told them to put her off until this week. I wanted her to have time to hear everyone talking about it so that she'd be dying for it by the time we made a selection. It totally worked."

Luke was concerned. "The planners don't know anything do they?"

Bella laughed. "No. No one knows anything, and I assure you that Glynn doesn't suspect a thing. I just got off the phone with her." She smiled. "She's the one who called me, by the way, and asked if we'd selected the host yet. I told her, 'That's so funny, I was going to call you later today' and that was it. She was hooked."

I was impressed. "Damn, Bella, you *are* a socialite whisperer."

Bella grinned. "Maybe so, but this wasn't even difficult. I told her that her fabulous abilities in fundraising and his oversight of the construction make them the perfect couple to head up the festivities. Plus, of course, they'd get a special award for all their hard work. Y'all would've been impressed at how thick I laid it on." She imitated herself fawning over Glenda in a sing-song voice. "'Oooh, y'all have worked so hard. The two of you are so wonderful. The two of you together have done more than anyone in Belize, St. Croix, and Puerto Rico combined...blah, blah, blah.' She totally ate it up."

Luke hugged her. "Bella, you're a rockstar. Thanks, so much."

She hugged him back and kissed him on the cheek as he released her. "It was my pleasure, Luke." She grinned at both of us. "Okay, so most of the big planning is being done as we speak, so all that's left is the details for the benefit itself. Now we all have to get together and finalize how, where, and when we were going to arrest them."

I grabbed my phone off the coffee table. "Is Sunday okay? We were planning on getting together at Mark and Sara's around four, anyway." Bella nodded. "Hang on, let's see if everyone's still available." I sent a text to Sara, Mo, and Lola and waited for an answer. "I was going to invite you so you could meet everyone, but this'll kill two birds with one stone."

Everyone confirmed they were still planning on meeting Sunday. I told Bella that we could pick her up if she'd like to ride with us, and she said she'd let us know.

Bella turned to Luke. "Do you think Agent Prince is available on Sunday?"

He shrugged. "I'll ask. Worst case, maybe we could all Skype or Facetime him while we are together. I know he's bringing one other agent with him to Puerto Rico, but he thought that having Daisy's dad there as backup would be a great idea. It turns out that Agent Prince's boss worked with Clayton before and had said that he would approve any paper-work to basically deputize him. I've already called him to ask if he'd like to come along as an official law enforcement agent, and he was thrilled to help out, so he'll be going with us, too. "

Bella agreed. "The more the merrier." She turned to me. "And Daisy, I love your dad, so it'll be great to have him there."

An alarm sounded, and Bella pulled out her phone. "Damn it. I've got to go." She shoved her phone in her pocket and turned to leave.

I opened the door for her and grabbed her hand as she headed out. "Bella, thanks again."

She squeezed my hand, smiled, and waved to Luke as she left. She called over her shoulder. "See y'all Sunday."

As soon as Bella left, I texted my Dad and told him we were getting together on Sunday at Sara's to go over details and asked him to meet with us. And by him, I meant just him, not him and mom. He said no problem. I thanked him and said we'd see him then. Luke texted Agent Prince and he said he'd be happy to Skype with us Sunday afternoon.

On Sunday, I spent the morning cooking for the week and I made some snacks for our four o'clock meeting at Sara and Mark's. Bella decided to drive herself, but the three of us got there right at four. Bella already knew Lola, Sara, and Mark, so I introduced her to Harrison and Mo. Mark was getting drink orders and I was setting up a tray with some of my cheese straws and cookies and a batch of red velvet cupcakes, which got me a big smacking kiss from Harrison as soon as he saw them, when I saw my dad come in. He greeted everyone, and then came across the room and hugged me off my feet. I had made him a batch of lemon blueberry scones, which are his favorite, and he happily settled on the sofa with a scone and some coffee. Everyone grabbed a snack and we settled in for an update from Bella.

"Okay, the gala is set up and ready to go. Our Puerto Rico organizers did a great job of finding a place and a group of caterers big enough to handle the size of the group, which looks to be somewhere between two and three hundred people. The good thing is that we're actually going to earn a ton of money on this benefit. We got the place and the caterer at a discount because no other group is doing anything like this right now, so they're desperate for business. The good part for us is everyone is coming because there are no other events right now." She nodded toward Luke and Lola. "With the amount y'all donated, the per plate amount from the dinner, and the amount from the silent auction, we should have enough to completely fund all of the projects we had proposed, plus a good bit more."

She looked at all of us. "So here's what we need to decide." She focused on my dad. "Clayton, when do you think is the best time to arrest them?"

He swallowed a bite of scone. "Well, since they're not violent types you've got options. Do you want to do it the easiest way, or do you want to have a little fun with it and maybe embarrass the hell out of them?"

Luke and Lola and I grinned at each other. I turned then and winked at Sara. "I think we should go for maximum damage and should just turn them over to Sara for a little alone time."

Sara nodded and everyone laughed, but my dad looked horrified at the thought. "That's a bad idea. We need to bring them back in one piece and I'm not sure I could explain that kind of damage."

Everyone nodded in agreement, and I said, "Okay, that's hilarious. That's exactly what Luke and Lola said."

Bella looked confused as she glanced over at tiny, innocent-looking Sara. Sara offered an angelic little smile, and then nodded with a shrug. "It's true. I'd tear his nuts off and then I'd kill that skank bitch where she stood."

We laughed at the expression on Bella's face, but all of us were used to Sara and her protectiveness toward everyone she loves. I once saw her kill a three-foot copperhead with her bare hands when it almost bit one of her kids. She left its body hanging outside on the fence so "his friends can see what I do to assholes that try to hurt my babies." I know Bobby didn't go over there for weeks after that incident.

Bella stood there looking at all of us, laughing and shaking her head. "Okay, so letting Sara take care of them is not an option, it seems. Clayton, what options would be safer?"

"Well, I'd say there's a couple of ways to do this. If y'all want to take them out with minimum fuss and effort, we can arrest them as soon as they get to Puerto Rico, or as soon as they get to the rehearsal. Bella, I'm sure y'all have a room backstage and you could get them both back there before everything starts. Prince and his partner could come in and arrest them there and no one will be the wiser. I'll just hang around in case they need me."

Luke looked at my dad. "Clayton, just out of curiosity, what if we did want to embarrass the hell out of them?"

My dad grinned at him and then winked at me. "I'll have to admit, that one kind of appeals to me. We could arrest them when they're onstage. As soon as they got the award, Prince and his partner could walk up and slap the handcuffs on them."

We all started laughing. That would be a pretty humiliating scenario for two people who are all about appearances. My dad was still turning it over in his head. "You'd have to check with Prince and his partner to see if they have any preference, but it shouldn't be dangerous or a problem for anyone." He turned to look at Bella. "Bella, what would you prefer? We know this gala is an important fundraiser for you. Would you prefer we do it behind the scenes, or wide out in the open so everyone has something to talk about?"

Lola pointed out, "You know they always say that any publicity is good publicity."

Every head turned to Bella to see what she thought. She shrugged. "Are you kidding? A huge scandal like that happening right in the middle of the party? I'm sure people would be talking about that for years. Check with Agent Prince, but whatever y'all want to do is fine with me."

Luke looked at his watch. "Prince said to call when we were all together, so we can find out right now what he thinks." He turned to Mark and pointed to the huge 70" television on the wall of the family room. "Didn't you say we can Skype on this thing?"

Mark grabbed the remote from the table next to him.

"Yep. That thing at the top is a camera, so the TV is basically a huge monitor." While Mark set up the TV, Luke texted Prince to tell him we were about to Skype him. Ignoring the raucous comments about how he and Sara probably used the camera to make 70" sex tapes, Mark took the number from Luke, and dialed Agent Prince's number. After a few confusing minutes, a tired-looking man in an FBI t-shirt and sweatpants answered the phone.

Luke introduced us all, and Prince acknowledged us with a weary smile. "Hey y'all. Sorry, I'm a little out of it. We just wrapped up a huge case last night and I came in today to finish all the paperwork."

"We won't take up much of your time." Luke outlined how the benefit was set up and asked Prince if he had any preference of when they should be arrested.

Prince thought about it for a moment and agreed with my dad that since they were white collar criminals and there had never been any evidence that they were dangerous, anything would work. He looked directly at Luke. "Luke, I know what they put you through and I've lived in New Orleans a long time, and it just pisses me off what they did. I would prefer to embarrass the shit out of them." He turned to look at my dad. "Clayton, you okay with that?"

My dad grinned. "Hell yeah. It's nice to have a job that we can have a little fun with." We all laughed and Bella told Agent Prince she'd get the event details and schematics of the building to him and my dad so they could make sure everything looked okay.

Prince looked at all of us. "Are all of you coming?"

We all looked at each other and then nodded at him. "That's not a problem, but if there was a chance that Glenda and Nick could recognize any of you from your college days, you need to stay out of sight until after the arrest."

Bella offered a solution. "There's a separate, smaller conference room we're using as a backstage office, so you can all stay in there until it's all over."

"That sounds great. Bella, just send over the details and the setup info and we'll finalize the arrest details when we get there. Otherwise, guys, see y'all at the beach." Prince waved and disconnected.

With that, my dad immediately stood and said he had to get home, so I hugged him and handed him a bag with the rest of the scones. My dad asked Luke to walk him out, and the rest of us stood around deciding what to do. It turns out everyone was either busy or tired, so we all agreed we'd talk later in the week. Bella left first, and we all hugged her goodbye and thanked her for all her help. Sara and Mark walked her to her car, Mo and Harrison went back to the living room to get their shoes and her purse, and Lola and I started toward the kitchen to put the leftover food away.

Luke was coming in the back door as I put the last of the cupcakes on a plate for Harrison. He smiled and hugged me from behind and kissed the back of my neck. "Hey baby girl. Those cupcakes for me?"

Lola plastered herself against Luke's back and hugged us both. "Or me?"

I laughed at their antics and told them that the cupcakes were for Harrison. Both of their faces fell. They are so pathetic. Like five year olds, they immediately brightened up when I told Luke I had extra at home and told Lola that her meals for the week were in the cooler in the garage and there were plenty of cupcakes for her, too. They both hugged me tight and thanked me excitedly, and I told them to let me go so I could finish up.

Lola let go and kissed us both on the cheek as she started toward the garage. "I gotta go. I've got a hot date with a big, dumb, pretty boy I met at the gym. If everything goes according to plan, I'm gonna take him to a nice hotel, wear him out, and then throw him out."

I rolled my eyes, while Luke shook his finger at her. "You just wait, Lola. One day you're going to find a man who will wear you out instead."

She stopped, turned toward him, collapsed back against the counter, and dramatically threw her forearm across her eyes. "Sadly, Luke that will never happen. Since you are already taken, I'm destined to roam the world alone and desolate." She straightened up, laughed and left, waving goodbye over her shoulder. "See ya."

Luke was shaking his head and chuckling. "That chick is a hot mess."

I agreed. "I know. She cracks me up." He helped me pack up the rest of the food while I cleaned the countertop and loaded the dishwasher.

"Did my dad have anything else to say?"

Luke studiously avoided my eyes. "Not much." He put the leftover cheese straws in a baggie and stuck it in my tote bag. I narrowed my eyes and looked at him and he sighed. "Fine. Look, it's not my idea, but..."

"Shit. I knew it. My mom wants to come, doesn't she? Who squealed? My dad?"

Luke looked pained. "No, it was actually Bella. Apparently, your mom is on her do-gooder mailing list, so she got the information about the benefit and asked your dad if he wanted to go and he couldn't really say no since he'll be there."

Damn it. "Does she know what all's going on?"

Luke shook his head. "No, she just knows it's a benefit

in Puerto Rico and, thanks to all the hype of being the event of the season, she wants to go and your dad said he'd take her. She doesn't know anything about Glenda and Nick and has no idea we're going or what's going on with us."

I looked him in the eye to see if he was lying. "Are you sure?"

He looked at me without flinching. "I promise, she doesn't know anything." When I still looked at him suspiciously, he rolled his eyes. "Daisy, think about it. If she thought you were going to a benefit for any reason, especially one that she's also attending, wouldn't she already have been bugging the shit out of you about a new dress, new hair," and now he scowled, "and smaller boobs?"

I relaxed. Good point. I will say this, the good thing about my mom is that she's been a cop's wife for a long time, so even if she found out, she'd never do anything to screw up an operation. That being said, she wouldn't hesitate to drive me freaking crazy, so I don't want her to find out what's going on. It's going to be bad enough with Sara and Lola, because those two won't rest until they have me trussed up in some fancy-ass dress, but if you add my mom to the mix, my life will be a living hell for the next few weeks.

Luke kissed my head, grabbed my tote bag, we yelled that we were out of there, and we went home. As soon as we got in, we took the dogs for a quick walk then went outside to sit on the glider together with a glass of tea and some leftover snacks. Luke grabbed a red velvet cupcake, took a huge bite, and looked around the porch while he chewed. "Hey, what would you think of letting me build you a fireplace or a deck for a firepit so you could use this place year round? I know you love sitting out here."

Awww. I leaned over to kiss him. "You are such a

sweetie, and I would love that. I'll tell you what, once this is all over, we'll do it." I patted his arm. "So, what do you think about all this? Just think...in less than a month, Glenda and Nick will be in prison and that part of your life will finally be over. You'll be ready to start with a clean slate."

He pulled me over and I snuggled against him, enjoying the cool evening air. He looked down at me with a serious look on his face. "You know, Daisy, as far as I'm concerned, that part of my life has been over for a long time. Now, I've moved here and hooked back up with all of my old friends from college, I'm starting a new business doing what I love, but without all the bullshit I hated, and I fell in love with someone I've known since I was a kid." He leaned over to kiss me and pulled back so he could smile into my eyes. "I'm so happy with my life just the way it is, that, no matter what happens with those two jackasses, I'm still the luckiest man I know."

I could feel my eyes tearing up, and I climbed onto his lap so that I straddled him and threw my arms around his neck and he wrapped me up in a big hug. I squeezed him so tight I could feel his ribs compress. We just sat like that for a while and finally we went in and went to bed.

15

SARA, MO, AND LOLA CAME TO PICK ME UP ONE
Saturday morning for brunch and shopping. They warned
me before we left that there would be no drunk shopping
and limited me to only one Bloody Mary. I told them that
brunch without alcohol was just some sad little breakfast for
people who don't get up early, but they didn't seem to care.

We went to Einstein's and sat out on their patio, where I
immediately ordered their eggs benedict special and one
extra-large Bloody Mary. Ha. If they were limiting me to
one drink, I was going to get my money's worth. The
weather was warm, sunny, and breezy, and we had a great
time, as always, but as soon as we were done with our meals,
Lola announced it was time to go, no hanging out for hours.
We had some power shopping to do.

Lola and Sara assured me that they knew a couple of
boutiques in Buckhead that had great dresses so we loaded
up in the car and headed out. I sat in the back seat, pretty
much pouting because I had to go shopping, wishing I'd
gone with the guys. "Okay, I'm doing this, but Lola, you
need to remember that I don't have your bank account and I

don't want to pay a fortune for some stupid dress I'll only wear once."

She turned around and shook her finger in my face. "Look, you are involved in an international caper, like one of those chicks in the movies. What if we end up in the paper? You are an international woman of mystery, and you need to dress like it." That made me laugh, as she intended. At that point, I decided I'd quit whining and get through it and, hopefully, it would all be over soon.

It wasn't soon enough for me, but it was fine. Thankfully, I found my dress at the first stop we made. The lady helping us saw me and immediately told me she had a perfect dress for me. It had been altered for someone else, but they accidently made it way too short. The person had big boobs and a big butt like me, or as the saleslady nicely put it, "was delightfully curvaceous," so it had been sitting on their sale rack for a while. Uh, yeah. I'm a very curvy 4'11", so I'm sure there aren't a ton of us walking in the door. She told me to try it and if it fit, she'd give me a great deal.

That dress fit like it was made for me. It was a beautiful sleeveless red dress with a low neckline, but it had some sort of miraculous built in bra that was obviously engineered for boobs like mine, because no matter how I moved or bent down, nothing was on the verge of popping out. The material was stretchy and sort of flowed instead of being clingy, so it was actually comfortable, and there was a slit up the front that was long enough to walk in easily, but not so high that I felt like my hoo hah was hanging out. As soon as my friends saw me in it, they all told me to get it. And the saleslady was right, she gave me a hellacious deal. Instead of it costing over eight hundred dollars, I paid two hundred and change. I told Luke later that the fact that I got a dress seventy five percent off at the first place I looked was a sign that Nick and Glenda were going to jail. He said he wasn't exactly sure that's how karma worked, but then he just agreed with me because it was easier. He's learning.

Three boutiques later, everyone found a dress, we all got shoes, and Mo even found a pair for me that was low-heeled and comfortable. Most importantly, we were done by three. I was thrilled. I told them they owed me another drink, and now I was hungry again, so we stopped in Inman Park for a little snack. We texted Bella and the guys and asked them to join us, but the guys had all decided to go to a bar so they could watch every SEC game at once and wouldn't be home till late, and Bella had a lunch date. We told them all to have fun and we spent the rest of the afternoon eating, drinking, and chatting about the gala.

Lola had talked to Bella earlier in the week, and Bella told her that Agent Prince confirmed that Glenda and Nick had booked flights and hotel rooms and were ready to go. Apparently, their flights were due in the night before the gala and then they were planning on staying for a couple of days afterwards.

We were arriving a few days before the gala and leaving the morning after. "Bella said they reserved all of our flights and rooms under the foundation's name, so our names won't appear anywhere on the official guest list."

Mo stole a strawberry off my plate. "So we'll just reimburse the charity after everything's over, or should we write Bella a check beforehand?"

I winced, knowing my news was going to cause an argument. "Uh, actually, Luke has already paid for everyone's flights and rooms, including my folks, so y'all don't have to worry about it."

Sara, Mo and Lola all fell silent and glared at me. I held

up my hands before they could start yelling and explained. "Look, Luke said that the only reason y'all are coming is to support him, so paying your way is the least he can do." They were all shaking their heads, and I continued. "He knew you would argue, so he said y'all could pay for all of our beer and food by the pool, so seriously, don't make it a big deal."

They each took a sip of their drinks while they thought. Finally, Sara pointed out, "If you're included in the deal, you're right. He may make out like a bandit. You can eat an assload of cheese and drink a lot of sangria."

"Right?" Whew. That was close. I smiled at each of them and continued. "Seriously, ladies, Luke appreciates your support more than you know, and he wants to do this, so I say let him." I took a sip of my drink. "He can afford it, and it's really important to him that he takes care of y'all. And if it makes you feel better, I promise to eat and drink as much as possible so all y'all will be totally screwed in this deal."

They all laughed and the tension drained away. Whew. That is, until Sara shot up straight in her seat. "Oh, shit. So your mom's staying at the same hotel we are? How are we going to avoid her seeing any of us?"

I rolled my eyes. "Wouldn't that be a nightmare? No, I specifically called Bella to make sure we weren't staying in the same hotel as my parents. There are three different hotels with blocks of rooms for organizers and guests. My parents are staying at one hotel, Bella is staying at the hotel where the event is going to be held, along with all of the organizers and event participants, including Glenda and Nick, and we're staying at the third one, which is a few hotels down the beach. Bella told my mom she'd asked my dad to help out with security and that's why the foundation is paying for their room, so she's perfectly happy with the situation."

Everyone looked relieved at not having to spend three days ducking my mom. That woman scares the bejesus out of all us.

Lola said that Agent Prince had said we just needed to stay out of sight. "He said to stay at the hotel, don't go wandering around Puerto Rico, stay off the beach, and he and his partner would keep an eye on Glenda and Nick as soon as they got there. Bella assured that she could keep them busy, so hopefully there won't be any surprises."

Sara looked thoughtful. "So basically, our job is to hang out at a hotel at the beach for a few days, get dressed up and sneak into a hotel for a gala, watch Luke help catch a couple of criminals that totally screwed him over, then come home the next day?" She shrugged. "Sounds like a productive weekend."

We all laughed. It was pretty simple. Hopefully, everything would end up going that easy.

16

The day we were leaving for Puerto Rico was a perfect Georgia November day, sunny, bright, and cool. Everyone met at Lola's condo and left our cars in her personal garage because she had hired a driver to take us to the airport. Apparently, she had just bought a limo company and hired one of her former clients to run it, and she said we were going to try out their newest car.

About that time, a huge white Hummer limo pulled up and a tiny, little, blond guy in a suit with a huge smile, who looked about twelve, jumped out and rushed to hug Lola. She hugged him back, told him that he and the car looked great, and introduced us to "her friend and business partner, Darrell."

We all piled in the car while Darrell and the guys loaded up the suitcases. I was sitting next to Lola, so I whispered, "Business partner, huh? Awww, has Darrell been lucky enough to find a fairy godmother to go into business with?"

She shrugged, looked very uncomfortable, and whispered back. "Shut up. It was strictly a business decision. I got the company from a client who owed me money and I gave Darrell a piece of the business to make sure he stays. I sure as hell don't want to run a limo company. Don't make a big deal about it."

I smiled and patted her arm. She's such a sweetie. I told her once she's like an M&M with a hard candy shell and a squishy, gooshy middle. That pissed her off because she likes everyone thinking she's all shell, no goosh. I leaned over and kissed her cheek. "Your secret was safe with me." She just rolled her eyes and tried to ignore me.

They guys got in and the trip to the airport was uneventful. We ended up getting to the gate with an hour and a half to spare. While we waited, Mo and I went to get everyone a Starbucks, and we boarded right on time. Three and a half hours later, we stepped off the plane into a beautiful, sunny Puerto Rican day.

It turns out that San Juan sustained only moderate damage from the hurricane, mostly downed trees and flooding. All of the hotels and businesses still had a few boarded up windows and you could see where some trees had sustained damage, but overall, we were surprised that everything was in pretty good shape. Power was on, the stores were open again, and it was business as usual, for the most part. We were all glad that the money from the benefit would do a lot to restore normalcy to the rest of the island, which had been absolutely devastated.

We all checked into our hotel and changed into shorts and bathing suits so we could go sit by the pool. There was an empty table and chairs with a huge umbrella, and we ordered lunch and a round of Bushwhackers, an ass-kicking frozen drink with rum and Kahlua, to celebrate. We had just sat down, when Luke and Lola's phones indicated they'd received a text. Lola took a sip of her drink and read the texts aloud. "Apparently Bella wants to make sure we got in okay, and Agent Prince said we should all meet in my suite around eight this evening. That good with everyone?" We all nodded and Lola texted them back, confirming the time. We hung out a couple of hours and then all split to go back to our rooms until dinnertime.

When we got to the room, we set an alarm to meet everyone for dinner, and opened the doors so we could hear the waves and feel the breeze coming off the ocean. Luke and I both stripped off our clothes, climbed into bed, and cuddled up together under the sheet. If you could ignore the small fact that we were here with the FBI to catch a couple of thieves, it was a very nice weekend for a quickie vacation.

I could feel that Luke was tense, and I rolled over to face him. He looked tired and stressed and I stroked his cheek and kissed him gently. "You okay?"

He smiled. "I'm fine. I haven't been sleeping that great and I'll be very glad when this is all over."

"Yeah, me too." I got the feeling there was something else. "You sure that's all that's going on with you?"

He snorted. "Is that not enough?" I raised my eyebrows and looked at him. He sighed. "Fine. Let me say first, I know how stupid this sounds, but I can't help it." He absently ran his hand over me as he spoke. "I actually feel bad about sending Nick to prison."

I was incensed and jumped up on my knees. "Are you crazy? After he ran off with your wife, stole $13 million, and left you holding the bag? Luke, he would have let you go to prison without even thinking about it."

He rolled onto his back. "I know that. I didn't say it was rational, I just said I feel bad. I mean, yes, he did all that, but he also took Glenda off my hands. And yes, he left me with a huge mess, but at least I wasn't in prison."

"No thanks to him," I interrupted.

"I know." He shrugged. "Look, it's just the way I feel. And I'll get over it, but right now, I feel bad for him. Nick was never a bad guy, but he had bad taste in women and they could convince him to do just about anything. I'm sure he was putty in Glenda's hands." He laughed. "And having to deal with Glenda all these years, trust me, he's had plenty of punishment already."

That made me laugh. "I see what you're saying, but truly, they both hung you out to dry. I have no problem making them both pay for what they did to you."

He pulled me against him and hugged me. "Thanks for being on my side, baby girl." He pulled back and looked at my face, smiling gently. "I love you."

I rolled on top of him, kissed him, and squeezed him tightly. "I love you, too." I dragged my hands down his sides and wriggled against him. "Want to fool around a little and then take a nap? I know a couple of tricks that might relax you."

He started laughing, rolled me over, and settled between my legs, kissing my neck until I basically forgot everything except him. As usual, he ran his hands all over my body, down my back, over my butt, between my legs, over my breasts. I started laughing. He raised an eyebrow in question as I snickered. "That cracks me up when you run your hands all over me like that. It's like you're taking an inventory of all your favorite body parts."

He shrugged and winked. "Hey, I just like to make sure all of my toys are exactly where they're supposed to be."

We both laughed and I hugged him tightly. He kissed me and slid slowly inside me, holding himself still and then he began to move.

Both of us tend to like fun, sweaty, active, laughing sex, but this was different. It was slow, and sweet, and tender, and very intense. We spent a lot of time looking in each other's eyes. He kissed me with these slow, deep, wet kisses, and the entire time he just moved against me slowly, grinding against me at the end of every stroke. I could feel every thick inch inside me, and I could feel myself getting closer and closer, but I didn't want it to end yet. I wrapped my legs around his waist so I could move against him, he put one hand under my hips and tilted me up and pulled me higher against him. He started moving slightly harder. I closed my eyes and writhed against him, rubbing myself against him, just focusing on his big body and the way he made me feel. After a few minutes of that, I could tell we were both getting close, and he told me to open my eyes and look at him. I love his expression when he's inside me, so intent and focused and like he can never get enough of me. We smiled at each other, he bent over to kiss me, he moved in me one more time, then harder, and that was it for me. I swear, sometimes, I really do see stars and that was one of those times. I could tell he was right there with me. My arms and legs fell out to the side and I splayed out over the bed with him collapsed on top of me. He managed to move his upper body slightly to the side so I could breathe, but both of us fell asleep just like that, with him on top of me and softer, but still inside me.

We must have been exhausted, because when the alarm went off that evening, we were still in the same position. My first thought was that I hope we weren't permanently stuck together. Yuck. I really needed a shower. I was still half asleep, and when Luke moved off me to go to into the bath-room, I rolled on my stomach to stretch and pulled the pillow over my head. A couple of minutes later, I heard the toilet flush, the water run in the sink, and the door shut, and then I felt Luke get back onto the bed. I pulled my head out from under the pillow and winked at him over my shoulder before I dropped my head back onto the pillow. He smiled, crawled on top of me and kissed my neck. Unlike me, it was pretty obvious that all of him was wide awake and ready to go, and our high level of grunginess didn't seem bother him at all. I grumbled. "Fine. But you're going to have to do all the work, and you're going to have to hurry."

He laughed. "Deal." He got up on his knees, pulled my hips up in the air, and moved behind me. It was fast, furi-ous, and a great way to wake up, I have to admit.

Whoever says they don't like quickies must not be doing it right. I don't know, I always kind of think of sex like that old joke about sex being like a pizza. When it's good, it's really good. When it's bad, it's still pretty good. We had just enough time to take a shower and get dressed and meet everyone downstairs in the restaurant.

Lola smirked when she saw us. "Hmmm, y'all look well rested."

I ignored her, but Luke winked at her. "Thanks for noticing, Lola." She winked back, and the hostess came to seat us at our table. As we walked toward the table, Sara grabbed my arm and looked at me, then questioningly toward Luke. I nodded, letting her know he was okay. She smiled, squeezed my arm, and went to sit next to Mark. When we were seated, Mark ordered us a bottle of wine and we settled in for a nice dinner. We had a couple of hours until we had to meet Bella and Agent Prince, so we decided not to discuss any business until they joined us. We just laughed and talked and enjoyed our dinner and each other's company.

We were upstairs in Lola's suite by eight o'clock, and we had just gotten settled when we heard a knock on the door. Lola opened the door and Agent Prince, Bella, my dad, and a man we didn't know came into the room. Prince introduced him as Agent Mike Spencer and we all sat down.

Prince started the meeting by giving us an update. "Well, it looks like everything is going according to plan. Glenda and Nick have confirmed their flights and their rooms and are due in tomorrow night. We checked with the airlines and neither of them have declared a weapon in their checked luggage, so that's not an issue."

Lola was curious. "Bella, have you heard anything from them?"

Bella snorted. "Oh, yeah. I texted all of the organizers and participants to make sure they had everything they needed and Glenda texted back and asked if we could make sure she had a few special items, specifically a bottle of chilled Champagne, a fruit basket, some chocolate truffles, oh, 'and please make sure the linens are all white and I prefer Egyptian cotton'."

We all laughed as Bella shook her head in disgust. "I was thinking, who does she think she is? J-Lo? This is a damn charity event, she's not performing at the Grammy's." She sighed. "But what I actually said was, that I would be thrilled to take care of that for her, and I was so excited they were able to do this with us." She shrugged. "Truth is, I'll kiss her ass as much as it takes to get her here and make sure this goes off without a hitch."

Mo clapped and cheered. "Yay, Bella! Way to take one for the team."

We all laughed as Bella took a bow. "Yay, me. But all

kidding aside, it looks like they're going to be here, as expected, and they don't suspect a thing."

Luke looked at all of us around the table. "Before we get started on a final plan, I've been thinking. Although embarrassing them would be a whole lot of fun for me, I think we should do whatever is the easiest and the least risky." He looked at Bella. "I don't want to do anything to screw up your fundraiser. Maybe we should just arrest them as soon as they show up to do the walk through that afternoon. It wouldn't be as embarrassing as arresting them in front of their friends, but I'm sure we could still have a little fun with it."

Prince and Spencer looked at each other and shrugged, and Prince spoke up. "Bella, Luke, it's up to you. The truth is, I don't think this will be a risky arrest, no matter what we choose to do. There's never been any indication that either of them are dangerous, they don't have any weapons, and there are three of us, plus the regular hotel security if we need them, so we don't have to worry about them getting away."

Lola offered a compromise. "Maybe we could have the best of both worlds. Bella, you're recording this, right? Agent Prince, what if y'all arrest them during the walk through? Y'all handcuff them, read them their rights, and while they're standing there, Luke, you can walk in and say a quick hello. People are going to wonder where they are, so maybe that evening, Bella can show the clip of them being arrested and tell everyone what happened."

Luke shrugged. "Sounds good to me."

Prince clapped him on the shoulder. "If that's what you want, that's what we'll do. But I personally am going to make this as uncomfortable as possible for them. I'll make sure when we handcuff them, we put them both on the floor. As prissy as she is, you know she'll hate it. Then, you can say whatever you want and we'll head out to the airport."

Bella smiled. "Y'all are going to miss a great party."

Prince winked at her as he grinned. "Bella, I have no doubt, but I promise we're going to have our own party back in New Orleans with these two." His smile faded. "We all lost something in Katrina, and we get special enjoyment out of dealing with assholes who profited from others' misery."

I turned to my dad, eyes wide. "Dad, you're staying for the party, right?"

I must have sounded more than a little panicked, because he put his arm around me and gave me a quick hug. "Of course. Your mother would kill me if we didn't stay for the party. You don't have to worry, I'll keep her off you for the evening." He leaned over to whisper in my ear. "But, you know she's not going to leave you alone until you're married again, so you might want to keep that in mind."

"Ugh." I rolled my eyes, he laughed and kissed me on the top of my head. He turned to Prince and Spencer. "Y'all just text me the time and place to meet you and I'll be there."

Agent Spencer smiled and stood up. "Will do, Clayton." He turned to Prince. "Ready to go?"

They waved goodbye and left with my dad.

The next morning, we met for brunch and spent the rest of the day hanging out at the pool, taking naps, and reading. We had dinner together, and all of us turned in early. That night, I don't think any of us slept very well. I know Luke and I didn't.

The morning of the gala looked to be a beautiful day.

Agent Prince had texted us all the night before and told us to meet downstairs for breakfast at seven-thirty so we could finalize our plans. Luke and I woke up at around five and couldn't go back to sleep, so we made some coffee and went out on the balcony. We wrapped ourselves in a blanket and lazily fooled around a little while we watched the sun come up.

I was sitting on his lap, cuddled against his chest, and we were quietly sipping coffee, watching the sun creep above the water. I'm not a huge beach fan, way too much sand in weird places for me, but I love watching the water. I turned to look at Luke's face and was glad to see he looked relaxed. "Nervous?"

He kissed my nose. "Nope. I'll be glad when this is over, though."

I nodded. "Me, too. I want everything to get back to normal. I don't think I'm cut out for international intrigue."

He smiled and kissed me then put down his coffee and put his arms around me, hugging me close. We sat like that until the alarm went off at 6:30. We went inside, took a shower, got dressed, and went downstairs to meet everyone for breakfast.

When we got to the restaurant, everyone else was already there, including Prince and Spencer, Bella, and my dad. Everyone was nibbling on pastries and drinking coffee, and I gratefully grabbed what seemed like my eleventh cup of coffee as we took the two remaining seats between Lola and Harrison. Lola slapped a croissant on my plate, Luke grabbed a bagel and we settled in.

Prince smiled at us. "Well, the good news is that Glenda and Nick got in last night, right on time and with enough luggage to dress the Kardashians. They checked in, they ordered room service, and they left a wake-up call for 9:30. We had already installed a microphone in their room to make sure there are no surprises, and I can say with a pretty high degree of certainty that they don't suspect a thing."

Bella was nodding her head. "I agree. They called me when they got in last night to ask me what time we're meeting for the run-through and I told them I'd meet both of them in the lobby at 11:00 and we'd walk over to the ballroom together. Glynn said no problem and they'd see me then."

Prince looked at my dad. "Clayton, let's head over there after breakfast to check everything out. We'll need to make sure all of the doors are secured except for the one that Bella's going to use when she brings them down. We'd also like you to drive us to the airport afterwards and wait with us until our flight, if you don't mind." My dad nodded and told him that would be fine.

The rest of us looked at each other and then we looked at Prince expectantly. Lola asked, "What about all of us?"

Prince looked at Bella. "Didn't you say there's a conference room that you're using as an office and storeroom during the event?" She nodded and he continued. "No windows?" Bella nodded affirmatively again. "Y'all can wait back there. Bella already has it wired so she and the other organizers can see what's going on when they're not onstage, so y'all can actually see when we arrest them." He looked at Luke. "Luke, once you see we have the handcuffs on them, you're welcome to come out and say whatever you need to say. Actually, all of y'all can come out. I just don't want them to see any of you until they're actually under arrest." We all nodded in understanding. No one wanted to be the one to screw this up.

We ordered breakfast, and as soon as we finished, Prince, Spencer and my dad left to do their preparation at the ballroom. Bella hung around long enough to tell us good luck and that she'd see us later and took off for her room. That left the rest of us sitting there. Harrison and Mark convinced Luke to join them for a quick workout in the gym and all of us ladies ended up in Lola's room on her balcony overlooking the ocean with a pitcher of mimosas. We figured a pitcher would allow us 1-2 mimosas each, maximum, so we wouldn't have to worry about being loud or tipsy, which, as Sara pointed out, wouldn't be good for an international caper. Obviously.

We were staring at the ocean, drinking our mimosas, each lost in our own thoughts. Lola broke the silence first. "Hey, Daisy, any idea what Luke is going to say?"

I was confused. "Say about what?"

"Say to Glenda and Nick. What the hell do you say to people who totally screwed you over and left you swinging in the wind? People you trusted? You're standing over them while they're lying on the ground in handcuffs. You have an opportunity to say whatever you want. What do you say?"

I took a sip and thought about it, then I just shrugged. "Hell if I know. What would you say?"

Sara snorted. "I wouldn't say shit. I would jump on their handcuffed bodies and tear their asses up. I'd..."

I looked at her with a deadpan expression. "You'd kill them with your bare hands like you did that copperhead and then hang their bodies on the fence so their friends would know what you do to people who try to mess with your babies?"

Sara gave a self-satisfied smile. "Exactly! I'd give them a message they'd never forget."

I rolled my eyes and finished the last of my mimosa in one big gulp. "Which is exactly why you will not be left alone with them. We want the rest of their lives to be extremely long and ugly, not extremely short and painful."

Sara shrugged. "Tomato, tomahto. So long as there's plenty of pain, I'm fine with it either way."

Mo hugged Sara and kissed her cheek. "I'm very glad you're on my side." She stood up, left the rest of her mimosa on the table, and waved to us all as she went inside. "Meet y'all downstairs in a little bit then we'll go meet up with Prince and Spencer."

We all said it sounded good and left for our respective rooms. When I let myself into our room, I could hear Luke singing in the shower and went into the bathroom to brush my teeth. I called out a greeting and was reaching for my toothbrush when he turned the water off and jerked the curtain open. He winked at me. "Hey baby girl, would you hand me a towel?"

I handed him a towel, and I heard him ask me a question, but I was having a hard time concentrating. Damn that man looks fine without clothes. I realized I was standing there staring, not listening, when suddenly a snap on my hip startled me. "Ow!" I rubbed my hip ferociously.

I realized he'd popped me with the corner of his wet towel. "Hey, I was asking you a question, goofy. Did you hear what I said?"

I was sulking, rubbing where he'd hit me. "No, I'm not listening to you, you big jackass. Why'd you pop me?"

He was drying off, laughing at my expression. "Because you were just standing there, gawking at my naked body and not listening to a word I was saying, ADD girl. I asked you three times if we're still meeting at a quarter to ten."

I told him yes and stuck out my tongue. He laughed and followed me when I walked into the room to change clothes. I pulled out a T-shirt, a denim skirt, and a pair of Teva sandals and started to change. He pulled on a pair of cargo shorts, no underwear, of course, an ancient Lynyrd Skynyrd concert t-shirt, and a pair of running shoes. Both of us were ready to go and headed downstairs at nine thirty.

By nine forty-five we were all assembled in the lobby. I called Bella and told her we were about to head over. Unlike me, Bella didn't sound nervous at all. "That's great, Daisy. If y'all go around to the back of your hotel, there's an employee parking lot that your hotel shares with this one. If you walk through there towards the back of this hotel, no one will see you come in. Just text me when y'all get here and I'll let you in."

It took us about ten minutes to get there, and it turns out she was already waiting for us outside the employee entrance. We followed her back to the conference center, my dad let us into the ballroom as soon as we knocked, and Bella walked us through the stage area and had us tucked away in her little, windowless, meeting room in no time.

Harrison and Mark pulled in some extra chairs so we'd all have a place to sit, and Bella spent a few minutes plugging wires into a big TV, and what I guessed was a recorder with a microphone attached to it, which was sitting in the middle of a round table. Suddenly, a picture came on and we could see Agent Prince waving at us.

Bella stood up and walked to the door. "I'll be right back, I'm going to adjust the camera." Within moments, we could see Bella walking across a stage to a podium and then she placed a microphone in a stand. A few seconds later, she rejoined us in the room, hit the button on the microphone, and spoke directly into it. "Testing, one, two, three. Mic check, check, check." We could see Prince and Spencer in their security guard uniforms, touching their earpieces and giving her a thumbs up. She checked the recorder to make sure it was recording both video and audio and then, apparently satisfied, turned to us.

"Okay guys, make yourselves comfortable. There are drinks in the cooler. Y'all lock the door behind me and stay put until you see Glenda and Nick get arrested and Agent Prince tells y'all to come in."

We all nodded that we understood. Mark asked her if she needed us to do anything like start the recording, but she said no. "Here's how this works. As soon as we turn the stage microphone on, this machine will start recording everything that's said on stage until I come in here and stop it. All y'all have to do is watch and enjoy." She pointed to the microphone with the button on the base. "If you need to say something to Prince and Spencer in private, just hit this button on the microphone and talk, and they'll hear it in their earpieces. It won't come through the big speakers, so no one but the two of them and Clayton will hear it." Her phone dinged and she looked at it with a pleased expression. "Well, speak of the devil. Glenda and Nick are heading down to the lobby. Here we go folks. It's showtime."

She texted back, "Meet you in the lobby in ten minutes," squeezed Luke's shoulder, and headed out the door. We saw Bella on the monitor as she stepped on the stage, turned on the microphone, and then we could hear everything as she, Prince, and Spencer went over the details. Yes, all of the doors were locked except the one from lobby, and my dad was guarding that door and letting people in and out. Yes, Prince and Spencer would be stationed on each side of the stage when Glenda and Nick got there, and they would quietly come down while they were doing the run-through and arrest them while they weren't paying attention. Yes, the backstage area was completely empty except for us, so there wouldn't be any interference during the arrest.

They all looked at each other and smiled, then Bella moved off camera as she left the ballroom to go meet Glenda and Nick. Agent Prince turned to the camera and said to us, "As soon as we have them on the ground and the handcuffs are on, all of y'all can come out. Luke, you can come over and talk to them, but it would be better if the rest of you stay back just so we can keep the area clear."

Luke leaned forward and hit the button to speak into the microphone. "No problem. We'll stay out of the way until y'all say to come on in." Prince smiled at the camera and gave us a thumbs up, and he went to take his place at the top of the stage.

We all looked at each other, all of us obviously nervous. Harrison started pacing, Mo and Sara were both chewing their nails, and I had to keep reminding myself to breathe. Mark moved to the cooler and handed us Cokes and then sat back down. We all absently took sips of our drinks, but mostly we were staring at the TV, just watching an empty stage with Prince and Spencer standing like statues at either end of the stage.

Lola, God love her, finally broke the tension. She hit the button on the microphone. "Is it just me or is this the most boring reality show ever?" We all laughed and we could see that Prince and Spencer heard the comment because both of them were smiling.

Suddenly, we could hear Bella's voice. "...Well, they're finishing the decorations this afternoon, so it'll be much more festive this evening. I just wanted to make sure y'all know where to stand, what y'all will be doing, and where I'll be in case you need anything. This will just take a few minutes to run through."

Luke was leaning forward and I could see the tension in his big body. I put my hand comfortingly on his leg, and he patted my hand absently as he stared at the screen.

Suddenly, there they were. Bella and Glenda and Nick, in the flesh. I realized that I had been holding my breath again, and let it out in a whoosh. When I heard "whooshes" all around me, I realized I wasn't the only one. We all smiled at each other in relief. They were actually here.

Luke leaned forward and focused intently on the screen, not moving a muscle, so tense it almost looked like he was vibrating. His eyes followed them as they moved around the stage.

Bella walked them to the top of the stage and pointed out where they would be standing. "Y'all will be standing backstage at first. We'll play a video that shows the damage from the hurricane and what projects we are raising money for, then tell everyone about how much money we've already raised, and how much work has been done. Then I'll tell them how y'all have been some of the primary organizers, and Nicholai, I will tell them how you've been overseeing the construction crews and how we couldn't have done any of this without your amazing help."

Bella moved out of the picture. "Glynn, Nicholai, y'all will walk in from backstage together and move to the podium." They followed her direction and went to stand at the podium. "Glynn, give me a sound check, just a 'testing, one, two, three', then Nicholai, please do the same." They both did as she directed. "Then, we'll present you with plaques and an award." She motioned to Prince and Spencer to come forward. "We're going to use you two to present the awards since you'll be all dressed up and looking pretty and you're already standing there. Please stand next to Glynn and Nicholai." Prince and Spencer moved in close to both of them, who didn't really notice how close they were standing because they were looking to Bella for additional direction. They also didn't notice that both men had hand-cuffs in their hands and were in a perfect position to easily overpower them.

And then it was too late. In a blur of movement, Prince and Spencer took Glynn and Nicholai down to the floor, and before either of them knew what was happening, they were both handcuffed with their hands behind their backs with two burly FBI agents kneeling beside them. My dad moved forward, close enough to get involved, if necessary, but mostly just helping to monitor the situation.

Glynn was the first to react. She immediately starting screaming and thrashing around, trying to get off the floor. "Do you know who I am? Bella, where are you, you bitch? What do you think you're doing? You don't know who you're messing with!"

Spencer and Prince hauled Glenda and Nick to their knees and kept them there. Agent Prince got right in Glen-da's face. "Oh, I know exactly who you both are. Glenda Mathis, Nicholas Watson, I'm Agent Prince from the New Orleans office of the FBI, and you are both under arrest for all kinds of charges. Fun stuff like false claims against the government; theft of government property; credit card, bank, mail, and wire fraud; and I'm sure there will be a few more by the time we're done. And here's the best part. Since the money you stole was disaster relief funds for Katrina, and since y'all ran to avoid prosecution, there's no problem with the statute of limitations, so y'all are still on the hook for everything you've done." He read them their rights, read them the official charges, and then smiled at both of them.

Glenda snarled at him. "Oh really? Well, I know my rights and I know that unless the FBI is working with another country's government, the FBI can only arrest us if we're on American soil. Well, you'd better be ready to let us go, because I don't see anyone here but you. This is Puerto Rico, not America."

Prince and Spencer looked at each other and laughed. Spencer took a dollar out of his shirt pocket and handed it to Prince who immediately waved it in front of Glenda's and Nick's faces and shoved it in his pocket with a smirk. "You were right. I said they couldn't be that freaking stupid that they didn't know that Puerto Rico is a U.S. territory, and therefore it is U.S. soil, but you were right. They are that freaking stupid."

Glenda started shrieking and screaming, trying to get away from Agent Prince, but he controlled her easily with his hand on the handcuffs. Spencer hauled Nick to his feet and he just stood there quietly looking at the floor. It was total mayhem for a few minutes as Prince let Glenda exhaust herself with her struggles, but she finally became quiet, too. Prince hauled her back up to her feet, and she stood there next to Nick, staring at the floor and shaking like a leaf.

While all that was going on, Prince had motioned for Luke to join them, so he had quietly come into the room, with all of us right behind him. We stood to the side as he slowly walked forward until he stood directly in front of them. He didn't say a word, he just stood there, waiting for them to finally notice him. When they did, and saw who it was, Glenda gasped and Nick dropped his head again, shaking it silently.

Luke stepped forward, crowding Glenda so she had to tip her head back to stare at him defiantly. He stared back at her and finally started speaking. "Glenda, I just wanted to make sure you know that I'm the one who found you, I'm the one who helped put this whole thing together, and I'm the reason you're going to prison. There's a special place in hell for someone like you that would steal money from people who are suffering, just to satisfy your own greed, and I knew that someday your actions would catch up with you. I'm just glad I could help. I'm also glad to know you're going to spend a lot of your miserable life exactly where you deserve to be. In prison. I'll see you when I come testify about exactly what you did to the people of New Orleans, and I hope that's where you'll serve your time." He winked. "They're gonna love you there."

He switched his attention to Nick, who avoided his gaze at first, but finally looked him in the eye. "Nick, I have to admit I kind of feel sorry for you, because I think karma already kicked you in the balls when you had to spend your last years as a free man with Glenda, but that's the choice you made. You were like my brother, but you screwed me over and you screwed over the people of New Orleans when you did what you did, so I think this is just karma serving up justice one asshole at a time. Good luck in prison." Nick just nodded once and dropped his gaze back down to his feet.

Luke turned his back to them and walked over to all of us. Everyone smiled at him, and he grabbed my hand and squeezed it. He turned back. "Do y'all need anything else from us?"

Agent Prince smiled. "Nope, we're good. Clayton's getting the car right now and we're heading to the airport as soon as he gets back." He smiled at Bella, who had joined our group. "Nice job, Bella. Thanks for all your help. I hope y'all make a ton of money tonight."

She smiled at him. "Oh, honey, trust me, we will. I'll make sure everyone knows what happened here and it'll add a little intrigue to the event. We'll make enough money to fund everything we need, I'm sure."

I guess Sara couldn't take it anymore. She strode up to Glenda and all of us immediately moved closer in case we had to grab her. When Glenda refused to bend down to talk to her, Sara narrowed her eyes, stood on her toes, grabbed a handful of Glenda's hair and pulled on it until Glenda was forced to bend down to her level. As Sara whispered urgently in her ear, Glenda's eyes widened, her face turned pale and she tried to back away from Sara with a fearful look on her face. Apparently, that reaction was good enough for Sara, because she smiled at Glenda and patted her cheek, and then backed up with a few parting words. "Bitch, I meant every word. You'd better hope you never see me again, because if you do, I promise you that's the last thing you'll ever see." We all stood there with wide eyes and our mouths open as Sara walked back over to us and cheerfully asked, "Y'all ready to go?"

We looked at her smiling little face and then looked at each other. She wasn't offering, and we weren't asking. Luke smiled back at her. "Sure, let's go get some lunch." He turned to Bella. "Bella, can you take an hour or so for lunch?"

She looked at her watch and told us to hang on one second. She called one of the other organizers and then hung up and turned to us, relieved. "Hell, yes, I can join y'all. I need a damn break. I'm not cut out for criminals and arresting people. Let me stick to my socialite wrangling and fundraising. That doesn't make me want to throw up from nerves."

We all laughed as we walked down the street to a restaurant overlooking the beach, totally relaxing for the first time in days. In Luke's case, probably weeks. Maybe years. We ordered our meals, we ordered drinks, mostly fruity, island-y drinks, and we ordered one of every dessert. It was a great time because all we did was unwind and laugh.

Suddenly, I had a thought. I shot up straight in my seat. "Hey wait a minute. We've already caught the bad guys, we've already donated money. Does this mean, we don't have to get dressed up and go to the gala?" I was crossing my fingers and whispering in my mind, "please, please, please," but everyone immediately said, "NO!" so emphatically that I knew I wouldn't have a chance of skipping out.

I sulked. "Fine." But apparently I looked pitiful enough that Bella actually felt a little sorry for me. "Hey Daisy, if it helps, this really is mostly a party. We are going to have awards and boring speeches, but that's thirty minutes, tops, and I will be talking about the arrest, which could be fun. Especially since I'm definitely going to show a little of that video, just to keep it lively. The rest of the evening is just eating and dancing and bidding on fun stuff, I promise. We have this amazing app that handles the silent auction, so you can bid all night on your phone, but you don't have to run around checking on the stuff you bid on. I promise, it'll be a fun night."

Luke grabbed my hand and squeezed it. "You said your dress is actually comfortable, and you don't have to wear makeup or heels if you don't want to." He kissed me and winked at me. "You look most beautiful just like this. You don't need any of that girly stuff if you don't want to wear it."

Awww. "Fine. I'll go." I tried to smile sincerely, but I'm positive I failed spectacularly. "I'm sure with Bella in charge, it won't awful."

Luke laughed and kissed me on the neck and Bella laughed at the look on my face. "Daisy, that's not exactly a ringing endorsement, but I'll take it."

I could feel my face turn red. "Crap. Bella, I'm so sorry. You've been so wonderful and I know my attitude sucks, but I promise it has nothing to do with you. Please don't take it personally."

Bella laughed. "Daisy, trust me, I know that dressing up and having to go to a gala isn't your thing." She gave me a quick hug. "I'm just impressed you're still coming." She waved to all of us as she left. "See y'all at six-thirty."

After lunch, we all went to the beach since we no longer were worried about being seen. We rented a bunch of lounge chairs and umbrellas and ran our poor waiter ragged ordering drinks and snacks. By about four o'clock, all of us had had enough sun and liquor, so we gave our sweet waiter a huge tip, we all went back to our rooms to rest awhile and said we'd meet in the hotel bar at 6:15.

Luke and I immediately fell asleep and when the alarm went off we both felt great. We got up and took a shower, okay a shower with a little action, and then we started to get dressed. I put on my version of fancy makeup, which is bronzer, a little mascara, and some lip gloss, and enough product in my hair to keep it long and in ringlets, hopefully preventing it from ending up in a sweaty ball on top of my head by the end of the night. I finished my very limited makeup and hair routine and left the bathroom to get dressed. Fortunately, I was just in time to see Luke putting on a beautiful, off-white linen suit with slip on shoes and no tie.

I stood there with my mouth open. When I finally could speak again, I croaked out, "Sweet baby Jesus, Luke, you look amazing." I came closer and circled around him. "Seriously, you look like one of those gorgeous, badass, drug lords in some Miami cocaine movie."

He rolled his eyes and his cheeks turned red. "You're ridiculous." He came over and pulled me close to him. "I like your outfit better. Naked except for lip gloss."

I pushed against him. "Back away from the nakedness and the lip gloss. I've got to get dressed and you distracted me."

He laughed and kissed my forehead, then gave me a swat on the butt. "Fine. Got get dressed and I'll check the football scores while you finish up."

He turned on the TV and I grabbed my clothes and went back into the bathroom. I put on my slinky new light control panties courtesy of Ms. Spanx, which I'm sure is not her real name, and stepped into my dress. I fastened the halter top, and made sure my boobs were seated securely in the low neckline, put on my low, sparkly heels, and walked out to the living room to show Luke. He must have liked it, because when I said, "Ta da!" twirled, and struck a pose, he didn't say a word. He just stared at me with hot eyes, running his eyes over my chest, and standing up and walking around me to look at my butt, which I have to admit did look good in that dress. He reached for me, but I slapped his hands away. "Sorry bud, don't mess with the dress. You're going to have to wait till tonight."

He completely ignored me and backed me against the wall. He pinned me there and kissed me thoroughly, the whole time grabbing my butt with one hand and sliding a hand into my low neckline with the other.

By the time he let me go, he had almost changed my mind about heading downstairs. Fortunately, I caught a glimpse of myself in the mirror and gasped. My lip gloss was gone, one boob was halfway out of my dress, and I looked like I'd just rolled out of bed. Somehow, I found the strength to back away. I held a hand out protectively in front of me and started backing toward the bathroom. "Get away from me, Luke Mathis. If y'all are making me go to this party, I don't want to look I just got laid in the elevator."

He started laughing, and raised one eyebrow as he started slowly advancing toward me. "Come on Daisy, you're already a little messed up. A little more isn't going to hurt. Just a couple more minutes."

He pretended to try to grab me and I let out an embarrassing squeal and I bolted for the bathroom, slamming and locking the door behind me. I could hear him laughing on the other side of the door.

I got the dress back in place with everything tucked in and put on some more lip gloss. When I opened the door, I gave him my best stinkeye, which made him laugh, so he offered his arm and we left to meet everyone in the bar.

When we got there, the other guys were already there watching a football game. They all looked very handsome in their island finery. Mark had on a light gray linen suit, and Harrison was wearing a traditional guayabera, a formal Mexican wedding shirt, and a pair of lightweight pants. I batted my eyes at all of them and told them all they were the handsomest men I'd ever seen. They just rolled their eyes and laughed a little uncomfortably, which cracked me up, and we went back to watching the game.

The other ladies came down right on time, and they all

looked beautiful in their dresses. Sara and Lola were in black, but where Sara's was slinky and formfitting, Lola's had an empire waist with chiffon flowing to the floor that made her look like a queen. Mo's dress was green and hugged her long, toned, frame like it was made for her. All of the guys stood up and said that we would be the four most beautiful women at the event. We all smiled at each other, the guys and I chugged the rest of our beers, and we left for the gala.

Bella was right. We all had a blast, even me. When Bella first came out to start the evening, she said that, before we got started, there had been a change in plans and Glynn and Nicholai weren't going to be the hosts for the evening. She gave a quick summary of what happened and then dimmed the lights and put up a short video of them being slammed on the floor and handcuffed, Glynn screaming obscenities and ranting about Puerto Rico not being part of America, and then the part where Agent Prince read them their rights and all of the charges against them.

When the lights came back up, the room was dead silent and everyone was frozen in shock. Bella shook her head with a disgusted look on her face. "You know the worst part was that they stole the money from hurricane victims. The money they took was supposed to rebuild a levee near the Ninth Ward, the poorest area of the city, and when they took that money, they didn't care what happened to those people." She paused theatrically. "Those poor people were in the exact same boat we're in right now, and she and her husband had the nerve to act like she cared what happened to Belize and Puerto Rico and the Virgin Islands." She paused again. "I say good riddance, and I hope they rot in jail, and then rot in hell." Everyone started clapping, Bella rubbed her hands over her face and took a deep breath to compose herself.

"Okay, enough of this. Let's get down to business. We know how to raise money, we know how to get things done, and tonight is all about making sure that Puerto Rico, St. Croix, and Belize can return to normal as soon as possible. Let me show you what we've already accomplished."

The lights went back down and the video was very powerful, showing the storm damage, what rebuilding had already been accomplished, how much money had been raised, and how much more was needed. The lights came back up, and Bella immediately began giving awards to those in the audience who had helped the most. As she promised, the business part of the evening was over in less than a half hour. She announced where we could look at the items for the silent auction, reminded us that any items could be shipped to our homes, and then motioned for the servers to start bringing in the food. The DJ cranked up, and by eight o'clock, the place was rocking.

Even my mom was in a fabulous mood. She walked up to where we were all sitting, a large, almost empty, glass of wine in her hand, and I braced myself for her opening remarks. Instead of an immediate verbal attack, she smiled at everyone and came over to give me a hug. She pulled back and ran her hand over my still-controlled curls. "Daisy, you look so pretty and I love what you've done with your hair."

What?! I actually looked behind me to see who she was talking to, and Lola kicked me under the table and muttered for me to shut up and be nice. I felt completely disoriented. I whispered out the side of my mouth. "Holy shit, how much of that wine has she had, Lola?"

Lola shrugged at me and whispered back. "Shit if I

know. Maybe it's the type of wine. You need to find out what that is and invest in the winery."

I nodded my agreement, unable to look away from the sight of my mom being both supportive and non-judgmental. She hugged Luke and kissed him on the cheek. "Clayton told me the whole story and I'm so glad those horrible people are in jail, and I hope that now you can move on with your new life."

That's more like it. I relaxed as I waited for the next comment that now we could get married, or now he could accompany me to a new class to learn how to dress, or he could convince me that a breast reduction make me look fabulous, or something. But nothing.

She took a careful sip of her wine and smiled at everyone else. "And the rest of y'all look amazing." She tipped up her glass, finished her wine and put the empty glass in the middle of the table as she smiled at each of us. "Well, I hope y'all enjoy your evening. I'm going to go find some of my friends from Atlanta, and," she patted me on the head. "Maybe find your Daddy so we can do a little dirty dancing. Y'all have fun and I'll see all y'all when we get back to Atlanta." And she spun effortlessly on her high heels and left. No parting shot, no passive aggressive comment, nothing. Just a wave over her shoulder and she was gone.

We were stunned. And now I was seriously getting worried. "What just happened? Did y'all see that? Did anyone else just hear my mom compliment me on my hair? Should we tell my dad? Do you think she's had a stroke or something?"

Mo shook her head and pointed out my mom dancing with my dad. "She looks good to me."

I was afraid to turn around. "She's not really dirty dancing with my dad, is she?"

They all laughed, so I turned to see her looking happy and healthy. I was still doubtful and made a note to check on her next week after we get back to Atlanta. And possibly sign her up for a neurological workup and some kind of brain scan. At the very least, I'm going to buy her about twelve cases of that wine.

Between us dancing, drinking, and eating, Sara, Lola, and Mo stayed busy bidding on funky jewelry and artwork. I won a set of cookware and some new wooden utensils for my kitchen, and started trying to win a pair of custom cowboy boots for Luke. Harrison was bidding on a week at a vacation rental house in Florida, and Mark told us he was determined to win a custom shotgun.

The guys eventually took a break to go check the football scores, and Sara and Mo went to the bathroom and to take a look at the desserts. Lola and I were hot and wanted to cool off, so we each grabbed a glass of wine and went outside and stretched out in two lounge chairs by the pool.

"How's Luke?"

"He's fine. Glad it's over."

She nodded. "Yeah, me too." She turned on her side so she faced me. "So, now that this is all over, what about y'all? What's the plan? Are y'all going to move in together or get married anytime soon?"

I shrugged. "I don't really know. There's been so much going on with all this and his new business that we haven't really talked about it." I rolled over so we were both facing each other. "Truth is, we love each other, and I definitely want us to live together, but I don't know about the whole marriage thing. I don't know what I think. I'm certainly not in any rush."

Lola smiled. "That makes sense. Would you marry him, if he asked?"

I didn't even think about it. "Yep. In a second."

We grinned at each other and went back inside to rejoin the rest of the group. We hung around for another couple of hours, which was just enough time for me to slip in a final bid and win the custom boots for Luke. By the end of the evening, Lola had bought a custom designed necklace from a local artist, Sara and Mo each had a couple of paintings and some really fun jewelry, Mark had his shotgun, and Harrison had won a five-day vacation rental in the Florida Keys for ten people.

By the time the auction ended, we were all tired. Bella came out to thank everyone and said that, although the numbers weren't final, they had already surpassed all of their goals and all of the projects would be fully funded. She thanked everyone, told everyone good night, and asked the winners to come fill out the shipping forms for the silent auction items. We got in line, paid for our items, arranged for shipping, and went to find Bella before we left.

Bella was standing by the door, thanking everyone, and saying her goodbyes. She looked beautiful, but exhausted, then Luke walked up to her and hugged her off her feet. He let her go and stepped back so he could see her face. "Thank you for everything, Bella. None of this could have happened without you."

She was embarrassed and waved it off. "Glad I could help. It couldn't have happened to two nicer people than Glenda and Nick."

He grinned. "Well, I have some other good news. I just got a text from Prince and Spencer and they wanted us to know that they all landed safely and Glenda and Nick are now in a jail cell in New Orleans. It should be on the national news, and it's all thanks to you."

She smiled and patted his cheek. "Thanks for letting me know. That's a great ending to a great evening." She waved to all of us. "I'll see y'all when I get back to Atlanta." We all waved goodbye, grabbed a shuttle van, and went back to our hotel.

It was a beautiful night, breezy with a full moon, and we decided to go back to Lola's room to sit out on the balcony overlooking the water. Mark made us drinks with some rum that Lola had bought in a drugstore across the street, and we settled in to watch the waves and relax.

I had my bare feet in Luke's lap, he was idly rubbing my feet with one hand and sipping on his drink with the other. Mo hesitantly asked Luke how he was doing, and he thought about it for a moment.

"You know, it's really weird. It doesn't feel real. I thought it would be some big deal when they were arrested and hauled off, but it really doesn't feel any different." He took another swig of his drink. "Don't get me wrong, I'm certainly happy about it, but the actuality was kind of anti-climactic."

Lola was sitting on his left side, and she turned to see his expression. "What do you mean? You didn't feel any closure after they were arrested? Was that not a good thing?"

His answer was immediate and he rushed to reassure her. "No. No, it's a great thing and I'm really glad those two are finally having to face the consequences of what they did." He took another sip of his drink. "I'm very glad they're behind bars, and I'm extremely glad this is all finally over. But really, I told Daisy the other night, for the most part, I moved past all this a long time ago." He smiled and tipped his head back, enjoying the sea breeze against his skin as he thought about what he was trying to say.

He looked at everyone, and smiled. "I'm in a new city, and thanks to all of you, I'm around people I love and care about every day, and I'm about to start a new business. Everything in my life is new and exciting, and all this other stuff is just old bullshit I left behind when I left New Orleans. I'm just glad that, except for testifying in their trial, that chapter in my life is over."

"I doubt that you'll ever have to testify," Lola predicted. "It would be tried in the U.S. district court for the eastern district of Louisiana, which is right there in the middle of downtown New Orleans. The evidence against them is pretty extensive and, trust me, you wouldn't want to be on trial for stealing Katrina funds in the middle of New Orleans. I'll bet they'll do some kind of plea deal."

Luke looked at her skeptically. "I'm sure that's what Nick will do, but I can't imagine Glenda will go to prison willingly."

"She'd better," said Lola. "Mayor Nagin got ten years for the shit he pulled, some lady politician just got five years, and some scam artist chick got 43 years. She'd better take the best deal she can get because those prosecutors aren't playing."

"Will they end up in that cushy low-security prison where Nagin ended up?" Mo asked.

Lola shrugged. "Who knows? I'm not sure what's available. I know Glenda can't go there, because that's a men's prison, plus it's low security with no fences. They've already proven to be a flight risk, so I'm thinking that will not be the prosecutor's recommendation. They'll probably end up in some medium-security federal prison somewhere in the South." Lola smiled and held up her drink in a mocking toast. "Maybe they'll sentence Glenda to one of the work camps. That would be a perfect hell for her, wouldn't it?"

We all laughed. Luke was shaking his head at the thought. "I can assure you, she will not be one of those let out early for good behavior. If she gets in trouble every time she mouths off, that mean bitch may be there the rest of her life."

He stood up and held out his hand for me to join him. I stood up and took his hand and he pulled me in close and put his arm around my shoulders. "And on that note, I'm ready to call it a night." He turned us to face everyone. "Thanks for coming with me. It really means a lot to have all y'all here and I appreciate it more than you know." We started toward the door as everyone said goodnight.

When we got to our room, Luke was still quiet. When I asked him about it, he just said he was tired and wanted to grab a shower and get some sleep. We took a quick shower, dried off, got in the bed, and Luke rolled on his back and cuddled me up to his side. He didn't seem stressed, but I figured that he had been through a hell of a day, so I decided to finish it off with a bang.

I rolled over and sat up so I could see his face. He looked at me and raised an eyebrow. "What's on your mind, Daisy?"

I smiled at him. "Well, you've had such an exciting day that I wanted to make sure it had a great ending..."

"Would that be happy ending?" He asked, bobbling his eyebrows and winking at me as he laughed.

I wrinkled my nose at him and stuck out my tongue. "Well, yes, as a matter of fact, that would be a happy ending, but I also have another surprise for you." I showed him a picture of the cowboy boots I'd won for him. "You get to pick the colors, the type of leather, everything, so I hope you like them."

He looked at the picture and grinned. "Daisy, I love these. Thanks so much." He pulled me down over his chest so he could kiss me.

I kissed him back, and then put my hand on his chest and pulled back up. "Wait, I have another surprise. Well, actually, it's a question. And it's on a totally different topic." I took a deep breath. "Would you like to move in with me?" Before he could say anything, I started babbling. "I know your lease is up in January, and I didn't want you renew it because I wanted you to move in with me instead. Well, actually, I'd like you to move in now, even though you'd have to keep paying your rent for another month or so..."

He put his finger on my lips to shut me up, and I stared at him with big eyes. He pushed up on one elbow and looked into my eyes. "Daisy, are you sure about this?" I nodded emphatically, his finger still against my mouth. He smiled slightly, and it turned into a grin. "Really?"

I pulled his finger down and grinned back at him. "I'm totally sure. We're practically living together now, but I think we should make it official." Then I frowned at him. "But I've been thinking about it and we're going have to add some stuff to the house. It makes the most sense money-wise to run your business out of the house, so you need an office."

He started laughing. "My Daisy is always so practical." He sat up and faced me on the bed. "First, let me be clear. I would love for us to live together, so yes, I would love to move in with you. As soon as we get back, not when my lease is up. I was hoping you'd want us to eventually live together, but I'm really excited you want to do it so soon."

He looked a little embarrassed. "Actually, I think I've figured out something that will work great for both of us. I started out just trying to expand your screen porch, but I kind of took off with a couple of other ideas while I was playing with the plan. Check this out." He jumped off the bed and went across the room to grab his laptop, and came back to sit down again, tapping on the keys as he spoke. "I drew up a plan last month, and I figured I'd show it to you when this stuff was all over." He turned the laptop around and pushed it towards me. "And, since it's all over, I think now would be a great time."

I looked at the plans, stunned at his ideas. "See?" he pointed to the drawings. "I can expand your office out into the backyard to give us enough room to make two offices and I'll put a barn door between our areas so we can leave it open or close it off, whatever we want. With the extra space, I can also expand the screen porch and I'll put a little fireplace on the far end so we can sit outside when it's cold."

It was beautiful and I just stared at it, picturing how the space would work and how the new extension would fit in the backyard. I still hadn't said anything and he frowned. "Daisy, this is just an idea. If you don't like it, we can change whatever you want to change."

"No."

He started to look worried. "No? What the hell does that mean? No, you don't like it? No, you don't want to do it?"

I placed my finger over his lips like he'd done to me. He stared at me, concerned, and I smiled at him. "No, I wouldn't change a thing. This is gorgeous and I love what you've done with the screen porch and the fireplace. When you reconfigure our offices, you think you can make it so the entire wall can open onto the screen porch with big French doors?"

He grabbed the laptop from me and slid it onto the

bedside table. "Baby, we can do it however you want it. Hell, I'll add a porch all around the back of the house, if you want, you just tell me what you want and we'll figure it out."

He grabbed me and rolled us over so he was on top of me. I smiled up at him. "I've already got what I want. You. The rest of it is just gravy."

He kissed me and pulled back so he could see my face. "You're right, baby girl. This is a very happy ending."

17

So, as soon as we got back to Atlanta, Luke moved in.

It was the easiest move ever, because he still doesn't own anything. When he moved to Georgia, he wanted a fresh start, so he sold his house fully furnished and walked away with a rocker from his grandmother and some personal pictures, his clothes, and a ton of tools, and that was it. We put the rocker in the living room, hung his clothes in the closet with mine, and that was it. He was moved in.

He taught his last class in the middle of December and on January third he officially opened his new business. He had leased a warehouse to store tools and materials and his new work truck in, but he needed space for his office, so he said his first order of business was to get our house in shape. For the next six weeks, we were overrun with him and his crew, so the house was a loud, muddy mess, but at the end of it all, the addition was even more beautiful than I imagined. Our office was wonderful, with built-in bookshelves, work areas that could be closed off to hide any mess, and a barn door to separate the two areas, if necessary. The screened porch was straight out of a designer magazine with a small, stacked stone fireplace on one end, a built-in fridge and sink, and an enormous TV designed for use under a covered porch. I'd seen a swing that was basically a suspended twin sized bed with a wooden frame around it, and Luke had made one for me and he and the dogs and I had spent hours hanging out on that thing. Luke had even managed to find room to give me a bigger pantry and a very small laundry room, so we could get a full-sized, high-efficiency washer and dryer. With his line of work, there's always a ton of very large, very dirty laundry to do, so the laundry room was a welcome addition.

He bought a new desk and an Aeron chair like mine, and he was ready to go. We went shopping and bought some nice patio furniture for the new porch and some new furniture for the living room. He had never complained, but I knew my living room furniture was too small and girly for him, so we bought furniture that was a little more macho, and I sold my old stuff to one of Mo's sisters whose daughter was moving into her first apartment. It worked out great for everyone.

Luke loves his new business, and the only problem he's having is that he's already having to turn work away. He knows that if he's not careful, he'll end up with a huge business again, and that's not what he wants. He's got a list of contractors whose work he likes so he can refer out any business he doesn't want to handle himself.

I ended up writing a story for the paper about Nick and Glenda's saga and it was very well received, but investigative journalism is not my thing, so I've just been sticking with my column and an occasional fluffy story, much to my dad's disappointment. The good news is that my column is being syndicated in a bunch of new papers, so I'm making more money than ever for the same amount of work, which is awesome.

I quit my TV gig, though. The TV station I work for changed management and I wasn't crazy about the changes they were making, so I gave notice. I'm not the only one. Billy Ray left to work for a local company that produces films for pro sports, which should be right up his alley, and Mandy's husband got a job in Charleston, so she's going to produce for the local affiliate there. It's a lot of changes, but in the end, I'm still just writing my column, hanging out with my friends, and living with Luke, so my life is pretty great.

Luke and I discussed the fact that we didn't want to drift apart like Bobby and I did, so we've made a real effort to spend quality time together. We both take off early on Wednesday afternoons to do something fun, we eat dinner together almost every night, and we spend a lot of time together with our friends. We do some things separately, of course, but not most things. We've really happy.

So when Luke seemed uncharacteristically stressed one Wednesday in April when we were working together on the porch, I was concerned. Obviously, something was bothering him, but I had no idea what it could be. I figured he'd tell me when he was ready, and finally, he put down his laptop and turned to me. Out of the blue, he asked, "Daisy, how do you feel about the way things are with us?"

What? That's not what I expected and I looked over at him, concerned. "I don't like the sound of that. Do we have a problem?"

He looked confused. "No. That's not what I meant at all." Then he started to look annoyed. "Why? Do you think we have a problem?"

I sat up, faced him and placed a conciliatory hand on his chest. "Hang on, buddy. Let's stop here a minute." I reached up to pat his cheek. "I think we're great. I love you, I love living with you, and I love the life we've made with each other. I think everything is great." I reached up to hug his neck and squeezed him tight. He hugged me back and finally I pulled back to look into his face. "Now what has you so freaked out?"

He took a deep breath and grabbed my hand. "Sorry I'm nervous and I overreacted. I just wanted to talk to you about something. Well, ask you about something."

I looked at him. It was weird to see him so flustered. "Look, there's nothing you can't ask me, so just ask."

He nodded. "Okay, then." He took a deep breath, grabbed my left hand in both of his, and squeezed it while he stared in my eyes. "Daisy, I've been so happy since we've been together. I think you're the kindest, most fun, beautiful person inside and out I've ever met and I can't believe we were lucky enough to find each other." He looked at me with a beautiful smile and an intent look on his face. I felt him slide something on my finger. "I love you and I want to know, baby girl, will you marry me?"

What? I was speechless. I looked at him, then I looked down at my finger, which now featured a beautiful antique platinum filigree band with tiny diamonds spaced all the way around it.

I finally choked out a strangled, "What?"

He started laughing. "I asked if you wanted to marry me. I'm hoping by 'What?' you mean yes."

My mind was blank. We've never talked any specifics about getting married, so this came totally out of left field, and I was confused. I looked at the ring. It was beautiful, so I squeaked out a question. "Where'd you get the ring?"

"It was my great-grandmother's wedding band. I know you're not a big jewelry girl, and you're always cooking and using your hands, so I thought you'd like something that didn't get in your way. Plus it's so pretty, I thought you'd like it. My great-grandmother left it to my mom, and she and I thought it was perfect for you." He started to look nervous. "Daisy, if you don't like it, we can get something else."

I curled my hand protectively over the ring and shook my head. "Over my dead body, big boy." He started to smile. "Let me start over. What I mean is yes. Yes, I love you, and yes, of course, I'll marry you. And yes, I love this ring. It's perfect. It's so delicate and so beautiful, and I love the fact it was your great-grandmother's." I looked up at him. "I'm sorry for the delayed reaction. I was just shocked. We've never really talked about getting married."

His eyes widened. "You've never thought about it?"

"Well, of course I've thought about it in general." I said. "Honestly, I always figured we would eventually, but I didn't know you were thinking about it happening soon. And I sure didn't know you had done all this." I was curious. "Did you talk to my dad?"

He nodded. "Last week. I called him and stopped by his office to ask for his blessing. He assured me your mom wouldn't spill the beans, but he knew I was asking you today, so I promised you'd call them as soon as I asked." He shrugged apologetically. "So you'll have to give her a call today or I'll be on her shit list."

Fine. I grabbed my cell phone and called my mom to get it over with. As soon as she picked up, I took a deep breath. "Hey Mom. I just wanted to let you know that Luke asked me to marry him and I said yes."

She sounded genuinely happy for me. "Congratulations, honey. We're so thrilled for both of you. Call me later this week and we'll all get together for dinner."

"Okay. Thanks, mom. Love y'all and we'll see y'all next week."

"Great. Love you, too."

I hung up the phone, completely baffled. "What the hell? Luke, I'm really starting to get worried. There may be something bad wrong with my mom."

He looked concerned. "Why? Did she sound weird? Did she sound like something was going on?"

"She just congratulated me and told me she loves me and we should get together for dinner. No interrogation about a big wedding, no comments about having to get a fancy dress or doing something with my hair." I started pacing. "Luke, that's the second time my mom has surprised me by not acting like herself. I'm not used to her being supportive and normal and I don't like it. It's freaking me out."

"Maybe your dad talked to her and she decided to turn over a new leaf."

I was doubtful. "Maybe."

"What else can you do other than go with it and enjoy the change for however long it lasts?"

He was right. But I'm still going to pay close attention next week when I see her. Maybe check to make sure she doesn't have any odd marks or new tattoos. I've seen those alien movies.

My excitement level started to tick up. I told Luke I needed to let the gang know what was going on, so I took a picture of the ring on my hand and texted a quick group message. "Guess who's getting married. Details later. XOXO" and turned off my phone.

Both of us agreed we wanted something very small and

casual with just our friends and immediate family. I suggested the two of us should go to the courthouse and then have a big party later, but Luke suggested that maybe we could have a beach wedding, since he'd been to his cousin's wedding at the beach and she said there's no waiting period in Florida for non-residents. That all sounded great to me, so I told him we'd figure it out later and for now, we should seal the deal the old-fashioned way.

Luke laughed and put out his hand. "A hearty handshake?"

I took his hand and stuck it under my Tshirt as I climbed onto his lap. As I threw my arms around his neck and went to kiss him, I told him, "Well, we can certainly start with that.

EPILOGUE

WE GOT MARRIED A FEW MONTHS LATER ON THE BEACH in Key Largo.

We were all together one evening, trying to decide where to have the wedding, and Harrison pointed out that the vacation rental house he'd won at the auction was right on the beach. We looked up the listing and saw that it had an enormous deck that ran the entire length of the house, and, according to reviews from previous guests, the sunsets from the deck were absolutely stunning. Harrison and Mo suggested we have our wedding on the deck at sunset and then have a big party afterwards. That sounded great to us, so Harrison called and it turned out that the owners had a cancellation for Labor Day weekend, so we booked it.

The best part for me, well, other than marrying Luke, was that we didn't have to dress up. Everyone was going to wear a white t-shirt and jeans and bare feet or flip flops, so everyone, especially me, would be relaxed and comfortable.

They have a ton of wedding planners in the Keys, so, in late April, I went on the Internet and picked one with great reviews. Then all I had to do was call them, tell them what kind of ceremony we wanted, pick a cake from a bunch of pictures, select a menu for the party afterwards, and it was done. I did spend a little extra time making sure the food was presented well, but even that just took a few minutes. Honestly, it took me more time to install the new monitor on my computer than it took to plan my entire wedding. It was awesome.

And so was the wedding. The weather was absolutely beautiful. Not too hot, there was a lovely breeze coming off the water, the humidity was low, and the water was calm. The weatherman said it would be eighty degrees by sunset, which was at exactly seven-forty, so it could not have been a more perfect day.

We only had immediate family and our best friends with us, so there was plenty of room for everyone to stand out on the big deck at sunset. Lola had gotten ordained online so she performed the ceremony, and she did a great job up until the end. When she said, "You can kiss the bride," she and I both started to cry and laugh at the same time, so Luke laughed, hugged us off our feet and kissed us both.

The food was perfect, so my inner Martha Stewart was very happy, and the red velvet cake was great, but honestly, it was not as good as mine. There were a few posed pictures, but most of them were just pictures of all of us having fun. The best picture is one where Luke is hugging me from behind in the middle of the picture and every one of the wedding guests is standing around us laughing and holding on to us and each other. That picture, with Luke and I laughing together, surrounded by family and friends, with love and happiness shining out of everyone's eyes, is my favorite picture ever. It is now blown up and sits in the middle of the mantel above our living room fireplace.

The first time Luke saw the picture, he said it represents everything he wants for us. For me to be happy, for him to be happy, and for us to be happy together. I told him that I loved everything about that, and I loved him. And that made us both happy.

BEFORE YOU GO...

Join my newsletter for news about new books, what's going on, and a chance to win some fun free stuff! There's also a link so you can get the second book in this series for FREE!!

https://laneykaybooks.com

If you enjoyed this book, please remember to leave a review! Authors appreciate it more than you know!

ACKNOWLEDGMENTS

For my grandmother Betty Platt, who instilled in me the love of reading and writing.

Thanks to Kendal Delaine Hall and Rita Perez for your wonderful editing. Your attention to detail and ability to reel in my love for commas and excessive adverbs makes for a much better story.

Thanks to my dental peeps who gave me a chance to try something new!

Thanks to my parents, who never gave me any crap about only practicing law for two and a half months (that was *totally* worth $30,000...) and were always confident I could accomplish anything I set my mind to.

Thanks to my friends and family, who are all hilarious and allow me to shamelessly steal their words for my dialogue. And especially to Hillary who always answers my call when I need help with a word, a title, or to discuss why any given situation is batshit crazy.

And most of all, to my husband, who totally supports me no matter what kind of dumbass idea I come up with.

I love all y'all!

ABOUT THE AUTHOR

Laney Kay writes all kinds of stuff, both fiction and non-fiction. She's a good Southern girl, a huge Georgia Bulldog fan, and a lover of dogs, coffee, and books. (She's also a Taurus.)

She and her husband live in Georgia.

This is Laney's first book.

I love hearing from readers! You can email me here

Or reach me at my website: https://laneykaybooks.com

COPYRIGHT INFO

Publisher: Porkchop Publications, LLC
    Editing: Kendal Delaine Hall, Rita Perez
    Cover designer: Fantasia Frog Designs

Made in the USA
Lexington, KY
02 December 2019